Headlong

EMLYN WILLIAMS

Headlong

A novel

HEINEMANN : LONDON

To my family: Molly, Alan,
Brook, Antonia, Owen.

William Heinemann Ltd
10 Upper Grosvenor Street, London W1X 9PA
LONDON MELBOURNE TORONTO
JOHANNESBURG AUCKLAND

First published 1980

© Emlyn Williams 1980

434 86605 9

Printed and bound in Great Britain by
Morrison & Gibb Ltd., Edinburgh and London

Contents

CHAPTER ONE

The Nightmare

I think the moment has come when my story should be told.

And told by me. When I remember the staggering sums I was offered, at the time, to have it written for me, in the first person, by one prominent journalist after another . . .

The time? The year 1935, during which I had my twenty-fifth birthday. I've just looked up, from my typewriter, at two piles of press cuttings: at the two top headlines. One of them reads: SON AVENTURE MIRACULEUSE! The other, IT WAS LIKE HURTLING OVER NIAGARA IN A BARREL! AND HE LIVED TO TELL THE TALE!!

I lived, but I didn't tell the tale. Even if I had tried to, it would have been too soon – too much smoke between me and the paper. How would anyone feel who is one day indistinguishable from the rest of the London millions leading an everyday existence, and who next – overnight – is pitched into fantasy? And not fantasy, either, as you or I understand it: no underground Wonderland such as Alice chanced upon, nothing like Jules Verne's Captain Nemo with his deep-sea extravaganzas – no, while everything and everybody around me stayed as real and as rational as before, in *my* fantasy I found myself . . . alone.

Well, the smoke – which at the time would have been between me and the story – has cleared away and here I am, surrounded by the cuttings and by letters, diaries and memoranda. I have, I hope, over the years, learnt to use words well enough to express myself on paper, with the punctuation fairly competent – and it was hard

work! – but there are bound to be lapses into roughness and un-
orthodox style; for such lapses I now ask indulgence. I'll make a
start.

The fateful date, in 1935, was Saturday, May the 11th. And my
first premonition of it – though I could not, then, have recognized it
as such, nobody could have – had come, oddly enough, on the first
day of the year. I happened to leaf through an evening paper.

Star January 1st, "THE SKY WHALE *We can at last announce
that Britain's unique contribution to the modern world – the airship into
which have been poured, during the three years of its creation, millions
of pounds behind locked gates at R.B.A.C. (Royal British Air Centre)
Nuneaton, is in the final stages of completion.*

"*Last January there was conjecture as to why an obscure provincial
scientist – R. S. F. Hotting – had become* Lord *Hotting. We can now
reveal that he is the inventor of a new gas, the lightest known, much
lighter than Hydrogen or Helium, and christened, by him,* Elaphrium,
from the Greek elaphros, *light-in-weight.*

"*For Elaphrium is the power behind the new dirigible, officially
named the R.B. 100 (the initials standing, rightly, for 'Royal British')
but dubbed, by universal consent, the* Sky Whale.

"*The first trial flight of our aeronautical miracle is planned for
March.*" Then the details. "*. . . Over 1000 feet long, keynote aluminium . . . the 7 engines carried on gondolas, the latest from Rolls-Royce . . .
Using heavy oil, replacing petrol . . . Dining saloon to seat 100, 2 fire-
proof smoking-rooms . . . An aluminium grand piano . . . Etc.*"

Sunday Times, March 31st, "FIRST TRIAL FLIGHT
TRIUMPH *At the Nuneaton Air Centre, although the event had not
been publicized, a crowd of over a hundred cheered as the monster dirigible sailed lightly into the blue, circled majestically, and returned. The
Maiden Voyage is apparently planned for some time in May, destination
undecided . . .*"

Daily Mail, April 25th, "SKY WHALE SENSATION! *On
Saturday May 11th, 5 days after Jubilee Day (the climax of this
Silver Jubilee Year of their Majesties King George V and Queen Mary)
at Windsor Castle a dream will come true, namely a Jubilee Family
Party, the climax to a week which underlines the solidity of the British
Monarchy, including (as it will) the entire Royal Family.*

"*The very special week-end will be inaugurated by a Celebration
Luncheon held in the Waterloo Chamber, capable of seating 150. But –
and this is the great news – the Luncheon will be preceded by a ceremony*

*truly unique. It will be recalled that we announced the maiden voyage of
the SKY WHALE for some time this month, from Croydon Aerodrome
to Le Bourget.*

"*It may also be remembered that His Majesty the King has evinced
a particular interest and pride in this feather in Britain's cap, possibly
because our Sailor King was attracted by its being an air*ship. *It is
now official that the maiden voyage will start, on that very Saturday at
12 noon, from Windsor Great Park. The wafting into the air of the
J.S.W.* (Jubilee Sky Whale, *henceforth its unofficial name, inevitably*)
*will be watched not only by a holiday crowd of several thousand cheering
subjects, but by the Royal Family itself, from a grand-stand, specially
erected. Traffic arrangements on that momentous Saturday . . .*"

But I wasn't paying much heed – too busy with my life in London.
Like many other young people, at twenty-five all I felt for the King
and Queen was absent-minded respect, "anyway isn't it all a bit behind the times?" And on Monday May the 6th, Jubilee Day, I'm
afraid that neither I nor my two friends – I'll tell you about them
later – turned out for the processions or the fireworks.

Saturday May the 11th.

Sitting in our flat, we were having a late brunch, between eleven
and noon, with the wireless playing patriotic light music. This faded
out, and the announcer said something like: "We now take our
listeners to Windsor Great Park for the great Maiden Voyage of the
Jubilee Sky Whale." I thought of switching off, but we had trays on
our laps and I couldn't be bothered.

Here are bits of the broadcast, from the full account in the next
morning's *Times*. It went on and on, of course, with bursts of band
music in between, and us only half listening, ". . . Brilliant sunshine . . . I wish listeners could behold the multi-coloured summer
crowd, from the special guests crammed over every square foot of
Castle Hill and overlooked by the gigantic silhouette of the Castle
itself, to the general multitude roped off from the Long Walk leading
south to the mammoth shape of the Sky Whale soaring above its
gondolas and tethered to the mooring mast . . . At the heart of the
crowd, the vivid scarlet of the Guards Band; and near the airship
and isolated at some distance from the spectators, the Royal Grand-
stand, gaily decorated in red white and blue, makes a brave show as
it stands empty and waiting in the sunshine . . ."

(*Band Music, RULE BRITANNIA!*) ". . . And here comes the
Royal Procession, the first to appear being . . ." Etc. etc., to pro-

longed bursts of cheering. ". . . As they proceed slowly down the
Long Walk, there are too many for me to enumerate from here, but
they are all there, down to five-year-old Prince Paul of Kenilworth,
toddling along holding his mother's hand . . ."

(*Band Music, LAND OF HOPE AND GLORY*) ". . . They have
reached the towering Airship, where the Captain waits to be presented . . . Then steps forward the Reverend S. T. Bridpath, one of
the Royal chaplains. He bows, walks slowly up the gangway, turns
and opens a prayer-book, a signal to the multitude that he is about
to perform the brief ceremony of dedication, unfortunately in-
audible at this distance . . ."

The crowd certainly took the hint; throughout the broadcast it
had provided a continuous murmur of background noise, but now
all that died down quite quickly into silence. It was impressive, even
to us. And we distinctly heard what was commented on next day: the
twittering of a bird, a yard or two from the microphone.

". . . A moment of pride, and an impressive one . . . The Royal
procession turns and makes its way on to the Grand-stand, to such
cheering as to make me wonder if listeners can hear me . . ."

Then a description of the technicalities of the launching, ropes,
pulleys, wires, etc., then . . . "The Sky Whale moves! Slowly, gracefully . . . it rises! . . . The thousands who have waited so long,
watch like children, with bated breath . . . The Sky Whale, as it
wafts upward, veers – very slowly – as if feeling its way . . . As a last
loyal gesture of farewell, it is now moving, still very slowly, directly
over the Royal Grand-stand, where every head is turned upward. A
unique moment . . ."

Then, muffled but sharp, a clap of thunder. We all three looked
up. I said, "But he said it was sunny –" From the wireless, the announcer's voice, an unrecognizable strangled cry, "Oh God, oh
God . . ." Then a sort of great wind, which was the sound of agonized
breath being expelled by thousands of throats. Then the same de-
mented voice, "it can't have happened – God help us – God . . ."
Another sob, which was cut abruptly off and turned into a faint hum:
some man had had enough presence of mind to disconnect.

It was the hum of a silence such as you had never heard before.
We stared at the wireless set, as if something might spring out of it
and attack. Then we continued to sit, staring from it to one another
and back, for what seemed like a full minute. Then another voice
rapped out, very unlike the smooth B.B.C. intonations. "This is
Broadcasting House London, please stand by for emergency news,

which should come through any minute now, stand by . . ."

The same humming emptiness. We sat, still not daring to speak. At last – at last a voice, another man's. Breathless but controlled. "This is Broadcasting House. Word has just come through" – gasp – "officially . . ." A pause, and another tortured intake of breath. ". . . that the R.B. 100, known as the Jubilee Sky Whale . . . has been . . . by explosion and fire . . . has been instantaneously destroyed. While it is feared that there are many casualties in the front of the watching crowd, it seems more than a possibility that from the airship itself and from the grand-stand on which it fell, there may be . . . no survivors. There will be a further statement . . ."

A pause, then an indefinable sound. A sort of shudder, or a gulp, and after that, the same hum of silence. A nothingness, seeming as if it would last for ever. Then music crept in. Ghost music: somebody had pulled himself together and found the right record. The "Dead March" from *Saul*. Since then, the few times I've chanced to hear it, I jump up as if scalded and switch off. I know that a lot of other people do too.

The dirge crept around us, and into us. "The Royal Family? Isn't it all a bit behind the times . . . ?" One after the other, the three of us staggered to our feet and . . . just stood. With heads bowed.

The wireless trailed into more sad music, and we sat again, still not saying a word. Then I turned it down, almost to nothing, which made us feel guilty. Mechanically, I got up and looked out of the open window. In the window opposite, an older couple stood looking at each other. Then he put his arms round her and they clung together. They were both crying.

Oh, I don't want to go on about it, and those of you who went through it won't want me to either; anyway, you'll find it all – as I have done – in Colindale Library. For those who need reminding, I'll quickly remind.

First, it was immediately confirmed that the victims had all – in a flash, literally – "*perished by instant incineration: all that remained was a twisted tangle of steel girders*". Next, everything closed down – except for places of worship and essential services like food, post-offices and public transport – for a Week of Mourning which included continuous funeral services with no funerals. Seven days during which people in black wandered along like dazed ghosts, not knowing where they were going. Some looked as if they had been physically beaten, others feebly rubbed their hands as they walked, as if from the cold. In the warm sunshine of mid-May.

I had read about mass hysteria bursting into violence – but this was mass apathy, from deep shock. Worse than if war had been declared, because about this . . . there was nothing to be done. A yawning pit. It was as if what had happened had proved, with a certainty that froze the blood, that the supernatural does exist; every single stranger in the streets seemed to have felt the cold wind of it. Shock.

So one particular symptom of that shock, one which seems extreme from this distance, was taken for granted: the churches, permanently open, were crowded far into the night, with people sitting, kneeling or pacing, blank faces looking around as if searching for something, anything. Even the three of us queued outside the Brompton Oratory, our first visit to a London place of worship.

After a day or two, once the newspapers – bordered with black – had published tributes (endless photographs going back through the Great War to Queen Victoria, statements by President Roosevelt, President Lebrun, Herr Hitler, Signor Mussolini) the unprecedented situation came gradually into focus. I quote from a book published some time later, *Twentieth-Century World Disasters* by Maitland Price-Tenby, who devotes a whole chapter to THE GREAT HOLOCAUST.

"The first thought which chilled the whole British nation, was that if the vast watching crowd had been allowed two hundred yards nearer the airship, hundreds would have been annihilated; as it was, there were forty-seven deaths and many more hospital cases due to severe burns. Secondly, there flared up the monstrous question-mark – what had made possible an inferno which made the loss of two precious airships – the *Italia* seven years before, the *R101* five – sound like a couple of street accidents?

"Then followed the equally inevitable answer: a crop of wild rumours which travelled with the speed of light. *Some* individual, *some*how, had insinuated himself into the Sky Whale, armed with a bomb – sabotage, by a Foreign Power. And that sparked off a score of detailed theories, each flimsier than the last. Two men had been overheard in a bar in Nuneaton, conversing in whispers in a foreign language; a steward had been seen to give a drunken stagger, brandishing a sheaf of bank-notes and, at the same time, smoking a cigarette which provided a clue to the tragedy in store; thirdly, a spy had acquired a false passport, enrolled in the Air Force and landed a job as a member of the airship crew.

"And if none of that was tenable, somehow there *must* have been negligence, and for weeks a Commission sat sifting the evidence – or rather the non-evidence. Scores of people came under suspicion and were interrogated, from Lord Hotting the inventor of the new gas Elaphrium (there was even talk of stripping him of his title) to the humblest cabin-boy, and there were filed no fewer than twenty-two libel actions, all of which were won by the litigants.

"For the simple and appalling reason that there was no proof. Of *anything* – either of a plot, or of an accident. '*All that remained was a twisted tangle of steel girders*' . . . The Sky Whale Disaster was never to be explained, and will stand – till the end of time – as the greatest mystery of the twentieth century.

"Nothing to do but mourn.

"But where to go from there? For it next dawned on the British people that the proud announcement that the whole Royal Family would be gathered at Windsor Castle for a celebration had meant what it said: *the whole Royal Family*. Right down to little Prince Paul of Kenilworth, the twenty-seventh in succession.

"But it was when the newspapers came out with phrases like 'How long is the Royal Standard at Buckingham Palace, to stay at half-mast? – THE WORLD WAITS – WHAT NEXT? A REPUB-LIC? – that the nation, except for the left-wing minority, panicked as it faced an unprecedented situation. For the first time since the Protectorate of the commoner Oliver Cromwell, the throne was vacant and in danger. *Le Roi est Mort, ou est le Roi?*

"Once again the rumours chased one another with regularity, many of them – at this distance – fairly absurd. The *Daily Telegraph*: 'In view of the Great War (of dreadful memory) against Germany, we can only hope that a certain Teutonic widow, the head of a minor Principality and a great-great niece of Queen Victoria, many times removed, is not up for consideration. It is an historical fact that it was Victoria herself who, hearing that her grandson was to be chris-tened George, complained to her Ministers that 'the family, as we look back, could have done without that Hanoverian blood!' She could also have reminded them that on George the First's accession, he could neither speak nor write English, and was forced to com-municate in pidgin Latin.

"The *Daily Mail* put on a straight face when it announced that 'it is unlikely that the London visit of the Gräfin Sophia Lischmann-Freisonne of Luxembourg has any special diplomatic significance. The lady is here to visit her dentist'.

"The *Morning Post*. 'A Palace spokesman has emphatically denied that the Marquess of Rotherinsay (89) is the nearest in line for the succession, for the simple reason that the Marquess, in his Memoirs, has stated frankly that his mother furnished him with conclusive proof that he is the natural son of Mr. Giles Welles-Gleason the racing millionaire'. A statement which the author was able to check, at the time, by telephoning the Marquess. His answer to the delicate question was unequivocal: 'I thought *everybody* knew I'm the oldest bastard in Debrett!'

"And so it went on, for an endless succession of thirty-one days and nights: nearly five weeks. Halfway through the second of those weeks, the Archbishop of Canterbury hit the headlines with a sermon carrying the stern warning that 'the Ship of State is drifting danger-ously, nearer and nearer, to uncharted rocks'. During the third, one ominous word was quoted more than once, with a question-mark: COMMUNISM? Halfway through the fourth, there came a fairly unprecedented phenomenon: a demonstration outside the Houses of Parliament, twenty-thousand strong, waving banners, GIVE US AN IDEA, TELL US *SOMETHING*!

"Early in the fifth week, on the evening of the thirty-first day . . ."

It was Tuesday, June the 11th 1935. I heard a knock at the door. "It's the Police."

I was young, living in London, and my conscience was not crystal-clear. My heart gave a thump. What was I in for?

But first, in order that you can know my character and circum-stances at that moment, I must write for you a detailed idea of what my character and circumstances had stemmed from. My history up to that date. That is important.

And as it goes along, quite a colourful history, in a quiet way. Now that I come to think of it.

Chapter Two

On the Farm

My very early years were ordinary, completely so. I wasn't even destined to shine at school, just average: the opposite of the bookish pupils bent on bettering themselves by proceeding to college. And though I was already eight when the Great War ended, my father was never conscripted – I imagine because being a farmer, he was exempt – which meant that I stayed virtually unconscious of the upheaval.

An only child, I grew up where I had been born, on October the 18th 1910; if anyone had sent me a postcard, they would have addressed it to Master Jack Green, Ladock Farm, Tregonissey, South Cornwall. Not a big farm, on its own near the top of Tregonissey Hill and overlooking the village, five miles inland from the small seaport of St. Austell on the English Channel. It was a part of Cornwall noted for its scenery; from our gate I could see for miles, hills and woods and clouds.

I hasten to add that all that was to leave me sentimentally untarnished; I never looked twice at the view and couldn't tell one species of bird or flower from another, so I hereby refrain from Memories of a Rustic Childhood. Nobody likes pigs, but when I was five I was bitten by a dog, which meant I had no use for our mongrel Spotto. And as for cows, large galumphing beasts with all that luggage swinging – no, I was the one Country Lad who would have given the Country away, gratis. Already, I was hankering after the Town.

About my mother and father – how can parents be described when one was looking at them from a child's level?

It seems right to speak of my mother first because, without making any effort, of the two she was the one slightly in front. An inch taller than him, solid without being fat. When I was ten she must have been still under forty, but she seemed older through being the old-fashioned sort of mother with greyish fair hair, not bobbed as women were starting to wear it then, but scraped back to a bun. A nice fresh country face, very calm, with straight blue eyes that seemed to read every thought. Which didn't worry me when I was ten, though it wasn't long before it did.

But it needn't have: on most things she was wise, but concerning what she called "the bad side", she was . . . well, innocent. I remember her always in an apron (and always a clean one, I don't know how she managed that, on a farm) over a cardigan, and she wore old-fashioned dark stockings and old brown shoes.

The Sabbath, of course, was different, she was in her best black from Sunday a.m. to Sunday p.m., taking her apron off only for Chapel: three times during the day, Strict Baptist. (I used to wonder what other kind of Baptist there could be – Sloppy Baptist?) I couldn't take to Chapel.

Particularly the pictures on the walls, in terrible bilious colours depicting all the Biblical jollities. Boatfuls of sinners flooded up to the armpits, grabbing at the rocks for dear life and trying their damnedest to make up for lost time by repenting right and left; a lady by the name of Jael looking as if she got out of bed the wrong side and creeping into a tent to disturb some poor fellow's sleep by knocking an outsize nail between his eyes; Samson bringing the temple down, casualties by the thousand and not an ambulance in sight. All the fun of the Old Testament Fair. But I kept it all to myself, I didn't want to upset my mother.

Her maiden name had been Alice Lavinia Petherick – a good old Cornish name – but of course at the time I didn't know that, to me she was just my mother. I never thought, then, how people feel towards each other, but I must have known, without forming it into words, that she loved me. In her Strict-Baptist way. Which meant that she didn't spoil me, except with my favourite saffron cake, which she made to perfection, with currants and lemon peel. I loved her too, but was scared of her. I wasn't putting that into words either.

I did think about my Da, because I worshipped him: not the way my mother worshipped in Chapel, he wasn't right for that. A stocky handsome man with black curly hair and a bright easy smile, in breeches and brown leather leggings. He gave the Farm that much attention but no more; once, when he took to his bed with the flu, I asked her what he was ill from. "Doctor Pollard will knaw," she said. "One thing be for sure, it baint from overwork."

"Oh," I said – "but 'e do work, in 'is garden!"

"Go along there, diddlin' 'bout wi' flowers, that baint work. Gardenin's a 'obby. What 'e do work at, is the Bettin'." He certainly did toil, modestly, over the Racing Page, but his garden was his passion. And he did have green fingers. Interested folk would come from miles around to look over the wall at his begonias and phlox, whichever they were.

Mind you, she had her hobby too, as high in her thoughts as Chapel was: her Needlework, for which she – as well – had green fingers. It was famous throughout Cornwall, having been on view at many a Chapel Charity Bazaar: things to make you gape at the perfection of them – rugs, cushion-covers, Bible-markers. When not at her housework or farm tasks, she was bent over her needle, with above her, framed on the kitchen wall, a bad-tempered old lady named Queen Victoria, given away as a Christmas calendar by the *Western Morning News*. For me, my mother sitting there was part of home.

One day when I was almost eleven, something happened which was not quite so ordinary. I was due for St Austell County School, and had to produce my birth certificate. When I got home I said, "Ma, why does the Sustifficate put it that my name's John Albert Sandring when I'm Jack Green – I mean John Albert Green – an' you, Mrs Green?"

"That's simple," she said, going on with her ironing, "Bertram Green is your Da now, wi' you 'avin' took 'is name o' Green, but your proper father was Albert Sandring, the time I was Mrs Sandring, down along in St Austell when we lived over the cobbler's shop that 'e kep' in those days." This puzzled me, but no more than that, nothing could stop my Da being my father even if he wasn't.

I said, "Where's my proper father now?"

"I don't know." She was always a stickler for the truth. "You see, Jack, 'e passed away."

"'E did?"

"A year after you was born. 'E was killed."

I dropped the spoon. "By a *murderer*?"

"By lightnin'. It was Jehovah's will. You could 'a laid me flat with a feather." And she turned her eyes up to the ceiling as if expecting a return visit. I burst out laughing, I couldn't help it.

She gave me one of her godly looks. "You're a bad boy, what's funny 'bout lightnin'?"

"I don't know," I said, "but it *is* funny. Like when Mr Blamey the preacher slipped on my bicycle pump!"

She looked sternly down at me. "Lightnin's funnier, lightnin' kills people." Then righteous irony gave way to advice, gentle and valuable to an impressionable child. "It was natural for ee to laugh about the Reverend, it's healthy in a growin' lad, but after you *'ave* laughed, you just spare a minute to be sorry for 'im with 'is accident. It could 'a 'appened to *you*. It's important to think of other people, an' when you will be grown up always remember that, our Jack." And without being goody goody – nobody could give me that label – I *was* to remember what she had put into words that day.

Then she got stern again. "An' don't ee go tellin' the boys in school about 'im bein' struck by lightnin'. The day after it 'appened, there come out a piece in the Western Mornin' News with a photo o' me an' sayin' 'ow sorry folks was for me, oh I was offended." Offended by the invasion of her privacy: she was distrustful of the most harmless inquiry from a gossip in the shopping queue, "An' 'ow is Mr Green with 'is cold?"

She went on ironing, then stopped and considered. "Struck by lightnin' . . . Come to think of it, it *is* quite funny." My mother always tried to be fair.

At St Austell County School I was lazy but on the quick side, so didn't mind the lessons too much, when I got bored I just let my mind wander. I remember once doodling on the front cover of an exercise book and being rebuked by the Scripture master. "Sacrilege," he said, "my boy, do you realize what you're defacin'?" It was something stamped on all the exercise books: the arms of the Duchy of Cornwall. I thought how fussy he was, funny I should remember that.

The pictures on the walls were much more agreeable than the ones in Chapel; there was one which the Arts lady teacher called the Blue Boy, and a very cheerful boy he seemed to be, in knee-breeches and carrying a feathered hat and looking you in the eye, quite sure of himself. I thought of him as a friend.

Then there was a nice reproduction of a Renaissance painting – I think – one of the pagan-looking ones, with feathery trees and ruins and, lying in the middle of it all, what seemed to me a rather heavy lady, and with enough of her showing – except the crucial middle section – for the boys to snigger and the girls to go red from the sniggers. I sniggered too, but in my heart I warmed to her, lolling back sleepy from the sun. What did she care about sniggers or blushes?

One experience I did long for – a visit to the Odeon Cinema in St Austell, but my mother would not hear of it, not even *The Ten Commandments*. A second experience, of which she was blessedly unaware, evolved gradually and naturally. Sex.

That summer when I was thirteen – my mother had recently taken me into St Austell, to S. R. Clems Outfitters for long trousers – one early evening I somehow found myself in a haystack; more often than not, it's the place where rural sex seems to start. Perhaps straw is an aphrodisiac.

I was wrestling with Peter Wakefield the baker's boy, two years older, fifteen, when he suggested ministering unto me, and what with curiosity and the summer heat, I was happy to meet him half-way and learn a fact of life or two.

Which started me off, and a month later, on the way to school I turned to Chrissie Woodleigh from the public house and brought up the subject of the same haystack. I must have had a tidy mind. I appreciated both events as being enjoyable and educational, within limits. At that early stage, equality of the sexes. No discrimination to speak of.

It was during that summer that I accidentally made another dis- covery, a hobby of my own. During a Sunday school trip to New- quay, on the Atlantic coast, looking out of the window I caught a fleeting glimpse, on a hill-top, of an old windmill.

The morning happened to be a gusty one, and the sails were racing one another, up round and down, up round and down – the lines of them frail, and yet bold – against blue sky and scudding clouds. A grand picture.

Something clicked in me: I just knew I was in love with that wind- mill, standing bravely astride that hill, independent and *busy*: trap- ping the feckless useless wind, and using it. I would construct a miniature mill.

And I did. With my pocket-money I sent off for a book, bought balsa-wood and little tools; I had my hobby. "Our Jack," my father said, "you been blessed wi' your Ma's 'ands, wi' that needle of 'ers!"

I was offended that my talent was inherited from a woman, but he was right. With the months, the hobby became a private cult; I really had got magic in my fingers. A natural gift, though, is often taken for granted by the owner, I just wondered if it meant I was to end up as a joiner.

The following year, with me – aged fourteen – taking for granted, in my vague way, that the world was an easy place to live in, I was jolted out of my complacency.

It was towards the end of my summer holidays. Since, by that time, I was getting restless – long bike-rides, sleeping rough, etc. – my mother thought it would be a good idea to break up the long stretch by giving me a change of air; taking advantage of a three-day excursion offer, I was to travel by rail to spend them with her sister Harriet, married to Uncle Fergus. For years they had lived in his part of the world: in the town of Jarrow, in north-east England, near the estuary of the River Tyne. I didn't mind, indeed I quite looked forward to it with not having been further from St Austell than the nearby Atlantic on those Sunday-school trips. I felt I was going to foreign parts, on my first journey on my own.

My father saw me off at St Austell, on to the train, with in the cardboard box from the Outfitter's my best suit and a change of shirt and socks, also my pocket Bible which my mother hoped I would open. The train went through some beautiful scenery, but I would sooner have been looking at a place I had seen in a photograph. Piccadilly Circus, with the buses and the sky-signs.

After a long cross-country journey, which sadly included a dull transfer by Underground from Paddington to King's Cross, thereby preventing me from seeing anything of London, I was met at Jarrow station by Uncle Fergus, "straight from the office". He was nice and respectable but highly cheerful, more so even than my Da: bubbling over with it. I had never heard the Tyneside accent, much rougher than the Cornish one. I quite liked it, but the streets were grimy and depressing.

The bus turned a corner, and Uncle nudged me with pride. "That, Jack, is my office." My mother had been mysterious as to what he did for a living; the couple of times when I had asked her, she had answered, "Oh, your Uncle tries to make people comfortable when they need it." So I had imagined him to be a sort of doctor.

The front door and window-woodwork of his office were painted black, the curtains dark grey. Uncle was an undertaker.

"Tries to make people comfortable . . ." I could see what my mother meant, but I did feel that any efforts he might be making, in that department, were a bit late in the day. Also I wondered how he could be so chirpy on that bus, humming a song from the wireless, *When You and I were Seventeen* . . . With me being fourteen, that sentiment was wasted on me. I would have liked to ask him about his "office"; the only corpse I had ever seen was in an illustrated Bible: Lazarus dead in bed, in transit for the tomb but you can't count him, seeing that he worked his passage back. I never got to the bottom of that.

Oh, but Uncle *was* cheerful.

More than the scenery was. None of the fields I was used to, and bored with: row upon row of slum houses. The sun was still out, seven p.m., but I saw that sunlight can be cruel, it showed everything up. The little houses were all stuck together and looked as if they had sores they had caught one from the other. Bricks and dried mud and dust and dust-bins and mangy cats and wolfish dogs. And nobody about, were they all at the Pictures or something?

But Uncle's house was on its own, and pleasant, with a bow window and at the back a neat garden. Beyond it, silhouetted against the evening sky, a dramatic and unexpected sight: the funnels of a great ship, we were near the river. That roused my schoolboy imagination, I thought of Columbus and Francis Drake.

And Auntie Harriet turned out to be plump and quite as jolly as Uncle, nothing to do with coffins, we had quite a few jokes. I imagined that my mother might have been the same if the Old Testament hadn't got at her; Auntie Harriet seemed, in some way, to have got vaccinated against all that. I had a nice evening, with Uncle teaching me whist while we listened to the wireless.

In the lobby, sticking out from the wall, something quite new to me: a telephone. In the middle of the game, it rang out and he answered; he came back rubbing his hands at the idea of getting back to the cards. "That," he said beaming, "was a business call."

Next morning it was raining, but Uncle left smartly for his office, whistling. Then I sat peeling potatoes for Auntie Harriet, when she asked me what I wanted to be.

I said I didn't know. She shook her head, gently. "Jack, that's not a good sign, a lad *should* know. If he don't, it can lead to them bein' blown about in life, like them bits of paper in the road." I could see her point, but I still didn't know. At school, Woodwork was my best subject, and the master teaching it had once said – a joker – "There's gold in them there Hands." They were certainly deft. So for a bit I'd thought I'd be a joiner, then forgot about it. All I knew, from dutifully helping Dad during my holidays, was that I was not going to be a farmer.

Sitting with Auntie, I did wonder one thing. If Uncle Fergus's Auntie had asked *him* the same question – "what do you want to be?" – when *he* was fourteen . . . would he have answered, "When I grow up, I want to be an Undertaker?"

In the afternoon it cleared up, beautiful sun and the air fresh after the rain. I got restless and asked Auntie if I could go for a walk. She saw me to the front gate, and I turned to start off down the long straight road.

I stopped in my tracks.

Where, last evening, there had not been a soul about, now there were dozens, men and boys. But not moving: all in one long line along the narrow pavement, like stone figures. And, further on, they were lined up the same road where it climbed up again.

For the first time, I saw Auntie not looking jolly. I said, "What is it, is there to be some sort of procession?"

"No, Jack love, it's the shipyards."

"The shipyards?"

"They're the out-o'-works. Never you mind, you're 'ere to enjoy yourself."

"The out-o'-works . . ." It was a subject I had – of course – heard mentioned in Cornwall; but with our part consisting so much of farmland, to me unemployment was a vague word which had never sunk in. It was to sink in now. "Are the shipyards in trouble?"

"Trouble? Yes, trouble. Such as Palmer's over there, opened nearly a hundred years back, an' they say will 'ave to close before too long. There used to be hundreds of ships built here, that ship you see behind our garden been like that for three years, like a ghost ship, we're sick o' the sight of it an' will be for years. Them men you see 'ave been out of work for years, an' they say that in ten years' time – wi' nobody high up doin' a thing 'bout it – in ten years' time things will be ten times worse." The repetition of the word "years" sounded very sad. "An' Jarrow's not the only place, there's Sunderland an' Gateshead an' West Hartlepool. If it isn't the shipyards it's the coal-mines, don't be long now."

I looked across at the masts of the abandoned ship, and they didn't look picturesque any more. I started off. The nearest to a sign of life was on a waste-ground: between piles of broken bricks, two lads of sixteen were stabbing sullenly at a burst football, against a background of smashed windows.

To avoid the pavement, I kept to the middle of the road; no danger from traffic, there *was* no traffic. When I did glance sideways, I saw caps and skimpy scarves, patched trousers, boots down-at-heel. But the boots were clean, polished from heel to toe, let there be something to prove self-respect, *something* . . .

Then I looked at the faces. Dead pale; rows of dull eyes looking at me, a schoolboy wearing a strange cap. I had promised my mother I'd wear my best suit, and as I walked along, my face turned red. But they were not interested, the eyes seemed to say, "Why should we be, when the world is indifferent to us?" They were all ages, from fifteen to prematurely old; and of the older men, a few were either one-armed or lame, mutilated from the war which I had never known, and which had sent them home to . . . this.

I turned back. It was terrible, and almost funny, that one of the few steady-jobbers around here was my Uncle Fergus.

Sitting in Auntie's cosy parlour, I thought, that was something I can never forget. I thought of what my mother had said, "it's important to think of other people." Then that Sunday-school story came back to me, of Saul on the road to Damascus – of the scales falling from his eyes in front of the vision which was to change his life.

Not that this experience was to transform me. It had been my first brush with reality, and a shock; but if the scales *had* fallen from my eyes, it wouldn't have taken them long to get stuck back on again.

As for Saul, I can't see an improvement in him when he changed from a frolicsome young sinner into an old preacher calling himself Saint Paul, and forever sending off Epistles giving his parishioners hell. They must have dreaded the postman.

CHAPTER THREE

On the Move

And for two years, dodging any examination of my future, interested in little besides my windmill interludes, I coasted down the current carrying me, leisurely and unaware, to the age of sixteen.

April 1927, my Easter holidays. Two things happened, within a couple of hours and quite different from each other: the first decisive and the second incidental. Yet the two were complementary, for the second helped to make my decision even firmer.

Since I would be seventeen in October, I was due to finish in a few weeks at the County School. One morning at breakfast my mother held up a letter. "Good news, Jack, your Da been in touch with 'is auld mate Mr Trelitt over in the Lizzard china-clay pit, Mr Trelitt been brave an' kind an' 'ave promised an openin' for ee, an' they'll pay ee a pound a week."

I stared at her, then saw the pit yawning. "I'm to be a clay-worker?"

"That you be. Won't be far by bike, so you'll be able to live 'ere at 'ome, edn' that a blessin'?"

I went on looking at her, then turned quickly away. Finishing my potato stew I said to myself, I may not know what I want to be, but I do know what I am *not* going to be – a useful nobody who will, in time, become useless, then be thrown to the ground and run over. I was resolved not to be liquidated by a steamroller for which, in my ignorance, I had no name. Industry? Politics? Both? I must get out.

"Well our Jack," said my father, "penny for yer thoughts, will ee give me a 'and this fine mornin'?" Further up our hill there stood

Ladock Lodge, a big rich house which was being sold up; and they had asked him if he would convey objects, in our farm van, to be auctioned in the St Austell Public Rooms – furniture, pictures, ornaments. As we trotted up to fetch the load, my father said, "The great thing to watch out for, be when ee do 'andle any o' they lookin'-glasses."

"Why's that?" The only mirrors we had were the ones my mother kept in their bedroom, and the even smaller one he brought to the kitchen table to prop against the sugar-bowl for him to shave by, and which I was using by now, peering at corners of my face for the same purpose. And the ones I'd seen elsewhere had not been that much bigger, to be hurriedly glanced at in the school wash-room or through the window of a furniture shop.

"Oh," he said, "these ones is lookin'-glasses the likes o' which us 'ave never set eyes on, six foot by four, that's been 'angin' in the big 'all in the Lodge. If we wuz to crack one, it'd be the end o' the world." Which made me nervous.

When we got up to the courtyard, a lot of the stuff was already stacked outside the big porch. Dad said for me to follow him, and in he went. I was just turning to do so, when I caught sight of somebody standing in the sun, five feet away, looking at me. Straight in the eyes.

He was my height, tall for sixteen, with a school-cap like mine, nondescript country suit and country boots like mine. Then I looked back at the face, shining in the sun. Short hair, brown to fair, large blue-green eyes, dark lashes, red lips slightly open from surprise, fresh skin touched with pre-summer tan. I smiled at him, he smiled back. I puzzled as to where I had seen the face before. The lad on the class-room wall, the Boy in Blue.

Then Dad, in the doorway, "Come an' give we a 'and, Jack . . ." I turned quickly away from the boy, then stopped again, quite bewildered. I could see another one, just like him, looking sideways and away from me, with a straight nose and a curved chin. Then it dawned on me that they were both the same lad.

What was more, both of them were me. For the first time, properly, I had *seen* myself – not in one mirror but in two, the second reflecting the first.

On the trip to St Austell, as I sat next to my father my mind was a jumble, it had never occurred to me that I was a good-looker – it wasn't that I was becoming infatuated with myself, I was merely facing an unexpected fact. And with my eye fixed on the horse's left ear, and my thoughts on the Lizzard Pit, I said to myself again, mouthing the words this time, to the rhythm of the hooves, I – must – get – out. What the mirrors had told me had clinched it.

Why? My mind was then indeed a jumble, but looking back I can now work out why, unravelling what I felt, and what I did not feel.

Sexually, aside from the occasional harmless half-encounters, I was as yet an innocent: so there could be no question of even the vaguest plan to invade Vanity Fair and there market my new-found physical advantages – in that area I was without guile, and was to stay that way. No, I was merely determined to meet people I would be comfortable with, and who would find it easy to like me. I wanted to enjoy life. Which meant that I had to – get out.

As we lumbered into the town, I looked down at the people walking along as if they had all day: men, women and kids I'd been looking at all my life. Well, here they were, each of them a stranger, and me a stranger in their midst, who had been here all the time, by mistake. A stranger who was now to spread his wings, and . . .

The time had come.

When we got home, my mother handed my Da a letter she had opened; she was looking at him rather strangely. "For you, come by the second post." After reading it, he drew out a sheaf of notes and gave a joyous whoop, "Holy smoke!" Two horses had come in first and won him twenty pounds, at that time a fortune.

My mother's face showed a struggle. Her mouth was doing its best to disapprove, while her eyes were aiming to fill with pleasure. The eyes won. But as he was stuffing the precious pound-notes into his pocket, she put her hand out, sternly. "Into the post-office, first thing tomorrow. All but five pounds."

But tomorrow was Market Day, and she had a good idea that delay, where her husband was concerned, might be fatal. "Jack will pay it in." And she put the fifteen pounds into a separate envelope and handed it to me. I had never in my life handled a single pound-note, never mind fifteen. All through high tea, my mind was working.

If I was to go, it had got to be *now*, without them having any idea of my intentions; if I were to tell them I intended to leave in a couple of days' time, I'd be finished. I'd only once seen my mother cry, the day she heard her own mother had died, and I wouldn't be able to face that again. (I'm soft-hearted, I said to myself; it quite surprised me.)

I said my usual goodnight, went up to my little bedroom, and having done my mind-work, carried it into action. I got out the big cardboard box and the string, from that Tyneside visit, packed it with my best suit, shirt, socks, underpants, shaving things, etc. (but not my pocket Bible). Then I went to bed.

What with my heart beating, and my brain racing, I got very little sleep. Never once had I made a stand against Mam, I had never been anything but mild, almost meek. Yet here I was, in this bed for the last time, staring out of my tiny window waiting for first light.

Once the sun was on its way, I wrote a note. On the lines of – "Dear Mother and Father, I'm sorry if I am upsetting you, but now that I'm grown-up I want to get out into the world. Don't fret, I'll write and send you back the loan of the £15 as soon as I start work, Your loving son Jack."

I tiptoed down. A farewell look at my windmill work, then out and down the hill; then softly along the village street, with my card-board box to give me away, but there was not a soul about. And in ten minutes I was out in the open country, striding along in the sun and whistling to myself. The box under my arm felt like thistledown.

Too early for a bus, so the five-mile walk to St Austell, and after an hour even thistledown puts on weight. A car came along, I looked harmless enough to get a lift. He was a commercial traveller, and I told him I was heading for Plymouth (true) where a job was waiting for me in the Midland Bank (false).

Within ten minutes, I caught a Plymouth train. And sitting in it, as cool as spring water, I watched the telegraph-poles in the sun, tearing backwards to join everything now at the back of me – farm, chapel, school – yes, and my parents. Ahead of me, London.

Not immediately, but in time. Via Plymouth, where I'd get a job as office-boy, anything. Opposite me, a girl with glasses and an older flirty-looking woman. Quite separately, they looked at me. Remembering the mirrors, I turned to look at the scenery. So that they could see my profile.

Then I felt myself blushing and looked at the floor. Watch out, I said to myself, or you'll turn into that chap in the tale the teacher told, who saw his face in a pool and tried to kiss himself and toppled in and that was the end of him, sounds not very manly, didn't the teacher tell us his name was something like Narsissy-us, was that where "Sissy" came from, watch out.

I didn't need to. Overnight, I'm glad to say, I was to take my looks for granted.

Walking from Plymouth Station, down the nearest main street, I was working on a plan to buy a local paper and study the Situations Vacant, when I stopped at a busy crossing, and looked around to see where I was. PALACE THEATRE, THE PEMBERTON DE FRECE PLAYERS.

"Stage-door's up there."

I turned; it was a stout lady, forty sort-of, with painted cheeks plus scarlet lips and earrings. I could not credit my eyes. Then she said, "You up for the A.S.M?"

She might as well have said, "You down for the X.Y.Z?" But I wasn't going to give away my ignorance. "Yes, I am."

"You're very young. 'Ow old are you, sixteen?" She talked through her nose. (I couldn't recognize Cockney, yet.)

"Eighteen." At sixteen, I felt eighteen.

"Stage-doorkeeper's gone to lunch, I'm off shoppin', landlady doesn' cater, au reservoir." And she was off down the road, clickety-click. High heels! I hitched my cardboard box under my arm and walked in at the stage-door. What my mother would consider the entrance to Hell.

Into pitch blackness. Then it cleared a bit, enough for me to turn a corner and spot a bench with a naked light over it. Beyond, what looked like a broken-down warehouse with a dusty (bigger) naked light very high up.

Under it, something I was seeing for the first time. A man and a woman, their arms round each other – in public – and kissing for all they were worth. She was in a sort of fur coat, on the scruffy side. Three men stood looking on, one holding a watch as if at a boxing-match.

Then the two unclinched, he said to her, "If you marry that out-sider, you will rue the day, for I will put a curse on you both from the wedding-bells on!", the watch-holder said, "Right, break for lunch, back at two." They all trooped out without looking at me, and there I was.

On the bench next to me, a paper. *The Stage.* I sat down and ex-amined it.

It was open at a double page, with on one side a very full list of provincial theatres. (I've refreshed my memory by looking all this up in this particular copy of the paper in the Colindale Library.) *Harry Hanson Players . . . Salisbury Rep . . .* What was Rep? *Mrs Tan-queray . . . Birmingham Repertory Theatre.* Ah, *Rep* was short for Repertory . . . On the other side, a column headed WANTED.

"WANTED, Juv. Gent not less than 5ft 4, good feed, good ward-robe; WANTED, Soubrette, v. pretty capable of schottische, buck, high kicks, cartwheels must be refined, or useless; WANTED, per-sonable young Shakesp. actor capable of 4 plays weekly, state lowest terms to meet the times; WANTED, clever refined female Kiddie, v. cheap; WANTED, 2nd Comic with Front-Cloth Speciality, sobriety indispensable; WANTED, Heavy Lady, smart, good mover; WANTED, Stage Manager, also A.S.M. and Under-study."

A.S.M. again . . . Of course, Assistant Stage Manager.

I did a bit more careful reading, walked out to a café for a sand-wich, got back at five to two (still no doorkeeper) and settled down on the bench.

The man with the watch was the first back. "Yes, what is it?"

"Please, sir" – I was back in the County School – "I heard you want an A.S.M."

"You look very young, me lad. What experience?"

"Two months in Salisbury Rep, four with the Harry Hanson Players." *The Stage* was proving a friend in need. "Seven weeks' tour in *The First Mrs Tanqueray* –"

"You mean the *second* Mrs T.?"

"That's right, sir."

"From the sound of you, you're from these parts. Cornish?"

It sounded as if I were being charged with an offence. "That's right." How could he tell? . . . "I started off as A.S.M. with the Ilfracombe Players –"

"I never heard of a rep company in Ilfracombe?"

"They only lasted three weeks, sir, went bankrupt." Crafty, you must admit.

"You've understudied?"

"Yes, sir." What was "understudy"?

"With that accent?"

"Yes, sir." What was an accent?

He hesitated. "Right, three quid a week. There's a room going in the stage manager's digs." I had read about quids, in a comic paper – but *digs*?

The others drifted back, and the man said to me, "Get on that stool, and prompt." I naturally took "and prompt" to mean for me to jump to it quick, and I did. On the stool was a grubby old book with on it *A Woman Scorned*. Then when the lady in the fur coat called to me, "Don't prompt me, unless I snap my fingers", I got the meaning. The script had a bookmark, and it was the right page. So far so good.

The actor stepped forward (Juv. Gent) and his voice rang out again. "If you marry that outsider, you will rue the day, for I will put a curse on you both from the wedding-bells on!" Then back to the scorching kiss. The leading lady said, "In the name of our child, Roger, I implore you to think again, oh you do smell of beer ducky!" And everybody laughed.

May 3rd, 1927. I was on the stage.

CHAPTER FOUR

On the Boards

"C/o Pemberton de Frece Players, Stage door, Victoria Th, Burnley, Lancs. May 13th 1927.

"Dear Mother and Father, This is my first letter I ever wrote to you. I am sorry to have been a nuisance and to wait over a week before writing, but I had to wait for salary before enclosing this postal order for 10 shillings on acct of the £15 I owe you, so you can see I am in clover.

"You will note from above address that I am in the Theatre Profession, and though I liked Home this is where I belong. I hope my father will not mind that my name is now not Jack Green but my real one Jack Sandring, being not so ordinary.

"A nice Co., God-fearing too. I do interesting jobs behind the scenery, such as striking a clock, copying horse's hoofs or a dog barking, or shouting HIP HIP HOORAY or HELP HELP, depending on the play, which is diff. every 3 nights. We have a stock of 6 plays, so we stay in each town 3 weeks, with *A Little Bit of Fluff, White Cargo, A Woman Scorned, Bunty Pulls the Strings, Damaged Goods.*

"I miss Spotto and think of him when I do any barking. Your affec. Son, Jack."

Notes. (a) I was careful not to disclose my salary of three pounds a week. (b) "God-fearing" was not the word to describe the Co. (c) You may have observed that of the six plays, I only named five. My mother could hardly guess that *Damaged Goods* was about syphilis, and might wonder if *A Little Bit of Fluff* could be about spring-cleaning, but I had a feeling that she would have been alarmed by *He Walked In Her Sleep.* (d) I did not miss Spotto. Not even when I was barking.

Reading their answer, I tried to harden my heart; not easy. Not so much from what was said, as from what was left out. My mother had written the letter, in her firm clear hand, which was to become a pattern, with my Da occasionally adding a P.S., including something to tease her.

> "Our dear Son Jack, Well here I am, your Ma ritin her 1st letter to you, escuse spellin, twas a pleisure to recieve yours. First, we are glad you are with Godfearin folks considerin the places where you have to work, pleise see that they give you reglar meals.
>
> "Mind you, it has been a worry but I have faith in you, with you meanin no harm. We been tellin folks that you are all rite, now we can beleive it. Spotto still goes scratchin at your door, he thinks a brave lot of you. I will keep your Postal Order for when you will be needin it, Your lovin Mother, Alice Lavinia Green.
>
> "P.S. Your lovin Da speekin. She has been takin a pill off Dr. Pollard to make her sleep, but last nite without a pill she slep rite through – if I baint mistook your letter was the rite medicine. Since the Rev Blamey's 70th birthday, the old chap's sermons gets longer & longer & that's not rite, long in the tooth is one thing but long in the pulpit is another."

I felt tender towards them. But I was realistic enough to be glad that no tour could bring me near enough to St Austell for me to have to visit. Having broken the bonds, I must – for quite a time, at any rate – stay away.

But I did send the ten shillings every week, till the fifteen pounds was paid off.

To think I'd once wondered what "digs" were: I stayed in furnished rooms in back streets stretching from Inverness to Dover; the only difference being that some had indoor "conveniences", some not. Which was nothing new to a Country Lad.

It was a communal life, one that was to be mine for several years: a gypsy world of shared dressing-rooms, shared digs, shared bedrooms, shared jokes. I enjoyed the jokes, people liked me and I liked them. I hoped to do well, but with no positive ambitions gnawing at me, I was happy. I fitted in.

I did understudy, short parts, and once went on as a chauffeur, which earned me a fan-letter. A weirdish one. "I happen to like leggings." Oh, and talking of sex – with all the moving around and the hard work, that was only occasional and on the casual side: ships passing in the touring night, between one Sunday train-call and the next.

I'll pilot you on, as if reading out from my entry in *Who's Who in the Theatre* (if I'd ever got into it). *The foll. yr. (1928), commenced his short career as actor in Musical Theatre, by touring in "Rose Marie" as Black Eagle.* A Red Indian part. I was miscast. I also got a couple of bits in quartets, etc., and found I had quite a pleasing singing voice; also two of the chorus-boys gave me dancing lessons. They said I was quick and graceful, and I liked that.

Aug. 1929, toured as Leander in "Katja the Dancer". In this I joined in a duet in which I had to sing the words *I'm your Leander, your Goosey-Goosey Gander . . .*

Xmas 1929, pantomime "Puss-in-Boots", Hippodrome St Helen's, Lancs., A.S.M. I also sang as one of THE THREE TOM-KIT-TENS, and had a short tap-dance.

In between these engagements I was happy to be based in London, looking for work, even if it meant unappetizing digs in Pimlico. A week after *Puss-in-Boots* finished (March 1930), I was sitting in the outer office of the Akerman-Patch Agency when the girl came out from the Holy of Holies and went up to a chap in a corner who was wearing a soft hat and said, "Jack Sandring? Mr Patch will see you for a minute –"

By then I was on my feet, you bet. "*I'm* Jack Sandring."

She looke᪐ ᴛt me. "So you are, sorry . . ." Then the other boy got up and took off his hat with a courtly bow. "And I'm Eric Dandy, how d'ye do?" You couldn't blame him.

"Sorry, dear," she said – she was snooty to the girls, but partial to Juveniles – "you looked like him with your hat on."

Well, with his hat off he didn't. Same height, granted, but with bright ginger hair, while mine was brown with sort of fair streaks. I thought no more about it and followed the girl into the sanctum, putting on the Smile: Mr Patch wore an inferior toupee and he too was partial to Juveniles. Among ourselves, we called him "Patch the Thatch".

He said, "I haven't much time, can you dance?"

"Sure" – I'd got that from the talkies – "I did a tap in *Puss-in-Boots*."

"With a partner? Another boy?"

"Solo."

"The reason I ask is that Archie Pitt has just seen the Rocky Twins at the Folies Bergère and wants to groom an identical act for a revue he's sending out – forget it, pop in in a coupla weeks in case something turns up."

I was walking out through the crowd in the outer office, with a jaunty look as if I'd landed a tour of *Journey's End*, when an idea struck me. I went up to the ginger fellow in the soft hat. "Can I have a word with you, outside?"

He looked a bit surprised, but followed me. On the stairs hung a dingy old mirror. I said, "*I* don't think we look alike, do you?"

He took off his hat and we stood, side by side, looking at ourselves reflected. It was a poor light, so his red hair didn't show up that much, and we were both in our best dark suits: even we could see a likeness.

I said, "Can you dance?"

His face came to life. "Can I dance? Since I was ten, me Mum an' Dad was the Footloose Fazendas."

I'd seen their name on posters. Walking downstairs, I explained the situation and we retired to a Lyons Corner House (Coventry St, actually) to work out a plan. I was by no means lazy in my job, but neither was I a ball of fire where donkey-work was called for; in that department, I had to be pushed. Well, over tea and buns I quickly got the message that I was dealing with a pile-driver. Dull as a yawn, but a fanatic about one thing. Dancing.

We went straight to his room off the Tottenham Court Road, where he produced two pairs of tap-shoes. I tried a pair on, it fitted; he pushed back the furniture, flung a record on to a portable gramophone and got to work.

I had been under the impression that I could tap-dance; he soon put me right on that, gentle but insistent. "No, no, don't start bouncin', that's not tap, it's 'orrible – *press*, into the ground!... On the rhythm for the Shim-Sham, you gotta relax more..." After an hour I was whacked, but learning. "Watch that triple wing, you're not flicking the wing out to the side enough..." His final verdict was "Pal, you got the idea, you got natural rhythm!"

Next morning I phoned Patch the Thatch, and he promised to arrange an audition with Mr Pitt. I took Eric to Clarkson's ("The

Theatrical Costumier's"), where I'd once been sent to refit a panto wig and done a spot of charm-school on one of the assistants; he agreed to lend us identical straw hats and bow ties. Then, for Eric, we unearthed a wig almost my colour.

We gave the audition at the Victoria Palace – the fourth of seven prospective Rocky Twins – and as we strutted on, my hand on Eric's shoulder, faces out front, matching smiles, you could feel (from the hard-hearted little group in the stalls) a gasp of surprise. Those slavish hours had paid off. Eric danced better than me, of course, but – it's not conceit – I had more personality. We both covered up what we lacked, which the other had got. (An awkward piece of prose!)

We got the job. Ten quid a week each, my biggest pay-packet yet. We worked up a patter routine – terrible, now I look back – based on one being Cockney and the other Cornish. And since his name was Dandy and mine Sandring Mr Pitt decided we were to be DANDY AND SANDY, THE INSEPARABLE TWINS.

The engagement was for eight weeks; well, we toured for more than eighteen months, and I enjoyed it. We were never high on the bill, but the applause was terrific even on the first house Monday. Eric and I shared digs, got on pretty well, and at the end of all those months shook hands and both had the feeling we'd not meet again.

How wrong can you be.

December 1931, Pantomime,"Cinderella", Prince's Theatre Bradford. I was vaguely aware of "Pantomime" as a very British institution and a theatre entertainment produced over Christmas, based loosely on one fairy story or another, and was now agreeably surprised to find it was a high-spirited pot-pourri of song, dance and spectacle. It was, moreover, decidedly puzzling to realize that – following strict tradition – the Ugly Sisters were played by two male comics and that Prince Charming was a buxom lady in tights, the star of the show.

As well as working in the chorus and as A.S.M., I had one tap-dance and understudied both Broker's Men. On Boxing Night, in the middle of the second house, a failure in the electricity: total darkness. Standing at the back of an invisible and paralysed cast, I stumbled forward towards the muttering audience and surprised them, and myself, by remembering I'd once sung *O For the Wings of a Dove* at a Chapel Social and then going right through it without a quiver. Then the lights came back on.

My success was such that I was promoted to Understudy to Buttons. One night two weeks later, Buttons got drunk, fell into Cinderella's fire before it turned into cinders, couldn't get up again and was sacked. I was engaged for the part for the rest of the run (twelve pounds a week), and with a passable voice, light feet and a tight page-boy suit, I attracted not only Bradford but Prince Charming herself. Miss Celia Gold.

Funny, as the run progressed, Buttons's Cornish accent became gradually less pronounced, due to speech lessons from – no less – Miss Gold. This was in between coaching of a more intimate nature, which was inaugurated during my second week in the part. After a matinee, Buttons was summoned to the star dressing-room for notes. I expected such requests as "In the Kitchen Scene, when I say 'Answer me' please look at me", etc.; but there she sat stripped to the waist, and in her mirror I saw two prince-charming breasts.

She was sort of thirty and married to the management, so the coaching (both sorts) had to be at that time, i.e. between matinee and evening perfs. And since the show played twice daily . . .

There were no laughs with Miss Gold, which I missed, but she was nice, though conscious of her status; she asked me always to call her "Miss Gold", as before. In the dressing-room I didn't call her anything.

The other boys guessed and pulled my leg, but I didn't mind. The only time I took umbrage was when somebody said, "Jack, you're on to something there, her old man's rolling in money, why don't you play your cards while the going's good, and wangle a Gold watch out of her?" I was conscious of being on the weak side, but – I'm glad to report – opportunism didn't occur to me.

I did get to speak better, and in my second subject, I have to admit that Teacher, by the end of the course, was giving me full marks. No fireworks, but it was restful and complimentary and you can't have everything.

Immediately afterwards, *April 1932, made his first West-End appearance in "Helen" at the Adelphi, chorus & A.S.M.* From then on, it was London all the way. *Oct. 1932, "Wild Violets", Drury Lane Th., chorus & A.S.M.* I enjoyed the stage-management part, and was considered efficient.

Dec. 1933, Pantomime, "The Sleeping Beauty", Lyceum (with Marianne Lynn) chorus & A.S.M. That was important. To explain why, for a minute I'll skip a few weeks.

"82a Yeoman's Row, London S.W.

"Dear Mother and Father, Many thanks for letter, I'm glad the Rev is over his cold, I hope you also are taking care. You will see that I have moved from that one room, and now share a small flat with a married couple, she is a good cook so you don't have to be worrying that your wandering boy might be starving . . ."

If the phrase "a married couple" suggests an old character actor and his plodding wife, it was meant to. They weren't old, or married. Or plodding. Back to *The Sleeping Beauty*.

I met Kathy first.

It was A WALLY PETTIFER LYCEUM PANTOMIME, which stood for the best; and since the label automatically promised adjectives like "spectacular" and "dazzling", you can imagine that rehearsals were strenuous. Particularly when I tell you that besides my chorus work and duties in the prompt corner – one hundred and twenty light cues – I was doubling as Prince's Equerry and Bad Fairy's Demon Slave. (Salary though, up to fourteen pounds.) So it was quite a while before I became properly conscious of Kathy. Not till dress-rehearsal time.

Oh, I had noticed her; I'd watched her being taken a couple of times through a solo dance (ballet) during a transformation scene, and thought her rather good as she coped with an intricate routine. Pretty, but they were all pretty; she had nice fine fair hair. I'd also been struck by her name, on the call-sheet: sandwiched between Mimi Vandeleur and Greta O'Carrington, you had to look twice at "Kathy Tripp".

And one remark sticks in my mind, a comment she made about our producer. The ENTIRE PRODUCTION was, of course, IN THE SOLE HANDS OF WALLY PETTIFER HIMSELF. Himself was fifty-ish, and at the height of his success as an impresario: a vulgar lecherous brick-faced bully whose power was hated throughout the West-End theatre, where he was known, by great and small, as the Beast. Noël Coward had once remarked that Wally Pettifer would have reduced W. C. Fields to tears.

It was his automatic habit to make a pass at his leading ladies – ours was unavailable, the Principal Boy Marianne Lynne being bespoke to the Bad Fairy, a stalwart baritone – but no girl was safe.

During a coffee-break when I joined the kids huddled off-stage, we listened to the latest Beast story.

We got it from a girl who had got it from Kiki Larousse, who had played a small part in a recent Pettifer revue, *New Roman Scandals*. One matinee, during Nero's Orgy While Watching The Fire, he had waylaid Miss Larousse on the back-stage stairs, and taken advantage. The one American chorus-girl in our cast whispered, "What did you say he did? *Way* laid her?" Then a boy who had been onstage for the Orgy-Fire insisted that the scene had lasted only three minutes.

"Oh," explained the story-teller, "he only wanted her to fiddle with him."

"Of course," says Kathy Tripp, painting her nails, "what else could she do, while Rome burnt?"

I had to look at her then; she'd said it in a flat Cockneyish way, quite a drawl, and with no expression, almost absent-minded, big thoughtful brown eyes. You just had to laugh.

Came the dreaded working dress-rehearsal, starting at 10 a.m. and going on through the day and into the small hours, something like 6 a.m.

Dreaded because it was the Beast's big day, and night. And this the biggest, working up to tomorrow's First Night, the most ambitious he'd ever tackled.

By the tea-break the twenty-four Tiller Girls (dressed as Toy Soldiers) were shaking with fright, and by midnight tempers were steaming. You could smell gunpowder. Any minute . . .

One a.m. The Tillers, by now Court Ladies, were halfway through a difficult routine with crinolines, put in only two days before; one girl, extra-tired, stumbled and they all got out of step. A bellow, "Hold everything!"

Two Tillers burst into tears, as the Beast lumbered to the pass-door and on to the stage. "You stupid bunch of amateur nitwits!" Then he showed them the step, moving them around like an elephant shifting furniture. From the prompt corner, I could see the whole company, including the star, standing about like scared rabbits.

Then he said, "Now get on with it!", started again for the stalls, hesitated, then hurried off through a back door. Miss Lynn announced, "He's been caught short and let's hope he's peed himself." Everybody laughed and felt better.

Silence: the Beast was clumping back. "Now get on with it, and any girl who goes wrong this time gets the sack!"

As he walked to the pass-door, not a sound: just the respectful silence, bursting with hate. Then a voice, clear and cool. "Please adjust your dress before leaving."

The cheeky drawl sounded familiar, it came from a girl sitting cross-legged on the floor, her back against the proscenium arch: in itself an insolent pose. Kathy Tripp.

The Beast stood stock-still, as if a pellet had been shot into the bulging back of his neck, and looked down at himself. His flies were undone. And in those days of buttons, there was no chance of instant correction. He went as red as an ugly oversized turkey, looked round at the staring company, then at the girl, his mouth open. She was looking at him with big saucer eyes as if it hadn't been her at all. His mouth still wouldn't shut. It was glorious.

He found words in the end. "If we weren't opening tomorrow night – no, tonight – I'd kick you out, now. You'll play the first performance, then out! Won't be easy to get a girl ready for the second night – but – but I'll manage – somehow – you're out – out . . ."

As he started to babble and stammer, it was a delight to watch the cruelty dissolve into a puddle, before those unblinking eyes of hers which seemed to be saying, "You're a very rude man, who are you?" She was dead calm, completely sure of herself. So much so, it was almost weird.

Then she spoke again, as if giving a piece of advice, take it or leave it. And this time the voice had no trace of Cockney. Clipped and cool. The accents of a superior addressing an inferior. "Why not try Kiki Larousse, who was in *New Roman Scandals*? Everybody knows Kiki will do *anything* for Mr Pettifer."

The whole stage, blazing with light, was as still as a graveyard waiting for Judgement Day: I could see the orchestra sitting staring, and stage-hands standing staring. I thought, she's out of her bloody mind . . .

The Beast wasn't red any more. Chalk-grey. "Next scene please." The words came out as if in a trance, the stuffing was out of him.

We got to the end of the show, somehow. Disbanded, we were not so exhausted we didn't give Kathy Tripp a quick look. Everybody was admiring her – at the same time it was scary, like somebody you've just watched stroll into the tiger's cage and out again without turning a hair.

She and I happened to be at the stage-door at the same minute. I couldn't help saying, "You must have known he was going to sack you?"

The saucer eyes focused on me: not rude, just not interested, not a flicker. And I wasn't used to that. "I had a *ghost* of an idea he might," said the Cockney drawl – and yet it had a grandish ring to it, somehow – "but the game seemed worth the candle. That man is beneath contempt. Totally." She said it simply, but to me – not used to that sort of language – she sounded as if she were in rather a good play.

"Are you going to turn up tonight?"

"I wouldn't miss a Pettifer first night for anything." She said it in a wooden way, as if issuing a statement to the Press. "I intend to make my performance a memorable one, ta ta." And off she walks, in control, taking her time, to Covent Garden Tube.

The First Night. What with everybody being on their nérvy toes, we all forgot about Kathy Tripp. Early on, she was just going on for her ballet speciality, when Ron (Wicked Fairy) Drew, standing at my shoulder in the prompt corner, between light cues, mutters, "God, suppose she's hatched up some funny business, to spite him!"

It was only then I remembered, and I watched the act with both hands over the light switches. Was she planning a faint? Or an announcement? "Ladies and gentlemen, my employer is beneath contempt, totally." . . . For a stage manager, it was a tense moment.

Not at all; she sailed through in fine form, and with the curtsey at the end, a dazzle of a smile. It lit up the whole face, and – after last night, that contemptuous stare at the Beast – made it unrecognizable. There could be a dash of mischief there, very fetching. I thought, pressing a switch to healthy applause, she may be a clown – Cue 58 B – but she's not only sexy, she's attractive. The two not being necessarily the same thing.

So on with the show, the audience loving it; the Beast was into another smash success. We get to the Finale First Half. "The Big Sleep."

This scene was the Beast's ace card, the sort that had put him up where he was, and couldn't fail. On stage – bar stage-management – everybody, including students and guardsmen (half a guinea a perf) standing in lines up a giant staircase watching – to start with – the Beauty and her Court as they danced to glorious Tchaikowsky music: the ladies waving gossamer scarves – I was working the wind-machine for that, at the side – as they waltzed with courtiers. Coloured lights, fountains, acrobats, fireworks – the bag of tricks.

During this, two spontaneous bursts of applause. The waltz came to a climax, crash, enter Wicked Fairy, silence. Then the "magic"

music, the spell started and gradually the whole cast, starting with
the Beauty, moved in drugged slow motion: footmen, soldiers, pages,
courtiers, sank down into slumber. Then the ladies. Standing in the
wings, easing off the wind-machine and watching the last scarf drift
slowly down and the whole thing freeze into a painting, I thought I'd
never seen anything so hypnotic. The music died away.

Then the beat of silence, which would have to be shattered by a
roar of applause. My hand was ready to signal the slow dim-down of
the lights, then the curtain.

But . . .

Suddenly – I couldn't believe my eyes – something moved. Some-
body. One of the sleeping girls. Kathy Tripp.

She sat slowly up, looked straight at the audience, gave a loud
long snore and flopped again on to her back as if she had been shot.

One more beat . . Then the audience laughed. And laughed. A
noise for which any comic would have sold his mother. Lights out,
and the curtain came down.

To pandemonium. The Beast was through the pass-door like a
fat arrow on fire. "Where's that blanking blank?" (To skip the
obvious four-letter words.)

And *where* was she? The Second Half had to be got ready and
gone through, and nobody had time to wonder. But it was reported,
later, that two seconds after the curtain fell on the unforgivable
crime, Miss Tripp had been seen to glide to the stage-door, pick up
her (pre-packed) suitcase and coat, and vanish into the first-night
night in her stage finery. Somebody said, "Christ what an exit!"

It was also an entrance. Into my life.

CHAPTER FIVE

Kathy and Bruce

The next morning, for the first time in living memory, a First Night hit the front pages. PANTO GIRL'S REVENGE!...REBEL MAID WALLOPS WALLY!...THE SNORING BEAUTY!!! That last one was to go into the West End language for several weeks. And "The Rebel Maid" hit the nail on the head.

They tracked her down, of course. Just before the second night, on the stairs, I stood looking at the *Evening News*: a blown-up photo of her in a sort of kimono, hair all over the place, they must have woken her up.

Underneath, *"Miss Tripp looked, and sounded, vague. 'Being a dumb blonde, I'm puzzled by the brouhaha, it's just that it occurred to me that with the entire cast sound asleep on stage, the scene might look a wee bit static and the audience might go to bye-byes too, so I thought if I gave it a lift Mr Pettifer would be grateful, I did it for him, I'm deeply sorry . . .' "*.

By the time I was standing on her doorstep in Battersea, it was just on midnight.

She lodged in a shabby side-street, worse than mine in King's Cross. That drowsy look again. I said, "Hello".

"You have the advantage of me." Cool and clipped again, as if any minute she might address me as "young man". "Are you another journalistic intruder?"

That riled me. "No, just a back-stage blur."

"Sorry, I'm getting sleepy."

"D'you remember *any* people you work with?"

She didn't answer. A ploy as simple as it was defeating. I went on, "Did you see today's papers?"

"In point of fact, I chose not to. Emphatically."

"You're described as the Snoring Beauty."

Her eyes cleared in a flash, she looked straight at me, and laughed: a joyous gurgle, and with a smile which took me back to her sparkle at the end of her solo dance. "Oh," she said, "I *like* that!" Cockney. Then she went drowsy and grand again. "Why have you come to see me?"

"To congratulate you."

"Nobody else has. What on?"

"Your guts."

"Ooh, you are common."

I thought I'd show off with a book-word. "Well then, your courage."

"I wasn't being courageous. I was enjoying – totally – getting him by the balls, the vile old bugger."

Now that was unexpected. I said, "Who's being common now, totally?"

"That wasn't common, it was invective."

Invective? Where had she got that from? Did she mean "effective"? Behind her in the little room, I could see a shelf of shabby old books. Was she a *reader*?

Her kimono thing was undone; she fastened it. In no hurry.

I said, "But it's put you out of work."

"I've been that before. In the morning I'll go round the agents. The long, long trail awinding."

She stood there, in absolute command. Unusual. Her fastening of the kimono had pressed it against her nipples, and even in the dim light I could see them, jutting nicely out.

I went on looking, as if deep in thought. Not a bad technique, I have proof of that. Makes a girl say "Penny for 'em" or some such, then you know the doorbell's working.

She said nothing so normal. "You're looking very abstracted."

She sounded drowsier than before. And grander. *Abstracted*? Swallowed a dictionary.

For something to say, I said, "Are you keen to get on?"

"No. Well, yes, I want to be a writer."

"Not a dancer? You're good enough for ballet."

"Covent Garden, would you say? Kathy Tripp? Hardly. Would you suggest, maybe, Katya Trippova?"

That made me smile. "Well, I'll be off."

"I've been in bed for an hour, reading, d'you want to get in?"

I thought, that's not out of *any* dictionary. I nearly said, "Don't mind if I do," but didn't. Common. But I couldn't compete with her, not in words. I said, "Are you feeling that way too?"

The eyes cleared again, and twinkled. "I do sometimes, when I'm at a loose end."

The bed was still warm. She smelt warm too, plus a trace of eau de Cologne. She wasn't fat, neither was she thin. It was lovely.

Then there was Bruce.

All she had told me about herself, at breakfast, was that she had started life in an Orphanage in Stoke Newington, outside London, that the Matron had paid for her to have ballet lessons, that she'd saved enough out of her first job to go in for half-a-dozen speech lessons – from which she had evidently learnt wonders – and that Bruce was as near being a steady as anybody. "But it's not an involvement. It's my belief one should never become irremediably entangled." Like last night, she sounded so much in control – plus the long words – that I was put off, for a minute.

But when I left in the morning, another surprise.

Over the Snoring Beauty business, she had seemed tough enough for me to feel it was safe to say, "Good luck with the agents, but I'm afraid you won't find things too easy."

She looked at me a second, then – with no warning – burst into tears. It was so sudden that it knocked me sideways, and without even thinking what I was doing I put my arms round her and laid her head on my chest, as if she were ten years old. I'd never done such a thing in my life before.

I could just make out what she was trying to say, "Why did I do it – ruining the show – putting all those people out of work – I'll never get another job, never – why, why . . ."

And as I smoothed her hair, I knew in a flash that all that funny self-possession of hers, off-hand and almost insolent, including the juggling with the long words – that all that was a protective front, carefully built to protect the insecure child inside. A child who had started life surrounded by strangers, and now looked out with wary eyes: not sure of anything, ready to resist the lot. It was my guess too – and again I knew I was right – that a lot of insecurity came from the fact that she had had even less education than me, and the long words weren't just an affectation: the only person she was showing off to was herself.

I could set her mind at rest on one score. "Believe it or not," I said, playing with her ear, which some instinct told me would comfort her, "your snoring act has somehow had a healthy effect on the box-office, the advance is terrific." That perked her up, "Forgive the self-pity, not a typical habit of mine." The defences were up again, and we parted on a cheery note. Casual.

But on the bus, my thoughts were with them both. Kathy. And Bruce.

Bruce Renfrew, as Scottish as Kathy and I were English, and three months older than me: while she was three months younger. She had first met him earlier in the year (1933), when they were both in *Mother of Pearl* at the Gaiety with Delysia, and she had then got him an audition for *The Sleeping Beauty*. As a result, he was sharing the top dressing-room with me and twelve others. I had been so busy, and he so quiet in a far corner, that I had hardly glanced at him. That evening, I took a little more interest.

Most of us were good-looking, but Bruce was the best, and seemed not to know it. Like me, he was neither tall nor short, neither burly nor thin: a fair Scot, almost flaxen, but with sudden liquid-brown black-lashed eyes, from – as Kathy told me later – a half-Neapolitan mother.

After the show, I asked him to the Strand Corner House for kippers.

"Thanks, prrovided I pay my whack." The Scottish accent was firm without being aggressive. As we entered the crowded restaurant, our looks drew a few glances which said, they look like a pair of struggling actors, shabby but neat. I didn't mind, but it made Bruce self-conscious; as he ordered coffee from the waitress – "wi' milluck" – he was blushing. I was a stranger. Studying the menu – pretending to – the perfect face, with the rounded lips pressed together so as to look thin and sensible – was as closed-up as one of those diaries with a lock which you long to snap off. Seeing him as a rival, I wondered what he was like in bed, I must ask her. If he was her steady, he couldn't be too bad.

All I got was that in character he seemed as immoveably Caledonian as Arthur's Seat, and as silent. As I made conversation, I doubted if we had anything in common. Except Kathy. I asked him how he had got into the theatre. Which opened him up a bit.

"When I was eighteen, in Glasgow. I was standin' outside the Alhambra, at the stage-door, when a fella gets on the chat wi' me, very friendly, his hair dyed black as I remember, an' says, 'Would ye like to go on the stage?' An' I say, 'Is that where the leak is?' "

I looked up from my kipper. "What d'you say?"

"I was a plumber's mate. Well, this fella takes me up to the dressin'-room where the wash-basins were."

"And he hangs about while you mind the tap?"

"That's right. Then he takes me down to the stage, and a mon says, 'Can ye dance?' and I say, 'No, but I can sing 'Annie Laurie', which I did, an' next day I was a Mountie in *Rose Marie*."

I told him I'd been in it too, also on tour. Would either of us have been, if we each hadn't been asked a question in the street by a stranger? "Would you like to go on the stage?" "You up for the A.S.M.?" And here we were.

I asked him if he liked being an actor. "It's better'n plumbin'."

To hell with making conversation. "Got a girl friend, Bruce?" It worked. "I'm verra attached to Kathy Tripp. I'm afraid that on the firrst night she drawed attention to herself."

"So I noticed. But didn't you think it was a brave thing to do?"

He shook his head like an old deacon. "Verra ill-advised. I nearly went over after the show last night to tell her so."

Then, just as I was thinking, funny if we'd met on the doorstep, he said, "Funny if we'd met on the doorstep."

I looked at him; and suddenly, the whole face opened into a wide, shiny grin across perfect teeth. Like Kathy's smile, his brought him three feet nearer to you, just like that. "I phoned her today." In his own way, he was as unexpected as she was.

I said, "Do you mind?"

"It's a free country. I'm worried about her, though."

"So am I." Then more chat – but I'd made headway. As we walked to the Tube, I said, "In *Rose Marie*, did you see much more of your chum with the dyed hair?"

"Only once, when he asked me to the pub for a drink. That was when he tole me I was a Greek statue, I didn't know how to take that, the only Greek statues I know of bein' pretty much bashed about. Anyway, that night he told the other boys he'd gone off me."

"Why?"

"Said I was dull."

"Silly old bastard."

"He was right. I *was* dull, still am." He nodded, thoughtfully. "I know what's the trouble with me."

"What?"

"No sense of humour. I've tried an' tried, but if it's not there, it's not there, is it? Goo' night Jack, thanks for askin' me out."

It was then I knew I was going to like him.

The Panto thrived and – again unexpectedly, and an immense relief – Kathy's escapade was so much condoned by the profession that the very next week, in the teeth of the Beast, Jack Buchanan offered her a nice little dancing part in *Mr Whittington* at the Hippodrome. The next day, she asked me over to Battersea, to celebrate over eggs-and-bacon cooked on her gas-ring. She was warm, simple, relaxed. And no Parade of the Long Words.

In bed after lunch I mentioned Bruce, knowing that he'd occupied the same space last Sunday. I asked about earlier in the year, how it had started.

"Took ages. You see, he was a bit of a muddle. An Italian grandmother but two Presbyterian parents, kirk-ridden, they make your mother sound like a Free-thinker. They're fighting Grannie, which means that to the end of his life he'll be serious. Asked me back one night after the show, to his bed-sitter for coffee. And coffee it was, I was a guest and not one to make the first move. The following week *I* asked *him* for coffee. Politeness really, and I didn't expect him to make a pass, but he did. I was careful not to rush him, to leave the moves to him – but at the same time I felt I was Sadie Thompson leading John Knox astray. Only this one was prettier."

"But not much fun?"

"None at all, nothing happened, you'd have thought there was a bobby at the key-hole. So a few nights later I was surprised when he asked himself back again, and produced a quarter-bottle of rum as a present, plus ginger-ale. We both had a drink, I'd never tasted rum, rather nice. I could tell he doesn't drink a thing, normally, but he had another, and that broke the ice. That wee drop of Mediterranean blood came to the boil and all hell broke loose, it was dreamy. And it's stayed that way. You said how good he looks when one's lucky enough to get that smile. Well, in bed, in the middle of everything, he'll suddenly laugh – a bit mad but not a bit scary, one chuckle after another, like a happy baby."

"On rum and ginger-ale?"

"Only that first time. But I keep some in that cupboard; you never know."

The following Sunday, Bruce and I went over for lunch, then we talked. At least Kathy and I did, she was very funny about the girls she'd dressed with in *Mother of Pearl*: not maliciously so, affectionately, which I liked. Bruce listened, weighing every word. I remembered "To the end of his life, he'll be serious." I also remembered the bedtime moment when the Neapolitan grandmother took over. The abandoned chuckle, like a happy baby.

Moreover, Grannie must have been good company, because in between the seriousness, Bruce showed glimpses of unexpected fun, accompanied by the straightest of faces. I picked up an open book, was impressed that Kathy was reading *Eminent Victorians*, and showed it to him.

"Would ye care," he said, "for a ferrst-hand report on Queen Victoria? . . . Nae, I wasn't born but my gran'father was, an' preachin' in the village of Crathie by Balmoral. One day on a walk he stops to light his pipe close to a pair of individuals leanin' over a gate, deep in thought. Says one mon to the other, who was wearin' a kilt, 'Tell me, Mr Brown – what is she like?'

"Mr Brown thinks for a wee minute, then – 'Not a bad auld soul,' he says, 'prrovided she keeps her place.' My gran'father called it a subverrsive asserrtion, but I'm partial to it meself."

"So am I," said Kathy, "a nice change from the kow-towing that still goes on – two years ago, when they came to see *Casanova*, the fuss outside and inside the Coliseum – ludicrous!"

After tea, Bruce and I stayed on. She wound up an old portable gramophone, we listened to "Let's Fall in Love", then to numbers from *Mother of Pearl*. One of them was a chorus song – "Bruce, that ghastly routine we all had to go through, let's see if it'll come back" – and they lugged the furniture round and recreated the dance for me, exaggerating the silliness of it until we all collapsed like children in a nursery.

Then it was six o'clock, and Kathy produced a bottle of sherry, "Only three-and-six, but not bad." I asked Bruce if he would sooner have a rum and ginger-ale, wondering at the same second if he'd be offended, but he wasn't. He stared, gave Kathy a quick look of mock embarrassment, then – "Sherry's safer". We toasted one another, and worked on an unfinished jig-saw puzzle.

During the easy conversation, we happened to compare notes on the childhood memory that stays with you for ever. Bruce had once seen a dead body floating in the Clyde, Kathy had stood at a window in the Orphanage watching a spectacular midnight fire – then they made me tell of *my* memory – the Tyneside visit to Jarrow, the ghastly spectre of Unemployment, the haunted starving faces, the start of the March on London. I was getting – for me – quite heated, till Bruce, rightly, pricked the balloon. "Steady on – cheer up, the Red Army, this is a par-rty, cheer *up*!" He was right, and we did.

At seven I said, "Must get back to my cockroaches." Bruce's face lit up. "Have ye got cockroaches in your digs – same here, that's ter-rrific! I must get back to mine too, afore they get anxious an' star-rt phonin' the police-station." Kathy clapped her hands, "What a *splendid* thing to have in common, cockroaches!" In passing, I puzzled as to when it had occurred to me that Bruce and I had something else in common – what was it? Her, of course. Kathy.

As we got up to go she asked us what we would be doing about a meal, and we answered, together – "Tins". There was a delicatessen next door, if we two would shop there she would cook dinner and then we could wash up. In the middle of dinner we all three had the same idea: it seemed ideally practical for Bruce and me to break faith with our cockroaches, and for the trio to pool resources and settle into a flat.

82a Yeoman's Row, a little street off Brompton Road, near Harrods. The flat was a small top one, unfurnished and very dingy, so the three of us set to and washed it right through.

Then Bruce told us he had been an apprentice house-decorator as well as a plumber's mate, and proved it by expertly distempering every square yard of the place, till it looked as fresh as a daisy. We bought a minimum of second-hand furniture, including a big double bed, a bargain. Turns would be taken with shopping, washing-up and cleaning; also we could all three cook, so we'd have a nice house-warming supper. No presents – but Kathy said that wasn't so, since we each had a present of the other two.

One problem had to surface sooner or later: besides the sitting-room and bedroom with the bargain of a double bed, there was only a box-room, small kitchen and tiny spare room with a single divan. In the middle of our pre-move spring-clean, during a breather for tea Kathy said, "So we'll eat at that table and put it under the window – and next, where do we all sleep?"

Nobody said anything, we just looked at one another, smiling. "Och," said Bruce, "not like our Kathy to tur-rn perr-nickety!"

He was as fond of her as I was, but I knew too that his feelings, at that moment, were no deeper than mine. Or than hers for either of us. At that moment. "Well," she said, looking amused, "as the lady of the house I am clearly entitled to the best. And the best is the double bed. And since it's hardly practical for you two to share that single divan, and there's also no charlady to threaten to leave-this-minute-unless, I modestly suggest that you toss up for the bed."

We did. I won.

I wonder how things would have turned out if I had lost.

". . . Your Da was readin' out of the Daily Express about that rude lady snorin' & persecutin' your poor employer Mr Pettifer. Oh we are properly releived that you been & found a home wi this married couple to look after you . . ."

While 82a was indeed our home, Bruce was usually out a couple of nights a week, leading his own life and well in control of it; and though it was not in his nature to be secretive, he was always tactful and it was mostly anybody's guess which way the odd rum and ginger-ale might have drawn him.

And even in my case, it would be wrong to give the idea that, at this point, I led a completely domesticated life. I still – once in a while, usually of a Sunday evening – got restless and wandered off to join a couple of the others from the top dressing-room in a pub-crawl which tended to include one or two bars with what the papers called "a dubious reputation".

Dubious or not, they were very colourful and always good for a laugh. One Sunday when Kathy had a dinner date – she was tactful too – Bruce and I ended up in the public bar of the Bag o' Nails across the road from Buckingham Palace. Getting into conversation with Harry Kellow, a guardsman a year or two older, I discovered to my delight that he was not only Cornish, but hailed from St Austell and had even strolled up Tregonissey Hill to have a look over the wall at Dad's garden. Harry was a lively customer and good company, so Bruce and I were glad to run into him a couple of times over the next year. And once, at the Fitzroy Tavern, I was offered a drink by a couple of chaps who took me to a grand party in Mayfair, given by a Sir Simon Rawson.

It was grand all right; but by one a.m. it was fair sizzling. I should have cottoned on to Sir S. when somebody whispered that he was a bosom pal of Tallulah's. Well, he came up to me with a fresh whisky-

and-soda – which he had well spiked with something, a real Mickey Finn – and the next I knew I was naked on the carpet with two naked girls and Sir S.'s camera clicking away like nobody's business. "For posterity, darlings, posterity!" For the time being, we draw a veil over that. Back to Kathy and Bruce.

The three of us got very attached: perhaps it helped that each was an only child, also we were so different that we suited one another.

Kathy. All her life, from that Orphanage on, she had ached to give affection, and for it to be given back to her. And she knew that, from Bruce and me, she was getting that affection. Also, she was forging ahead, very slowly. When she had mentioned to me that she wanted to be a writer, she had meant it, and was now making a start.

A secret writer, at the moment. She had bought a little desk and under a blotter ("I got the idea from Jane Austen") she kept copy-books in which she had started a novel, which you could tell meant much more to her than her dancing. I once asked her – if she had to choose between the desk and the bed, which would she settle for?

She thought about it. And finally drawled out, "Darling, the bed. I could always sit up in it with a writing-pad on my knee, but try and enjoy the other on that desk . . ."

One morning a week, at my suggestion, she gave me and Bruce an hour's speech lesson – at least she gave *me* the hour, because after twenty minutes Bruce, the obstinate Scot, declared that he had no ear and it was his turrn to get the lunch. After that I was the sole pupil, one hour a week. A bit lazy, but I made progress. And Teacher did agree that it was right for Bruce to stay Scottish, it was a part of him. He used the hour to do odd jobs around the flat.

Yes, we were attached.

I mentioned a box-room. I had once talked to them both about my obsession with windmills, and one day I got back from understudy rehearsal to find they had got in a big work-table and set up the little place as a first-class work-room. I was thrilled, wrote to my mother to send me my windmill tools and went shopping for neces-sities – balsa wood, beechy wood, surgical blades, enamel paints, emery boards – I'll stop there.

I also bought a book, Trenchard's *Windmills, Their Historical and Technical Evolution*, studied others in the British Museum Reading Room, and spent hours in the Science Museum, Exhibition Road. Then, every spare moment I had was given to "the Windmill Room". Kathy once said, "No wonder you're a good stage-manager, I've never seen such microscopic attention to detail!" It was a funny talent, but it was there all right. Windmills, and watermills, are beautiful things. When you have finished a model and press a button and then watch the wheel turn, slow and graceful, then faster, and then the water drip or the flour start to stir – beautiful.

The Panto finished in February; Bruce went into a musical play at the Coliseum, *The Golden Toy*, and I into *Music in the Air* at His Majesty's. Then the splendid summer (of 1934): excursions by Green Line bus to Virginia Water and Henley, down the Thames in a punt. On non-matinee days, while Bruce went swimming at the Y.M.C.A. or exercising at the gym, Kathy took me for walks in Hyde Park and Kensington Gardens – always the same route, round the Serpentine.

One morning, when I was crossing the living-room from the Windmill Room to make us a cup of coffee, Kathy looked up from her manuscript to find me staring in her direction. "What's the matter darling, aren't I tidy?"

"It's the desk."

"The desk? I bought it in a sale, I told you . . ."

"I've never really looked at it. It's different."

"How?"

"Well, it's . . ." I was self-conscious. "It's better-looking."

"It's a beauty, it's Sheraton. You'd never have guessed that, it was so cheap."

"Sheraton? I didn't know he made furniture, I thought he wrote plays." (I had stage-managed *The School for Scandal* in rep.)

She explained. I said, "I'm not artistic." "You don't have to be artistic to enjoy art, you just use your eyes. You think you're a Philistine but you're not."

I nearly asked, "What's a Philistine?" then thought the question might prove I was one, whatever it might be. I looked it up in her dictionary. "A person deficient in culture . . . one whose interests are material and commonplace." Well, I thought, that's me.

But since she wasn't in complete agreement, on several afternoons I accompanied her to the National Gallery. And scanning the procession of framed riches, I saw them through her sensitive loving eyes and learnt a lot.

One of our excursions that summer was to Hampton Court, to look at the treasures in the way of antiquities. We walked through the rooms: a bit overpowering for me, even more for Bruce, but Kathy was absorbed. After a hotel lunch near by, with wine, we wandered into a sort of park, sat under a tree, then – from the wine – we fell asleep. I woke up first, sat up and looked at them. Her head was at rest on his thigh, her face and breast turned straight up as if wanting to reach up to the blue sky. He was smiling in his sleep. With the trees and the grass, they were two glowing Babes in the Wood.

I was to think of that 1934 day, a lot. During the following year. Which was getting nearer.

CHAPTER SIX

Up to the High Dive

October the 18th, of the same 1934, my twenty-fourth birthday; at supper the three of us had a bottle of Algerian wine. Kathy said, "Jack, you're Libra, nearly Scorpio."

I said, "And what does that make me?"

"Optimistic, tolerant, line of least resistance."

"That's me. Superficial."

"Oh no!" I looked at her in surprise, she had said it so forcibly. She went on. "You *think* you're superficial. But you're not."

"Prove it."

"Easy. That experience you told us about, when you were fourteen – the unemployed on Tyneside. The way all that sank in – you haven't forgotten and never will. It's just that since then you've been dormant, with nothing happening to dig into you. I'm afraid it takes a crisis to wake up a Libra."

"Such as the lighting board catching fire in the middle of a first night?"

"Could be."

"Interesting. I must get those buckets of water into the prompt corner."

Kathy's turn came; her birthday was December 31st, "the Orphanage wasn't sure, so my guess is as good as anybody's . . ." We had all three worked consistently through the year. Looking back, I noted that I seemed to wander less and less and to spend more and more time – without in any way committing myself – in Kathy's company.

"In twenty minutes," she said dreamily, "it will be 1935."

I had turned off the top light, and in the glow of the gas-fire the three of us were sitting on the floor, in fancy dress, Kathy as Columbine, Bruce and I as the Two Pierrots: after midnight we'd be off to the Albert Hall, to the riotous annual event known as the Chelsea Arts Ball. (The boxes were a byword; a couple of years back, a dancer we knew in the Sadler's Wells Ballet had entered one of them dressed as a sailor and emerged, a couple of hours later, as Lawrence of Arabia.)

I had wound up the portable and put on "Let's Fall in Love"; in the flat, it had gradually become a kind of theme song. *Let's fall in love, now is the time for it, while we are young – let's take a chance, why be afraid of it* . . . "In front of us," I said, "is a crystal ball."

Kathy pondered, her hands round her knees, her hair drawn back to a knot, looking very pretty. "One thing it can tell *me*. By the end of the year I'll be twenty-five. One year nearer to thirty."

Was she going to get sad? But she brightened up. "Bruce, what's *your* wish? For Gaumont-British Studios to groom you as Jessie Mathews's new leading man?"

You could almost hear him putting his mind to it. "I'd luke guid in the test, but the rest wouldna stand up to it." It was true, and would apply just as well to me. But I had my stage-management, and my windmills, even better.

Then Bruce said something; you never knew what that flat prosaic voice might come out with. "It may sound a bit crazy" – it wouldn't, nothing he said could ever sound crazy – "but what I wude really like," – he was looking into the gas-fire, as if absent-minded – "is for the both of you, in 1935, to get *your* wish."

Kathy and I looked at each other. And she said, "Bruce love, if Jack and I, in 1935, hear anything as nice as that from anybody, we'll be lucky."

The record finished, I clicked it off and turned on the wireless. "Kathy?"

"I sound cold-blooded, but what I'm hoping for is a pleasant rich older man. Not rich enough to dominate me, but rich. Any age up to forty-five – listen, they're playing my tune!"

They were: on the wireless, the Tchaikowsky music from "The Big Sleep". We laughed. It faded into "Auld Lang Syne", then the midnight boom of Big Ben and the gurgle of more Algerian wine. I said, "Here's to the Snoring Beauty, and the forty-five-year-old Prince who's going to wake her with a hit on the head with a cheque-book."

"Thank you, love. And you?"

"Oh," I said, "very dull, I just wish to keep working through the year and for us to stay as we are." We all kissed under the mistletoe, but for a minute she had depressed me. Had she meant it? Thinking of that orphanage, I understood her fear of being poor at thirty, so the sugar-daddy did make sense . . .

Big Ben died away, we clinked glasses and cheered up. We were into 1935. And off to the Chelsea Arts Ball.

Dancing with Kathy and bumping into a theatre couple we knew, I asked what had happened at midnight, which was usually marked with a ceremony, novel or comic, or both, to introduce the New Year. They both spoke together – "The Sky Whale!"

And we both said, "What's that?" "We didn't really know either, it's a new airship that's coming out during the year, they'd made a pretty good rubber model of it with 1935 right across, and it floated down from way up there, not bad, happy New Year!"

Star, Jan. 1st, THE SKY WHALE! *"We can at last announce that Britain's unique contribution to the modern world . . ."*

In February, Kathy went into *Stop Press*, a revue at the Adelphi; and in March Bruce and I auditioned for the big Ivor Novello musical play at Drury Lane (himself, Mary Ellis, Liz Welch) and we both got in. *Glamorous Night*.

Sunday Times, March 31st, FIRST TRIAL FLIGHT TRI-UMPH . . .

We rehearsed through April; both Bruce and I in the chorus, as usual – courtiers to the King of Krasnia, sailors on S.S. *Silver Star*, gypsies at the Gypsy Wedding. I was also A.S.M.: a great challenge, involving a sinking ship. In mid-rehearsal, in the big scene of the ball given by the Baroness Lydyeff I was given two separate speaking lines. *This has proved something of a bolt from the blue!* and *You must have been sorely disappointed.* It indicated that my accent had improved considerably, a compliment to Kathy as well as to me.

Daily Mail, April 25th, SKY WHALE SENSATION! *"On Saturday May 11th . . . Jubilee Family Party . . . Windsor Great Park . . . Entire Royal Family . . ."*

But in Drury Lane Theatre, we were all too busy and could think of no date beyond May the 2nd, our opening night. A big success, and during the next days it was good to relax.

Saturday, May the 11th.

Late brunch, if you remember: we all three had matinées. Listening idly to the wireless commentary. "And here comes the Royal Procession! . . . The Sky Whale moves! . . . It rises! . . ."

Then the horror. And the Week of Mourning. THE WORLD WAITS, WHAT NEXT, A REPUBLIC?

"... Your Da was just remarkin, to think our Jack be within walkin distance o that sad & empty Palace . . . You mind how cheerful he is allways, well he sets for minutes on end starin at the 1910 Coronation mug we got for ee, it bein the same year of your birth. Even Spotto looks like he knows something is wrong. The hens are layin, thank Goodness."

But even after a Holocaust, in the end life has to simmer down to near-normal. On the Monday week the theatres reopened, and audiences crammed in looking for relief; but you could tell they weren't really escaping, by the fact that the jokes which normally got a roar went by in silence, while in every theatre, before reopening, any line which could remind people, in the slightest degree, had to be cut out. Such harmless chit-chat as "A cat may look at a king" or "Who do they think they are, Royalty?" would have got a gasp.

The Old Vic had to drop the Shakespeare historical plays like hot bricks; one West-End play couldn't reopen, a revival of *The Sport of Kings*; while another musical one, in rehearsal, had to be abandoned. *The Student Prince*. People could not have borne those words shouting at them from the posters. And at Drury Lane, Ivor had to rewrite. King Stefan of Krasnia had to be demoted to President, etc. It was a weird time.

The Friday of the fourth week – June the 7th – was the birthday of one of the boys in our chorus-room – if you could call him a boy, he was quite a bit older than us others, somewhere in the shadowy forties: Bill Dell, known affectionately, back-stage as "Belle Dell". He was as thin as a pair of scissors, and had been plagued, since the age of twelve, by a big nose. To which problem, his solution was two small dabs of mauve on the tip of it. He called them his "invisibles".

Two or three days before the event, Belle announced – after being in continuous tears – "If I 'ave to stand it a minute longer, I'm going to lock meself in the loo and scream – *I'm going to give a birthday party!*"

And he did.

"My twenty-first dear, keeps *on* coming round, the monotony of it!" That evening at the end of the show Belle skipped the call (not my place as A.S.M. to give permission, I turned a blind eye) so as to rush to the 11 bus for Chelsea, to get the special punch-bowl on the brew: "it's the aphrodisiacs that take the time, dear . . ."

Kathy joined Bruce and me at the Lane stage door, and a bunch of us (boys and girls) bundled into taxis with bottles discreetly hidden: we had all been careful not to discuss the party, but though we felt guilt we also felt immense relief.

At Belle's flat, the door was opened by a lady's maid, in cap and apron, who curtsied – "Oh sir, oh madam . . ." – curtsied again, and said: "Bugger off upstairs, the lot o' ye." It was Belle.

What with the gramophone and the booze, it was wonderful to let off steam. The party revved up, and at a well-chosen moment Belle made a stage entrance from the bedroom. The lady's maid, fairly sloshed by now, was brandishing a violin.

Belle's fiddle was famous, and – you'd never have thought it – he was a good player. "A present from Heifetz, dear, we're just good friends, oh yes I could ha' been a concert hartiste, but no scenery an' no footlights, you must be mad, if I catch me fiddle in me streamers just sort me out . . ." Accompanying himself he belted into one of Mary Ellis's big numbers in the show, *Fold your Wings around me, Fold them close till they have bound me, I'm your Slave and your Defender, I Surrender!*

It was a riot. Somebody said, "Belle always plays best when she's pissed, come on Belle, 'In a Monastery Garden'!" And "In a Monastery Garden" it was. Then with a bow, "You must all talk Ivor into writing a show for Yours Truly, Belle Dell in *Hello Dragtime!*"

Everybody was thankful for the party, and at about four it came to a pleasant close. The three of us walked home and fell into bed.

Three evenings later . . . No, four, I must get this absolutely accurate. Tuesday June the 11th.

During that day, as sometimes occurs just before a crisis, two very nice things had happened to me. In the morning, the stage director who'd been my boss in *The Sleeping Beauty* (I nearly wrote "Snoring") rang me to say he'd been consulted as to whether I'd make a good stage-manager for a big new New York musical show coming to London, and he'd given me a boost.

And secondly, when I got to the evening show, it turned out that my present Stage Director had given the same recommendation. I seemed to be on the crest of a wave, and nobody rocking the boat.

The crisis started in the middle of the Second Half. I was up in the dressing-room, during one of my ten-minute breaks from the prompt corner; we were all changing from sailors on S.S. *Silver Star* to gypsies at the Gypsy Wedding, all half-naked and out of breath, pulling trousers off and on. A babel of silly chat.

A sharp knock. The stage-doorkeeper, known as Grumpy; he was out of breath too. Still grumpy, but with a light in his eye. The light of bad news. "It's the Police. On the phone."

The chat was cut off as if by a switch. Nobody in that crowded room was a criminal, but this could mean trouble for any of us. Somebody said, "Are you sure?"

"Sounded like the Police to me. Wouldn't give a name." Grumpy was enjoying himself. "It's for Jack Sandring."

They all turned and looked at me, in one swivel. I saw Bruce get up. "Oh?" I said stupidly, "well . . . I can't come now –"

"I'll tell 'em to ring again when the show's over." And he went, colliding with the call-boy, "Ev'rybody down, late call for the Gypsy Weddin'!" We tore down the stairs like a line of trained seals; the others were longing to question me, but no chance, we were on, *In ev'ry gypsy's heart, There's a place for Cupid's dart . . .* And what with the lighting cues and the routines, I just had to forget about the Police.

Almost. How could anybody forget about the Police? And as soon as we were back in our places, taking off make-up, the pumping started. "Now come clean Jacko, we thought Bruce and Kathy had turned you into a home bird, what you been up to?"

"I can't think of a thing." And I couldn't, not anything special; my conscience was clear.

"What happened to that guardsman you met in the Bag o' Nails?"

"Harry Kellow? Haven't run into him for over six months, anyway he's a nice chap, from my part of Cornwall, and he'd be the last to say anything to make trouble –"

Then I remembered something I just happened never to have mentioned to them. The party where the host had spiked my drink and I'd been photographed with those two girls. My conscience was not clear.

Somebody said, "Jack, didn't you know that Neil Wendlebury?"

"Not well enough to worry about. I was having a drink with Harry in the Running Horse when this Neil bloke asked me for my phone number, but when he rang up I took agin him and never saw him again –"

"Had he written your name in his address-book?"

"Yes, why?"

One of the others piped up. "He was in the *News of the World* on Sunday, arrested for having a friend of sixteen. Well *my* friend Stanley is scared stiff, out on bail."

"Bail? What for?"

"For bein' in Neil Wendlebury's address-book."

I looked at Bruce, and felt a bit sick. The sharp knock. "Jack Sandring, Police again." I stumbled down the stairs, buttoning my flies, passed Ivor's door, crossed the vast empty stage as if I was on the Last Mile, and got to the stage-door phone. Grumpy was holding it out to me, all ears.

"Mr Jack Sandring? My name is Fawcett." Rather a posh voice.

"I was told it's the Police, what's it about?"

The man laughed, quite smooth and friendly, which made me even more apprehensive. "No, no, all I said to the doorkeeper was that it was a private matter, and urgent, I'm afraid he jumped to conclusions. No, not exactly the Police, this is Mr Fawcett, Special Investigation Department, Home Office, Whitehall. We're anxious not to attract unnecessary attention by calling at your place of employment, would it be convenient to call for you at your residence, tomorrow morning, eleven thirty?"

Mechanically I gave the address, hung up and turned to Grumpy. *His* attention had been attracted all right. "It's nothing, a friend of mine's had his car stolen." Bruce appeared and we proceeded to the bus: a subdued walk.

And a subdued supper; I told them about the party and the photos, and the address-book. We slept badly. In the morning it was a relief that the only envelope was in my mother's writing.

The relief didn't last.

"Your Da & me are terrible worried. This afternoon 2 gentlemen come up along our Hill, so well-spoken that you could tell straight away they werent from anywhere hereabouts. Pleise, they ask, could we go over the house?

"Oh I was vexed, no I says but out they bring a warant or

some such & go through the big desk, not much there, deeds of Farm, Savin Sustificates receets etc, they seemed to be sniffin for anythin to do with *you*, famly groups, your theetre photos, your leters home, did we know any of your London freinds ect, then they fetch a camra out of the motor car & take photos in your bedroom.

"Whatever ave they got against you? Your Da & me do believe you got no harm in you (well, not a *lot*) but we do know about the Temtations, what have you been up to?" . . .

The doorbell. I said, "Don't leave me alone with him, not to start with." Bruce drew himself together, put on his Scots face and went down to the front door. He came back followed by a man. Then another. Two of them.

Well, if these were policemen, the Force must have gone genteel overnight. Two quite elderly City-type twins, identical in black tie and striped trousers: each with tie-pin, each carrying gloves, brief-case and black bowler. Except that one (old-fashioned even in 1935) wore grey spats.

Then they spoke, together and posh. "Mr Jack Sandring?" Then one said, "I'm Mr Fawcett, we conversed on the telephone last night, this is my colleague Mr Cairns."

A pause. Kathy spoke. In her dictionary voice. "Will you gentlemen kindly excuse me and my fiancé, Mr Renfrew – do sit down – we have to busy ourselves domestically." Even under such stress, she was able to keep up the style.

"Please don't go," said Fawcett, or was it Cairns – "we'll be very brief. It's just that –" he turned to me, smooth as silk – "it would be of enormous help if you would see your way to co-operate with us, so sorry to incommode you . . ."

At the word-game, he was beating Kathy at the syllables – but why the sarcasm? Why couldn't they come out with it, "We're here to see that you help the Police with their inquiries"? They sat eyeing me in a peculiar way, as if I was some kind of . . . specimen – as if they knew I was a murderer and were angling for a confession. Almost wary, not a bit like two older upper-crust gents up against a lower-class chap young enough to be a son, and a wrong-doer at that . . .

Then one of them said, "So in order that the situation can be clarified, if you wouldn't mind accompanying us this morning . . . er . . ."

They'd got to the crunch at last. They got up. I got up. Kathy and Bruce looked stricken. I walked to the door, turned – "I'll get into touch with you, somehow" – and followed the Twins as their shiny shoes pit-patted down our shabby stairs.

Outside, a Daimler, with a liveried chauffeur holding open the back door. I got in, the Twins settled in the front. I was in solitary confinement. Anyway, better than the Black Maria. No noise, just the swish of the wheels. It was a beautiful London May morning, everybody walking happily along, and the car smelt of rich leather. Of success. I stared at the thick rug, past my hands clumped together between the invisible handcuffs.

At Hyde Park Corner the car (as I had expected) turned down Constitution Hill: I somehow knew they were taking me to Bow Street Police Station, just up the road from Drury Lane Theatre.

Then as the Mall swung into sight – I was just able to catch a glimpse of the length of it, of the two endless rows of flagpoles in mourning, stripped of the Jubilee flags – the car went right instead of left, and all of a sudden everything turned very outsize.

The only word for everything I saw, is "great". Great iron gilded gates, with at the top a row of great spikes, between tall stone pillars each holding up a great iron tree with lamps in its branches: a great courtyard, which we crossed, then another courtyard leading to a wide stone staircase. Above it, three great doors. There the car stopped. On the steps, two footmen; one moved down and opened the car door.

In my movements I was always a scrambler, like a schoolboy – Kathy and Bruce were teasers about it – tearing in and out of buses and Tubes and stage-doors. Here I was moving slowly out of a Daimler and placing my two feet on the first step of a staircase leading up to . . . ? As if under water. I heard the footman close the door and the car drive slowly on.

I turned to the Twins. Each held his bowler. I stared at them standing there, bare-headed. I must have looked about twelve. One of them said, "I'm sorry, Sir, but we couldn't talk in front of your friends, or the chauffeur."

I had to say something. "There's some mistake. My name's Jack Sandring. Who are you taking me for?"

The Twins both smiled, and spoke together. "The King of England."

CHAPTER SEVEN

Quite a Day

Then they bowed their heads. I looked, from them, to the great middle door, a double one, which the two footmen were slowly opening. I climbed two steps, then hesitated.

It was as if there was a hand on my shoulder. Suppose I took my top foot off the step, turned, walked back through the courtyards, out past the sentries, up Constitution Hill, and caught the 14 bus to Yeoman's Row?

The footmen stood waiting. I looked down at the Twins, they had not moved. They now stepped up and stood one on each side of me; I waited for them to move. They spoke, together, formally. "After you, if it please your Majesty."

I walked into the Palace.

They followed me, and as the door closed behind me they both gave a sigh of relief. Now that I knew where I was, and who I was – while hardly believing it – I understood the strain they had been under, this morning.

Then one of them made a little rehearsed speech. "We must crave your indulgence, Sir, for all that mysterious cloak-and-dagger stuff, doncher know, you see we had to do everything to prevent a leakage to the Press before the signal can be given . . ."

"It's quite all right." What else could I say?

I looked round. Everything still outsize: immensely tall marble columns, and a great staircase sweeping and winding solidly up. The real thing, not like the ones in Panto. We climbed it, me in the

middle. Looking down, I saw that the cuff of my shirt, though clean –
Kathy had washed and ironed it yesterday – was frayed. And I remembered her reminding me I could do with a couple of new ones,
people notice these things at auditions; what was more, Bruce should
have his shoes heeled . . .

I looked further down, at my own brown shoes. I'd once left a
pair of shoe-trees behind in the theatre in Dundee and never possessed any since, and my instep had a corrugated look. I remembered
I was wearing a bow tie, also that the inside of my shirt-collar probably had a trace of stage make-up from last night. A wave of shabbi-
ness came over me.

At the top, we entered rooms as big and as high as churches,
walking on carpets that looked like flower-beds. I did notice that, for
May, it was quite a draughty journey. Also the feeling recurred of
being in trouble: the Twins on either side of me could have been the
politest of policemen. We came to the biggest room. Said one of the
Twins, with pride, "One hundred and fifty feet long . . ." With
pride, but in a hushed voice; I noticed, not for the last time, that
people tended to speak, hereabouts, as if they *were* in a series of
churches.

We proceeded between oak panelling, with on it rows and rows of
paintings in gilt frames, some enormous, some tiny, all crammed
with powdered wigs and silks and satins and jewels and medals. And
on either side a mish-mash of priceless stuff, I was later to read it all
up. And it sounds like the richest Auction Sale in the world: Rem-
brandt, Frans Hals, Van Dyke . . .

Aubusson carpets, tables of gold and lacquer, Queen Charlotte's
bureau-cabinet, a Chinese supper-table (oak and lacquer), Boulle
escritoires, clocks of marble and ormolu, bronze and ormolu, ebony
and ormolu, tortoise-shell and ormolu – I was to get a bit tired of
ormolu – the Prince Regent's grand piano, a vase of gros-bleu Sèvres
with turtledove handles, a monumental barometer, pot-pourri jars,
Fabergé. Name it, we've got it.

To the left, one of the great doors was open; we stopped, and one
of them breathed – "The Music Room". High, high above, a vast
chandelier, a glass thicket with a thousand twigs, each made of
gleaming crystal. Across the room, five great bay windows.

It was then that I felt sure I was dreaming. The windows overlooked the heart of a countryside, bathed in sunlight: clumps of
green, a great expanse of green grass, in the distance a great curved
lake. Of course – the Garden, where those Garden Parties go on:

with in the furthest distance, the high wall with behind it Grosvenor Place, from where – if you were quick – you could catch a glimpse of the Gardens as you skimmed past on the top of a 16 bus.

We came to a door with a lot of gilt on it. One of them opened it, the other said "The Royal Closet", and before I could think what a rum name it was, I was inside.

The room was smaller without being small, with a big marble table with lions' heads underneath, but quite bare on top. Against the wall, a sort of gilt throne, very stately; the two of them lugged it up to the table. They seemed to expect me to sit at it, so I did.

One of them unlocked a drawer, took out a portfolio and laid it in front of me as a footman came in (one of the ones earlier? they all looked alike) with a silver tray and silver things on it, coffee for one. As he poured out, one of the Twins said, "If your Majesty, having spent a moment studying these papers, would have the goodness to press this button . . ."

They left me. The footman left me. I opened the portfolio.

"HIGHLY CONFIDENTIAL." Page after page of typed rig-marole: I turned them, way out of my depth. *Emergency measure heretofore without precedent – whereas yet another interpretation (see Wilkes and MacMahon, pp. 1781) of the Laws of Succession – videlicet* Case of Somebody V. Something re Statute of 1765 . . . Then – "Minutes of EMERGENCY MEETING at 10 Downing Street, evening of Tuesday June 11th, 1935." Last night. The typists must have worked till dawn. "The Prime Minister, the Right Hon. Stanley Baldwin, presided.

"The P.M.: 'In view of the mounting national bewilderment, a momentous decision must be made tonight: every hour counts. First let me read you the directive from the Cabinet. "It is our un-animous opinion, having examined the list of minor foreign royalty (and morganatic quasi-royalty) lined up in decreasing stature as candidates for the British throne, that it is imperative to find a Monarch of British blood. Which brings us to a subject –' "

At that second my eye happened to catch the heading of the document underneath, and it was one to make me sit right up. Though I was obviously not meant to read this one before finishing the Minutes, I couldn't resist it. "THE JACK SANDRING REPORT."

"Our immediate concern, of course, was the Report of our two officials who called on the mother of the said *Jack Sandring* (now Mrs Green) and his adoptive father *Bertram Green*. Both Protestants; no trace of Catholicism on either side. The latter is a gentle-manly peasant, not markedly industrious and with a leaning towards conviviality, but of sterling character.

"But it is the mother who constitutes the candidate's strongest recommendation. *Alice Lavinia Green* is a remarkable woman, of good Cornish stock and moral character, who has brought up her son with the prime idea that he should develop into a decent human being.

"It was next arranged, under the direction of Messrs. Fawcett and Cairns, that the discreetest inquiries should be implemented, sepa-rately, by no fewer than 27 trusted agents.

"First, the Cornish background. Ten of the agents proceeded, separately, to St Austell, Tregonissey etc. and interviewed ten separate sources (headmaster and teachers, Sunday-school teachers, former fellow-pupils, etc.) with the idea of ascertaining whether young Mr Sandring would 'make a secretary'. His scholastic record was apparently unimpressive, but since all agree that he is slightly above average intelligence, that can be helped. The consensus was favourable. It should be added that the discreet inquiries as to health were also favourably answered, in particular with regard to *haemo-philia*.

"Second, the London background. On this we employed the same procedure, employing the other (17) agents with the pretext of ascertaining whether the young man would make a suitable employee as Stage Manager for an American musical play (imaginary). Among those consulted were the impresario Mr Archie Pitt and the actress Miss Celia Gold.

"From the 17 combined comments, we confidently report that the candidate is an extremely reliable worker, meticulous, conscientious and well-mannered: and, in spite of his youth, unlikely to allow sudden success to go to his head.

"MORAL CHARACTER."

I sat up. All right, let's have it.

"Needless to say, the fact that he has been involved with the theatrical profession was hardly encouraging. But we have been pleasantly surprised.

"He smokes very little, drinks socially but in moderation. Has never married or been engaged, and – again despite his youth – has no sentimental affiliations which might constitute future embarrass-ment. Has for 18 months shared a London home with 2 close friends, a young lady and her Scottish fiancé. So we must conclude that his moral record is a satisfactory one."

Feeling fairly shaken after listening – as it were – to twenty-seven witnesses pronouncing on me – I went back to the EMERGENCY MEETING at Downing Street. The Prime Minister still speaking. ". . . Imperative to find a Monarch of British blood. Which brings us to a subject which has been, for exactly 50 years, a mystery: a mystery because the facts, by adamant order of *Queen Victoria*, were suppressed and consigned as 'private papers' to the Palace Archives. But this week, owing to the unique features of the crisis, we have been allowed access to those papers. I refer to the *Clarence Case*.

"Tonight, for the 1st time, I am able to present to you the incontrovertible facts. People nowadays have to be reminded that *Prince Albert Victor, Duke of Clarence*, was the eldest son of *Edward VII* and therefore (until his death in 1892, at the age of 28) the heir-presumptive to the British throne, to which his younger brother George (V) was later to succeed. Clarence was a cause for concern to his parents, being a young man of charm but of singularly unstable character, forming violent but unlasting attachments to one young lady after another.

"In early 1884, aged 20, he was an incognito frequenter of disreputable houses in *Cleveland Street* W.1.: in the street outside one of these, he engaged in conversation with a Miss *Faith Pasco*, a member of a (Cornish) Quaker family and a social worker who concerned herself with the welfare of the unfortunate women: a girl (21) good-looking enough for the Duke to fall violently in love with her, possibly on the rebound from the same women.

"Miss Pasco, evidently a young lady of strong character, rejected both his advances and his subsequent insistence on marriage (by then she knew his identity) but he was so persuasive that she finally relented. The Duke, after an artful sequence of large bribes to 2 or 3 dependable people (solicitors, clergymen) was able, without detection, to change his name by deed-poll to *Albert Victor Sandring*, a prankish abbreviation of the Royal country estate.

"Again without detection, he married Miss Pasco at *St Botolph's Church, Aldgate*, on April 17th 1884; he then disappeared completely (to the alarm of the old Queen and the whole Royal Family) to a remote hide-out in Cumberland.

"It took the authorities much ingenuity to explain that disappearance to the nation: it was given out that stricken with tuberculosis, he had been forced to retire for 3 months to a Swiss sanatorium, in complete seclusion, then a long sea-voyage, etc.

"During which time Mrs Sandring became pregnant. But by the date of their child's birth (a boy) on Jan. 30th 1885, the Duke had tired of his wife, and was back in *Marlborough House*. Presumably, to his erratic mind *Mr. A. V. Sandring* had never existed; but we have in our possession a letter, in his hand, to his wife, from which it is clear that he planned to visit his baby son, for whom – in his impulsive way – he expressed affection.

"But that was all; Clarence was probably, by then, caught up in the sort of feverish infatuation he was to show later for Princesse Hélène d'Orléans and Lady Sybil St Clair Erskine. Mrs Sandring, refusing any compensation beyond an income just enough to support her son and herself, moved back to her native town of St Austell in Cornwall; there she died 3 years later, of influenza. (In passing, it is interesting to note that had she lived, her existence could have become an acute embarrassment to the Royal Family when the forgetful Duke became engaged to *Princess May of Teck*, later Queen Mary: a formidable possibility of Royal bigamy which would anyway have disappeared by reason of the Duke's death before the marriage could take place.)

"Mrs. Sandring left the child – *Robert Albert Sandring* – in the care of her aunt, and the boy grew up in St Austell, where, at the age of 15, he became a shoemaker's apprentice. In 1909, aged 24, he married *Alice Lavinia Petherick*, aged 27, who had worked as housemaid at Staverbridge Priory, outside Mevagissey.

"During their occupation of a cobbler's shop, in St Austell, on October 18th 1910 their only child was born, a son. A year later the husband died; three years after that, the boy was adopted by his mother's second husband *Bertram Green*, who gave the child his own name of Green.

"And it is this child, *John Albert Sandring*, at present aged 24 and employed at Drury Lane Theatre in several minor capacities, whom we are gathered here to discuss.

"The next step, the routine identification of the said *John Albert Sandring*.

"Two of our officers, in the course of a routine examination of the farm where he was reared, took possession of his birth certificate, of his mother's marriage certificate and of a locked cash-box left with the mother by her first husband. (One has to wonder whether he could have had a premonition of the present situation.)

"On forcing the box open, the 2 officers found 3 documents of vital importance, which will be found attached to the next page." (They were.) "(a) the birth certificate of the boy's father bearing the signature 'Albert Victor Tudor' in the handwriting of the *Duke of Clarence*, (b) the Certificate of Marriage between the boy's grandmother *Faith Pasco* and the same *Albert Victor Sandring*, the latter signature again in the handwriting of the *Duke of Clarence* (there can be no question, therefore, of a morganatic marriage) and (c) the letter – previously mentioned – from the Duke to his wife, alluding to his affection for his child. Gentlemen, any questions?"

I took up the last document. The important one. "At the end of the Emergency Meeting at 10 Downing Street, it was agreed that the following statement should be issued concurrently to Reuters, World Press and World Wireless. 'May the 11th, as the world knows, was a day of the blackest tragedy; but let us now rejoice in the knowledge that on that day – at 11.41 a.m. Saturday May 11th 1935 – *John Albert Sandring*, great-grandson of *King Edward the Seventh* by direct male descent, became – without his knowledge as yet, indeed without the knowledge of anyone living – *our only lawful Liege Lord, John the Second by the grace of God, King of the United Kingdom of Great Britain and Northern Ireland, and of the British Dominions beyond the Seas, Defender of the Faith, Emperor of India. God Save the King'.*"

I looked down at my hands, holding the document. They were shaking. They had always looked ordinary to me. I spread them out. They still did. Kathy had once remarked they were sturdy peasant hands, and you'd swear they were. I thought back, to other hands. Back and back. To a name I'd not heard since school. William the Conqueror.

I went on staring, until I said to myself, If you don't start trying to turn this morning into reality, you'll go mad. I pressed the button.

The footman must have been just outside the doors, they seemed to open immediately. A man walked in carrying a briefcase and dressed like the Twins, in a long coat shaped like a swallow, over striped trousers. It could have been a uniform. Only this chap was older, quite an old man. I thought, I know that face . . . The footman announced, "The Prime Minister, the Right Honourable Stanley Baldwin."

I got up. Mr Baldwin bowed. "Your Majesty." I said, "Please sit down." He said, "Thank you."

I said, "You're welcome." Again, I had to say something. And it may not have sounded too bad, it could have meant "To my new home, I bid you welcome."

A Prime Minister is somebody, and here is where I should be giving you a pen picture of Mr Baldwin which would go down in History. I can't remember anything about him at all, I was so busy behaving. Except that he looked like an amiable country squire, with a pipe in his pocket. (I had heard of the pipe.)

What did we talk about, or rather he? "Such a relief, Your Majesty, that the suspense is over . . . The essential priority is to settle things down . . ." et cetera. The next I knew, there was another swallow in the room complete with briefcase and striped trousers, only this one was wearing pince-nez. "Sir Godwin Rodd . . ." "Sir Godwin," said Mr Baldwin, "is eager to do anything to help."

The new arrival gave the creak of a bow, and didn't look in the least eager. The Prime Minister took his leave; I said, "Please sit down."

Sir Godwin was small, thin, bloodless: one of those spinster-men you couldn't believe had either a wife or children. I was to discover that he was a legal legend and now "extremely high in the Cabinet" – practically ran it – had been right-hand man to the previous Prime Minister, MacDonald, and was now in the same capacity with Baldwin. A figure sharp as an important knife, and just about as friendly. I took a dislike to him.

I could tell he was sizing me up: the wild card in the pack, the cuckoo in the Royal nest. I also knew that if I made a special effort to be pleasant, it would be in vain: merely an attempt to impress by a vain young actor-chap. What he was sizing up was not my face, which could mean nothing to him, but my spotted bow-tie and frayed cuff.

He opened his briefcase, with a snap which said, "Let's get down to business." Then a dead sort of smirk. But he would never have said anything as compact as "Let's get down to business"; I was to find that he talked more fancy than Messrs Fawcett and Cairns put together. "May I venture, your Majesty, to give voice to my sympathy on the considerable psychological shock which this metamorphosis must have occasioned you?"

I thought, now that's not conversation, it's a speech. As if he was in a play. But not like Kathy's style – not a good play, just an old-fashioned one.

I was about to say "You're telling me!", then decided it wouldn't sound right. Then I thought, you're behaving as if he's a manager and you're up for a job – relax, you've *got the part* . . .

I couldn't relax, but I did get the idea to put on the voice I used to use in the show, for my two spoken lines. (Used to? I used it *last night*!) And by a happy coincidence, the first of those fitted now, and I spoke it. "This has proved something of a bolt from the blue."

Sir Godwin looked (for him) surprised. He could hardly guess I wouldn't be able to keep *that* up for long. "Yes, it is indeed. I had planned for your Secretary to be with us, but he reports pressing business on your behalf, highly inconvenient but of course there is considerable ground to be covered. So I am here, Sir, in the endeavour to act in an advisory capacity vis-à-vis such problems as Protocol and so on."

I tried to remember something out of Kathy's dictionary. "It is my wish to ascertain my immediate future."

"Precisely. I would hazard the guess that you will find these notes of considerable help, allow me . . ."

At the moment of taking the paper from him, I was trying to work out his manner. It was 100 per cent unhuman all right, but on top of the sizing-up there was an attitude. The nearest I'd got to the upper classes was a couple of times after the Drury Lane curtain was down, when I'd gone into the stalls to bring somebody through to visit Ivor or Miss Ellis or Miss Welch, "This way, sir, mind the step." Once, one of them had tipped me. Why not?

They had been quite friendly. What was the word for this chap's manner? I could see what he must be like with people he worked with: impersonal, condescending. But with me, on top of the disdain for the cuff and tie, there was . . . Then I got it. Something I'd never experienced from anybody.

Respect. And him old enough to be my Grandad. He was respectful. Just as he must have been through all his visits to this place, over the years.

I looked down at my notes. *HIGHLY CONFIDENTIAL, to be distributed to Palace staff involved, including Messengers already alerted for shopping.*

11.30 a.m. H.M. expected to arrive at B.P. (approx.)
11.35 a.m. Courtesy audience to the P.M.
11.40 a.m. Audience to Sir Godwin Rodd.

12 noon H.M. will be escorted to his apartments, where he will be
awaited by skeleton (emergency) wardrobe. Dark suit, suitable tie,
. pyjamas, slippers, dressing-gown, shirts, socks, underpants, black patent
shoes (2 sizes), 2 hair-brushes – (the list made a slow dwindle-down,
you had to smile) *– comb, toothbrushes, tooth-paste, toilet water,*
scissors, nail-file, 2 varieties hair-oil, shaving cream, badger shaving-
brush, safety-razor, Players cigarettes, baby oil. Well, the one thing
I'd always hated was shopping, in and out in a jiffy ... *Razor,*
cigarettes, baby oil? For a smoking, shaving baby?

I decided to go into the remaining appointments as they cropped
up, laid aside the list and looked across at the grey face and the
gleam of the glasses. "Quite a schedule."

"It is indeed." I had a feeling that I was going to be agreed with,
in those words – like an echo – by many people, many times. It is
indeed, they were indeed, he could indeed ...

Sir Godwin leant forward. "Any questions, your Majesty?"

"Two. Suppose the dark suit doesn't fit?"

"It will. An hour ago my staff had someone consult a person at the
theatre in question – the Mistress of the Wardrobe, am I correct?"

"The wardrobe-mistress, yes."

"We obtained measurements from her, on the pretext of furnish-
ing you with clothes for what I understand is termed a Film Test."

I thought, that'll make a small topic of conversation, backstage.
Which reminded me, "My second question is the important one. I
have a matinee today."

He looked puzzled. "I beg your pardon ...?"

"The show I'm in has ... The theatre where I was ... is giving
a performance in a couple of hours' time."

"Of course. One sympathizes with your Majesty's solicitude for
your former colleagues, and I am happy to say it has been fore-
stalled. One of the Household telephoned your place of residence,
also the offices of the theatrical firm presenting the entertainment in
question, apprising them of the fact (a challengeable fact, but no
matter) that you are detained in hospital with a sprained ankle, but
no cause for immediate anxiety."

A pause. I sensed that he was waiting for me to draw our meeting
to its close. I got up, which meant that he got up. I was learning. I
bowed, he bowed, I put out my hand, he gave it a faint chilly shake,
and went. Sir Godwin Rodd and I had cemented a firm non-
friendship.

Down the corridor, to dress. The Private Apartments, which had
sounded forbidding, turned out – to my relief – to consist of a comfortable study, with a Bechstein baby-grand piano, books and many
family photographs in silver frames, plus bedroom and bathroom.
None of it small, but not depressingly large either. One of the photographs gave me quite a twinge: it was of Queen Victoria, the identical one reproduced on a wall at the Farm. And on her home ground,
she didn't look one bit more pleased with life than in our kitchen.

In the dressing-room off the bedroom, I was awaited by a smartly
dressed man who introduced himself as Quelch, one of my two
valets. He helped me into two pairs of shoes, and one of the pairs
fitted perfectly. Then he held out the trousers of the dark suit, then
the waistcoat and jacket; all that too fitted perfectly.

The tie he handed me was black, which reminded me I was in
mourning for relatives I had never met. He let me tie the tie myself,
then let me part my hair and brush it; both hair-brushes and comb
were of silver. There were also shoe-trees. I quite expected them to
be silver too. I guessed oak.

It was evident to me that from now on I was never to lift a hand;
I imagined that if I asked for it, in the bath I could get my back
soaped, a footman to each shoulder-blade. I wouldn't mind, I had
nothing to hide. Might make an item of gossip in – the pantries, are
they called? On second thoughts . . . no. Leave that stone unturned.

Quelch scooped up my old belongings – shoes, socks, bow tie,
everything – and started to go. It was as if he were taking away the
effects of a man who had died. Behind the stables, had they already
dug my grave?

"Don't!" I said, quite sharp. He turned to me, and here was another look I'd not seen before: a look of fear. And that depressed me.

"I'm sorry," I said, "leave it all there, will you, I'll put it away
later." And he did. It was childish of me, but I couldn't help it.

*12.15 p.m. H.M. will give a brief audience to Lord Dawson of Penn,
the King's Physician, who will be at His Majesty's service.*

Lord Dawson's service consisted of requesting me to take off all
the clothes I had got into with such care, and then – after some
elaborate business with a stethoscope, etc. – respectfully scanning
every corner of me. The sort of procedure which, presumably, had
helped him on to the House of Lords. I was glad I'd had a bath this
morning. (*This* morning?) He pronounced me A.1. and bowed himself out as if he hadn't come within three feet of me. I dressed
quickly, for my next scene.

It turned out a small scene. *1 p.m. As an interim, His Majesty will have luncheon in his study, unaccompanied.* I appreciated somebody's kind thought: for the first time, I was alone, and idle. Footman. On a silver tray, a silver tureen with a silver top (soup) and a silver dome with fish underneath. Like fish and chips, only much more select, and I had my first acquaintance with fish knife and fork. (My guess now, is that it was Goujons of Sole, something like that.) A silver salt-cellar (I'll stop that from now on, please assume that everything is silver that is not gold). A small carafe of white wine.

The footman bowed and left. In the silence, I ate and I drank. What's the phrase? *In solitary state.*

I turned on the wireless. The best tone I'd ever heard. It was playing a quick medley of popular songs: "Night and Day", "Heat Wave", "The Continental". I sat down to unwind, but was to wind right up again when Mary Ellis's voice rang through the room, *let us kiss and recapture . . . that rapturous Glamorous Night!*

There was a matinee, today. I looked slowly around and said, aloud, "It's a dream, a dream . . ." I felt so unreal that I jumped up and turned the wireless off. The sun was making a criss-cross pattern on the rug. No sound, except the sleepy tick of a wall clock which must have been there for generations. And priceless.

I wandered to the books. *Who's Who, Debrett's,* the *Oxford Dictionary,* a world atlas. Quite a few detective thrillers, several by Edgar Wallace. The Prince of Wales's? . . . On the desk, next to the leather blotter (mine now), a book that looked as if it had been put there for me. *The Royal Family and the Palace.* I sat down for a skim through.

". . . 600 rooms . . . 45 acres of garden . . . The King's Allowance amounts to just under half-a-million pounds a year . . . The second biggest land-owner in Britain, with 180,000 acres in England alone . . . The King pays no income-tax . . . The King never carries money . . ."

I felt dizzy. The clock chimed. 2.30. In Drury Lane Theatre, the orchestra was in mid-overture, *Fold your Wings around me, Fold them close till they have bound me . . .* I'm late, never been late before . . .

2.30 p.m. His Majesty will await Hair-dresser for Haircut, Shampoo; also Manicurist.

Not a sound, and no faces: just fingers, satin-smooth and soaked in invisible respect. I closed my eyes, lay back and felt like a rich whore. The only thing I remember is the hairdresser murmuring, "A stray lock might be pleasant, your Majesty, shall we try it?" I was at a loss until he explained that he was suggesting a flat curved cowlick of hair on one side of the forehead. I didn't mind, it looked rather saucy.

3.30 p.m. Photographic Session with Mr C. Beaton, Music Room. My last photo had been two years ago, for a half-page in the *Spotlight*, the theatre encyclopaedia, increasingly expensive for a struggler. As I came in, Mr Beaton murmured, "Your Majesty," but didn't say much after that, which I thought was right. Hard to know what he was thinking, but that applied to all the others too. He was professional, and quick. He approved of the "stray lock" of hair, and said the plan was to give the finished pictures to the papers next week.

4.30 p.m. Conference with Palace Press Office, in King's Audience Room. I told the Press Secretary everything he wanted to know about my early life, and the more facts I gave, the less real they sounded.

5.30 p.m. Session with Tailor and Cutter, Private Apts. Fittings for 10 Lounge Suits, 2 Outfits with Knee-breeches, 3 Morning Suits, 4 Evening Suits (2 Tails, 2 Dinner Jackets), 1 Uniform of Field Marshal, 1 Uniform of Air Marshal, 1 Uniform of Admiral of the Fleet, 3 Overcoats, 3 Dressing-gowns.

Tailor, Hawes and Curtis; I'd never been fitted before, quite tiring. The Cutters had two assistants. They whispered measurements, again as if in church.

There came one moment when I knew I was blushing, and hoped they weren't noticing. It was when the older assistant took a tape between fingers and thumbs, dropped on to one knee – for a second I thought it was some sort of ceremony – and applied the tape between my legs. At the top.

Then he said, "May I inquire on which side your Majesty dresses?"

It was as if he had asked me which shoe I get into first. What was the answer . . . "Depends on the mood I'm in . . .?" Or "Let's say the *Conservative* side, shall we?"

Or "Can't you tell?"

I murmured, as if absent-minded, "I've never thought about it." They smiled in appreciation. Too much appreciation. Back into the dark suit and back to my quarters, rather jaded.

6.30 p.m. Preparation of Speech for tomorrow, H.M.'s 1st Privy Council. It is not customary for the Sovereign to speak at a Privy Council, but in the unusual circumstances it is considered fitting that His

*Majesty should speak the few words, here appended, before the cus-
tomary oaths are administered by the President of the Council.* "Customary oaths" sounded promising. What in Hell's name, damn and
blast . . .

The idea of the speech alarmed me, but I was a quick study. About
fifteen lines of rigmarole, "My lieges, it is our deep-felt honour, at
this solemn moment . . ." I got it pretty pat in twenty minutes.

My eye caught, on the list of the day's appointments I'd already
got through, *11.35 a.m. Courtesy Audience to the Prime Minister.*

I thought again of Drury Lane, less than twenty-four hours ago.
One day, you play to an audience; the next, you give one.

That thought cheered me up, but only for a second. I was on my
own. And scared.

7.30 p.m. Informal audience to Private Secretary. I was tired; this
could make me more tired.

I picked up a sheet of paper. "*PRIVATE SECRETARY, PAR-
TICULARS FOR H.M. Mr William Farley Millingham, only son of
Mr R. J. Millingham and grandson of Mr Francis Parkes Millingham,
both with pronounced Radical views which, happily, are not shared by
the third generation, his mother having apparently insisted he should be
educated at Eton and then Magdalen College, Oxford. Married, to
Lady (Anne Deborah) Swann-Cavendish, cousin to the Duke of Devonshire. Age 34. One son, John, aged ten.*

*2 yrs. Sec. to British Consul in San Francisco, 3 yrs. Sec. to British
Ambassador in Vienna, 5 yrs. Sec. to British Ambassador in Madrid,
for the last two years attached to Royal Household. Now unanimously
proposed as Private Sec. to H.M.*"

Stuffy as hell. Well, anything's better than Sir Godwin.

Knock. Footman. Enter Private Sec. to H.M.

Tall. Too tall, six foot two, to my five nine-and-a-half (ten at a
pinch). I sat down, quickly.

"Your Majesty, allow me first . . ." Was this to be a younger,
better-looking version of Sir Godwin? As I waited for the pompous
pronouncements, I felt the same dislike rising up inside me, like ice
forming on a wind-screen.

"Your Majesty, allow me first to interest you in a particularly dry
martini, American style, gin with just a whisper of Noilly Prat."

There was a discreet twinkle in his eye, and my dislike blew away.
It was as if a window had been opened. The long figure hovered
elegantly over the drinks-tray. He was languid and yet lively: the

voice pleasantly clipped and cordial, the manner friendly without being ingratiating. He was convivial, and yet showed no effort. Here was a man who had already spent years with crowned heads swirling round him, ermine from wall to wall: George and Mary, the Emperor of Japan, Marie of Rumania, the Lion of Abyssinia, he must have been at home with them all. His family may have turned Radical but one could not mistake the breeding.

In the middle of mixing, he turned suddenly, with a smile. "Tell me, *how* did you find Sir Godwin?" Then back to the drinks; it was as if this morning we had had a long talk about Sir G., and were going on from there. I liked it, and took the cue from him. "He was heavy going."

"I bet he was. Behind his back, when he's not called 'Grey Eminence', he's known as Sir God."

"I must remember that."

"I'm sorry, Sir, that I wasn't there, but somebody had to do the shopping." He handed me my martini, with a flourish.

"The shopping?"

"I did the tailoring end of it down to the socks, while one of the footmen, a bright one, did the sundries. Do excuse me while I check the props."

He vanished into the bedroom, while I savoured my martini as I had never enjoyed strong drink before. I was untensed. Check the props?

He hurried back. "Looks all right, I hope you'll find the shaving cream to your taste and the toilet water tolerable, some of them make one smell like a brothel in Bengal."

I picked up his potted biography. "Anything more I should know?" I felt at home with him.

"Not much. I've been everywhere, and done nothing. At Eton, since I was a rather pretty little fellow and my name was Millingham, I naturally answered to the name of Millie, but mercifully not for too long. I have no political views, having inherited nothing from my Radical family background, and no particular ambition, which is just as well since I have no outstanding talent. Unless you count a flair for looking after people more important than myself. To be a buffer, Sir, between you and the outside."

I asked what I should call him. "I should be happy, Sir, to be known as Willie." He turned serious. "It's been a ghastly thirty days. But you know all about that – it was like getting to the brink of the first night, and . . . there's no leading man, how can there be a first night?"

"But you haven't worked in the theatre . . . ?"

"Not professionally, but I have frequently trod the boards as an amateur in Gilbert and Sullivan. Invariably on the note, but rarely audible, untalented but undeterred. I once played the Duke of Plaza Toro at a dump by the name of Windsor Castle. Thomas Beecham's comment was, 'My boy . . . you may have the breeding, but where's the brio?' Which took me aback, just a millimetre. I should have told that to Kathy and Bruce."

I looked up from my glass. "Kathy and Bruce?"

"I just left them, they had tea with me."

"Here in the Palace?"

"No, in Lyons Corner House. I walked them back for their evening performances, quite the stage-door Johnny."

I was moved, and puzzled. "Why did you want to take them out?"

"I knew they hadn't an idea what was going on and were miserable, also I felt you were worried about them. So rather than have the thing land on them in a matter of hours, like an avalanche, I thought I'd break it gently."

"How did they take it?"

"They didn't believe me. Insisted it was an elaborate joke. I do believe they're still not sure, they're in a daze. Two very nice people; if she could take on some of his stability, and he a bit of her *change-ability*, they'd make a good marriage." (Of course, Bruce was Kathy's "fiancé".)

Then I remembered my parents. "It's my family I'm worried about, it'll be a terrible shock to them –"

"They'll have heard about an hour ago, this morning I sent your Second Secretary down to Cornwall by car, to hint to them that you have a new job, and to say that you send your love."

"Is that why he wasn't able to do the shopping?"

"No matter – oh, and in order that their letters to you won't get lost in the shuffle, I've arranged for all four of them to have a code-number to put on their envelopes."

My eyes turned damp with gratitude. And gin. He consulted notes. "To ease the pressure for you, Sir, I've made a couple of suggestions to the powers that be. I can't tell you how inflexible they can be when it comes to Protocol or tradition, but I think, through pleading that the situation has no precedent, I think I've got away with it." The Powers-That-Be . . . I thought, he and I are going to be using that phrase quite often.

He went on. "In view of the shock to the country during the last weeks, it has been decided that, in order not to prolong the reminder of them – more than is decent – the usual mourning period of six months will be shortened to five weeks, ending this Saturday, June the 15th. Secondly, I pointed out the immense task your Majesty faces in adjustment to the Palace and its ways, and suggested that it would be unrealistic to expect you to tackle the rest before next January at the earliest – so no Presentations at Court till then, and no Garden Parties till next summer, after the Coronation."

"The Coronation?"

"It's too late to plan it for this summer, and since it's traditional to avoid the bad months it'll have to be next summer. It's not official yet, of course, but the date will be Wednesday, May the 6th."

"Where?"

"Westminster Abbey."

He let that sink in, then continued. "Also postponed till after the New Year are Windsor Castle, Sandringham and Balmoral. May I doubt, Sir, if grouse-shooting is a passion with you?"

"I haven't handled a gun since a wooden one in the Boys' Brigade."

"So that can wait. Less important, but immediate, at your first Privy Council tomorrow, which will be particularly crowded, members will not be expected to stand throughout – if you ask me, a most uncomfortable tradition. I may have some more tiresome bits-and-pieces for you in the morning, but till then . . ."

"You spoke of my immense task." I took the plunge. "Willie, what have I let myself in for?"

He looked at me, quite sharply, for him. Then into his martini. Deep into it. I said, "Well?"

"Sir . . . I'm being fanciful, I know, when I compare you to a butterfly which . . . You don't mind?"

"Better than being called a moth. Go on." I looked into my glass, trying to get as deep as him.

"The butterfly, without warning, finds himself . . . caught."

"In a net?"

"In a machine."

"A big machine?"

"Gigantic. And very old. But no rust, well-oiled."

"Do I lose my wings?"

He hesitated. "Yes."

"Anything left?"

He kept me waiting, then shrugged and smiled. "Too early to tell."

"That's fair enough." We drank. I sensed we'd got deep enough for a little gossip to be welcome. "Does the machine ever stick?"

"The occasional lurch. Last year Mrs Northing, the Head House-keeper, found a pantry-boy in bed with a housemaid. And three months ago, a page in bed with a page. Two pages glued together, as it were. A great finder, Mrs Northing. At the last Christmas staff-party, at two a.m. a boot-boy drank a shoe-polish and tonic and had to be rushed to St George's Hospital on the floor of a Daimler. The gossip columns missed that one. These things happen in the best-regulated households, and this one is certainly regulated."

I had enjoyed that, was hoping the scandals would move Upstairs, and finished my martini. Then the gin, on top of strain, brought on a wave of dizziness; my head just flopped. Willie gave a nifty jump-up, which got me sitting straight.

"I'm sure, Sir, you'd welcome my cutting along now, it's been quite a day. Tomorrow, I hope, will not be quite so taxing, apart from the Privy Council . . . Oh, would it be agreeable to you to attend at the Private Chapel here on Sunday morning?"

"Not that agreeable, but I suppose I'd better?"

"It would make a good impression, not a long service and needn't be habit-forming. The Domestic Chaplain will be officiating." As he turned to go, he looked at a clock. "You may care to turn on the News. Goodnight, Sir. Sleep well, it's been quite a day."

Alone, I concentrated on the wireless. It was nine o'clock, and Big Ben was doing the usual. After the last stroke, "This is the News. A time of tension is at an end. It is officially announced, from Buckingham Palace, that at three p.m. tomorrow afternoon, in St James's Palace according to ancient tradition, the new King will be proclaimed, by heralds and trumpeters. King John the Second by the grace of God. He is the great-grandson of King Edward the Seventh . . ."

I was so nervous that I turned it off. Alone in that room again, in silence, I felt creepy again. I thought of my parents, and dreaded what it might do to my mother, however carefully she had been pre-pared. I remembered the time she had told me about my – real – father being struck by lightning, and how upset she had been with it being in the local paper. I thanked God for her sound heart.

But I enjoyed the thought of the wireless being on in the chorus-room at the Lane, and hoped they were all quick-changing at this minute. "What was that . . . *What?* . . . Jack Sandring in Buckingham Palace, somebody's pulling somebody's leg . . . WHAT?"

9.30 p.m. H.M. will be served dinner, unaccompanied, and will be free to retire. A knock, footman with tray, lamb cutlets, carafe of red wine. As he closed the curtains, another knock: Quelch the valet. He went into the bedroom, closing the door very gently. What was his task? To position the two toy ducks on the steaming bath-water? And last thing, by the bed, the Ovaltine?

The footman bowed and left, the valet re-entered, bowed and left. I ate and drank in silence, then walked to the bedroom, lurching slightly. The curtains were closed, the bed turned down. On the pillows, pyjamas next to a dressing-gown, quilted. At the foot of the bed, slippers lined with fleece.

I slid my tiredness between the sheets, which were not crisp like on the Farm – they felt like water, they were so silky. Before turning out the bedside lamp, I looked up; the bed was a four-poster, under a canopy with a faded tapestry – must be ancient – with on it a group of old-fashioned dusty plain people in grey wigs, etc. It felt to be weighing down on me, like the lid of a coffin. I thought, I must be one in a billion: the bloke who does *not* want a roof over his head.

In the silence, I could hear the sheets, whispering. Then, very far away, so faint that I thought it was in my head, a ghostly choir. But it wasn't. It was a crowd outside the Palace gates, singing "God Save The King".

I turned out the light, and in my fuddled head it seemed as if it was the world singing. Then it faded away and I fell asleep. No, I didn't fall, I dived.

I half-woke once and put my arm out to touch Kathy's breast and draw her to me. But there was nobody there. Just the Bed of Ware.

But I was soon asleep again. Quite a day.

CHAPTER EIGHT

Growing Pains

Thurs. June 13th, 2nd Day of Reign.

When I woke up in the morning I put my hand out again, from
habit, and it took me a moment to get my mind organized.

Just as well I was awake, or I'd never have heard the footman's
knock, it was so discreet. Breakfast on a tray, and the tray on a little
wicker table with stumpy legs that lowered on to the bed on each
side of you. My first breakfast in bed, and very nice: eggs and bacon
under a cover. But first, two glasses of water: those unaccustomed
dry martinis had left me with a morning thirst.

The footman opened the curtains to the sun, and started to go. I
said, "Any newspapers?"

He hesitated. "Mr Millingham wasn't sure, Sir, whether you'd
care to see any."

Could my notices be as bad as that? "I'd like to see them, please."

He was back in a trice with a pile, it must have been on a chair
outside the door.

The picture papers were on top, and my knees shot up so abruptly
that I nearly knocked my breakfast over.

Daily Mirror, front page. I thought how it had looked a month
ago, just the giant words THE WORLD MOURNS: nothing else.
Well, this time there was one word, even taller, thicker and blacker,
then the blob of an Exclamation Mark, the whole thing underlined.
KING!

Underneath, not that much smaller – JOHN THE SECOND!!

Daily Mail, ditto, only more matey. KING JACK!! *Sketch*, a variation on that – UNION JACK!!

The Times and the *Telegraph*, both respecting their own dignity, had the front page smothered in the usual small print, Births, Marriages, Agony Column, as if anybody cared this morning. But the inside pages were shaking with excitement. A NATION SIGHS WITH JOYOUS RELIEF, FULL ROMANTIC STORY . . .

Back to the inside of the *Sketch* and the *Mirror*: headlines in hot competition. FROM THRESHER TO THRONE! . . . FROM COWSHED TO KINGSHIP! (Those cows . . .) They both had a page of photographs of the legal documents: my birth certificate, my father's, and my grandmother's certificate, of her marriage to Clarence. On one page, an ingenious photo of the outside of the Lane: the sign THEATRE ROYAL DRURY LANE, with the word ROYAL picked out. Then I darted from one paper to another, landing on phrases.

I could tell that Sir Godwin's staff had attended the Press Conference, and that their guarded answers had acquired a certain amount of colour on their way to the printed page. *"They insist that he will be a breath of fresh air . . ." ". . . strikingly handsome . . . quietly charming . . . musical Cornish lilt . . . intelligent . . . brought up in the Baptist faith, a chapel-goer who will attend on Sunday at the Palace Chapel . . ."*

Then they got on to *"the King's mother"* and I started to worry – what was she feeling at this moment, with half St Austell running up Tregonissey Hill with these same newspapers? *"She has the face of a Madonna . . ." ". . . a West Country farmer's wife of few words . . ."*

Then a couple of tit-bits. *". . . How striking the origin of the name Sandring . . ." ". . . The Duke of Clarence had also had his son christened after his own grandfather, a name given also by the son to his, the present King, John* Albert . . ." I hadn't thought of that. *"The last member of the Royal Family to be struck by lightning was an aunt of Queen Anne, in 1692 . . ."* Where had they fished that one up?

Then a bold fiction. *". . . As the King stood bewildered by his surroundings, and looking younger than his 24 years – 'Strange,' he mused, 'that as a child, on the red-letter day when I was allowed to hold a sovereign in my hand, it never occurred to me that one day I would be one . . .'"* I had never mused any such thing, but it did sound neat. At the top of an item about my doing well in the Woodwork class, JACK JOINER!

Endless photographs, somebody had done the most thorough job of Instant Research, starting with a picture of my mother which I had never seen, looking very young outside the cobbler's shop, arm in arm with a strange nice-looking young fellow, for a second I thought it was me, then I read underneath, "*A wedding picture of the King's father with his bride.*"

Me at six months, lying on a rug, nude but – thank God – upside down. Me at eight, in a group, the County School choir. ("*His musicianship was quickly apparent.*")

Me at twelve, at a school picnic, "*the idyllic open-air Cornish Lad*" . . . Me at thirteen, standing in front of a haystack: the same stack in which Peter Wakefield the baker's boy piloted me on my first skirmish with Sex. Peter had taken the snap afterwards, perhaps as a memento; you could see bits of straw clinging to my trousers. "*From the clear blue eyes* (Royal *blue!*) *there radiates the innocence of boyhood . . .*"

Then a snap without me, taken by Sir Godwin's snoopers: a big open book, in the background my narrow monastic bed. ". . . *Here's the Family Bible, handed down by the King's grandmother (wife to the Duke) and always kept in Jack's bedroom so he could (every night before going to bed) read a passage aloud to himself. It was his mother's idea . . .*" It was indeed, one of those ideas that stays an idea.

"*. . . And now his Stage Career in the Chorus . . .*" Photos of me in shows, in groups of course, my blurred head picked out inside a white ring. Black Eagle in *Rose Marie*, an Apache dancer, a Foreign Legionnaire, a Gypsy, tap-dancing as Sandy, with poor Dandy (who had, of course, been next to me) cut out; and finally a Courtier in *Glamorous Night*. "*Ah, a Courtier! Shape of Things to Come?*"

Me at a party, playing the fool pretending to drink champagne out of a girl's shoe, and that drew a fairly roguish caption: "*SOWING HIS WILD OATS?*" Me in Miss Gold's dressing-room, a snap taken by her dresser, with her sitting in front of the mirror making up for the evening show, me standing behind her and looking on. "*PRINCE CHARMING WITH HER KING.*" Before the snap, I'd had to comb my hair owing to a roughish session on the couch. "*The female star of his first Big Show smiles encouragement at the shy beginner. Miss Gold – the voice of experience – assured us of his thoroughness and eagerness to learn . . .*"

Then a snap of Kathy and Bruce, taken by me "*Outside a Royal Residence by the name of Hampton Court, which he was visiting as an obscure tourist!*" Both of them looked very nice, I was proud of them. Underneath, "*Miss Kathy Tripp reports: 'One could say unequivo-*

cally' – I could hear her stretching it out – *'that he was very close to me and my fiancé'.'*" Now that was bright of her. No mention of the Snoring Beauty, such is notoriety.

"*Mr Bruce Renfrew, a dour Scot, was not very forthcoming.*" At last, an understatement. " *'Nothing unusual about Jack, just an average chap'.*" Thanks a lot, Brucie.

Then *MORE QUOTES FROM THOSE WHO KNEW HIM.* I made a face, this again sounded as if I was dead. "*Mr Novello : 'He was always cheerful, and a most reliable stage-manager'* " . . . "Stage-doorkeeper, *Drury Lane Theatre : 'Everybody liked him, including me : both the ladies and the gentlemen took to him'* . . ." Grumpy, you don't say . . . Even Belle had got into the act. "*Mr Bill Dell, a fellow artiste : 'The reason we all loved him in the dressing-room, was that he was so quiet and dignified'* . . ." Untrue. " *'He had a love of good music, would sit at my feet while I played my violin, till I had to say Jack, we'll miss our entrance!'* . . ."

And – what? Kathy's – and my – former employer, the Beast. "*Jack was a good little artist when I used him, but I felt in my bones he deserved a higher sphere.*" Higher than a dressing-room five hundred stairs up? A place on the roof?

I was bathing in it all, in an agreeably embarrassed glow, when – wallop. There's always one rude review. The *Daily Worker* allotted the event a six-line paragraph in a bottom corner, headed EX-CHORUS-BOY ASCENDS THRONE.

"*Jack Sandring (alias Green), a chorus-boy fresh from singing and dancing in the West End, is apparently the grandson of a royal duke and therefore eligible for the vacancy. We understand Mr Sandring displayed no marked talent on the stage, but maybe he will now do better in a job for which he is as overpaid as he is undertrained.*" Ouch . . . "*Are we to expect a chorus-girl as Queen Consort? Queen Babs the First?*" Proletarian sods.

I looked down at the crumpled avalanche of print which had overtaken my breakfast, cold by now, and had the urge to leap out of bed, hurry to the desk in the study, take up a pen – gold – and a sheet of writing-paper. It had a crest at the top; feeling it wasn't quite right for my parents, I decided on a plain sheet.

"Dear Mother and Father, I hope you are well as I am and not too upset with all this business, it has knocked me into a cocked hat I can tell you, it will take some getting used to, grin and bear it. I'll do my best. I have a very good Secretary, whose assistant visited you – he is a nice tall chap called Willie, will write more later, Your loving son Jack."

Not much of a letter, I agree. But you can't write to your parents the things I'm telling you, can you, now?

I looked at the words "I'll do my best" and thought, well that's true, I *am* going to do my best. The same as I tried to be a good stage-manager. And I was.

From them, my thoughts went to Kathy and Bruce. I decided on the crested paper, it would amuse them. It would by my first letter to them, ever. Normally I would have started with "Dear K. and B.", but I got emotional.

"My dearest Both, I haven't come to yet! One minute I feel like a cork bobbing about in heavy seas – the next, with everybody so quiet and polite, I think I'm in hospital. Looks as if the show will run. As you see from above address, the digs are nice. A bit roomy, but highly recommended. Must rush, write immediately, love love love, Jack."

Then I thought a second, and added, in big black letters, "R.I." I left the letter in a tray for that purpose, for "staff" to cope with. (I was learning all the time, *Daily Worker* please note.)

Then I saw the sun outside and felt a second urge: to walk out into the open air. And I hurried into the bedroom and dressed. Another long gulp of water, and into the corridor. All around me, there spread 600 rooms, how could I ever forget it? I reached a window overlooking the Garden – 45 acres – and found a staircase leading out of doors.

The morning was again a beautiful one, and I bounded down the steps and across to the great green sunlit meadow of a lawn. Here was I, who had turned my back on the countryside, hungry for a rustic stroll in the middle of London!

I walked; not a soul to be seen. I stopped, looked back at the dozens of blank windows glittering in the sun, and sat down on a stone seat next to a statue with no nose. I looked to the left: far away, under a tree, on a low folding chair, a dozing figure in shirt-sleeves, a helmet pulled down over the eyes. A policeman.

Beyond him, even further away, a high wall armed with spikes, they must be all round the place. Behind that, against the blue sky, the silhouette of wings: that big statue group on the top of Constitution Arch at Hyde Park Corner, which you pass on the bus. I listened. Yes, in between the twitter of birds I could hear the hum of traffic. Far, far away.

For the first time in my life, I was lonely.

"What *you* doin' 'ere?"

I turned. A face was peering between two big bushes with big yellow flowers. A very old, suspicious face. The rest of him parted branches and shambled forward, in a waistcoat and carrying a pair of shears. Must be one of the dozens of gardeners, and this one the Methuselah of them all. As he got nearer, I looked down and saw that in my haste to get out of doors, I had instinctively put on my shabby old flannel trousers and shoes. No jacket or tie, hair uncombed and an unshaven chin.

"What *you* doin' 'ere?"

Some mischief got into me. "I'm waitin' fer some laundry, see, the butler tole me I could 'ave a bit of a look round the plice." I was never good at Cockney, but I enjoyed having a shot.

"Oh . . ." But he stood firm. "Well, yew watch out the Secret Service lot don't nab yer. All this is the property of a private person." He looked round at "all this" as if he were the person in question.

"I know," I said, "what a 'uge place! 'E's in there, ain't 'e?"

He put on an impenetrable look. "I ain't sayin' yea an' I ain't sayin' nay."

"But I 'eard it last night, on the wireless!"

"Nobody's seen 'im yet. It could be an impostor."

"*Could* it?"

"You never know. Ah've known funny things 'appen in Royal circles. Ever 'eard o' the Monster o' Glarms?"

"Glarms?"

"In Scotland." He sat by my side, like the Ancient Mariner. "There was once a castle-ful o' guests, chock-a-block they was, not a room empty, well, they all knowed there was this Royal Monster tucked away *some*where – but where? Well, there was some jokester there, a drunken Juke I 'spect, well, one mornin' 'e made a plot that every room would 'ang a towel out o' the winder, an' then everybody to troop out on to the lawn an' check the frontage like."

"An' then?"

"Well, right at the top left-'and corner, there was one winder – just the one – *wi' no towel*. Shut. Sealed."

"Any bars?"

"What? . . . What would they need bars for, four storeys up? If 'e'd 'a jumped, they'd 'a found the poor thing squashed on the Terrace, not very nice for the family."

I felt I had to go into this. "Why did they 'ave to keep it such a secret?"

He looked round again at the property of a private person, and spoke lower. "Because 'e was next to be King. I mean, jus' imagine, a Monster on the Throne, covered in 'air, I mean what would the Garden Parties be like? Now the way I put two an' two together is . . . that *nobody's seen this new King*."

I said, "But it was on the wireless!"

"On the wireless, can you *see* a person? Yes or no?"

"Ah would say, no."

"An' nobody's mentioned any snaps of 'im bein' taken since 'e was . . . fetched in." I thought of the Beaton portraits. Snaps . . .

I said, "Supposin' 'im to be genuine – what d'ye reckon 'is chances are?"

"Nil."

"Nil?"

"In this business you gotta be trained from the cradle." I thought of the *Daily Worker*, "overpaid and undertrained" . . .

He looked across at the Palace front, taking in the six hundred rooms. "Oh, Ah've seen 'em come an' Ah've seen 'em go . . ."

"Are they very different from the rest of us?"

"*Naw*! Scratch 'em, an' they're jus' like anybody else."

I wanted to ask him when he had last scratched Royalty. I probed further. "D'ye reckon they're a 'appy lot?"

"*Naw*! It's a dog's life."

"'Ow?"

"Fer one thing, 'owever 'ard a King works . . . 'e can't *better* hisself, can 'e?"

There was no answer to that. "No wonder Teddy the Seventh went on the rampage like 'e did!"

"*Did* 'e?"

"'Course 'e did . . ." Methuselah, the Court gossip, shook a disapproving finger. "Look at that Lily Langtry, no better than she should be. Jersey Lily indeed, it's a libel on lilies . . ."

I said, "'Ow d'ye *know* she was no better than she should be?"

"Weren't she a hactress?" I had asked for it.

He looked me up and down, frowning. "Shouldn't you be gettin' back to your laundry basket?" He was dismissing me. I took the hint, got up and walked thoughtfully to my Palace. Turning my head, I saw him snipping sourly at some bushes. By Royal Appointment.

I'd given him a longer audience than I'd thought, and only got back just in time to change for my first Privy Council; luckily my clothes were laid out, and the bath steaming. It smelt of scent. I nearly looked for the two rubber ducks, then rang for the Valet.

10.55. With his co-operation I was scrambling to get ready when Willie called for me. I was glad it was him and not a footman, but sorry he was not in a suit like mine: he was dressed like all the others, as a swallow. "Sir, please don't give it a thought, they'll each be greeted by a note breaking it to them that your morning rig can't be ready yet. By the way, they've co-opted me as the only new Privy Councillor since the last reign, so I can be at your beck and call." I was relieved.

As I grabbed my typed speech, he said, "Would you like me, Sir, to brief you a little on this?" As we strode along the corridors, he did.

"I'll make it short. 'His Majesty's Most Honourable Privy Council' is a tradition dating from the Court of the Norman Kings, for the expression of the Monarch's wishes." The Willie of the two martinis had been left behind in my study, this was the King's Private Secretary at work. "The Council is by now a formal body meeting on formal occasions to transact formal business, such as approving and ratifying the work of the Cabinet, or discussing pressing Parliamentary issues; it mostly consists of dignitaries who have held high office, mostly either political, judicial or ecclesiastical. The main question at the moment is Mussolini, because it's becoming obvious that he intends to invade Abyssinia. End of exposition."

I asked how many members. "Varies, well over a hundred. Attendance varies too, depending on the occasion. More often than not, Privy Councils are held in the smaller 1844 Room on the ground floor, but this morning's is in the Throne Room. And it'll be a full house."

"Mussolini?"

"No, Sir, you."

The Throne Room. As we approached, I was just conscious of Willie delicately picking one hair off my shoulder. Outside, trestle tables groaning under stacks of memoranda, bowlers, sticks, umbrellas and folded copies of *The Times*.

As doors opened to let me in, I was again reminded of the theatre. As you know, I had never played a leading part – unless you count

Buttons in *Cinderella* – but I was now aware of what it feels like to
key yourself up inside, for an all-important entrance. I was helped by
being dressed, from head to foot, in a new rig-out in an immensely
expensive production, with limitless backing, of which I was the
star.

The Throne Room was another outsize church, and a Roman
Catholic one at that, all gilt and candles and paintings. And Willie
had been right, they were there in full force, a massed flock of
swallows twittering discreetly under a vast chandelier. Which was to
the good, they were too many for each to be presented. Then stepped
forward (I might have guessed) Sir Godwin Rodd, greyer and
stiffer than yesterday. As he bowed to me, the twitter died into a
silence even more discreet: a happening which was to become completely familiar.

Behind Sir God, two figures. From yesterday, I recognized Mr
Baldwin the Prime Minister; then "May I present to your Majesty
Mr Ramsay MacDonald?" He was tall, and looked tired. Our conversation was so tactfully general, and I was again so intent on behaving, that I can't recall any of it. All I said was, "I see . . . Of
course . . ." and such-like. I once caught myself saying, "It is indeed . . ."

Quite soon Willie nodded and escorted me to a dais, on which
waited a gilded throne. Mine. I stood before it, a schoolboy in a
class-room of one pupil facing one hundred masters. With Prefect
Willie as moral support, I stepped forward in a spotlight splintered
from many many pairs of spectacles.

A robot voice: the Clerk of the Council, Sir Maurice Hankey,
reading out the called-for proclamation. Well, booming out; in the
theatre he'd have been asked to cut down on the melodrama.

" . . . We, the Lords Spiritual and Temporal of this Realm, do
now hereby, with one Voice and Consent of Tongue and Heart, pub-
lish and proclaim, That the High and Mighty John Albert is now
become our Liege Lord, John the Second, by the Grace of . . ." etc.
Then the Lord President, Mr Baldwin, got me sworn in as a Member
of the Privy Council; I bowed, stepped forward, and made my
speech. My first ever.

"My Lords and Right Honourable Gentlemen, It is my deep-felt
honour, at this solemn moment, to pay tribute to my Predecessors,
and reverently to bow to your Proclamation . . ." I was nervous, but
I could tell my voice was ringing through the spacious room, and I

only had to look at my paper once. Even then I tried to make it look like a pause for effect.

I finished up word-perfect; I had also struggled to speak clearly without sounding Cornish, not easy when you *are* Cornish. So I was taken aback by the pocket of non-applause, until I remembered where I was. A footman bowed, and as I sat on my throne there was the general flurried sound of the swallows perching at a long table.

Looking down at the notables, I saw – apart from Willie and a handsome chap of forty whom I recognized from the papers as Anthony Eden – only rows and rows of careful colourless faces; the ones who weren't wearing glasses had lost their hair, while quite a few qualified on both counts. Between the heads catching the light of the table candelabra, and the spectacles, my first Privy Council looked quite a glittering affair. Sorry if I sound tough on the older generation.

But they were all dignitaries-who-had-held-high-office. Political, judicial or ecclesiastical. A smattering of clerical collars and black aprons and gaiters. I looked round for a ratty grey wig from the Old Bailey, but no luck; I did spot one bonus – a prop I'd seen shamelessly used in rep. A monocle. Drop it at the right shocked moment, and it's a sure laugh. Whoever was wearing one here, wasn't dropping it.

I have the names before me, and here are a few. Besides Baldwin, MacDonald, Simon, Hoare, Halifax and Beaverbrook, there were Lord Maugham, Sir Austen Chamberlain, Mr Neville Chamberlain, the Marquess of Huntley, Earl Beauchamp, Mr Winston Churchill, Lord Dawson of Penn ("If I may say so, Sir, you appear to be in the pink"), Lord Howard of Penrith, Mr George Lansbury, the Earl of Shaftesbury, General Smuts, Mr Herbert Morrison, Mr J. H. Thomas, the Archbishop of Canterbury, the Archbishop of York, the Earl of Balfour, the Marquess of Bath, the Duke of Atholl. That will make you understand why I said "notables".

The Council got under way. I settled down to swimming about in it: completely out of my depth, just swimming. Even when it was not Sir God droning on, the language was still Sir-God talk. "To refer back to the aforesaid anomaly . . . er . . . between the grant to the Armed Forces . . . er . . . and the prodigious dispensation of Parliamentary salaries . . ." I let the muddy waves of words eddy round me.

An Archbishop sailed to his feet. I had never before heard the Anglican half-wail. "It is my solemn prayer that . . . er . . . the

Almighty will reveal to Signor Mussolini the error of his ways . . .
er . . . in his breach of the Kellogg Pact and the Tripartite Treaty of
1906 . . . and I adjure you . . ." I waited for him to say "My
brethren . . ."

On and on. Once, whoever was speaking turned to me. I could tell
this was not entirely in order; he was trying me out. "I feel sure that
your Majesty will concur that . . . er . . . a war of aggression is to
be . . . er . . . unconditionally deplored?"

They waited. "Totally," I said, loud and clear. He bumbled on.
Thank you, Kathy. I had scored.

Later – much later – I was again addressed. "May I respectfully
suggest to your Majesty – er – that we present our considered appro-
bation of this proposal by the Cabinet?"

"Oh," I said, louder and clearer, "emphatically."

On. And on. Then, at the core of my being – literally, because it
was at the base of my stomach – a faint warning signal. This morning, if you remember, I had drunk a fair amount of water. And in my
anxiety not to be late for all this, I had forgotten to make sure that
his Majesty – at his first Most Honourable Council – would be physically at ease.

I needed to pee.

Speaker after speaker. "My lords, an't please you to move to
Point Four." Miserably, I thought of the Beast caught short, and of
Kathy humiliating him.

On, and on. Being – that morning – headline drunk, I miserably
visualized A PUDDLE AT THE PALACE . . .

Finally, in the silence between one speech and the next, I raised
my hand. And with the calm of the panic-stricken I turned to my
Prime Minister. I tried not to say the inevitable, but I did. "Please,
sir, can I leave the room?"

It was, I suppose, my desperate hope that after a dumb-struck
pause, there might be a general guffaw which would save my bacon –
they might even say to themselves, he's proving he's human – that
he's just like *us*!

No, there was just the pause, and rows upon rows of raised eyebrows. A country bumpkin had misbehaved. Totally.

Then a voice, loud and clear. Willie's. "Come to think of it, Sir,
I'm in a spot of trouble too – my lords, might you not welcome a
breather, for coffee?"

I got up, he got up, they all got up. He opened a side door, and
followed me out. I said, "Willie, thank you."

"My pleasure, Sir. Actually, what's the point of a Privy Council without a Privy? I'll wait for you . . ."

Standing in the lavatory, I looked up and noticed – and it was a bad moment to notice – that the window had bars. In my mind I saw, outside, the giant gilded gates topped with giant spikes.

As we returned to the Council Willie murmured, "Stupid of me, Sir, I should have reminded you of the late King's advice to the Prince of Wales. 'Take every opportunity you can,' he said, 'to relieve yourself.'"

Willie had left the door of the Throne Room open; inside, a background of polite murmur and tinkling coffee-cups. Willie was just standing aside for me to precede him, when we both heard the P.M. speak, slowly and with concern. "It's an alarming thing to say, but . . . I don't think he'll do."

The three others looked at him. Then they spoke, as one. "Oh dear . . ."

Willie and I waited a moment, then walked in past them. Everybody got up, I sat down again, they sat down again.

For the rest of the meeting I stared dutifully at whoever was speaking, but this time not a phrase, not even a stray word, got to me. My head was as empty as if I was sitting in a slow train staring at the telegraph poles sliding by. No, not quite empty: inside it, five words were running round and round, one on the tail of the other. It's not what people say to you about yourself that you remember, for good; it's the things you overhear. I-don't-think-he'll-do-I-don't-think-he'll-do-I-don't-think-he'll-do . . .

I felt a pain in my fingers, and looked down to see that both fists, on the table, were clenched tight and white, as if in a boxing-ring.

My eyes didn't move from them, but the words in my head seemed to get fainter and fainter, and give way to others that got firmer and firmer.

Oh-yes-he-will-oh-yes-he-will-oh-yes-he-will . . .

I got up, they all got up, I bowed, they all bowed. And Willie and I left.

We still had not spoken when we entered my study, and even then there was nothing we could say, two housemaids were dusting and sweeping. I could tell by the way they scuttled out, that they shouldn't have still been there for me to see them "at it". And by the time they were gone, Willie was gone too. Again I wasn't hungry; I had a poached egg on a tray which I hardly noticed, my mind was working so steadily.

2.30 p.m. Willie, with pad and pen. And we were alone.

"You're thoughtful, Sir."

"Last evening you described me as a butterfly caught in a machine. Then I asked you whether the butterfly, once he'd lost his wings, would have anything left. You said it was too soon to tell. Well, after this morning, you can tell. There's nothing left."

"You mustn't exaggerate, Sir. At a long meeting, anybody can be distracted by the call of Nature. Even a butterfly. On consideration . . ."

"Yes?"

"Before you came here, the wings were in full play and the solid part wasn't getting much attention. I have a feeling the body's tougher than one might think."

"And now the wings are gone, could it get . . . tougher?"

"I don't see why not. This morning – at your first public appearance – before the little contretemps, you did better than you imagine. You have natural behaviour."

There spread over me a nervous glow. If this fellow's the public-school product . . . thank you, Playing Fields of Eton. You could be *seven* foot three, I'd still like you. "Willie, I've got to catch up, I've got to be told. The lot. At school I didn't have much use for spelling or grammar, being quite happy near the bottom of the class. Will you lend a hand?"

"I will."

I was excited. "We start three seconds from now. Is there a dictionary here . . ." He got up, took one from a book-shelf and placed it before me. I said, "I'll spend the afternoon with this."

"And I'll spend it mapping things out. Shall I be back at five?"

"Suits me."

"That would fit in, would it?" That was his artful way of correcting me without seeming to: a way I was to get to recognize. "That would fit in, perfectly . . . But before you go, Willie, back to the big machine. Give me a couple o' tips."

He reflected. "Beware of the boot-licking, I've seen flattery play hell with the truth. Second, watch the old tongue."

"Except when you and me are alone?"

"Exactly, except when you and I are alone." I said, "I'll remember that – except when you and I are alone."

"Otherwise, if anybody's within earshot, censor your every word.

For instance, a footman is trained to look deaf and dumb, but he's not; it's a discreet staff here, but only human. The Press is human too, and things can get distorted in transit."

"I realized that from this morning's papers. I'll remember. Any time I need to speak my mind, it'll be strictly between you and I."

"Exactly, strictly between you and me. I'll be back at five."

Grammar isn't easy.

An hour later, with me deep in the dictionary, with paper and pencil next to it, a letter was delivered, with a code-number. It was addressed, in my mother's flowing hand, to HIS MAJESTY KING JOHN THE SECOND, BUCKINGHAM PALACE.

Well, she had to call me something. And not even "London". The letter had crossed mine, and I prepared myself for the bewildered reaction of two simple people knocked sideways: dazed by an event far beyond their grasp.

"Our dear Son Jack, The London genleman has just aquainted your Father & Self with the news of your promotion.

"It affords the both of us great pleisure & suprise to adress the envelop by the Title which it has pleised God & the Law to place upon you. What a blessin they did not spot earlier who you was, you would have been under that Sky Whale & by now in Abrams Bosom.

"Your Father & Self baint in any doubt that you will behave as to the manner born & be a credit to us & to your Empire. It is a big relief to us that you are in Buckingham Palace & not in Jail."

It would seem that the only tangible effect of the news was her feeling that from now on her husband – formerly referred to as "your Da" – should now become, on paper, "your Father".

"Your Father would add his blessin only two lads are callin him this minute to the back door. they bein here to fetch the manure, I am sorry to say that Spotto is gettin quite blind and we do ave to think of the future, Your Lovin Mother & Subject, Alice Lavinia Green."

Except for the spelling, it might have been from a farming Queen Victoria to *her* son, my great-grandfather Edward.

Then an afterthought.

"I did have the idea that my 1st usband had somethin to hide, such as a convict in the family. But I would never have suspect it was Royal Blood, he seemed to me quite normal."

CHAPTER NINE

Cramming at Court

At four p.m., a letter. "From D. Lloyd George, Private and Confidential."

It was in his own hand.

"Your Majesty, May a commoner from Carnarvonshire, North Wales, aged 72, surreptitiously approach his King, aged 24, from Cornwall, South England, to offer his homage?

"My approach is surreptitious for the simple reason that I have no wish to alarm my colleague Mr Baldwin, or that Tory bastion with feet of clay Sir Godwin Rodd, who has been sitting on the fence so long that the iron has entered into his soul. Can a bastion boast feet, and then sit on a fence? No matter.

"They don't care for me. Sir God, in confidence, has informed certain gossiping intimates that *the Welsh Wizard has a morally disintegrating effect on all whom he has to deal with*. Moreover, Sir Godwin, who claims to 'have His Majesty's ear' – there are times when one wishes the Monarch was deaf – each time I have hinted at a private audience with your Majesty, he has evaded the issue. (Would the word 'shifty' fit the case? Surely not.)

"From which I conclude that the two of them, and the enfeebled cohorts behind them, fear that your Majesty – in the hands of the Wizard – would turn into juvenile jelly and . . . morally disintegrate.

"Is there a Conservative fear that having buttonholed you, I would drug you and inject you with the Liberal spirit? The possibility must be horrific.

"The outlook is made more threatening by the libellous rumour that I am plotting to get back into office. It happens to be true. Good luck my boy, long may you reign over us, Your Uncle David.

"P.S. If you ever feel the need of my advice, please send for me."

The splendid dig at Sir God, I found later in a book about L.G.; it was worth a repeat. I kept the letter.

And had no idea, then, that the day would come for me to go back to it.

Willie was back on the dot of five, with under his arm a dozen books which he deposited in front of me. I said, "Anything to declare?"

"Yes, Sir. I've just come from the House of Commons, where I was able to have a constructive talk with the P.M."

"Oh . . . Does he still think I won't do?"

"Once I'd reported to him the conversation I'd just had with you, he changed his mind; your attitude has impressed him. He then showed me a cutting from an afternoon paper, a third leader."

He took it from a folder and handed it over. "Now that yesterday's first flush of jubilation has died down, a question must arise: is a young man – whom we all wish well, but with a sketchy small-town education which terminated at 16 – equipped for a task more than formidable? Only time will show . . . His first public appearance – in the next couple of days, we trust – will give an indication . . ."

Willie went on. "The P.M. sees that as a straw in the wind. So I suggested that in order to forestall more wind, a special announcement should be drafted, ratified and given to Broadcasting House and given tomorrow to the Press. I have the draft here." He read out. "Tomorrow morning, Saturday June 15, 1935, the King will sign the proclamation by which the Monarch signifies his consent to the State Opening of his first Parliament. Since the Opening cannot, by law, take place earlier than seventeen days after his signature – the date therefore being fixed for Tuesday July 2nd – the Prime Minister and the Cabinet are agreed on the following.

"That the State Opening of Parliament should mark His Majesty's first public appearance before his people; and that, in view of the extraordinary circumstances of his Accession, he should spend those twenty days giving himself – with the help of an expert advisory board – a solid grounding in the ramifications of Royal duties, et cetera. A Royal cramming course."

He looked up. "Between you and me, Sir, on all that traditional stuff you will be briefed as each occasion arises, it's the 'et cetera' that covers the ground we're thinking of."

"I understand."

"You approve, Sir?"

"Not half . . . I mean, totally." I looked down at the pile of books he had brought: at the top book. "Did you think of adding that the cramming course includes Thurloe's *Elementary English Grammar for Beginners*? . . . Expert advisory board. How many?"

"Not many. Actually, one. Myself."

"Suits me. I mean, that would fit in . . . Willie, it's a marvellous idea!"

"It just seemed obvious that you needed a period of – sort of – incubation."

"Totally. On top of my Elementary Grammar?"

"An hour a day with Miss Fogerty –"

"*Elsie* Fogerty, the speech teacher? Big stars have been to her, she's *good*! On just what I need, the King's English!"

"Quite . . . Next, social scene. I understand from the Novello management, that you don't need dancing lessons. Any languages, at school?"

"French. But not much, half the time I wasn't listening."

"A little Spanish and German can also, on occasion, make an impression."

"And after your years in Vienna and Madrid –"

"I hope, Sir, to cope."

"And Willie, grammar and vocab.?"

"Ah . . . The most important, and with your nimbleness of mind, the simplest. It's merely a question of absorbing the elements which would have been part of you long ago, if you hadn't had to get out and earn your living."

"Nicely put."

"Thank you, Sir."

"Thank *you*, Sir." I held out my sheets of paper. (I have them in front of me now.) "Willie, I've just been on a Dictionary Binge, can I show off?"

"You may certainly show off."

"Willie, *may* I show off? . . . First, I've made a list headed 'Fancy-words with tricky spelling which I might be called upon to utilize in writing'."

"Called upon to use in writing – good idea . . ."

"What's wrong with 'utilize'? Sounds fancy enough to me!"

"That's the trouble with it. My advice would be, don't utilize 'utilize', use 'use'."

"I will. But I do realize (spelt with a Zed) that if I did write 'utilize', I'd spell that with a Zed too. But 'surprise', I'd spell with an S."

"Go on."

"Likewise 'exercise', and 'paralyse'. 'Embarrass' has two R's, *and* two S's. 'Fulfil' has one L at the end, 'forestall' has two. 'Descendant' ends in *A*, N, T, 'Independent' in *E*, N, T. 'Existence' ends in *E*, N, C, E, 'Tolerance' in *A*, N, C, E."

"Splendid."

"And here I've made a list of words I frankly didn't know, and ones I knew just well enough to nod to, but *not* on speaking terms with. Which I now am. I've memorized them. With a Zed. Also invented, for each one, a good Privy Council sentence using the word in question."

"Quite the best method." Willie shut his eyes, to listen. "Yes?"

" 'Manifestation': a public act on the part of a government. Example: 'Such a manifestation, Prime Minister, would hardly be in our interest'."

"Excellent."

" 'Substantiate': to prove correct. Example: 'The rumour, Prime Minister, that Sir Godwin –'."

"Ah . . ."

" 'The rumour that Sir Godwin is the life and soul of any party, has yet to be substantiated'."

"Capital!"

" 'Cunctatious'."

Teacher opened his eyes. "What was that again?"

" 'Cunctatious': prone to delay."

"Example?"

" 'Would you not agree, Prime Minister, that the fact we've been waiting three bloody hours for Sir Godwin proves he's a trifle on the cunctatious side?' "

"Sounds delightful, but I think I'd side-step that one. It's a trifle on the rare side."

"I'm glad," I said, "what's more, it sounded to me a trifle on the rude side."

"I agree."

" 'Ostentatious': means you like to show off. 'If I may say so, Sir Godwin, that parasol you are carrying looks somewhat ostentatious.' "

"I like that."

" 'Ineluctable': describes something from which one cannot escape. 'When the warder locked the door, the prisoner knew his cell was ineluctable'."

A pause. "Sir . . . I don't think that's *quite* it. If I were you I'd duck that one."

"Right."

Then Willie got thoughtful. "D'you know, *I've* always thought 'surprise' had a Zed in it . . ."

And so we went on. It was interesting.

It was to go on like that for (nearly) three weeks I was to be under wraps, before becoming Public Property. Sorry to bring in the theatre again, but to me it's inevitable (I nearly wrote "ineluctable"): I threw myself into my three weeks of slogging as if rehearsing for a big First Night.

The Gram and Voc hour (Grammar and Vocabulary) was a daily feature: I made the acquaintance of hyphens, brackets, dashes, colons and even of semi-colons. When it came to my French lesson, I was gratified that much more of my school grounding came back to me than I expected; and I found – to do with singing, I suppose, and my native Cornish vowels – that I had quite an aptitude. Then I went from Spanish grammar to German phrase-book.

Then Miss Fogerty, deferential but strict. "You must be careful, Sir, to pronounce *subtle* without the b . . . No, when one has not understood – or quite heard – the other person, it is incorrect to say 'Pardon?', one says either 'I beg your pardon?' in full or, less formally, 'I'm so sorry, what did you say?' . . . No, the word *bath* in standard English, rhymes with *hearth* and not with *hath*, and since the 'g' in *recognize* is not – I repeat, not – silent, the word is *not reconize*, also I would remind you, Sir, that while it sounds charming to pronounce *yesterday* with the accent on the last syllable instead of on the first, it is incorrect. And a minute ago, Sir, you read out the words 'law and order' – it would be wise to bear in mind that the word 'and' does not begin with an 'r' – 'law-*rand*-order'. Again please, 'Law *and* order' . . ."

Fri. June 21st 1935, 10th Day of Reign. A letter on my breakfast table. Ah, Kathy and Bruce . . . No, from the Farm. Strange that K. and B. hadn't written by return . . .

> "Our dear Son Jack, Oh your Father & Self are pleised to get our 1st leter from B.P. & in your own writing. Yesterday a polite genleman from Lond. Times paper called along up here & said how strange I must ha felt on learnin I was the mother of the King. Why should I feel strange, I said, when I ave been his mother all his life? I did not mean to sound sharp. What has ocured to us as a famly is all v. intrestin. Your Auntie Arriet & Uncle F. (Jarrow) send love & congrats.
>
> "Our only plague is the crowds achattin up along our Hill mornin & nite, what they expectin to set eyes on, freaks? Your Father has put a notice on the gate, WILD BULL ON PRE-MESES, it baint true but in this case the Lord will look the other way, Your Lovin Mother & Subject, Alice Lavinia Green.
>
> "P.S. From your lovin Father. You will note from above that your Mother is the most looked-up-to-woman in Cornwall."

In the cramming course, History and Geography were vital and daily subjects, and I could see why there was a World Atlas about; it was clear to me that it would be unsuitable to go on imagining that Brazilians spoke Spanish and that the Prince Regent and George the Fourth were two different people.

And once, when I mentioned that I expected Mr Lloyd George and Mr Ramsay MacDonald must be close friends, Willie looked puzzled, "What makes you think that, Sir?"

"Because they're both Liberals."

A pause. "Ramsay Mac's Labour." He suggested gently that I should undertake a daily scanning of the political news and leaders, "just to keep abreast". Hard going, but advisable.

Bewildering as well, for I would often find myself in a muddle. *The Times*: "The Abyssinian problem can be solved only by stern intervention – *pro bono publico* – by the League of Nations." *Express*: "If the League thinks Mussolini will kow-tow to a feeble rap over the knuckles from a bunch of idealists, the League is eating its hat." So where do I go from there?

Then two books which the Cabinet had recommended "for intensive study": Bagehot's *The English Constitution* and Kerr-

Mallinson's *The Monarchy and the Constitution*, I did try, but found them both very heavy going indeed.

In preparation for the Trooping of the Colour, gentle riding lessons outside the Stables; I had never been on a horse in my life, not even a cart-horse, and I found I had a good seat; then tennis – singles with Willie on one of the Garden courts. "On an Empire tour, a touch of Royal athleticism works wonders . . ." He was good. I started hopeless, then the fact I could dance helped, I got better, then better still, and at the end of the second week I won 9-7. Then, in the evening, a Bridge lesson: "Terribly useful, means that for hours you don't have to talk *or* listen."

Willie was the perfect tutor, watching over his charge impersonally and yet with a guarded affection. He was especially adept at manoeuvring me into asking him for enlightenment on a subject. "I'd like your views, Sir," he would say, "on the House of Lords – or, as I like to think of it, the Old Curiosity Shop . . . Do you feel there should be stricter rules about attendance?" And in twenty minutes I acquired a reasonable grasp of how the Old Curiosity Shop was run: essential for the future.

My chief distraction (except that it was still work) was the Red Boxes. They were exactly that, leather despatch-boxes which arrived every morning from Whitehall, locked, and to which I had my key.

They disgorged State Documents, Orders in Council, Lists of Government Appointments, Signed Commissions for Armed Forces, Foreign Office telegrams, "submissions" from the Prime Minister, the Cabinet and various Government departments which it was my duty to "master" (master? half of them I couldn't make head or tail of) and finally sign.

Willie explained that the papers had piled up, which was why the first day had to include at least three hours of solid sifting. He also impressed on me that the Red Boxes were top-private, and that I must never leave them unlocked, and I never did.

With him at the blackboard, the cramming course was enjoyable even when it came to the important points of Etiquette. "At feeding functions, one is expected, after paying attention for a bit to the lady on one's right, to make contact with the other side. Sounds like Spiritualism, but there it is . . ." Small points too: I learnt to cure an unconscious habit, when sitting with one leg over the other knee, of wiggling my foot, and so looking nervous. Useful habit for Royal males, on long official walks: hands loosely clasped in small of back, somehow gives impression of being at ease and at the same time attentive. Etc. . . . Interesting.

Item, useful short cuts to popularity. I learnt that Baldwin was fond of talking about "Astley", his retreat in Worcestershire, that his favourite author was Mary Webb (who was she?), that he and his son Oliver didn't see eye to eye politically and it was a sore point; that Sir John Simon was not Anthony Eden's favourite character . . .

A typical nudge from Willie was the time he looked at a note he'd made – "P.W. Cigars, now what did I mean by that . . . Oh yes . . . The Prince of Wales, Belling. Belling's the Chief Butler, been here since the Boer War and the Prince used to give him two boxes of Havana cigars for his birthday, which is next Tuesday, may I put your Majesty down for two boxes?"

"Thank you, Willie."

I found one tip interesting. "Can you believe it, Sir, that if you fasten the bottom button of your waistcoat, the Powers-That-Be may label you as an outsider? Because your great-grandfather King Edward (since his valet's duties didn't extend to button-fastening) tended to forget to do up the one in question. We can only be grateful that presumably he wasn't quite so careless with his flies."

A momentary side-track: my fittings, for everything I was ever to wear in public. The tailoring staff must have worked for forty-eight hours solid, like they're said to do in Hong Kong.

Behind a screen and out again, to and fro (there had to be a screen so the assistants wouldn't catch a glimpse). I must have got into, and out of, thirty pairs of trousers, with the same assistants pulling and tweaking and diving with pieces of chalk, while I was to try on every variety of headwear, from top-hat to sporting cap – everything but a turban and a bishop's mitre. Except for the aura of whispered homage, I might have been a dummy. I certainly looked like one.

The second distraction was more fun, though it lasted for only ten pleasant minutes. Three days later, at breakfast. Every paper displayed, on its front page, the announcement THE KING'S POR-TRAITS, INSIDE!

The Beaton photographs. As I scuffled through the pages, to get to the middle spread, my only thought was . . . will I look like a chorus-boy?

Well, I didn't. Mr Beaton had seen to that; he had done me proud, full-length, full-face and profile. They were pictures which would have got me straight into Louis B. Mayer's Hollywood empire, if I weren't already tied up with my own.

The full-lengths of King John the Second displayed a trim erect figure, coupled with a dignity which did not make him look a day older than his twenty-four years. In the close shots the eyes were lit so that you got just a glimpse of the shadow of eyelashes: bedroom eyes really, yet with a hint of "Although I'd be a hell of a guy if I weren't behaving myself, I *am*, so keep off the grass", and balanced by the chin, firm without being hard. The mouth was soft without being weak. Two smiling ones, the smile not too wide. Tentative, implying "I hope you'll approve of me".

Which meant that I felt the inevitable mixture of embarrassment and gratification. I tried to feel less gratified as I absorbed the comments underneath, but didn't succeed. "Photogenic . . . sensitive . . . appealing . . ." One paper used the portmanteau word "sex-appeal". Another reproduced a faded photo of the Duke of Clarence. "*One may detect a resemblance to Grandpapa.*" I couldn't see it – those poppy eyes! – but Willie did.

Three days later, the *Daily Sketch*. ROYAL SALUTE! "*Following our publication of the Royal Photographs, we have experienced an unprecedented flood of letters, mostly from women readers. The following are a few of many . . .*"

Among the few: "*No good pretending, I'm in love with King Jack!*" "*. . . He knocks spots off Clark Gable and Gary Cooper, younger and more boyish, oh how I'd love to set eyes on him close to, where has he been all my life?*" Living on a farm, ducky, and then in a chorus dressing-room. "*There's a look in his eye of a real king, and yet you just ache to cuddle him and mother him and ruffle his hair – oh yes you do, as sure as my name's yours sincerely Gladys Potter.*" Steady on, Glad . . .

The same day, in the *Mirror*: COINCIDENCE? "*It is announced that next Wednesday will see a revival, at the Gaumont Cinema Haymarket, of a Courtneidge-Hulbert film made a couple of years ago. But there is no truth in the rumour that there will be a gala opening attended by His Majesty the King. The film? 'JACK'S THE BOY!'*" The *Express*: "*Postcards of the Beaton photos, now on sale, are in unprecedented demand all over the country: half a million have been sold in the last five days.*"

All that, in between the slogging, was nice.

On the second Saturday morning, after our Gram and Voc hour,

Willie said, "Would you mind, Sir, if I went home for the week-end?"
I said, "Of course not, I did appreciate your giving up the last one,
but you mustn't do that again." His request almost startled me,
making me realize that since his account of his career on our first
meeting, he had never mentioned himself or his family. All I knew
was that he lived in a house in Surrey, with his wife and small son,
and during the week used a small flat in Knightsbridge. I sensed that
he was devoted to them both, but was shy of talking about his home
life.

On our way to tennis before he was to leave, he had to deposit
papers in his office, across the corridor from me, and there he presented "Captain Sellison": my age, pleasant, elegant, vaguely good-
looking. I noticed, behind him, a large table laden with sacks, half-a-
dozen of them, all bulging. As we walked on I asked who Captain
Sellison was. "My assistant, Sir, your Second Secretary." "Ah," I
said, "Sec-Sec." And for me and Willie, Sec-Sec was to be his name.

"Works hard," Willie said, "keen. Very keen." I got a faint impression that he himself wasn't so keen – on his assistant, personally,
I mean.

Descending the stairs, I tried to remember what Sec-Sec looked
like, and failed. There was nothing to remember. I thought, "Is he
what they hope to turn me into?" That depressed me, but only for
a minute, the tennis restored me. (My two alternating Equerries
turned out to be of the same stamp as Sec-Sec, just as elegant, just as
pleasant. Must have been, or I'd remember something about them.
Willie, and Willie alone, was my life-line.)

Walking back in from the tennis, I asked about the sacks in the
office. "Your mail, Sir."

"*What?*"

"That's only the first day. From all over the country, and by next
week from all over the world, it'll be a roomful. The sorters say half
of them are proposals of marriage."

Over me came the same feeling of being in mid-dream, which I'd
had on first entering this place: then I struggled with it, and shook it
off. It scared me.

"Lots of boxes of chocolates," Willie said, "nice for the hospitals.
Now, Sir, you must see why the people close to you had to be given a
code number."

That, of course, sent my thoughts straight to Kathy and Bruce:
every morning when I woke, they were immediately in my mind, for
the simple reason that I expected a letter which was never there.

Then the day's work would pile up, with me getting more and more absorbed – the German session was really tough – and I would forget about them. Once or twice I mentioned their silence to Willie, but all I got was a non-committal "Oh, really?"

The following Thursday, *June 27th 1935, 16th Day of Reign.* And since it had been a gruelling one, our martini half-hour between six and seven was to be looked forward to. Only two martinis each, but good ones, and I hoped they would loosen Willie up. They did: after the first one, I found him – at last – talking a bit about himself.

We had somehow got on to the subject of Temper. I said that although I mostly take the rough with the smooth, I sometimes wonder whether, in an intolerable situation, I might not lose control. "Willie, have *you* ever lost your temper?"

He said serenely, "I don't seem to have one to lose. My wife once asked me to have a try, but as she's never given me cause, it would be difficult. The nearest I ever got was when I'd sat up all night working on the intricate minutes of a Cabinet meeting, snatched an hour's sleep, then found that a housemaid had lit the fire with them."

"Willie! . . . What did you say?"

"I said: 'My dear girl, *what* did you think they were?'

" 'Rubbish, sir,' she said. I said: 'You may have something there, but *not* for lighting the fire with.' "

He reflected a moment, then: "Oh, I'm lucky to be the placid type, so is my dear Anne. Once the first flurry is over – the creation of a son-and-heir and all that – the restfulness makes for a happy marriage."

"That's good. Quite a price to pay, though . . ." Then I did a complete non-sequitur. "I know what I'll do. I'll phone them."

"Them?"

"Kathy and Bruce."

He was immediately on his guard. "I shouldn't do that, Sir."

"Why not?"

He hesitated. "I went to see them after their Wednesday matinees, yesterday."

"You *did*, Stage-door Johnny, did you? Corner House?"

"Yes."

"Well . . . how were they? Did they ask after me?" And I thought, what an idiotic question . . .

"Oh they did, and they're fine. But they very definitely feel you mustn't be bothered until . . ."

"Until I've opened?"

"Precisely, your *Opening* of Parliament."

"Not even with a letter?" I was vaguely hurt. And puzzled.

"They seem to feel it would be an intrusion. And I don't think a phone call would be satisfactory, Sir, do you?"

On consideration, I agreed with him. I imagined the conversation – "But tell me about *you*, how's everything with *you* . . ." No.

The official Speech arrived, which I was to make at the ceremony; prepared by the Prime Minister, it was factual and short, but needed careful rehearsing. With it were the very detailed *Instructions re Procedure*. Until my three weeks were over, I would postpone Kathy and Bruce. Work, and wait.

CHAPTER TEN

Good Evening, the World

London was waiting too. And by the middle of the third week of the Cramming Course, patience was wearing thin. *Daily Sketch: "The King's subjects are beginning to feel deprived – starved. As the days drift by, a dozen charming Beaton studies seem meagre fare."* One bold headline, HAS THE PALACE BALCONY GOT DRY ROT, OR WHAT?

Next day, Willie issued a statement. "As promised, next Tuesday July the 2nd, on the occasion of the State Opening of Parliament at 10.45 a.m., His Majesty will drive from Buckingham Palace to the Palace of Westminster." Which, Willie explained, is another way of saying "Parliament". "On his return, there will take place an event unprecedented on such a day, one traditionally reserved for the Coronation: the King will make an appearance on the Palace Balcony. In addition, at 9 p.m., a second unprecedented happening. From his study in Buckingham Palace, His Majesty will speak to his people, and to the world, by wireless."

I asked Willie if George the Fifth had written his own Christmas speeches for the B.B.C. "Oh yes, taking advice from any source he chose to consult."

"Good, I'll choose to consult you." Later in the day, however, he reported to me that "in the unusual circumstance of the young King's inexperience", the Powers-That-Be had decided that I should have the speech ".drafted" for me. And when he told me who was to do the drafting, my face fell. Sir God. Predictably, the draft did not arrive till the day before the Opening. As Willie placed it in front of me he said, "I'm afraid, Sir, it is some distance below Mr Lloyd George on one of his off days."

It was. "It is with a mind heavy-laden, that I move forward to face my people: heavy-laden by reason of the monumental tragedy on which it would be too distressing to dwell" – then why bring it up at all – "though my mind be heavy-laden" – three heavy-ladens – "my *heart* stays buoyant with hopes for a united people. I humbly pledge myself to explore every opportunity . . ." Why not "every avenue"?

I returned the script to Willie. "I know," he said, "the word is 'pedestrian', and Royalty has no business to be travelling on foot. But there we are . . ."

"Tomorrow I'm supposed to go through this rubbish with Miss Fogerty. Will you be there so we can try to take some of the horror out of it, starting with the explored avenues?"

> ". . . It is v. intrestin for your Father & Self that you will be on the Wireless July 2nd, we will not ferget to turn it on. Take care of your Health, your Wealth is no good without your Health.
>
> "So with openin your Parliment it do seem to us that you must not let them take advantage of your kindness. Though we reckon you will only be requird to lay down the law pretty & loud, then turn some big key in the door & then bow to the Members of Parliment on their knees . . .
>
> "Your lovin Father speekin. Last Fri in St Austell, Market Day, I strolled down along Fore St to the P. Library & copied detales of your Family Tree on back of Farm Accts Book. Well Jack, if you had knowed you was related to all that, the time you was at school, you would have been top o the class."

July 1st, the eve of my unveiling. After forty-five minutes with the Red Boxes – I was getting the knack of skimming them at just the right speed, signing away fortunes, sealing the fates of thousands of human beings on the other side of the globe, how could I know? – I was glad of the Fogerty Hour, a rehearsal for tomorrow night, 9 p.m. Just as we were about to start, a knock and Willie walked in. I looked at him. "Oh . . ."

"I'm sorry, Sir, you implied yesterday that you'd like me to help –"

"I know, Willie, but I'm afraid on second thoughts – I'd feel less self-conscious without a third person, I know you'll understand . . ." He had been about to sit down, but now shot up again. "Of course!" And he was gone.

My "second thoughts" had nothing to do with feeling self conscious. Last night, sitting up in the Bed of Ware and scanning the text of Sir God's "suggestion", I had made a decision. Then I had taken pencil and paper, shut my eyes and talked. To people. People at the foot of my bed. Millions of them.

And as I talked, I had written the words down, later making two fair copies. And at this moment Miss Fogerty was holding one, I the other. For Willie's sake, I wanted him, when the time came, to be able to say that he knew nothing about it.

I rehearsed, and Miss Fogerty was thorough. "No, Sir, don't fill your mouth with the vowels, clip them rather, keep them pure . . . It is correct – and I think attractive – to use 'an' before 'historic', 'an historic coach', please repeat . . . You have a natural sense of sentence-rhythm and variety of intonation . . . Not so *stiff*, say it *not* to that sheet of paper, and *not* to an audience, but to *me*, me sitting here . . ."

It was a good run-through.

In the evening, so that I could relax before tomorrow, no work: a quiet dinner with Willie and his wife, Anne; I had insisted on meeting her, knowing that he was not the type to suggest it. She was exactly as I had imagined: delicately handsome, friendly but shy, though she liked me enough, I could tell, to relax into warmth. She obviously shrank from the social life which could have been hers, and loved the country, as he did; they were nice together, easy and affectionate.

Tues. July 2nd 1935, 21st Day of Reign.

As Wilkins opened the curtains (by now I was identifying the footmen) he said: "Royal weather, your Majesty!" And it was, the Royal sun was streaming in.

Bath, shave, then a steady silent procession of visitors: haircut, shampoo, manicure: special valet to lay out robes and insignia. It would be all so hot and heavy that I was to stay in my dressing-gown till the last minute.

Willie arrived, slim as a lamp-post and quietly impeccable in morning dress; he was as poker-faced as ever, but I could tell from the way he drummed his fingers that – for him – he was excited.

"Would your Majesty care to walk along and glance out of the windows?"

Past the paintings and the treasures, past the Blue Room and the White Room and the Green Room and the Great Gallery. The clocks were unanimous: 9.30. The front windows were crowded with Staff, taking turns to crane their necks and have a peep. As I got nearer, they melted to each side, discreetly ignoring my dressing-gown. Willie drew aside a corner of curtain and I looked down past the Palace Balcony.

And gasped.

First, up in the sparkling morning air, with just enough wind to make them graceful, the two long straight lines of brilliant flags against the light-green blur of summer leaves, receding down the Mall for – as it seemed – mile after mile. Lower, bathed in sun, it was as if decorators had spread a huge carpet of flowers, a glowing multi-coloured mosaic overflowing into Green Park on the left and St James's Park on the right. The flowers were moving gently, thousands of them, as if in a breeze. But down there, there was no breeze.

I looked at Willie, quite stupid. And what I said was silly too. "But . . . those flowers – are people!"

"They are, Sir," said Willie. "Your people."

The way he spoke that, it was a fact. I felt dizzy. Back in my study, Willie suggested I put my feet up during the hour of waiting, "as you must have done in the theatre before your first nights." As if I had played Hamlet and Othello in the West-End for years. I did put my feet up, and even dozed for a few minutes. My heart slowed down.

My two valets dressed me, with the utmost care, from head to foot; I nearly wrote "underlings", because in an account of that day, the word does not sound absurd or demeaning, you just felt that the world – just for July the 2nd 1935 – had got one foot in the Middle Ages. My costume – I am able to quote, from a subsequent newspaper article on the whole morning – was "the full dress uniform of an Admiral of the Fleet with sword, medals and (hanging from the neck) the Badge of the Grand Master of the Order of the British Empire, also (hanging from the shoulders) the collar of the Order of the Garter". And when I looked into a long mirror, I saw that those scrupulous fittings had been worth while.

Walking slowly down the sweep of the stairs, I could tell that my attendants were impressed. As we reached the glass doors opening on to the Portico, I remembered that since the morning I had first walked in through them, nearly three weeks ago, I had not been out of the place.

The coach was waiting: I had read it up: "built at the behest of George III, known as the Irish State Coach, and drawn by a team of four Windsor Grays, with on each side a postilion". And perched on the back, four footmen in glowing scarlet and plush, with – I remember – pink stockings. As I sat upright in the coach – it was lacquered and enamelled – there was a musty smell, mingled with a scent of soap.

Out into the sparkling sunlight of the Forecourt, accompanied by the cheerful measured clatter of horses' hooves: in front of me, "the First and Second Divisions of the Sovereign's Escort of Household Cavalry and behind, the Third Division." Then one State Landau after another. But the rest of the journey would never be quiet enough for me to hear the clatter again: as I emerged between the two flashes of red from the sentry-boxes, there was a roar like a giant waterfall.

And as the coach rolled slowly on, down the Mall to Trafalgar Square, the roar never stopped: neither did the flutter of handkerchiefs and of flag-sticks darting to and fro. I kept my smile going and my hand waving slowly towards me and back, the way I had rehearsed with Willie. Under Admiralty Arch, past Nelson and into Whitehall, every window packed and applauding and waving, not an empty seat. It was endless, and glorious.

The Palace of Westminster. At the Norman Porch, a sedate flurry of robes and I was received by the Lord Great Chamberlain and the Earl-Marshal of England. A battalion of photographers and newsreel cameras. "A fanfare of trumpets, and his Majesty entered the House of Lords." In complete silence; my ears had got so accustomed to the journey's non-stop cheering that my boots sounded to me like small claps of thunder.

From then on, everything in slow motion. "The King proceeded up the staircase, behind heralds in scarlet and gold, to the Robing Room," where I became a revered object to be draped with my "Parliamentary Robe, crimson trimmed with ermine". Then the silent Procession – with persons in front of me walking backwards, I didn't envy them – through the Royal Gallery and into the Chamber, both packed to suffocation with dignitaries and their womenfolk: judges in full wiggery, bishops, ambassadors, diplomats, all in their robes. There was a distinct smell of moth-balls.

"In the Procession were carried, by three separate dignitaries, the

Cap of Maintenance, the Sword of State and – above all – the Imperial State Crown which the King will assume at his Coronation next year.

"Next, His Majesty was escorted up steps to his Throne, from which, through the Lord Great Chamberlain, he commanded the Usher of the Black Rod to let the Commons know that it was His Majesty's pleasure that they attend him immediately in this House. Once they had arrived, the Lord Great Chamberlain knelt on one knee and handed the King a copy of his speech, the speech being preceded by His Majesty's reading aloud of the Declaration of Faith. 'I, John the Second, do solemnly and sincerely in the presence of God, profess that I am a faithful Protestant . . .' etc."

The "speech", as I had discovered on checking through it with Miss Fogerty, was a pure formality, outlining in vague terms various future Parliamentary policies. "My Government will confirm that they earnestly commit themselves to . . . My ministers will work towards stability between the nations . . ." More a recitation than a speech, no problem. I was looking forward to the drive back.

And that turned out, if anything, more deafening; as the coach turned in at the Palace gates, I looked up and saw, for the first time, the Royal Standard floating high above the Palace Balcony. The heat was by now oppressive. I smelt a whiff of sweat from the horses, was back on the Farm, and felt another giddy second of unreality; I was glad to get back in, and out of the regalia.

State Luncheon in State Dining-room, preceded by a quick visit to my bathroom. I was gratified to note what strides I had made during my Cramming Course; I found myself conversing with the Lord Chancellor about the dilemmas of the League of Nations. "Evidently a crucial issue in the question of Re-armament has to be . . ." Sir Godwin gave me a glacial bow; I made no reference to his suggestions for the evening's wireless speech.

At three o'clock, I proceeded with the guests to the Palace Balcony; at the appropriate moment the doors were opened and I made my appearance. My official entrance into my new world.

There seemed more people even than this morning; the applause and the waving went on (somebody timed it) for six minutes, and I had to make two reappearances. Both times, as I smiled and waved back (try smiling and waving for three goes of six minutes each, it's hard work) I wondered if Kathy and Bruce were swallowed up in the middle of all that, then decided to leave all that till tomorrow.

During the rest of the afternoon I put my feet up, did my Red

Boxes, studied my speech, then two sets of tennis with Willie. On the way back he said, "I don't know, Sir, whether you'd welcome hearing something about Sir Godwin –"

"Why, Willie – has he been arrested?"

"It's just that he was always invited to the Palace to each of the Christmas Broadcasts, with a glass of wine afterwards, and it was difficult –"

"I don't mind, so long as he's not in the room with me."

No martinis: my baptism of fire was going well, but not yet over. The real test was to come.

At exactly five to nine, I was seated at my desk in the study, in dinner-jacket and black tie: in my position I had to be correctly dressed, even "on the wireless".

I heard my overture: a portable set in the corner was playing a record of Malcolm Sargent conducting the London Symphony Orchestra in a medley of suitable pieces, the one I remember being the one supposed to have been composed by Henry VIII, *Greensleaves*. All over the world, people had sat up, or risen early, to listen to me.

Too nervous to be moved, I insulated myself and settled at my table facing the curtained windows, with behind me Willie, the two footmen and the B.B.C. crew; I had asked for them all to be so placed, so I would not be tempted to look at their faces.

The music faded; Big Ben. The quarters, then the ruthless strokes, nine of them. The last boom died away. Trumpets.

Silence. All over the world. In front of me, between me and the curtains, in the half-dark I saw the seated figures of my parents, Kathy and Bruce; and behind, the shadowy millions, a bigger audience than all the players in London, put together, had ever faced. I felt suddenly calm, and happy, as I checked the two sheets of paper before me and slid them so they were side by side and wouldn't rustle. My hand was steady.

From the portable, a voice. "From Buckingham Palace. His Majesty the King." The portable switched off, in front of me a small green bulb flashed on, then off. I talked.

"I want you – each one of you – to put yourself in my place. Can you imagine being born again? Twenty days ago, that is what happened to me; and overnight, I had to readjust.

"You will have read a lot about me, some of it true. I was born in Cornwall, lived on a farm, went into the theatre and at that moment twenty days ago I had a good job, in London, my best salary so far, fourteen quid a week – all true." I could feel, behind me, Willie's startled eyes fixed on my shoulder-blades.

"But in between, a fair amount of exaggeration. I am not – I hope – a fool, but I have been described by some as being of superior intelligence, by others as 'cultured'. It is my duty to inform you that I am neither. At school I was lazy, I have never been a great reader, and the day I entered Buckingham Palace my knowledge of politics consisted of being able to give you the name of the Prime Minister, and little more.

"So overnight, I had to start from scratch. For just on three weeks I have been back at school, in the best hands, making up for lost time, twelve hours a day, becoming every minute . . . not perhaps more intelligent, but a little nearer to being cultured.

"And this morning I sat for my exam, in an historic State Coach, before an examination board of thousands; and one might add at this very moment I am undergoing my oral interview, before a board of millions. I hope I pass – not necessarily with distinction – but a pass. To put it another way: the French tell us, *C'est le premier pas qui coûte*, it's the first step that counts. I hope that, today, I have not stumbled.

"The British monarchy is the oldest in Europe, older even than Parliament; my family has been there, to serve you, for over nine hundred years. I promise to do my best. Goodnight."

A pause, then an orchestra played the National Anthem. During it, my back-stage mind was thinking, the French bit didn't sound too dragged in, considering that it was.

The chandelier blazed up. The B.B.C. lot had, naturally, been too absorbed in their job to listen, and were just relieved it was over without a hitch; but you never saw a face showing such a mixture of feelings as Willie's did. Consternation, disapproval, a dash of amusement, a hint of "I take my hat off", then back to disapproval.

I got up, thanked the others, and left with Willie for the Music Room. On the way he said nothing; he just didn't know what to say.

Sir Godwin was waiting for me, bolt upright in the middle of the room, a column of grey ice. Unlike Willie's, his face was an open book, with written across it VOTE OF CENSURE. I had defied the Headmaster. When he bowed, I could have sworn I heard the creak.

I made an attempt at a smile; even if it had been sincere, it would have had no effect. "Sir Godwin, I must first make it clear that my Private Secretary here knew nothing of the change until he listened just now; you can surely tell from his face. It's just that when I came to study your kind suggestions, I realized that you had credited me with more expertise in public speaking than I as yet possess, by composing a speech distinguished for its literary style. I shirked the challenge."

A feeble suggestion of thaw. "It was, I'm afraid, a shock. I take it, Sir, that we got our wires crossed?"

"I beg your pardon?" Not "Pardon?". Miss Fogerty would have been pleased.

"You did make an attempt to consult me beforehand?"

"There seemed no time for red tape." I tried to look innocent. "I hope I said nothing out of place?"

"I feel strongly that the conversational approach – both in subject-matter and in delivery – such expressions as 'exam', 'scratch', 'job' – the mention of salary, involving the use of the word 'quid', and on the wireless – a far cry, a very far cry, from the Royal broadcast speeches of the past."

"That was the intention. Did you like the French bit?"

"The Royal Broadcasts are aimed primarily at the Sovereign's Empire, which happens to be English-speaking."

"I did translate it."

He was stung into declaring himself. "It was, if I may say so, a regrettable and flippant impulse. May I ask what excuse it could claim?"

I knew I was being cheeky, but couldn't help it. "The Royal Prerogative?"

He bowed. I bowed. He went. Willie followed me into my study, which was empty and tidied up, and we each had a stiff whisky. I said, "*Was* it a regrettable and flippant impulse?"

He considered. "I'm so close to it that . . . I just don't know. I was too taken aback by the unexpectedness to listen coherently, then it was over. We'll know in the morning."

And in the morning, when Wilkins knocked I had been awake for some time, *Wed. July 3rd 1935, 22nd Day of Reign.*

Breakfast, and the papers. I picked up the *Mirror*, and turned to the front page as if it might bite me.

CHAPTER ELEVEN

When Ladies Meet

Front page headline: GOD BLESS OUR KING, SENSATION-
AL BRILLIANT SPEECH, *see p. 5*! And a picture of me on the
Balcony, waving. Inside, a two-page spread of the crowd: the vast
carpet of flowers.

Headline after headline. MOVING SIMPLICITY...I HAD
A GOOD JOB, 14 QUID A WEEK...DISARMING HON-
ESTY . . . STARTING FROM SCRATCH . . . BACK AT
SCHOOL . . . AFTER A DAY OF TRIUMPH, ANOTHER
SUCCESS...I PROMISE TO DO MY BEST...MODESTY
50%, STEADINESS 50%...

One leader particularly delighted me, in a paper which – Willie informed me afterwards – was edited by Sir God's first cousin. The
heading was A GODWIN WIN! "*Before His Majesty concluded a
glorious day with a speech over the ether, no-one had any idea of its
contents, except the King himself and – we hazard the guess – Sir Godwin Rodd, who – it is strongly rumoured – has a hand in these events.
Beforehand, some people had wagered that Sir Godwin would play for
safety with the traditional generalizations, 'the mantle which has fallen
on our shoulders', etc.*

"*Instead, Sir Godwin has displayed a flair of which his detractors
may not have thought him capable. He saw to it that the Boy King
spoke from his heart, in what could have been His Majesty's own words.
An unforgettably moving experience.*

"*And the quotation – in impeccable French, flavoured with a delicate
Cornish sauce – was an inspiration. Those six words* C'est le premier

pas qui coûte – *will have done more for the* Entente Cordiale *than three hours of blethering at the League of Nations.* Vive le Roi Jean Deux!"

When Willie arrived, his pleasure warmed me as much as the yards of print put on end. Later in the morning I attended an emergency Privy Council, Hitler trouble this time; on our way to it, Willie and I agreed that last evening after my speech, outraged Sir God must have seen to it that everybody round him should know the facts: "I had *no part* in all that!" So I would have enjoyed a photo of him picking up the morning papers.

And when I walked in, there was – no mistake – more than the token respect. The real thing. "The Council wishes to congratulate your Majesty on last evening." Sir God bowed to me as if wound-up from the back, but no comment. He did not even draw attention to the praise lavished on him by his cousin's newspaper. To the Head-master, full marks for Modesty.

As the meeting progressed, I did notice that the genuine respect was tinged with something else: they were all looking at me with a sort of wariness. As if to say, "You got away with it this time, but – what next?" Let them wonder.

Once or twice my opinion was asked, politely, and I managed. After Hitler, came the discussion of the draft of a letter to be sent to a Trade Congress in Hong Kong; one sentence read, "That the proposal may not be acceptable to the Board of Trade in London, is not unlikely." I suggested that even to the Chinese mind, a triple negative might sound a little tortuous.

On Willie's discreet face, a glimmer of approval. I wasn't doing so badly.

From Affairs of State to a puzzle which was, to me, becoming important. Walking back from the Council I said to Willie, "If I don't get a letter soon from Yeoman's Row, I'll have to do something about it." He said nothing, and at my door left me, to work in his own office. It was irritating.

He had thoughtfully realized that with me, after the strain and excitements of yesterday a reaction would set in, and the rest of that day was planned accordingly. A light midday snack, alone, a pleasantly strenuous afternoon of Gram and Voc interspersed with Spanish; my schoolmates in St Austell County School would have been amused at this diligent bookworm. I was taking to the words, emphatically. And taking pains, really meretriculous. (I think I've got into a bit of a muddle there, the Editor will see to it.)

In the middle of a Spanish conjugation I said – I quite surprised myself – "I see the afternoon post is in. Still no letter from Yeoman's Row."

"Really?" Then he seemed to hesitate. "Er . . . We haven't touched German for a day or two, *nicht wahr*? Where's that copy of *Deutsches Leben*?" And *Deutsches Leben* it was.

In the middle of "*Ich habe ihn lange nicht gesehen, wir haben sie lange nicht gesehen*", I remembered his face when I had said "Still no letter". A look I had not seen there before. Till then, nobody could have looked as direct as Willie – well, in that flicker, he had looked . . . yes, evasive. And had changed the subject.

Something dawned on me, with a dire certainty. The Powers-That-Be were keeping Kathy and Bruce away from me.

I could see it all: they were an embarrassment, and must be eased out of my life. They had been ordered not to muscle in. My mind went dark.

Willie turned a page. "Here are four very tricky irregular verbs –"

"I'm worried about Kathy and Bruce. Very worried."

"Oh, they're perfectly well . . ." His voice had trailed off.

"How d'you know?"

"I . . ." Yes, he was shifty. I was angry, and disappointed. In him.

"Willie, you've seen them again. Haven't you?"

"Yesterday morning. After you said you'd have to do something about it, I took a taxi to Yeoman's Row."

"To tell them to keep away from me?"

"No, Sir."

"Have they been offered money? Is Sir God behind all this?"

"No, Sir." Six foot two, red and stammering. It was ridiculous.

"But Willie, there's something wrong! You're shielding somebody, or hiding something. How were they?"

"Drinking, Sir."

I stared at him. "Drinking? I thought you said you called on them in the *morning*?"

"Noon."

"But they never drink that early, unless for a birthday or something . . . And it was Wednesday, they had matinees! Were they drunk?"

"A little, but not unattractively so. It would certainly wear off by the afternoon. She was in a dressing-gown."

Kathy in a dressing-gown, at twelve noon . . . "What were they celebrating?" Then I thought I'd got it. "My wireless speech, of course – the newspapers!"

"No, they weren't celebrating. They looked very sad."

Had somebody died? Had she been sacked from *Stop Press*? "They surely mentioned the speech?"

"Oh yes, said it was marvellous."

"Then . . . What's wrong? *Why* haven't they written to me?"

"Because they don't want to." He had blurted it out.

"They don't *want* to? Why?"

He sat down and talked. And I could feel his relief: he was a diplomatist all right, but it wasn't in his nature to deceive. It all came out.

The time before when he'd been to see them, between shows, they had insisted – as he was to report to me afterwards – on not bothering me till I was under less pressure. This time Kathy had started by being just as evasive, even stiffer, but in the end Willie's charm had worked, and she had explained for them both.

"Explained what? Hadn't they had my letter?"

"Oh yes. She opened a drawer, and there it was, crumpled up."

"Crumpled up? But *why*? It was a loving letter – and to make them laugh I made a silly joke about being in nice digs –"

"I know, she insisted I read the letter."

"Well?"

"She said it sounded . . . put on." I must have looked as incredulous as I felt, so he tried to make things clearer. "The phrase she used was, 'He's playing down to us'."

"What? But they know me – no two people know me better!"

"I definitely got the feeling . . . that they don't think they know you now. She said that at the end of the speech, she felt you had just said goodbye."

"But I *want to see them*!" I shook my head, helpless. "Willie, get me to understand . . ."

He thought a moment. "All this has been extraordinary for you, Sir – but I did realize, listening to Kathy, the immense psychological shock it is to two people as close to you as they have been . . . I'll put it like this – suppose it had happened the other way round – suppose it had not been you, but *Kathy* who suddenly found herself in this situation – not inconceivable, it happened to the young Victoria, when she was mysteriously whisked off to end up in Buckingham Palace. Queen Kathy sends not another word to you and Bruce, all you get is an official phone call leaving a code number to write to. You and Bruce talk for hours, for days – 'Will it turn her head – *what will it do to her*?' Then that letter arrives. From her. Might you not feel that the Queen of England was playing down to two old chums?"

"Don't . . ."

"You see, Sir, you think you haven't changed, but they can't be sure."

I had to take that up. "I *think* I haven't changed? Willie, do you mean I'm not necessarily right, in believing I haven't changed?"

He smiled. "I didn't say that, Sir."

I considered, grimly. "There's only one thing to do. I must go and see them."

Willie got up, sharply. "I beg of you, Sir, not to think of such a move."

"Why not?"

"Because nothing could keep such a visit a secret, and for it to leak into the Press would be highly inadvisable."

He looked straight at me: the poker-face. The Press had certainly (and luckily) assumed that I had been sharing a flat with an engaged couple, whom the King would hardly be visiting at this moment. Willie must have a faint idea that the patron saint of the top flat, 82a Yeoman's Row, had not been Plato.

I said, "I'll think about it."

"Please do Sir, I beg of you . . . Is this your first visit to the Palace, *Ist dies Ihr erster Besuch zum Palast*?

After the lesson we broke for tennis, so by our relaxation time I was nicely tired, enough to get that conversation off my mind for a bit.

And there was always something to distract me. Unwinding with Willie, I happened to scan the *Daily Express*. The William Hickey Column, *These Names Make News*, a paragraph in the familiar clipped shorthand style. "Rumour has it that unique occasion on cards tomorrow: meeting between King and only other surviving member of Royal Family. May be remembered she unable, through indisposition, to be included in fatal journey. *Princess Victoria Matilda of Meiningen-Amnisch* (88), grand-daughter of one of Queen Victoria's uncles, who has for many years lived in retirement, Hampton Court."

Hampton Court. Last summer, a hundred years ago, the three of us. Staring wide-eyed at the treasures, then half-asleep under a shady tree . . .

Willie arrived, I showed him the item. Rumour, for once, had it right; the Princess had written to Sir God, asking him to arrange an audience. Willie had never met her. "Nobody seems to have, for years. She must have one of those little Grace-and-Favour houses. If she's anything like the sisters my Mama knew when she was a girl, she's a tartar."

He handed me a few notes, to brief me. "Never married, fiancé the Duke of Saxe-Lippburg, killed in action in the Franco-Prussian War; in the Great War, 1914, although in her 60's worked in France, own Red-Cross unit" et cetera. A bossy old maid, well well . . .

"Willie, what's the Protocol?" I was getting used to that word, it was like asking what time your train left.

"Pretty formal, I should imagine. I suggested tea in here, but she said she'd like to see the Music Room again."

"Tea for two in the Music Room? But it's enormous!"

"She said she'd like to sit in it again. Since she's the only one left of her kind, my guess is that she sees herself as important and will be on the look-out for anything treating her as less. I had thought of tea in here, but in spite of there being only the two of you, I would suggest the Music Room."

"You'll be there?"

"I'm afraid not, she specially asked for a tête-à-tête."

"Oh no . . . Do I wear Court dress?"

"Just the dark suit. Wilkins will bring in tea and leave it to you."

"Then I turn to her and say, 'Shall I be Mother?' " No reaction. "But I *do* pour out?"

"Difficult – you see the Queen has always presided at tea-parties, because there hasn't been a new King without a Consort since the accession of Charles the Second. It might be tactful to ask her to pour, depends how shaky she is."

" 'The King Without a Consort', not a bad title!" This was the first time *that* subject had been skirted since the Daily Worker had been rude about "Queen Babs the First". It'll come up properly, one of these days. Leave that bridge to cross later . . . All I knew was I was dreading the "tête-à-tête". At tea-time, not even a glass of sherry . . .

But that was not till the day after tomorrow, and tomorrow was to be a big day, when I was to get launched on the first of my Routine Public Engagements; Willie had warned me that they would be pretty heavy, since they included jobs normally shouldered by the rest of the Royal Family. I now consult my Engagement File of that time: every evening, Willie was to leave me the list for the next day.

Thurs. July 4th 1935, 23rd Day of Reign. 9.30 a.m. His Majesty will sit for his portrait by Mr. Gerald Kelly, R.A., the first of 5 sittings. (Boring but restful, restful but boring.) *11 a.m. First INVESTI-TURE of Reign, in Throne Room. His Majesty will be attended by the Lord Chamberlain, the Master of the House, the Comptroller, an Air-Marshal & several Admirals (list appended).*

Now this I was looking forward to. Willie explained to me that an Investiture meant a distribution of Honours: I would stand in front of my Throne facing a gathering of around three hundred recipients and their wives or husbands, and after breakfast I spent a strenuous hour committing to memory a typewritten list of some forty or fifty names – personages whose achievement I should become acquainted with. "Colonel Pennington, quelled a riot in Calcutta; Roderick Parsons, climbed the Matterhorn in record time; James Franscombe, won the George Medal for rescue work at the big Portsmouth fire; the Rev. Christopher Venables, 25 years' missionary work in the Congo" – and so on.

Waiting to make my entrance, I could hear a tiny disembodied string orchestra (housed in the chandelier, it sounded like) playing popular tunes. I waited for them to strike up "Glamorous Night", and when they did, my reaction in no way resembled my feeling of utter unreality when I had heard it, on the wireless, that first day.

Was it only a little over three weeks ago? Today I was taking the music for granted, an affectionate memory out of a quaint theatrical past, years away. *Was* I changing?

It wasn't the moment for a soul-search. An Equerry gave me a signal, the strings struck up my tune and I was on.

All over the packed room, a soft rustle as they all stood slowly up and looked at me. Respect. I gave my smile, and my shy eyes saw the respect blossom into admiration. And although, as I stood there, my mind was clicking over two or three of the names I had memor-ized, it would be no good to pretend I wasn't thoroughly enjoying it.

It was beautifully stage-managed – I couldn't have done it better myself – the recipients being quietly beckoned out and shepherded, in batches, into the Picture Gallery, to have their names called out in turn; then they were *on*, and then made their exit into the Green Drawing-room. After a dozen presentations, the whole thing felt exactly like Prize Day at school, with me as Visiting Celebrity.

A series of nervous faces. Apart from a minority of Women's Institute ladies, they were mostly politicians, civil servants, high-ups in the Services or successful business magnates whose names were unfamiliar to me. All middle-aged or elderly.

And mostly in hired morning dress they weren't used to. (I wasn't used to *my* wardrobe either, but – for the first time in my life – it had been made to measure.) Each time I had to murmur, "And what are your plans at the moment?" I felt the urge to follow with "When you send the suit back, love, say hello for me to the Moss Brothers . . ."

But at no school could it ever go on as long as this. The nervous faces approached in interminable procession; Willie told me afterwards there had been three hundred and twenty-seven of them. It began to seem a long time since I had enjoyed the room looking at me; my face began to ache, and the smile can't have gone on looking as spontaneous as when I'd made my entrance. My Glamorous Morning was clouding over.

Sinking on to the sofa in my study and taking up my list for the afternoon, I gritted my teeth.

2 p.m. Will leave to inspect 2nd Battalion of Coldstream Guards, Wellington Barracks. 3 p.m. Back to change & visit British Post-Graduate School of Hygiene, Bloomsbury . . . 4.30. Audience (and tea) with Princess Xenia, also Dean of Windsor & Maharajah of Patiala. I made a note to consult my World Atlas. *6 p.m. Mr Gordon Latham will kiss hands on appointment as Governor of the Leeward Islands. 8 p.m. Dinner with Private Sec.*

By 8 p.m., I was whacked; my right arm ached, my jaw ached, I ached all over, and had a feeling that the Smile could do with being laid off for repairs. So I was somewhat taken aback when, over the two martinis, Willie told me he'd kept the first day as light as possible, just to get me "played in". Tomorrow would be "a little heavier".

I thought, can I last the course?

But I slept the sleep of the exhausted, and woke up refreshed and ready for work. I knew there'd be no letter, but I had to look.

Fri. July 5th 1935, 24th Day of Reign 9 a.m., Haircut. 11 a.m., H.M. will receive in audience Bishop of Truro, introduced by Sir John Simon, who, as Sec. of State, will administer oath, when the Bishop will do homage on his appt., the Bishop of Oxford – Clerk of the Closet to the King – being in attendance. 12 noon, H.M. will receive in audience Lord Trenchard, Marshal of the Royal Air Force.

Then the engagement Willie must have meant when he called the day "a little heavier": *Luncheon, in the Dining-room, in honour of . . .* an Ambassador from somewhere in the Middle-ish East. (No names, in case I get personal and the country loses some valuable Oriental contacts.) Seven courses, seventy-five guests.

Willie had composed my speech, with my collaboration; this was to become routine, and included introducing a couple of jokes of which we were never to be proud, but they were always to get a laugh. On this first occasion . . . "In the presence of our distinguished guest of honour, let us forget the commercial importance of an historic country steeped in romance – we will be neither oily nor gushing . . ." That sort of thing – I'm afraid – was to get me consistently good notices, "*His Majesty produced the unexpected shaft of wit, and the Ambassador visibly unbent . . .*"

Beforehand, Willie would usually supply me with helpful hints as to what topics to avoid. I remember one: "Memo, re Marchesa di Piri: in view of fact that her husband recently shot his mistress dead, it might be advisable to avoid the subject of Capital Punishment."

During the same first occasion, I had the feeling that the conversation, before and after the speech, was typical of the functions which were to face me most middays or evenings, sometimes both; and I made notes of it. (This Luncheon was also important because at it, I met an older lady who was to become – well, important.) But I was never to make notes again: first because the talk was to go on being so repetitively trivial as not to deserve attention, secondly because of the noise.

On my entrance there was always the expected reverential hush; but once I had sat down, there would be let loose the empty ear-piercing prattle of hundreds of voices being polite to strangers. This was to become helpful to me, being usually so deafening that I acquired the technique – via a series of nods and smiles ("of course" – "really?" – "oh no!") – of concealing the fact that I could not hear one word in ten.

At that first Luncheon, the guests on both sides of me happened to be expert enough to override the general din. On my right, of course, the Ambassador's lady, a rather beautiful short fattish dusky person awash with all the colours of the spectrum. A square rainbow. With a moustache.

I had been briefed that she was half-Persian, and started off – as was to happen frequently – with an untruth. "I've been dipping a lot into Omar Khayyam lately." (That morning Willie had read out a couple of verses to me, while I was shaving.)

"Your Majesty, Omar Khayyam is not – I regret I make the statement, no thank you, waiter, no sherry – he is by no means my favourite poet. On the whole, as one might say moreover, the FitzGerald translation is somewhat lousy, if you follow me. Your Majesty, please your pardon most sincerely if I am forward, but you are a half-caste?"

She had been so forward she had knocked me sideways. I said something like, "I'm afraid not. English on both sides, from the West Country."

"Ah, Greenland? Iceland?" She too should have had a few things read out to her. While *she* was shaving. It seemed the moment to turn to my left-hand neighbour, Lady Haddlewick, a relative of Willie's. "I'm afraid," he had said, "she insisted on sitting next to you, my Aunt Rose is a very insistent woman."

Aunt Rose was fifty-ish, sharpish pretty and sharpish elegant, with quite a smattering of jewellery, in a summer dress but with a brown pattern so she looked as if she was covered in autumn leaves, and a small nothing of a hat. Her manner was very grand and busy and twitchy, not helped by a shrill voice, clipped together and hitting the words very high, one after the other like a chatty typewriter.

"Your Majesty, this is *too* thrilling, to be one of the first people privileged to meet you *privately*, I never dreamt!" We were scarcely meeting privately. "Of course the horror of it – no sauce thank you, just the cauliflower – it was all such a nightmare, *un vrai cauchemar*, having known them since I was a tot, cried for days, just lay in a darkened room, my daughter will tell you, and then the romance of *you* turning up, out of nowhere, a *Fairy Prince!*"

The waiter's hand, pouring the water, stopped in mid-air for a second. I was glad that nobody was around from the top dressing-room in Drury Lane Theatre.

I hadn't taken to her for rushing to "the nightmare" as an opening gambit; but I didn't have to worry how to appear agreeable, the typewriter was clacking away. And she was flashing a steady smile, on and off, then on again; but the eyes didn't match the smile. Not a gleam, it was as if something had fused. I waited for the patronage, and it came.

"Your Majesty, I couldn't help overhearing that unfortunate description of your good self, though I think I know what was meant, because it *is* a splendid stroke of luck that we have a monarch of *mixed blood*, as the snobs put it – waiter, would you pick up my napkin, thank you – I remember saying to Queen Mary, à propos of the dreadful Kaiser and some very bizarre minor Continental royalty one could mention, that our wonderful Victoria was so right when she said, 'Too much intermarrying!', no wine thank you, just the water . . ."

I began to know the meaning of "small talk"; hers was so small you needed a magnifying glass. And the names were dropped like top-drawer confetti. "Poor dear Ena of Spain was another one who should *never* have been farmed out, she's as English as the cliffs of Dover . . . I always think the *ambiance* in Sandringham so much more – how shall I put it – so much *cosier* than Buck House, particularly York Cottage which I was taken to tea to as a little gel, though Queen Mary as Duchess of York did find it *un petit peu* poky, no sugar thank you, just black . . .

"I have such a soft spot for Cornwall! As children we spent holidays there, near Mevagissey I think it was, I was always so amused by the dialect, so quaint, and we stayed one summer with Lady Staverbridge at Staverbridge Priory, a heavenly house, do you know it, Sir?" She rested a second, to take a sip of water. Staverbridge Priory . . . I remembered my mother having worked there.

"No," I said, "but my mother knew it, quite well."

"How fascinating – what a small world – Now tell me, Sir – you with your unique knowledge of the London theatre – what would you recommend for a daughter who came out a year ago? She *adores* the theatre and is, *en même temps*, though I sez it myself, terribly intelligent, would you say the new Shaw play . . .?"

And on and on and on. 4.30 p.m. Tea, alone, with Princess Victoria Matilda, of Meiningen-Amnisch (88).

It was a hot day, and standing in the Music Room in my dark suit and plain blue tie – no mourning, thank God – waiting for a battle-axe, a rusty one at that, I longed to be in shirt-sleeves in Yeoman's Row. A footman opened the doors, and she came forward.

She was tallish, thin, walked with a stick, and in her black looked frail enough to break in half and blow away. Her clothes were, of course, modern, "for the older woman," summer coat, blouse, skirt to the ankles; but you knew that in this she was humouring the quirks of a new generation. In her mind's eye, she was in a dress trailing the ground, with a bustle below corsets like a suit of armour. She could well, at this minute, be wearing corsets, she was that upright: shoulders held back, like a retired athlete keeping it up all the way. One cameo brooch, with pearls round it. Black lace gloves, and you could tell why, the hands had had their bones pulled about and then wrenched, God can be a cruel old thing.

But the bones of the face were perfect. It was one of those profiles you see on coins: too firm to be beautiful, and yet saved from hardness by a gentle old-maid dignity.

I could tell that Willie was relieved to find her not what he had expected. "Sir, Her Royal Highness Princess Victoria Matilda."

She curtseyed. And it was clear to me that she'd been doing it since she could walk, and doing it right. Willie bowed, and went. I motioned her to a chair. She gave a timid fluttery smile which for a second turned her into a girl. And when she sat down you expected her to give a little dainty kick to the train that wasn't there. When she said, "I have so much looked forward to this moment," the voice was slow but firm, with round it a vague guttural fog, not quite English. German? You believed every word.

I made a gesture towards the teapot (Worcester, I knew); she bowed slightly, and poured. With a hand crippled but steady as a bird. In that great room, the two of us must have looked like a tea-party on a well-appointed raft in mid-Atlantic.

"Your Majesty is a beautiful and vulnerable young man, and I have prayed for you."

I knew I wasn't bad-looking – so do you, by now – but the remark startled me. Particularly the second part. My mother had prayed for me too. Did I *need* praying for?

She handed me my cup as if she had just said, "I put in two lumps, is that right?" She turned and looked around, her eyes lingering here and then there, and I understood why she had wanted to sit in the Music Room again. She wanted to talk a little but needed coaxing. "Your Highness, is it long since you were here?"

"I remember the last time. *And* the first time . . . The last was seventeen years ago, towards the end of 1918, the Victory Ball after the Great War. It was such a big affair there were two orchestras, one in the Ballroom along there, the other in here, I was sitting in one of those chairs. They were dancing a new dance I'd never seen, and I remember King George's face as he watched it: his look of utter disbelief. 'Good Lord,' he said, 'it's as ugly as its name – the Fox Trot!' Then it struck me, doesn't he look like Nicky, quite a shock . . . The Prince was dancing past us at that minute, d'you see, and I had the feeling that Papa had said it so that he would hear. Poor David went quite red."

"David?"

"The Prince of Wales. He was twenty-four." My age. "A beautiful young man." She said it as if she hadn't just used the phrase: as if, in her mind, she was fusing two people together. She looked round again. It was so quiet you could hear the faint whisper of traffic, in the Mall. In the long empty room I could see faint figures gliding past and round, round and past: ghosts dancing to music that wasn't there.

She turned back to me. "So kind of Sir Godwin to arrange this pleasure, so kind . . ."

"He seems to arrange a great deal."

That sounded indiscreet, but she again surprised me. "He always has. I remember him as a playmate of the Battenberg children, I mean the Mountbattens . . . Can you imagine a child of twelve being pompous in a sailor suit? Well, he was . . . Yes, the Prince was twenty-four. He was never pompous."

I said, "When was the first time you came here?"

She put her nose to the steam from her teacup, sniffed, and smiled. "In 1870 – I was twenty-three – Mama brought me to tea with the Queen – Victoria, of course – and the tea smelt just like this, did they have Earl Grey then? I'd been so frightened of meeting her I hadn't slept, but she was like a little jolly aunt. Until Mama mentioned the Franco-Prussian War, which had just broken out, d'you see, then the Queen showed her mettle, a regular little spitfire, 'Oh those Germans, how ashamed my poor dear Albert would have been!' "

Her voice weakened a little, and she stirred her tea. I thought of the Prussian fiancé fighting on the wrong side, whom she had been about to lose. Was *she* thinking of him too? . . . I said, "You mentioned Nicky . . . ?"

"King George's cousin, the Tsar." She stopped, and a shadow seemed to fall across her face.

"Was he still alive then?" As soon as I'd said it, I knew I shouldn't have. Her head made a slight move, like a flinch, and she closed her eyes: then quickly made an effort and opened them again. "He was dead, they were all dead. Murdered." That word, spoken in this place, sounded like broken glass.

Then she seemed to wander off. "You've heard of Princess Alix of Hesse – no, why should you, she was another of Queen Victoria's granddaughters. Five years after Eddy – the Duke of Clarence, your grandfather – well, five years after he married your grandmother, and two years after your grandmother died, d'you see –" The old lady had certainly got her facts right. "Though of course none of us knew anything about that – the old Queen was most anxious that he should marry dear Alix. A nice girl, I was years older but she liked to come to me for advice. And did, about that. I mean about . . ."

"About whether she should marry my grandfather Prince Eddy, or not?"

"Of course. Now I could tell she didn't want to. He was very . . . unreliable, you know . . ."

"I know."

"So I said, 'If you have any doubts, don't.' And she didn't."

"Oh?"

"Alix married Nicky and became the Tsarina. It's haunted me ever since. Those dreadful peasants . . ."

I hoped she wouldn't notice what she'd said, but she knew. "Oh," she said with a nice old smile, "there are *good* peasants, I've known many . . . But I can't forget poor Alix, d'you see . . . Oh dear, I'm becoming a bore . . ."

Her voice trailed off again, as if she couldn't think what next to put into words. I thought, well, she's eighty-eight, it's got to show somehow.

Not a bit, she knew exactly what she was going to say. "Are you enjoying it?"

It was a direct question all right; but the way it came out, with shyness, it didn't put me off. And I could see why: because at this minute she wasn't looking up to me as King, or down at me as Jack Green, she was having a private talk with an equal.

While she waited for my answer I thought, *am* I enjoying it? She said, "I know you said on the wireless, and splendidly, that you are determined to do your best – but happiness is so important."

I said, "It's all so new. Complicated, of course, but my Secretary is the most enormous help, and I don't mind the hard work. Yes, I'm enjoying it."

"Ah . . . I'm delighted."

"You sound relieved."

She hesitated, then looked straight at me. We might have been old friends. "I was thinking of David."

"The Prince of Wales? Yes?"

"We were very close, I was one of his godmothers. He was an-

other who came to me for advice, I seem to have always been somebody people picked on to talk to. Oh, but I couldn't advise him. It
was too delicate."

"How?"

"He just didn't want to become a King. Oh, he had great difficulties . . ."

All of a sudden she seemed to sag, just a little bit, and the eyes
closed. I said, "Would you like to rest?"

In one go, the eyes flicked open and the ramrod sprang back into
place. "No, thank you, I'd like to see the Front Balcony."

For the first time, she sounded a bit bossy. No, I know English
better than that. A trifle imperious.

"Of course."

Quite apart from my own appearance on that Balcony, I knew all
about it. From the Princess's childhood on, it had been there, for
birthdays, marriages, Coronations, Jubilees; Victoria, Edward VII
and George V and their families had crowded on to it and waved to
the multitude. And for most of those occasions, this old lady had
been there.

We were preceded on the long walk by a footman (there was
always one about somewhere) and I slackened my speed to hers. I
noticed she put her stick down most carefully, so as not to make a
clatter on the parquet.

While the footman opened one of the big French windows, she
stood right back from it, as they must all have done before making
their appearance in the open: as I had done myself. Then I watched
her stand even more erect, life seemed to flow into the spent body,
she smiled – not the shy tentative look she had given me, quite
different: a public smile, one for the millions. She made her entrance. I followed her.

The weather had clouded over, and under a summer drizzle,
everything was uniformly grey. Not one soul peering upwards for
the magic; half a dozen scuttling brollies. I looked at Princess
Victoria Matilda of Meiningen-Amnisch.

Since my Ma's look when she was told her mother had died, I
never saw anything as sad as her face. She was staring down at the
Mall, a star facing an empty house. As she stood there, I thought of
the names slowly crossing her brightly flickering old mind, like those
electric signs in Trafalgar Square gliding along, ROOSEVELT
SPEAKS OUT DEADLOCK IN RUHR HITLER DENIES
ATTACK ON JEWRY CHELSEA FLOWER SHOW . . .

Only with her it was MARINA OF KENT GLOUCESTER LASCELLES ALICE OF ATHLONE SAXE-COBURG-GOTHA KAISER WILHELM MAY OF TECK ALBERT DAVID . . .

She looked up from the emptiness, and focused on me; the bright mind, for the moment, was misted over. Uncertainly, she shook her head. "What's happened? David . . . where have they all gone?"

I left it to her to blow the mist away, and she did. "Oh . . ." She looked back at the Mall; even the umbrellas had vanished. "I'm so sorry . . ." Then she smiled at me, the shy look. "It's high time I went."

I said, "My Secretary will ring down for your car." But I knew she hadn't meant that. I helped her back into the room.

With me holding the arm that wasn't coping with the stick, we took slow steps down the Picture Gallery, miles high, miles long: slow enough for her to take in some of the paintings. "Oh look, I've always loved that Canaletto."

Then I spotted, in the distance in front of us, two approaching figures.

A stocky man, the woman a little taller. As they got near, I saw that she was in black, and the silly idea came to me that it was the Princess seen in a mirror, looking more robust. As they got nearer still, I saw who they were. My parents.

Behind them, Willie. "A little surprise, Sir." My mother looked at me, then smiled and curtseyed. Then she took another step and kissed me on the cheek. My father was beaming. I held out my hand, he took it gingerly, then – in sheer high spirits – pumped my arm.

Willie stepped forward. "Your Royal Highness, may I present Mr and Mrs Bertram Green?" My mother was in her Sunday – Baptist – best, the black relieved only by the old-fashioned white-lace fichu; above grey hair neatly back to a bun, a black straw hat with faint white spots and white band. Except for those relieving touches and the Princess's heirloom cameo, the two women looked startlingly alike. They could have been mother and middle-aged daughter.

The Princess's face came to life with a warm smile. "Mr and Mrs *Green*? But of course – His Majesty's mother!" Once again she looked years younger. "This is a very great pleasure, we've all been reading about you both, you must have just arrived from St Austell – but you must be longing for tea –"

"We 'ad our tay along on the train, Your Royal 'Ighness." My mother had taken her own cramming course. So far, so good.

"Then before I take my leave, let's sit here a moment!" Oo-er, here we go . . .

We all sat, in the centre of the Picture Gallery. After exchanging a look with Willie, I decided to keep a watching brief: to step in only when the boat needed baling out.

"I was most interested in the *Sunday Times* article, and must ask you a couple of questions." Hello, the Royal patronage?

She seemed to want to lean back, but her chair was too deep. Willie got up – "a cushion, Ma'am?" – but the old lady said, "No thank you" and sat straighter than ever. Willie was replacing the cushion when he saw my mother looking at it. She turned back to the Princess. "Excuse me, but I've never seen . . . It's beautiful!"

The Princess looked pleased. "Really? I'm so glad you like it, I made it for Queen Mary."

My mother was startled. "*You* made it?"

"For her fiftieth birthday I think it was, she was still in mourning for her cousin the Grand Duke Adolphus and I thought the colours would cheer her up." She turned to me. "I'm afraid, Sir, that one of the drawbacks of Royalty is that one is for ever in mourning, which is easier to get into than out of! That was why I was so relieved when they made an exception this year, and yet here I am, still in mourning, customs die hard . . . I'm afraid, Mrs Green, I've had to put away my needle, my sad old hands – but of course, that's what I want to ask you about – you do *petit point* too?"

My mother looked puzzled. "Pity . . . ?"

"Oh dear, I should never embark on French, my accent is atrocious, I do apologize." She had pronounced it perfectly. "I'll tell you one thing about us Royals, we are *not educated*. I'm sure your son here got a much better grounding in his Cornish County School than he would have done here!" She had taken her cramming course too. "I'll just call it needlework . . . Now when they wrote in the *Ladies' Home Journal* that you do half-cross-tent-stitch, and yet are left-handed – now isn't that practically impossible?"

"It wasn't easy at first," my mother said. "Shall I show you what I do?" And there were the two of them, doing phantom needlework as if killing time in the St Austell Women's Institute. I looked at my father, who was smiling broadly. Then at Willie. I could tell from his eyes that he was enjoying it too.

The Princess turned to my father. "There's a second matter, Mr Green, which I'd like cleared up. The magazine stated that on top of your farming, you are the best gardener between John O' Groats and Land's End – that's their claim. Now, Mr Green . . . I thought *I* was. I have quite a few decorations at home which I haven't earned – forgotten what most of them are for – but I do deserve one for my gardening. Well, what I want to know is –" she leant forward and tapped his knee – "do you deserve a medal more than I do?"

"Well, your Royal 'Ighness, I 'aven't any medals unless I count me Farmers' Association Badge – but I *am* a gardener."

"In your part of the country, what is the soil?"

"Loam mostly, but by some freak, on the Farm ours be chalk."

"Ah!" She was delighted. "That's what the article didn't say, and that explains it. When they wrote that your lilacs are famous throughout the West Country, I felt positively jealous. You see, I've been struggling at mine for thirty years – but my soil in Hampton Court is clay, acid. And lilacs – as you well know – thrive in a chalk soil, alkali – and that's where the good Lord has favoured you! That makes me feel considerably better . . ."

During this, just as I had watched her take in her surroundings, so now I was studying my mother as her eyes travelled around: over the ornamented ceiling, the scores of paintings, the gleam of gold frames, the fussy conglomeration of treasures – vases, boxes, clocks, swords, coats-of-arms – what must she think it all looked like?

The Princess now turned back to her, and she too caught the eyes moving slowly, in wonder. "My dear, what do you think of it?"

My mother thought a moment before she spoke. "It's . . . like one of our Chapel Charity Bazaars – everything on show, it's *lovely*!"

The Princess didn't bat an eyelid. Just looked round. "I do see what you mean . . . Did they have much trouble persuading you to make the journey?"

"Oh no," my mother said, "it was my idea. I wanted to make sure he was being looked after."

"Quite right!"

"And that he was behavin' himself."

I turned to Willie. "Is he?"

"I think, Sir, one could say yes. So far."

The Princess patted my mother's hand, "Of course he is, he has already made a great impression. That wireless speech, I can't forget it . . ." She got up slowly, steadily; so did the four of us. "Mr Green, I'm especially proud of my herb garden and I would enjoy showing

it to you both, but I'm afraid I don't entertain any more. I've enjoyed my afternoon very much, thank you, Sir."

She curtsied to me, my mother curtsied to her, and we watched
the fragile figure become small in the distance, with the back as
firm as Willie's by her side.

"Well," said my father, "that's what I call a nice lady."

CHAPTER TWELVE

Enter Two Chums of Willie's

I suggested taking them to my quarters. As we moved on, my mother took a last look at the Princess's cushion. "She's made some grand needlework. Bertram, you don' think of any of 'em *doin'* anything, do you?"

I decided to rise above that. We walked. "Well," I said, "where 'ave they put the two of you?" My Cornish accent was well and truly back.

"Oh it's nice! I said to Mr Perry – the genelman that travelled to see us an' make the arrangements – I said we'd come so long an' nothin' in the papers – oh them papers, I never knowed they could be so greedy to use up all that print! An' we knowed that wi' us lookin' like anybody else, folks wouldn't bother us. 'E said that in 'ere we'd be safer from the busybodies than in lodgin's, so I said only if they give us the smallest bedroom in the place."

We turned the corner into my study. My mother looked calmly round, went to a mirror, studied her hat in it, to make sure it was still at the severely correct angle, sat with her black hand-bag on her knees and looked at the paintings opposite; they were smaller and fewer than in the Charity-Bazaar Department, but all in gilt frames.

She then opened the bag, took out needlework, set it out on her knees, put on her glasses, and picked out a needle. Dad sat near her, winked at me, took up a *Daily Telegraph* and opened it at the Racing Page.

I looked at Queen Victoria on my desk, while the corner of my eye caught – as it had done, so it seemed since the day I was born –

the slow steady rhythm of my mother's needle. And in front of me, the Palace paintings and tapestries and carpets and the rest of the treasures – the Palace walls themselves – melted away. She looked strange, sitting there sewing in her best hat. Because the three of us were in our farm kitchen, and Queen Victoria was not framed in silver on a Chippendale desk, but scowling down from the wall, on an almanac.

And conscious of the rhythm of that hand, and of my father's concentration on the printed page, I knew that they had both – in their different ways – adjusted to a situation which must still seem, to most people, unimaginable.

I said, "Did you like what I said on the wireless?"

My mother answered without looking up, and almost with disapproval. "That do go without sayin' – it was handsome, Jack." She talked as she did in the evenings at home: thoughtful, leisurely, with comfortable spaces. "It was like you was i' the room with us, only your voice a bit diff'rent, we could tell it was our Jack but a bit more grand. I reckon it's nat'ral, the change that come over ee 'as got to come out some'ow."

I asked her how long she had practised her curtsey.

"Good gracious, I was curtseyin' long 'fore you was born. When I was in service at the Priory, many a lord an' lady come to stay an' Lady Staverbridge liked us to curtsey, she was terrible ole-fashion like that, quite right too. T'es nice when folks do show respect, it be nat'ral."

A pause, for a difficult stitch. "Bertram, thinkin' 'bout this . . . Oh I'm glad that our Jack do seem to take more after my side than the side o' my first 'usban'!" Another stitch. I knew why she referred to my real father as her first husband: out of consideration for her second, sitting there. I asked her why she was glad.

"Your father 'ere was readin' out some stuff 'e'd copied from a 'istory book i' the Public Library, 'e do say they'm all in it. There 'as been bad blood, mind you, along the way."

"You don't say?"

"Gospel truth. There was that poor George the Third, soft i' the 'ead from the age o' forty, poor soul, should 'a' been in a 'Ome where he could 'a' been looked after an' scolded for wand'rin' all over the shop all night . . . Cromwell was godly, but o' course no relation . . . Victoria was good, we know that, but you can mope about for too long, it ed'n nat'ral, when will you be goin' along up to Balmoral?"

I explained that Willie had said all that would be in 1936.

"Then it'll be somethin' for 'em all to look forward to i' the New Year. Oh that Richard the Third, by rights he should 'a' 'ad the Society for Cruelty to Children on 'is tail, oh that side o' you!" I could see them all, in the witness-box one after the other, desperately trying to make a good impression on Alice Lavinia Green.

I said, "Did Willie talk about the future at all?"

She looked up. "Willie? Oh, the nice tall gen'leman, does 'e get enough to eat? . . . Yes, 'e did mention a Pension, I said weren't due for the Ole-Age Pension yet, then 'e explains that it was to do wi' Royalty. I said, But we baint Royalty, so we couldn't fancy that, it wouldn' be right. We're all right while we got our 'ealth, eh Bertram?"

"'Course we are my dear, we're all right sure enough." Well, he wasn't sure, being by nature – what had the report called him – "convivial", so a Pension would have been more than welcomed. But his wife was his wife. "'Course we are, my dear . . ."

I could tell they were tired, so we had a quiet early dinner, in my study. More of a high tea, really. No footmen. My Da and I got quite rosy on the wine.

I saw them to their bedroom, in spare staff quarters. My mother was very interested in the bathroom next door, not having seen one since Staverbridge Priory. As I was leaving, my father went to his battered Gladstone bag, produced a cardboard box and handed it to me, "from your Mother." A saffron cake.

I wondered if she would give me a good-night curtsey, but she knew where to stop. The old kiss on the cheek. I worked late on my Red Boxes, and in the night had one of those silly jumbled dreams.

First my mother doing her needlework, but sitting in Hampton Court, and looking up at a painting of her Prussian Duke and bursting into tears. Second, the Princess sitting in the farm kitchen doing *her* needlework, my Da sitting opposite her drinking from a gold goblet. The Princess then got up to go and milk them cows. (Sorry, *those* cows.)

The next thing, I found myself in a London street, in top hat and trailing ermine cloak, dashing to catch a train for a vitally important destination. But passers-by kept on recognizing me and rushing one by one in front of me, so I was held up each time they curtsied: men as well as women. Then each of them stayed in the curtsey, so I had to push them over to get past – "I must get there, I *must*!" – and the next thing was, there was another for me to fall over. Then dogs started running up, and they managed to curtsey as well. Just as I fought my way into the station, the train was puffing out.

My important destination? Balmoral.

Next day (*Sat. July 6th 1935, 25th Day of Reign*) Willie told me he had booked, for tonight, three theatre seats, for the Crazy Gang. I said, "Perfect, I saw the show last year, I'd love to take them to it!" My father would laugh himself hoarse at the naughty jokes, which would be well over my mother's head, while – in spite of herself – she would enjoy the music and the scenery and the high spirits. It would be a night out!

Willie hesitated. "I'm sorry, Sir, but the third seat is for me."

"For you? But you've got your week-end at home –"

"I could have Monday off instead, if you wouldn't mind, I don't think Sec-Sec is quite the right person to take them –"

"But *I*'m taking them. I want to see the Crazy Gang again, with my parents!"

"I discussed it with the P.M. I'm afraid he feels it wouldn't be quite right as your first public appearance at a theatre."

"But it needn't be public, we could just slip in . . ." As I said it, I saw how daft it was. How could I "slip in", anywhere in London – or, for that matter, anywhere else?

During the morning, while I worked (*10.30 will preside at Meeting of British Council for Relations with other Countries; 12 noon, Mr R. Campbell will kiss hands on appointment as His Majesty's Envoy Extraordinary at Belgrade*), Willie took my parents sight-seeing: Westminster Abbey, St Paul's, the Tower. The three of us had another simple meal in my room, then they rested while I studied: Spanish. Then, before high tea, a stroll in the Garden, where my Da lingered long over the flowers and shrubs. Then off they went to their first theatre outing ever: the first house at the Victoria Palace. "Funny," said my father, very straight in the face, "if it isn't one Palace it's another . . ."

So I spent the evening alone. With the late sun glowing through the window, I sat imagining myself at the Victoria P.: my first Official Royal Visit. I saw myself standing in the Royal Box in my Guards uniform, she on one side and he on the other, while the orchestra plays my Anthem, then we sit. Why couldn't it have happened like that?

No, the P.M. was right. If I had insisted on such a display, I knew enough, by now, to have a shot (in my mind) at the sort of newspaper comments I might have earned. "It is, of course commendable that the Monarch should encourage the Arts, but was he well advised to choose, as his first "show", a *music-hall*? And the Crazy Gang at that, with their low-brow antics and risqué double-entendres? No wonder His Majesty's mother never smiled, and his step-father's guffaws gradually subsided as the King seemed uncertain whether to smile or to frown . . ." How Sir God would have loved that . . . And I would have provided a peach of a headline. JACK IN THE BOX!

So I'll have to wait for *The Trojan Women* or a special performance (suggested by my mother) of Handel's *Messiah*. I remembered something the Princess had said. "The Prince of Wales had great difficulties . . ." I'd never been one for sitting for minutes on end, just getting depressed, but that's what I was doing, as I waited for my elders to arrive home from their night out.

Home . . .? Anyway, surely it should be the other way round: my elders waiting up for me, the young blade out on the town . . .

When the elders did arrive, they were delighted with their escapade. My father smiled when my mother said, "The colours was lovely, though I couldn't follow a lot of the talk." Then he said, "Jack, did *you* use to work the lights like that in the theatre, before you retired?"

Retired?

I went to bed thinking of Kathy and Bruce. Then, staring up at the canopy, I tried to describe my situation to myself, and got it pretty exact. A life sentence, with no remission for good behaviour.

I went to sleep more depressed than before.

". . . That nice Mr Willie gave your Father & Self a grand send off, & at home our new dog Corry was delited to see us (short for Coronation)". Then for my mother, quite forthcoming. "In the train your Father said, You must be proud of im, & I was suprise to feel 2 tears under my eyes & I said, *I be, I be*, but I am a terrible poor hand at speakin my felins, God bless our Jack Defender of the Faith . . .

"Your lovin Father speekin. Yesterday I backed a orse by name of Royal Visit, & he won!"

That gave me quite a zestful morning. *11 a.m., Preside at Annual Meeting of the Grand Military Race Committee at St James' Palace . . . 12 a.m. Receive in audience His Majesty's Ambassador Extraordinary*

& Plenipotentiary to Chile. 1 a.m. Luncheon for the Lady Maud and Captain the Lord Carnegie. (40 guests, list appended.) On our way to this last, in the middle of official talk Willie said, "By the way, Sir, would you mind two chums of mine being presented to you?"

"Of course, Willie, if they're friends of yours."

"Good – cocktails in your study this evening? Quite informal?"

"Fine." After the day's work (*3 p.m. Visit to Exhibition of Products of Ex-Servicemen, Imperial Institute, S. Kensington; 5 p.m. Fitting for special uniform for inspection next week of 2nd Battalion of the Gloucestershire Regiment at Catterick*) a change of pace would be welcome.

Back from the Institute, I had half-an-hour before the fitting, and before taking a cat-nap picked up an early edition of the *Evening News*. Not only for the political bits and pieces, but because there was nearly always something or other about me. Such as – "*People at fashionable gatherings are increasingly conscious of a new detail in the male coiffure: what barbers inelegantly term 'the cowlick', a short curve of hair on the forehead is, on the brow of His Majesty, more stylish than it sounds; the 'King's Curl' is being copied right and left . . .*"

I turned a page. HIS MOTHER DROPS QUIETLY IN! "*It can now be revealed that some days ago, without an outside soul knowing . . .*"

I turned another page. TEA FOR TWO, A ROYAL ROMANCE? I sat up. "*Yesterday afternoon, when at 4.15 a grey Rolls-Royce purred into the Palace Forecourt and through to the Quadrangle, and purred out again 1½ hours later, who was the sole passenger? Wearing a blue picture-hat and a mink stole, could she have borne a fleeting re-semblance to Miss Deirdre Haddlewick, who was (last year) presented at Court, only daughter of Lady Haddlewick, widow of the late Sir Rupert H.?*" Alongside, the photograph (by Dorothy Wilding) of a very pretty girl.

Willie popped in with a couple of papers for me to sign: "John R.I.", as to the manner born. I said, "Did you read about my little tea-party yesterday?"

He looked vexed. "I hoped your Majesty wouldn't see it."

"I was under the impression that the lady I was entertaining was white-haired and nearing seventy, eating scones between teaching me the King's English, by the name of Miss Fogerty."

"I'm sorry, Sir, the young lady came to tea with *me*."

"Alone? But Willie, you're a married man!"

"She's my first cousin, her mother being my late mother's sister. My Aunt Rose."

"Sorry, I misjudged you."

"Aunt Rose sat next to you, Sir, at that first big luncheon."

"Of course. You don't care for her?"

"Not too much, no two sisters have ever been so unalike. I would wager any money that she wangled that paragraph into the Press."

"The Press are certainly on the – what was the expression came up in Vocab yesterday – they're on the qui-vive, aren't they?"

"They are."

And he went. Settling down for my cat-nap, I found that the snippet of false gossip had set up a train of thought; hadn't I said earlier that there was a bridge I'd have to cross? Hell, it was getting near. I thought of Charles II, the last bachelor to ascend the throne. A King is expected to get married. Should get married. Must get married.

For no reason my mind flew, with a stab, to Kathy. Between her and me (now that's grammar, though it doesn't sound like it) there had never, for a second, been the faintest idea of marriage. But now . . . since there had to be *some*body . . . what was her proper name – Katherine. Queen Katherine, not bad . . .

Then I laughed, out loud. Queen Katherine the Rebel Maid, who was – at this very moment – rebelling against her King!

I could just see the Wedding: Westminster Abbey, lined with coronets and spotted ermine, the organ pealing, the Archbishop of Canterbury, the smell of incense and moth-balls, the bride exquisite from tiara to train, the two of us kneeling before the Almighty's Understudy. Then the mellifluous tones, "Dost thou Katherine, take this man John of England, to be thy lawful wedded husband?"

A fateful pause, broken only by the sniffing of titled noses into titled hankies. Then . . . the Bride turns sharply round on her knees, throws her bouquet at the nearest Duchess, and gives the loudest snore ever heard in any place of worship. ROYAL WEDDING SENSATION!! FROM SNORING BEAUTY IN LYCEUM TO SNORING CONSORT IN ABBEY!

A case of miscasting. I was asleep.

And it was a good nap; during it the tailor had telephoned my valet, the uniform for the Big Inspection was very elaborate, one little detail was incorrect and must be *just* right, so if he were a little late, would His Majesty forgive – etc. I was glad; they did not wake me up till he arrived.

And he *was* late; in the dressing-room I scrambled into the uniform. It was gorgeous but complicated, gold epaulettes and a lot of braid, and two rows of medals already attached to fit the measurements of the braid: gold braid on the peaked cap. Stiffly uncomfortable, more so even than the others, but in the long glass I looked good. In order to rehearse walking, I stalked awkwardly into the study, followed by the tailor and his two seconds, with note-pad and pencil. I stood still, for them to make notes.

One of them knelt in front of me, to adjust the trousers over the boots. He looked as if he were about to kiss my foot.

A knock at the door. A footman – Fielding this time – was followed by Willie and his two chums. For cocktails. Quite informal.

It was the second surprise, in the way of visitors, which he had sprung on me in four days. The chums were Kathy and Bruce.

CHAPTER THIRTEEN

When Lovers Meet

I looked at them, they looked at me. I heard Willie's voice, "Well, Sir, I'll leave you with your friends." And he left.

My first stumbling thought, after many days of balding heads and gleaming specs, was that these two were beautiful, beautiful . . . there can't be anything more beautiful than these two. My second, that I love her. I love him too, but not in the same way. I haven't seen her for twenty years, but she don't look an hour older. I love her.

My third thought, as they stood gaping at me, was how crashingly silly I looked: a bemedalled tailor's dummy got up in a musical-comedy uniform as stiff as a board, with the tailor grovelling at its feet. I gaped back, like a repertory actor who has rushed onstage in armour and finds that tonight it isn't *Henry V*, it's *Charley's Aunt*. We all three gaped.

The tailor scrambled to his feet – "thank you so much, your Majesty, so many apologies" – and glided quickly out with his assistants hot on his heels, looking as embarrassed as if they had been caught *in flagrante delicto*.

I muttered, "I'll get out of this," and stamped into the bedroom. As I pulled and pushed and panted – the boots were hell – my mind saw the two of them in the next room, perched gingerly on the sofa (gilt where it wasn't embroidered), as lost as two ship-wrecked angels.

In my fury, with the trousers I had whipped off my underpants. Stark naked, I looked at the Bed of Ware. And something which had been pent up for a month, boiled to the surface.

I strode back into the study, stood facing them and struck a pose: feet boldly apart, arms outspread. "The Emperor . . . without his Clothes!"

What I'd forgotten, was that I was still wearing the peaked cap. And my socks. Kathy looked me up, then down, and gave a peal of laughter. Which set Bruce off, then me. A timid knock at the door.

I was into the bedroom like a shot: just in time, it was the tailor back for his attaché-case. I got into a dressing-gown, heard the outer door close, and peered out. "I hear you're casting a French farce, anything for me?"

A pause, and we all laughed again, and through it I leapt forward and took Kathy in my arms. She smelt faintly of the familiar eau de Cologne, and when I hugged Bruce to me, there was a warm whiff of new soap, and of flesh. "God," I said, "this is good . . ."

But as I sat opposite them, I noticed that while I had embraced them both, neither had kissed me.

But I was in a dressing-gown, which helped me to imagine we were sitting around in Yeoman's Row . . . Willie must have in- structed Staff to leave the three of us alone; I hurried to the drinks table. "Booze time!" And as I took up a bottle, what I'd just said made a cruel echo in my head, "booze time!" Too jolly. Jocular, putting scared visitors at their ease. Proving I'm human.

They sat saying nothing, probably looking at each other, and as I made martinis – Willie had taught me – I thought, don't kid your- self, all that laughing was . . . hysteria.

When I turned back to them, Kathy was looking slowly round the room, her eyes moving from pictures to furniture: the loving look I had watched in the National Gallery and at shop-windows.

Then she turned to me, and I could tell she was thinking, but all this treasure – here he is in the middle of it, *it belongs to him* . . .

She spoke at last, quite primly. "What beautiful things."

I bustled up to them with three full glasses. "Oh they're not bad digs, a bit roomy but highly recommended – cheers!"

As I said it, I remembered it was the same poor joke I had made in my letter. They said, "Cheers" in unison, and we sipped. *Cheers* . . . The sort of thing you say in pubs to acquaintances, to strangers even – the three of us had never said it to one another, ever. Looking down at my glass, I saw the crest on my dressing-gown. They must have noticed it too. This was ghastly.

They were both dressed in their best, what we called "the audition number". He in his dark suit and black shoes, they still needed heeling; she in the navy-blue coat and skirt, and the white blouse with the Peter Pan collar and the halo hat I had liked and which made her look fifteen.

At the throat, her one piece of jewellery which had been left her by her old drama teacher. I had never seen the shoes before, very chic with high heels showing off the beautiful ankles. I guessed that she had gone out and bought them this morning. She had had her hair done, but not too done, neat but careless-looking. He had had a hair-cut and – again I guessed – a shampoo, in our little bathroom. Her make-up was slight, but perfect. They were both shining.

They had always been that. What hit me, with a wallop, was that between them and me, there was no current. I was cut off from them, they were unapproachable. It broke my heart.

On the little table next to her, Kathy saw a book, and her eyes widened, my *Oxford Dictionary*. I said, "Yours is *Cassell's*, isn't it? This one's good too."

"I'm sure." I could tell from the drawl that the long words were on their way. "I imagine that in point of fact, one would find most dictionaries fundamentally identical."

"Quite," I said, "I have a feeling that the demarcation is negligible."

For the first time, she smiled. So I thought another little joke might help. "Funny – there was Bruce and me kidding you about studying to be a good author, and here's me studying to be a good King!"

She stopped smiling, just looked at the dictionary. The joke hadn't come off. The word "King" had killed it.

Bruce said, "Ay, we saw 'bout that. Most morrnin's we take a perrsonal interest an' slip doon to the Chelsea Public Library an' go through the free newspapers."

We sipped, in polite silence. I could bear the pain in my chest no longer, sprang up again, went to the little piano, and played a few notes. "Let's Fall in Love." Then I played them again, at the same time singing softly. *Now is the time for it, why be afraid of it . . .* I hadn't sung solo since Panto, got discouraged, went off the note and trailed away.

Silence. I gulped my martini, turned and looked at them. Bruce was staring at the carpet, with the old trick of pressing his lips together to make them less full. Kathy was looking straight ahead, with a film of wet under each eye, like a close-up on the Pictures.

Desperate remedies . . . I jumped up – "But I haven't shown you the bedroom!" They followed me. I pointed to the bed, "There!"

It was neatly turned down, my pyjamas laid alongside. Not a crease. Immaculate. I looked at them looking at it.

This time the silence seemed to swing to and fro like a pendulum. Kathy finished her martini, then Bruce spoke, for the second time. Thoughtful, as always. "It's no' as nice a bed as your bed was in Yeoman's Row."

He had said it like a very grown-up lad of ten. I looked at Kathy, and we both laughed. Yes, it *was* hysteria. "Tell me," she said, "do they turn the covers down as early as this? Are you going to bed *now*?"

Which led to a last Desperate Remedy. "Come to think of it, not a bad idea! Kathy, why don't you and I make it an evening, then supper in here?"

A pause. Then she said, in a level non-voice, "I have to leave in ten minutes, so has Bruce, we're both in shows." I had forgotten.

I said to her, "How's *Stop Press*? Going to run for ever?"

"No. We finish next month."

"Oh. But it's had a nice run, hasn't it –"

She got up as if to go. Then sat down again, on the bed, and burst into tears.

Bruce and I had – of course – seen her sitting looking miserable – the nameless depressions girls seem to suffer from on occasion – when he and I had sat on either side of her and held a hand. But we had never seen her like this. And by instinct, we did what we'd done the other sad times – sat on either side of her and held a hand. "I'll be all right – I'm sorry – I'll be all right . . ."

The Royal Bed seemed hardly the setting for the scene, so Bruce and I coaxed her back into the study. I lifted a silver cover; under it, a big plate heaped with the daintiest little sandwiches you ever saw: or rather, *they* had ever seen. To counteract her martini, I placed the plate in front of her. She sniffed and munched, munched and sniffed. Bruce just munched.

It was my chance, the bull by the horns. "I don't see why the hell you're crying. You get me stripping down to the buff and then turn me down! If that isn't humiliation, I'd like to know what is. It's me should be turning on the waterworks. We've got to thrash this out!"

"Sounds like a terrible play – gulp, sniff – *Bulldog Drummond* –"

"That may be, but it's got to be done!" She ate another mouthful of sandwiches and quietened down.

I chose my words carefully. "I wrote you a very special letter, because I love you. I love you both, but you, being the female end, run the ship." More like a terrible play than ever, but I pressed on. "That's why the letter was to you. I'm sure it wasn't easy for Willie to persuade you to come today, but you did come, because of my letter. Because you knew I meant every word of it. Didn't you?"

She tried to say yes, but couldn't. Just nodded. I felt my way forward, cautiously. "The three of us loved one another, but it's only since . . . this happened that I've realized how much. You can't kill that – it would be as bad as yanking something out of the soil that's growing there."

Silence. I was making a point. "You told Willie that everything's changed. Certain things have changed, but *I haven't*. That's why I'm glad I made a fool of myself just now, I'm the same, I'm Jack – your Jack! Did you read that my parents spent two days here? Well, they behaved with me as they've always done, exactly the same! They accepted the situation, and my mother's a countrywoman, simple, unsophisticated –"

She was ready for me. "That's why she was able to accept." She picked up another bunch of the dainty sandwiches, and Bruce followed suit. A couple of stage-folk snatching a bite before the show.

She spoke again, slowly, with the sad deliberation of somebody who has lain awake, doing a lot of thinking. And she spoke simply, no long words. "And she's your mother, always has been, didn't she say so herself? This is different, utterly different. You said you're glad you showed us the Emperor without his clothes. I'm glad too, but not for the same reason. The opposite. I'm glad because it proved to me, one hundred per cent, that we can never go back. Of *course* the body's the same, but the Emperor . . . is the Emperor. It makes all the difference . . . in the world."

I got up and paced up and down; I had to fight this. "But darling, it shouldn't make *any* difference – not to you! Who was it who despised wealth and privilege? Who defied the most powerful producer in the West End? Who was nicknamed 'The Rebel Maid' by the Press? Above all, who described the fuss over the Royal Family when they visited the theatre as 'ludicrous'? Of all people, it's you who should be dismissing all this, with contempt, it should mean nothing to you – why aren't you sending the whole thing up?"

She thought. "You're right, of course, in that I don't hold with it at all. But . . . it's like religion, which I don't hold with either. I remember reading somewhere about one of the great philosophers –

I forget his name, a real old atheist, no wool over his eyes – well, he was in Rome and went into St Peter's. And standing at the heart of it all – the Jewel, worth billions and billions, and all based, as he put it, on centuries of superstition – he looked round and said to himself, "Well, you can talk against it till you're blue in the face . . . it's there.' "

And like the old atheist, she looked round: taking in the rich secure little haven of a room, from the silver-framed photographs, each with the firm flourish of a legendary signature, to my dressing-gown crest: then the six hundred rooms hemming us in. I was losing ground.

She turned to me again. "In the same way, *we* can't pretend. You can't pretend that because you call Bertram Green your father, he *is* your father – he's not, you are the son of the grandson of a King. And behind him, quite a family. That Public Library's got history-books as well. Hasn't it, Bruce?"   ·

"It has." The last of the baby sandwiches. "Verra interestin', in view of the sittyation."

"You must have seen the article," she went on, "in the *Sunday Times*, headed 'The Magic of the Crown'. About every monarch having been anointed, and made sacred, for close on a thousand years. You'll be anointed, and sacred. *The Magic of the Crown* . . ." She spoke the words flatly, but they seemed to boom round us. Then she added, "We can't fight that."

I must take charge. Now or never. "May I remind you of last New Year's Eve?"

She looked puzzled. "Yes?"

"The three of us were discussing our wish for 1935. You dreaded getting to the age of thirty and still being insecure. Remember?"

"I remember."

"And then you said you hoped to meet a nice rich older man –"

"Who'd keep me. I remember."

"*I'm* a nice rich man. Very nice. And very rich."

"A millionaire. The second biggest landowner, owns Sandring-ham and Balmoral –"

"And," put in Bruce, "a verra valuable stamp collection, worr-th more than a million."

She was looking down at the Aubusson carpet. "Now," I said, "since I'm a nice millionaire, and not even an older man, a young one –"

"A young one?" Her voice was flat, factual. "When you were

brought into this place, you left your youth behind. No King can be young."

She made it sound so true that I brushed it aside. "Since I'm a nice millionaire, what's wrong with *me* keeping you?"

She gave me a steady look which told me this was the question she had been waiting for, and she answered slowly, carefully. "I've thought about it, of course. A cosy little love-nest, *not* in Mayfair, too noticeable – tucked away where least expected, shabby old Pimlico. But the last word in luxury, very different from Yeoman's Row, with a lady's maid with a weekly salary ten times the rent.

"Once a week, at about nine p.m., there creeps up a nondescript car, driven by a rather shady character, paid through the nose to do nothing else: rather like the man employed to drive your grandfather the Duke of Clarence to shady nights in Cleveland Street."

The Chelsea Public Library must be the best in London.

"This goes on for months, a year even. Then the Royal Wedding. Westminster Abbey, crammed to the doors with the Cream de la Cream. But who is that sad figure in black, behind a pillar, weeping into her black handkerchief?" A pause. "*No!*"

There had been a spice of parody in it, in words and delivery, but the "No!" had rung out like the crack of a whip. She got up, and put on her dictionary voice. "We must both be journeying to our respective destinations. Otherwise, we'll be keeping the curtain waiting, at two theatres."

I stood looking at them both, in my crested dressing-gown and stockinged feet. By now her eyes had dried, but his were blurred. I had nothing to say.

She said, "Goodbye." He said, "Good luck." She added, "Good luck." I said, "Thank you." Not a memorable farewell scene. I was relieved that she hadn't curtsied.

The door closed after them. It should have been my turn to burst into tears, but I fought against it and won.

CHAPTER FOURTEEN

All Work and No Play

That evening was my one free one that week, so Willie stayed and dined with me. To keep my mind occupied, I talked fragmentary Spanish to him which he corrected as we went along; but once the footman had gone I said – a bit ginny by then, understandably – "Willie, it was no good."

He looked into his glass; the deep serious look. "I begged them," he said, "to come and try it, but I was afraid it wouldn't work."

"They had told you it wouldn't?"

"Yes. They're the salt of the earth, you know, those two."

I was pleased at that, but in no mood to stay pleased. "You talked of this as being a machine. Remember?"

"Yes."

"I've got my coat well caught in it, haven't I?" No answer. "Willie, shall I slide my coat off, and . . . walk out?"

"No!" He was – for him – quite vehement, then he loosened up. "The machine runs so smoothly that at the slightest hint of trouble it glides politely to a halt, adjusts and glides on. Not a scratch. Permit me, Señor, to tell you that it is the truth, *permita le diga que es verdad. Continuamos en español?*"

The work piled up, and I was glad. Next day, *Wed, July 10th 1935, 29th Day of Reign. His Majesty will tour Special Services Centres in Lancashire, Luncheon, Mayor of Preston. Next day, will visit Social Services Centres in Lancashire. Next day, will visit Portsmouth & inspect Royal Naval and Marine Establishments, attended by Admiral*

*of Fleet Sir Ffulke Brentwood, received at city boundary by Lord
Mayor. Will visit H.M.S. EXCELLENT and 5 other ships. Etc., etc.
Tues. July 16th 1935, 35th Day of Reign. Daily Express*, William
Hickey. *"Is understood Miss Kathy Tripp been offered £5000 by
Sunday paper for story of what was clearly close friendship with King,
and turned offer down.*

" *'Anyway,'* she told us on phone, *'no question of romance, my fiancé
Mr B. Renfrew and I realized he was shy, lonely, and we suggested his
staying at flat, he did.' Asked when she and B. would marry, she smiled,
shrugged, 'You never know.' Mr Renfrew unavailable for comment.*

"*Asked if King is marrying kind, money-scorning Miss Tripp answered, 'How would I know, I never asked him. I would hazard the
guess that he would be a trifle on the critical side.' "* She'd got through
that well. And turned the money down. Taste. My chest ached.

What did emerge was that everybody was watching, and thinking
of marriage.

Next evening, seven p.m., end of Gram and Voc session. I had
just said, "I'm getting to be a dab hand at spelling, aren't I?"

"Yes, Sir, but to match your spelling, it would be pleasant if you
could say something like, 'I'm getting better at spelling, am I not?' "

"I'll practise that. Willie, I'm expected to get married, am I not?"
He looked up. "I'm afraid so."

"As soon as possible?"

"Within reason, Sir, yes. May I ask if you have any ideas?"

I considered. "Any I have, not unnaturally, tend to veer towards
the theatre and the flicks. What are the requirements?"

"Firstly, Protestant. Secondly, free without owing that freedom to
Divorce. And ideally, a year or two younger than yourself."

We concentrated on the stars. I said, "Jessie Mathews?"

Willie examined the idea as he sipped. "Queen Jessie . . . ?"

"And married."

"On consideration, as a theme-song for a Queen-Consort, 'Over
My Shoulder Goes One Care' does sound a shade irresponsible."

I pondered. "Celia Johnson? Married . . . Anna Neagle? Married . . ."

Willie shook his head. "Anyway, aren't all those charmers a year
or two older than your twenty-four? Also, unfortunately, they're
none of them quite . . ."

"Good enough?"

"Not quite . . . suitable."

I felt my back-stage heckles rise. "Why? They'd all carry it off more than well. Didn't Gertie Millar turn into the Countess of Dudley?"

"This is different. It's that bugbear Tradition."

"Am I forbidden by law to marry a commoner?"

" 'Forbidden' is a strong word . . . Let's say that it's 'done' for the wife of the King to be, if not royal herself, of aristocratic birth . . . In the meantime, Sir, do you miss sex?"

It was sudden; but he *had* finished his second – and last – martini. He went on, as direct and impersonal as a doctor. "I am only asking because in my job I have to face facts, and the fact here is that in the matter of sex, other chaps may not have the luck to find themselves as untroubled as myself."

A pause. "Willie, I salute what must be rare. A diplomat who gets to the point."

"A King, Sir, is a human being." *No King can be young.* But still a human being?

"I suppose," I said, "now and again. Nell Gwynne had proof of that. And Alfred the Great can't have spent his whole time burning cakes . . . Do I miss sex? Not that much, I'm too busy. It's true that I can't remember how long it's been since I went without it for five weeks. I have, once or twice, woken up with the accent on 'up', but by then the curtains are being opened and all is well. What's your idea, Willie – could it be an illicit shack-up with a Deb?"

"Not really."

"You're right, of course. Not much fun bending your knees in a curtsey, and the next minute being expected to separate them."

"True." He took a paper from his pocket. "I have here a list . . ." I waited for a menu, and for the grandest head-waiter in London to murmur, "Well done, Sir, or medium rare? White meat, or dark?"

He opened the paper. "A list of six ladies for whom I can vouch."

"But what –"

"The logistics?" Must look that one up, must mean where-and-how.

Willie explained, carefully. "Side by side with their hobby, if you know what I mean, they have their work, which could bring them to the Palace on occasional afternoons. One is a lady decorator who would be here to check on the wear and tear of furnishings, another a lady photographer requiring rather intensive sittings, another a lady journalist writing an exhaustive profile, and so on."

I stared at him, I was tickled pink. Could this be a throwback to

my great-grandfather's youth under Victoria's eagle eye, when
Necessity had to be the mother of Invention? "Willie, I salute more
than a diplomat. We take off our crown to the best-bred procurer in
the business."

"Thank you, Sir."

He'd got me thinking: the idea of a pretty woman measuring curtains, and then tumbling back on to the Bed of Ware with nothing on
under her skirt, was to be dwelt on for a moment.

Only for a moment. I said, "Are you going to see Kathy and
Bruce again?"

"I don't think, Sir, there'd be any point, do you?"

"You're right."

Work, work. *Fri. July 19th 1935, 38th Day of Reign. Luncheon to
King of the Belgians after H.M. has personally invested the King with
the Insignia of a Knight of the Most Noble Order of the Garter . . .
3 p.m., will visit Int. Exhibition of Chinese Art, Royal Academy. Will
be received by President of R.A. and Chinese Ambassador. Equerry-in-
Waiting, Lieut. Col. the Lord Alastair Innes-Kerr . . .*

The Cornish branch of the Royal Family.

". . . You mind Sir Gerald Winthrop-Smith, Stone Manor, the
gambler? A good 13 yrs ago, you aged 11, he & his Lady owed
us a 2 yrs Bill for eggs & butter, & 3 times we sent you down
along there to collect, in the hope that a little Child would lead
them, but no go. Well, this very week, who do you reckon
called on us? Sir Gerald & Lady, comed up all that way to deliver the cash in person, evry penny. No mention of Interest.
They asked after you.

"They showed us in a newspaper a peice statin that as regards
a Bride you would be choosy. I should think so, in your position
your wife got to be the rite one, & must love you true. It would
be nice to travel to London again, there would be no trouble wi
the crowds by reason of your Father & Self bein ominous" . . .

It took me quite a time to work out that "ominous" stood for
"anonymous". English is not an easy language.

Choosy I might be, but I must choose. At one of our breaks between work, Willie arrived with a pile of magazines and heaved it
on to the table between us. They were all numbers of *Country Life*.
Of course . . . after thumbing through stately *Old Properties for*

Sale, in Excellent Condition, you get to the frontispiece page, consisting of one big "photographic study" of a single stately *Young* Property. One of the year's Debs. Also, presumably, in excellent condition. *For Sale?* Don't let's put it like that. *For Private Viewing*.

It was fun to examine the field. "The Honourable Marcia Lymington-Wemyss, daughter of Lord and Lady Fressington, The Old Place, Worcester"..."Lady Grace Pangbourne, daughter of..."

I said, "They don't look very sexy, do they? And as they're in there, on show, in the hope of hinting that they *are* sexy, they can't be."

Up came "Lady Queenie Vavasour de Lacy". "Willie, she doesn't look bad."

"A school friend of a cousin of mine. A crafty photograph, she's a titled iceberg. Anyway, are we ready for a Queen Queenie?"

Turning a page, I came slap up against a large photo, in colour, and my strong reaction to it quite startled me – no, it wasn't of Kathy, she wasn't in any way important enough to be in *Country Life*. I was looking at a windmill, in Dorset somewhere, with opposite the picture a finely detailed drawing of its inside. And I actually saw my fingers twitch forward to pick up the tiny tools of the trade which were lying idle in Yeoman's Row. Forget it . . .

I switched to another frontispiece. "Lady Mary Crawshay-Moreton, daughter of the Earl and Countess of Winfield, Winfield Abbey, Rutland." I said, "Not bad, amiable efficient face, capable mouth . . ."

"She was at Girton with another cousin. And known throughout Cambridge as the L.M."

"The L.M.?"

"Ladies' Man. A capable mouth verily. Capable of anything."

"Willie!"

"Sorry Sir, I forgot myself."

"Kindly forget yourself oftener, I like it . . . No, she is *not* for the Abbey, I don't see the wedding-veil going with the rest of the outfit. Jodhpurs and a cigar. Who's next . . .?"

But I stayed choosy. The pile of magazines exhausted, Willie said, "It looks, Sir, as if we'll have to look further afield. We must just keep the old eyes skinned."

"And where do I do that? Strolling in Piccadilly?"

"No Sir, waltzing in the Palace. In a few weeks' time. At your first Royal Ball."

"Oh. How will the invites be worded, "Audition for Female Lead'?"

Fri. July 26th 1935, 45th Day of Reign. Willie was in his office across the corridor, I was learning a speech. Finding I needed a reference book of his, I walked across to find him sitting opposite a visitor. A lady, fifty-ish, smart, who shot up and bobbed. In the past weeks I had met enough fifty-ish smart bobbing ladies to last a life-time, but I thought – don't I know her? As Willie got up, he looked almost annoyed. "Your Majesty, may I present my aunt Lady Haddlewick, she sat next to you at a luncheon –"

Auntie was off, the whole face crackling with metallic smiles, the voice underlining every other word. "The *King*, as I live and *breathe*! Far from the madding crowd, this *is* jolly – but Willie, you told me His Majesty wouldn't be back till this afternoon, *what* a happy chance!"

I took the hint, "The second meeting was postponed." And I sat down, so that she could sit down. Which she did, happily. "Oh, those *boring* functions, don't you sometimes dread them, Sir – the people one can get landed with, pretending to be interested in this and that!" I thought, at that particular function she'd been mostly landed with *me*, and felt like shaking her. "Oh, the superficial *chatter* that goes on, don't you agree there should be night-schools opened, for intelligent table-talk? You and I discussed Staverbridge Priory, didn't you mention that your Mama knew it, what fun if I once met her there!"

This time I just had to tell her. "I would doubt that. My mother was second housemaid." It stopped her in full spate, it was as if I had yanked the needle up from a gramophone record.

But not for long. "But how quaint – how *killing*! I must tell –"

Willie intervened, gently. "Aunt Rose, I'm afraid His Majesty has an appointment."

"Of course, *ça va sans dire*!" She got up gaily, choosing to forget that I had just mentioned a cancelled meeting. "What a scrumptious talk, Willie we *must* arrange something, it would be heaven, this has been such fun, goodbye, Sir, goodbye . . ." She curtsied and re-treated.

"Willie, she's not your favourite."

"No harm in her, but they can be the most tiresome. An ace climber. There's never been a Christmas when I didn't long to send her an alpenstock."

"But she sounds pretty high up herself, a title and all that!"

"I'm afraid that doesn't affect it. If a climber's already three quarters of the way up, more than ever he or she is determined to get to the top."

A knock at the door; return of Ace Climber. "I *do* beg your pardon, Sir, but my daughter – Willie's first cousin – has called for me, I had left a message at the Portico that he'd like to say hello to her and here she is – Deirdre dear!"

Willie's face was a polite mask, but when his cousin walked in he gave her an easy peck on the cheek, which meant he didn't dislike her. She was really pretty, with golden hair: a bit of a chocolate-box, but all right. About twenty, not too tall.

Mummy crackled away. "Willie dear, such a lovely morning and Deirdre's only ever seen the Garden alive with *nouveaux-riches* dying for a glimpse of Royalty, *do* you think we could persuade H.M. to take her for *une petite promenade*, ten minutes, she'd *so* love it!"

Cheek. I was only relieved that her daughter didn't look in an agony of embarrassment. Willie's jaw was very set. "I'm afraid he has an appointment – a fitting –"

"Oh, a *tailor*! They're used to waiting, do, Sir, please!"

Double cheek. No way out; I gave Deirdre my smile, she smiled prettily back and I followed her out. I heard the typewriter voice behind us, "Wouldn't it be fun, dear, if H.M. accepted a wee invitation . . ." I didn't envy Willie.

The Garden did look fine in the sun, as beautiful as on my first walk. As the two of us embarked on the lawn, a figure came shambling down a path, carrying a watering-can. Methuselah the gardener. He saw us.

I waved. He stared as if face to face with a sunlit ghost and scuttled between some bushes. The laundry-boy had gone up in the world. Deirdre had noticed nothing, and I was glad: too boring to explain.

As we strolled, I took a quick look at her profile: just a touch of snub in the nose, excellent. A bird sang on a branch, then flew down for a chat with a walking bird, just a yard from my feet; one of them gave me a look, then they both fluttered off. They couldn't care less, and I liked that. I decided that after the next of those Luncheons, I would walk straight out here and enjoy the non-company of the non-people. (This was to become a habit.)

We strolled. Deirdre smiled up at the wispy curls of cloud in the blue, like a little girl. And it was a relief that not only was she not chatting away, there was no trace of that damned Respect, or of nervousness. She was herself. Blessed are the silent.

We strolled. I thought, out of politeness I should say something, just as she stopped and studied a row of flowers. I said "Deirdre, I'm very bad on gardens, what are those called?"

"Begonias and phloxes." She didn't add the "Sir", and I liked that too. Nothing wrong with her voice either. Just a voice, no bother. I said, "Do you live in London?"

"No."

"Oh . . . where in the country?"

"Old Grange House."

"Where's that?"

"Oxfordshire."

She said no more, just looked around. It would seem that Mummy did the talking for both of them. And that if she ever got her daughter to the altar, Deirdre would find "I do" quite a mouthful.

I tried again. "You're fond of flowers?"

"Yes, quite. We have flowers in *our* garden." Pause.

Strolling by her side as she looked around, I took a quick look at her. She was wearing a sophisticated summer two-piece—I hope that's the phrase—but it now dawned on me that the reason she smiled like a little girl, was that she *was* a little girl. Of twenty. I was Uncle Mac of the Children's Hour, trying to interview a precocious tot.

"That's nice, Deirdre. Is it a big garden, Deirdre?" It seemed the right way to cope.

"Too big for three gardeners, Mummy says." Pause. "We should have twice as many." Pause. "Which would be six."

Silence. She stopped, bent down and examined a flower-bed. Which, just as I was settling for non-conversation, seemed to trigger her off. "I do think it's a shame that flowers have to go bye-byes."

"Bye-byes, Deirdre?"

"When they drop off and die. When one of them did that in one of Mummy's vases after a party – a rose it was – I had a little cry and buried it at the bottom of the garden."

"That was nice, Deirdre." I nearly asked if the three gardeners had attended the funeral. Could this be the daughter whose Mama had asked me for advice about a Shaw play? Twenty-year-old Deirdre would be out of her depth at *Peter Pan*.

She was still gazing at the flowers. My next question should have been "And what do you want to be when you grow up?" but I phrased it more tactfully. "Deirdre, have you any plans?"

She got up, smartly. "Oh yes, to get married. These are petunias, I like petunias."

She stroked a petunia. It wouldn't have surprised me if she had asked it which it would prefer, when the time came – to be buried or cremated.

I, the adult, stood there, at a loss. "*Why* are you planning to get married?"

"Because Mummy says so."

"Do you *want* to get married?"

"I haven't thought about it."

"Does Mummy want you to marry anybody in particular?

"Yes, you. Those over there are hollyhocks." She straightened up, and smiled again at the sky.

I said, "Would you enjoy being the Queen?"

"I wouldn't mind. I like dressing up."

I said, "Deirdre, we'll walk back now, shall we?"

And we did.

CHAPTER FIFTEEN

Audition for a Female Lead

J ii R

*The Lord Chamberlain has
received His Majesty's commands
to invite*

....

....

to a Ball at Buckingham Palace
on Thursday, the 29th August, 1935,
from 9 p.m. to 1 a.m.

Evening Dress   Decorations

Seven hundred names. Standing at the door of Willie's office and seeing Sec-Sec carefully copying them out, I felt a tremor of excitement, which I knew many other people were sharing. *Daily Express: "It is whispered that all ambitious Mamas in Debrett's or on borders of same, are falling over themselves angling for invitations."* It could have been more delicately put, but Willie assured me it was roughly true.

Since there would be a Buffet Supper, I would be spared the familiar ordeal of being clamped to a table for hours on end with a strange female on either side. No speeches! And gone the tinkling little orchestra, there would be real music like the theatre: a Dance Band! Back in my study, in front of a long mirror, I practised a couple of steps and visualized myself dancing, in the tails which particularly suited me. In between the dances I would wander free as a bird, dispensing quiet charm. I felt pleased with myself.

I asked Willie if his Aunt Rose was on the guest-list. "I'm afraid we can't get out of it, in spite of the fact that her candidate is out of the running." (He had told me that Deirdre was known, throughout his family, as Dreardy.) I asked if he had given Mummy a hint that Baby had lost the part.

"I did imply that you'd found her daughter a trifle immature."

"How did she react?"

"Very bothered, for a bit. Then seemed to accept the inevitable. She's now setting Dreardy's cap at one of the Devonshire lads. She's pretty innocuous, really."

From the Princess, "I fear, Sir, that I must ask to be excused, being a little frail for late festivities." I was glad, I wanted to remember her as she had been on that special visit.

I had asked for Ivor N. and Mary Ellis to be invited, but "they" (Sir God and Co) advised that while they felt sure that "the lady and gentleman were suitable guests", it would set a precedent and other theatre personalities would be miffed. I saw the point, reluctantly.

Kathy and Bruce . . .

Neither Willie nor I had mentioned them since the parting. As the names came up in my mind, there it was again, after all these weeks: the familiar tightening across my chest. And I wasn't pleased. It takes time.

Thurs. Aug. 1st 1935, 51st Day of Reign. A typical day, close-packed with engagements. Such as – *9.30 a.m., H.M. will sit, 4th Sitting for Portrait, to Mr Gerald Kelly . . . 12 noon, will receive in audience, and accept letters of Recall from their Predecessors, and their own Letters of Credence, from the Envoys Extraordinary from the Kingdom of Nepal and the Dominican Republic.* By now, my World Atlas was well thumbed . . . *8 p.m., Dinner for Crown Prince of Egypt, 67 guests, Court Dress, Speech . . .*

"... Your Father & Self attended the Annual Baptist Social, the Chairman of the St Austell Council as Special Guest, everythin nice till he gets up & speeks. Dear Friends, it is a honour to bid wellcom to Mrs Alice Green (or, to call her by her corect Title, the *Queen Mother*).

"They clapped like anythin & I could ha smacked him. And for not bringin in your Father. So when he sugests a big Reception for me I said, Escuse me, how much would that cost? £200 he says & I say, Thank ee but instead would you be v. kind & use the money for our Chapel Roof which is leakin terrible. And it baint rite for godly folks to come to Gods House to pray for good Health & then go ome with a Chill. Your Lovin Mother & Subject, Alice Lavinia Green.

"Your lovin Father speekin. Dont tell on me, but down in St Austell she is now known by the name of *Alice the Palace.* They start on the Roof tomorrow."

Fri. Aug. 9th 1935, 59th Day of Reign. 11 a.m., H.M. will receive the Maharajah of Bhavnagar Dhrangadhra. 1 p.m., Luncheon for the King of Greece. 3 p.m., will proceed by car to Portsmouth, where (7 p.m.) dinner with Lord Mayor (Speech), then at Tactical School, will witness a demonstration of the Battle of Jutland. (Naval uniform.)
And on. And on.

Thurs. Aug. 29th 1935, 79th Day of Reign. Tonight, the Ball.

Mid-morning, on my way to a Privy Council, it looked as if most of my six hundred rooms were in turmoil; the first dress-rehearsal of *New Roman Scandals* was nothing to it. Trestle-tables came clattering past, then music-stands, then candelabra, then carpets on shoulders, then battalions of little gold chairs. But – very different – as noiseless as on a normal day, no fuss, no haste. Decorum, decorum.

At 8 p.m. I sat down – immaculate in white tie and tails, red rose in button-hole – in my study for a quiet dinner with Willie: he had firmly suggested that I should tackle a square meal, rather than get ravenous at midnight and wolf the grub in front of seven hundred watchful eyes.

It had been planned, of course, that he should bring his wife Anne, but at the last minute she had begged off: at home in the country with a bad cold. I suspected that the cold was confined to her feet, at the frightening prospect of facing the Social Event of the Year, and knowing her I understood. I had an idea that Willie wouldn't have minded being at home too, with the same cold.

Over coffee, I studied my inevitable notes, on the thirty or forty non-illustrious guests I should learn something about. I read one out – " 'Sir Cuthbert Angell – Sir Godwin's list – last year performed delicate major operation on Sir Godwin, removing an internal organ which left the patient in better physical shape than before.' "

"I wonder," Willie murmured, "what part of him had to go . . . The funny bone?"

How to remember the name "Angell"? Easy, Angell attended Sir God . . . I ate without noticing the food. "Seven hundred . . . At these kinds of events, who's the first to arrive? There's got to *be* a first – what will he be like? Or she, or he and she?"

"You never know. At a big reception last year, for Queen Wilhelmina of the Netherlands, the first arrival – three minutes before the chap who announces the guests – was Queen Wilhelmina of the Netherlands: at five to nine, complete with entourage, a Dutch treat before its time. Somebody had goofed, thinking the thing had started at eight, which would have meant that at nine, as the guest of honour she was on time. They were all very put out, and insisted on being herded into a tiny ante-room."

"To wait for their entrance. Right and proper."

"The first are usually country gentry who've driven up from stately homes and are too impatient to skulk in their parked car until the right moment. It can also be the ones who aren't familiar with the routine and have an idea that to be late for Royalty amounts to lèse-majesté. So on Big Ben's first stroke of nine, up glides the hired Rolls. And once, a titled journalist – must have been Lord Castlerosse – arrived at ten to nine."

"Why?"

"He wanted to be able to describe who'd be the first to arrive."

9 p.m. I proceeded to my post, the top of the staircase leading to the ante-room leading to the Ballroom, and the Lord Chamberlain joined me for the announcing. In the Ballroom, the dance band were poised with baton and bows in the air. Then, from the several clocks, a delightful flurry of chimes, and the band made a spirited swing into "You're The Top". I formed the words "You're the Top, you're the King of England . . ." and felt a glow.

Sure enough, as if the moment had been rehearsed, a couple appeared, from nowhere. Elderly, and terrified. On his chest, a rash of small apologetic medals, while she was in a cape made of some pale frightened-looking fur, which hadn't lately seen the light of chandelier. They could have been a couple come to be interviewed about a post. He whispered to the Lord Chamberlain, who called out "Sir Cuthbert and Lady *Angell*!"

Angell, Sir God – hurrah, I'm in luck. Lady Angell curtsied as if her knees had unexpectedly given way. I said, "So glad to meet you both – Sir Cuthbert, we specially wanted you to come tonight, after the brilliant job you did on Sir Godwin . . ."

I gave them my best smile, and the terror left their faces like a mist blown away, leaving surprise and pleasure as they moved into the vast empty ante-room. I felt the glow spread all over me. I was going to enjoy myself.

Guests trickled in, to the sprightly strains of Gilbert and Sullivan; the band was holding back the modern stuff, saving it up for the dancing. Then a gentle steady flow which, by ten o'clock, had swelled into an in-pour. Sprinkled between the high-class nobodies – among them Sir God, a glacial entrance – the big names. "Lady *Oxford*!" . . . "Mr and Mrs Stanley *Baldwin*!" . . . ("It's good, Prime Minister, to meet you out of school . . .")

"Mr Lloyd George!" A bow of the old lion head, "Your Majesty . . ." As he moved on, a sly twinkle. In his day, those Privy Councils must have had more zing . . . "Lady *Astor*!" . . . "Mr and Mrs Anthony *Eden*!" . . . ("Mr Eden, I so much appreciate your cutting short your holiday . . .") Again I glowed.

When did the rot set in?

It was a matter of monotony. There were as many gentlemen, junior and senior, as there were ladies – had to be, for the dancing – but it became gradually obvious that the all-important element, underlining the purpose of the exercise, was the girls – the *Country Life* brigade – and their mothers or chaperones. You wouldn't believe there could be so much Peerage about.

I have in front of me nine closely printed columns of the next day's *Times*, all concerned with one subject: no, not an international crisis of prime urgency – the dresses and "ornaments" worn at my Ball, plus the dress-makers. I'll pick out a few details at random, just to give you an idea.

Baroness de Cartier de Marchiens, a gown of silver lamé, with train of real Brussels lace trimmed with silver lamé, the ornaments being diamond tiara and diamond necklace, large white ostrich fan (*Mme. Wyatt, 16 Clifford St, Mayfair*) . . . The Marchioness of Townshend-Raynham, a gown of pastel grey-blue romaine de soie with a sun-rayed skirt and close-fitting bodice, with a train of midnight-blue satin, and blue feather fan; jewels, diamonds. (*Debenham and Freebody, Wigmore St., W.1.*) . . . The Dowager Marchioness of Linlithgow, a classical gown of ivory and silver brocade, with a train of the same material lined with ivory chiffon: with ornaments, namely pearl necklace and earrings. (*Rosemary Ltd., 62 Brook St, W.1*) . . . Countess Ahlefeldt-Laurig, a gown of blue chiffon velvet, with a train lined with a deeper shade of chiffon; tiara of turquoise and pearls, and turquoise and pearl ornaments . . .

On top of that, an orgy of lace, velvet, gold tissue, ivory satin, ripple satin . . . Enough to stock a monster milliner's emporium.

The *Country Life* girls included several "Famous Beauties", each conscious of the label, you could tell from the studiedly vacant look. The others were mostly pretty, but also mostly insipid, which made it hard to tell one from another. Sadly, some of the non-pretty ones had flawless complexions, but what chance have peaches-and-cream against a lantern jaw? It was sad, too, when teeth stuck radiantly out and the bust failed to follow suit.

"How do you do, so happy to meet you, how do you do, such a pleasure, how do you do, how do you do . . ." It was rhythm without a trace of rhapsody, and I felt myself turn into an automaton, swaying politely and with a permanent smirk painted on its face. I felt as I had as that first Investiture wore on, only worse. In the distance, the buzz of low well-behaved voices. When I gave the occasional quick look, I saw the gleam of wine-glasses lifted. Champagne. But not for me. "How do you do, so glad you could come, how do you do . . ."

"Lady *Haddlewick*, Miss *Deirdre* Haddlewick!" Aunt Rose's curtsey was stiffer than it had been, and the smile as artificial as my own. She didn't like me. Dreardy bobbed cheerfully as a good little girl should, but I got the impression that she had never seen me before. On they sailed, into the main stream.

Ten p.m. After a solid hour at my reception post, I knew that the footman had put out the wrong pair of evening shoes, the ones that were a fraction too small: my feet started to throb. (At the Luncheons, I was at least seated.) I stifled a yawn, just in time, shifted from one leg to the other, lifted the free one half an inch, and swung it slightly to help the circulation. Not a Royal gesture.

The band, sawing mechanically away, was beginning to sound shrill, and hearing the distant clatter of plates, I got hungry. "How do you do, how do you do . . ."

Then, suddenly, it became obvious that I had inquired after the health of seven hundred people: my doorway was empty. The music came smartly to a halt, to a splatter of applause, and to my intense relief I saw Willie advancing. As we had arranged, I advanced too, and followed him into an adjacent ante-room where I fell into an armchair, while he uncovered a tray and poured champagne.

I guzzled. Willie looked sympathetic. "How do you feel, Sir?"

"Whacked. Our feet are killing us." In one double movement I peeled off my patent-leathers, hurled them to the floor, lay back and closed my eyes. If the Empire could see me now . . .

"A sandwich, Sir?"

I munched, then held my glass out again. He refilled it, I re-guzzled. "It's all right, Willie, I won't get drunk, but I do realize that out there I can only have one or they'll say I'm a toper, give me some more . . . You realize who's the wisest guest I've got?"

"Who?"

"The one who isn't here, the one who skipped it. Your Anne . . . What the hell happens now?"

"It would be pleasant, Sir, if when I present the first young lady to you, you would ask her for the first dance."

I glowered at him. "And when she says, 'Ta ever so' do I say, 'I'll shut my eyes and think of England'?"

"She's a good dancer, I promise you. My aunt vouched for that."

"Lady Haddlewick?"

"Yes, she made inquiries. I must say she's been the most co-operative, she's evidently facing facts about Dreardy." I drank, lay back and rested my eyes.

I must have sat there for a good five minutes, when I heard the door open. It was Willie back again, I didn't even know he had gone.

"Willie," I said, "God knows theatre people work themselves to a standstill, but even there the fifteen-hour shift is strictly for dress-rehearsals – in this lark it's fifteen hours every other day! And actors can at least belly-ache to Equity, where's *my* union? What am I called on to do next, to keep the Ball rolling – go out there and sing 'Bless the Bride'? Or recite the bleedin' Ballad of Buckingham Jail?" And more. Plebeian.

When I had worn myself out complaining how worn out I was, I opened my eyes. Old Poker-face was standing there, holding out a pair of black shoes. Not mine, half a size bigger. I blew a kiss and got into them, they felt snug and loving. Tying the laces, I pictured the lucky footman who'd been sent down to bed early, in his stockinged feet. "Willie, you're a marvel, sorry about that, once more unto the breach!"

"If, in the Ballroom, Sir, you would like to stand roughly under the middle chandelier –"

"I wouldn't like to at all, any more than I liked standing at those bloody doors for an hour of sentry duty!" But he didn't seem to notice my bad temper, which made the temper worse.

I got up, polished off a last glass and made for the door. Willie touched my arm and held out a tiny box.

I said, "What's that?"

"Cachous. Very pleasant to the taste, Sir, after shampers." I gave him a look, hesitated, took one, broke it between my teeth, and went. "Sir Digby, didn't we meet at the Opening of Parliament, your wife couldn't be there as I recall, it was a *boy* was it, I'm so happy for you both . . ."

As I advanced, heads seemed to turn automatically my way, having sensed the Royal re-entrance. I would have liked to give the impression I was returning from a telephone call on Cabinet business, hard to do; so I just looked shy and walked with Willie into the Ballroom, which was – by now – crowded all round the dance-floor. I followed him to the middle chandelier; he gave a beckoning look to a girl, and as she walked forward I heard the buzz of conversation die down, quite distinctly. People were trying to behave and not look, but I knew the eyes were swivelling.

"Your Majesty, may I present Lady Constance Wynstan-Arundell?"

I bowed, and smiled. Her curtsey was the right sort – quick, graceful, unselfconscious; and she was the prettiest in sight, with the peaches-and-cream complexion all right, but no lantern jaw, exquisite hair the colour of honey. Not tall, yet with what they call a willowy figure. I could tell she could dance.

My *Times* tells me that she was wearing a period gown of mist-blue faille, the bodice trimmed with clustered camellias of the same tone, and low at the back forming cross-over straps, with a train of silver lamé draped from the shoulders and lined with mist-blue chiffon. Ornaments: pearl necklace and white feather fan. I did notice that she carried a demure Victorian-looking posy of white flowers.

From the band, the roll of a drum. That, on top of the champagne, lifted me right up, the glow was back. The music slid softly into a seductive waltz, and suddenly everything fused into magic: the glittering crystal, the tiaras, the paintings, the wine – magic. Again I knew people were holding their breaths. I said, "Shall we?" She bowed her head, put aside her fan, and we waltzed.

Slowly, beautifully. I felt her cool breath on my neck, and was glad of Willie's cachou. And as we glided and swooped and wheeled, the whole room was as still and silent as a theatre auditorium. People at the back were craning their necks, including the waiters; even the band were fascinated. We waltzed.

I didn't want to talk, but felt I should; it would make the act look less conscious – because that's what it was – and more careless. Any conversation would do. I said, "D'you know the tune?"

"Very well, Sir." Nice voice, on the low side, "It was in a revue earlier this year, *Stop Press*, at the Adelphi." Kathy had got me and Bruce seats for an afternoon dress-rehearsal, she had a solo dance-spot to this very tune. Even at this great moment, I felt the ache. Damn . . .

I snapped my mind back to my partner. This girl was not only – obviously – eligible, she was a beauty. It only remained to be seen if she was fun.

She said, "It's called, 'You and the Night and the Music'. I forget what comes after that."

I said, conversationally, "You and the night and the music fill me with flaming desire."

A pause, a twirl and she looked up at me, I looked down at her. She giggled, I grinned. And we both knew that not a flick of an eye-lash was being missed by our public. She *was* fun, as well!

The last note died away, and as we moved to leave the floor, there came a burst of applause such as can never have echoed through these marble halls: surely their first spontaneous gesture. I just stopped myself bowing; instead, we both walked out from the dance floor as if unconscious of the heady ovation. The exhibitionist in me was back in form.

So much back, that the glow lasted for a good ten minutes.

But no longer. As Willie presented me with one prospective Queen Consort after another, and I accompanied her to the dance floor, it became clear that the delicious Lady Constance was a flash in the pan.

I had never in my life attended a dance, not even a humble hop – people in the musical theatre aren't often drawn that way; and all I'd heard about the fashionable London junkets was that during the long walks round the polite arena, the conversation was abysmal.

Well, it is. The blondes and brunettes, the tall and the short, the slim and the plump – they all said exactly the same things. If I had been told they had all been sent to one big finishing-school to learn by heart certain required phrases, and then be trained in varying the order, I'd have believed it. My own dialogue was just as vapid; I heard myself say, several times, "Nice little band isn't it? I'm told that once the pianist is good, you're halfway there."

"I'm Putting On My Top-Hat" . . . "Your Majesty, it must be jolly interesting to live surrounded by masterpieces."

"It is indeed, particularly when I have to confess that I couldn't even paint a *gate*." This sally was greeted by a tiny gale of girlish appreciation, and for a second I felt witty; but for no longer. I had struck the right note of facetious self-apology, knowing that I would be reported as "so modest and human, do you know what he said to me as we were dancing . . ." (Anyway, I had told a lie: on the Farm, I had been a wizard with a paint-brush and a gate.)

"Anything Goes, The World's Gone Mad Today" . . . Not this world it hasn't, or ever will. Fingertips touching, ever so slightly, other hand in small of back, ever so slightly. "May I say, your Majesty, that you dance beautifully?" Seven partners running said it; the last one used it a bit late, I was afraid she'd spoil the record – then out it came. And each time it happened I wanted to say, "So I damn well should, considering it was part of my job till I got into *this* lark." And I could imagine what Mummy's comment would be on that. "How jolly interesting darling, proves he's still a chorus-boy at heart, strictly below the salt my deah . . ."

"Let's Fall in Love". When that struck up, I tried – and failed – to switch off my attention. "I often think, Sir, how wonderful to be sophisticated like Gertrude Lawrence, is it naïve of me, you must have met her?" "Not at all naïve, no I never have." Once or twice during the intolerable gaps in the dialogue, I fought an urge to say, in the same chatty strain, "Lovely tune, by the way are you a virgin?" And I longed for a partner who would suddenly come out with Willie's phrase, "This music reminds me, Sir – do you miss sex?" No such fun . . . "I Can't Give You Anything But Love, Baby" . . .

Just once, for a flash, I was startled. I was trundling a young lady – a particularly ladylike one – past a portrait of Byron, and I had just made the expected inane remark about him, when she said "Mummy, Sir, says that Byron's downfall was his *bed* habits."

I nearly stumbled. "Really?" But what she had said was, "bad habits". She was refined. Too bed.

In the middle of all this, it was a relief to fit in a one-step with Dreardy. Knowing she would not utter, I enjoyed the quiet.

Between dances I kept myself on the look-out for Lady Constance, feeling that after these others, I deserved her. Settling down to my (allowed) glass of shampers, I found she was seated behind me, with her inevitable Mummy. Neither had yet noticed me there, and I heard a puzzling exchange.

"But Mummy I *need* to go!"

"Nonsense darling, you went ten minutes ago and the Ladies' Room is busy enough as it is –"

"Mummy I *have to go!*" I heard her get up, and she went. Mysterious. Did the one possible Queen Consort in sight . . . suffer from wonky water-works? Ah well . . .

But after a couple more duty-chores on the floor, my chance came. I caught sight of her approaching, evidently fresh from the Ladies' Room. Nothing could have been more graceful than her entrance: she did not walk, she floated. And as she floated, she put her exquisite face to the posy she was carrying, and sniffed the flowers. Then she saw me, stopped and smiled.

I said, "What are they?" She said, "Lilies of the valley, such a lovely scent," and sniffed again. Well, more of a sigh, a long sigh. Then we both held out our arms, moving very slightly to the music. They had just struck up "La Cucaracha": after our waltz, a tango would be the perfect switch. We were just about to glide on to the dance floor, slightly in happy rhythm, when I saw she had spilt face-powder on her upper lip.

"So sorry darling," I said, "but a white moustache isn't really you, excuse-moi . . ." I took out my crested handkerchief and flicked the powder away, leaving her more immaculate than before. And we slid on to the parquet.

The heads again turned. For a moment I thought dancers would begin to drift off, as before, and leave the two of us to give a second exhibition, which would have been tempting our luck. To my relief, they stayed put and were joined by other couples. The Baldwins made a stately duo.

My relief was not to last.

No tune could be more dance-able to than "Cheek to Cheek", and I looked forward to a second success.

But . . . something was wrong. Could it be that the future Queen Consort was strictly a waltzer? She was still floating, and the one thing you can't do to a quick-step, is to float. I faked a couple of steps, as I'd once had to do in Panto, with a poor lass who'd insisted on playing with a temperature of 103, when I had just got through.

And with this one, I was just getting through; I was grateful for the couples who kept hiding the two of us from the many watching eyes. And not a syllable out of her. I was searching for something to say, when there came a sudden throaty whisper, "This, ducky, is sheer fucking heaven!"

A minute ago I had longed for something unexpected. I'd got it.

More floating. The lovely honey-coloured hair floated on to my shoulder, while the beautiful manicured fingers of her right hand floated down from the small of my back. Down, and then round. To the front. And nested there, like a bird. And, like a bird, fluttered.

A headline hit me between the eyes. KING GROPED!!

Without removing my smile – a cardboard affair by now – I located the inquisitive fingers, hoisted them sharply into mid-air, and set out to float Lady Constance back to Mummy. Since her smile was as steady as mine, we must have looked a happy pair; it was a weavy journey, and – under the prying eyes – a long one. By dint of miming that people were inclined to bang into us as we went along, I made it.

Mummy, I thought, looked a bit tense. I bowed and moved on, making duty calls on the Devonshires, Lady Londonderry, the Westminsters, etc. Then I caught Willie's eye, and as I followed him into our little refuge I caught a glimpse of Lady Constance being grasped by Mummy and then floating out, homeward bound. When I put my hand out for champagne, Willie saw it shaking. "Anything happen, Sir?"

"On the dance floor. Lady Constance. Crutch trouble."

Anyone else would have reacted with a "Good *God*!" A slight wait, then, "Oh dear yes . . ."

"What d'you mean, oh dear yes?"

"A minute ago, in one of the cloak-rooms, I overheard a couple of chaps, both a bit squiffy. One said, 'Can Constance Wynstan-*Arundell* be a candidate?' Then the other said, 'Surely not, she's in the Dean Paul set!' "

I was lost, I could only think of the Dean of St Paul's. Then the penny dropped; the legend of Brenda Dean Paul and her brother Napper had reached the top chorus-rooms in Drury Lane Theatre. For they were the stars of what was, in 1935, a rare and exotic breed. "Drug fiends."

The penny dropped lower. On Lady Constance's joyous return from the ladies' loo, her white moustache had not been face-powder. "Then," Willie added, "the second man said, 'She's known to her friends as Cocaine Connie'."

I gobbled my champagne. I needed it. Then I said, "Doesn't quite go with a Victorian posy of lilies of the valley . . ." when the penny dropped yet again. Connie hadn't been sniffing the flowers for their scent.

Later Willie told me that the same male gossip had also muttered, "I'm told, though her people deny it, that she has quite a touch of Lesbian."

"You don't say," said the other, wiping his hands, and possibly not too bright, "mind you . . . that might not have been bad, the Royal Family was never any the worse for a spot of foreign blood."

Back to Square One.

"Life is a Song" . . . "La Cucaracha" . . . "Little Man You've Had A Busy Day" . . . The worst was over.

Was it?

"Zing Went the Strings of my Heart" . . . "Mad about the Boy" . . . "My Heart Stood Still" . . .

Three quarters of an hour after midnight. Older couples started coming up for the gracious farewell, but the dancing went steadily on, and I still had several prospective Consorts to pilot round the parquet. After Cocaine Connie, the staid little journeys were a relief. Then into the ante-room, for the medicinal breather with Willie.

Emerging from this, and turning round after bidding goodnight at the door to Ramsay MacDonald and Sir God – who seemed to have spent the evening seated on a sofa as if he had a desk in front of his stomach, you waited for the sofa to swivel under him, left right, left right – I noticed Lady Haddlewick, who was predictably here till the bitter end, pointing somebody out to Dreardy, with a gesture implying, "I wonder who she is?"

I looked, to see an older woman, tallish – no, not the Princess – showily dressed in an old-fashioned style, shaking a fan. Small tiara, white gloves; quite heavily made up, her hair arranged rather like Queen Mary's. I said to Willie, "She's well-known, looks familiar – what's her name?"

He looked. "I can't place her, the groom at the door told me she only arrived twenty minutes ago and said not to bother to announce her as it was so late, she'd been delayed at the Lithuanian Embassy."

Since the new arrival was alone, I felt it my duty to greet her; but just as I was crossing she saw a waiter with a tray, tapped him on the arm, took a glass, and walked sedately on. I thought, good, I needn't bother, forgot about her and joined Willie and Mr and Mrs Baldwin:

the P.M., conscientious as ever, had stayed late in order to straighten out, with me, a small but important detail of Protocol to do with some imminent ceremony. I said, "Prime Minister, I've seen photographs of you smoking your pipe, do please light up!" He smiled his appreciation, and fished out the pipe.

While I listened to him, Willie chatted to nice comfortable Lucy Baldwin. Our business over, we were joined by two Guards officers, from St James's Palace, in their thirties and used enough to their surroundings to relax – or near enough. So I too could relax for a moment, and even take a public glass of shampers. I felt I deserved it; I had danced with all the girls I was expected to invite, and had even coped with Cocaine Connie. We chatted. It was an easy moment.

The band finished playing "You are my Lucky Star". Faint applause. A break. Mr Baldwin got up, "Past my bedtime!", and we all got up.

Along the length of the great historic room there was wafted, on the night air, a new sound. The wail of a single violin. I tried to think what it vaguely reminded me of – so vaguely that it must be a childhood memory. I gave Willie an inquiring look, and we strolled towards the band, the Baldwins and the others drifting behind us.

On the dance area, a scattering of couples. But not dancing: looking. Watching the soloist. The whole of the band, including the violinist whose instrument had been borrowed, were watching too.

The soulful strains of "Liebestraum" reverberated among the classical paintings, the Rembrandts and the Rubenses, and well played too. The player? The mysterious aristocratic older lady who had arrived late, from the Lithuanian Embassy. Looking faultless against the background of a gigantic portrait of Victoria's Albert in his Coronation robes, she piloted "Liebestraum", without a tremor, into "In a Monastery Garden". Then I spotted, at the end of the nose, a delicate shade of mauve, to make it look smaller.

Belle.

Belle Dell the Fiddler, direct from her success in the top chorus-room, Theatre Royal Drury Lane. And it came to me why – earlier – the get-up had looked familiar. It had been borrowed – hem, line and tiara – from the Drury Lane dressing-room of the Baroness Lydyeff, of the Kingdom of Krasnia.

I had been sustained by enough champagne to imagine, for a moment, that both performer and Prince Albert were an optical illusion. Stupefied, I looked at Belle's captive audience. And thanked my stars that Sir God was out of the way.

That audience? They were fascinated. On the brink of being amused by the sight of a foreign lady of title entertaining her fellow-guests – she had to be foreign to be able to play the violin – they were also impressed by her performance. Mr and Mrs Baldwin stood politely attentive, he puffing at his pipe. They might have been watching a display at a church fête.

"Belle always plays best when she's pissed . . ." Well, she was pissed now. In Buckingham Palace.

I stole a look at Willie, he was completely at sea. I leant nearer and muttered. "*She's in drag . . .*"

Now Willie was a sophisticated man, but for once, between us, the tables were reversed: I was giving him a Vocabulary Test which was beyond him. In those days, to people in his circle, the word "drag" suggested a healthy country (and county) day with the fox-hounds. I'd got him further out to sea. "Sir, *who is it?*"

It was the moment to be explicit. "It's an elderly chorus-boy from *Glamorous Night*." The soul-searing notes of "In a Monastery Garden" wailed away.

Willie gulped. During his years of thin-ice diplomacy, he had found himself in a couple of ticklish spots; once, in a Schloss near Vienna, in the middle of the night he had been roused by an hysterical Grand Duchess in order to effect the removal, from her bed, of a Duke (not hers) who had been unexpectedly pitched, in the midst of busy Life, into idle Death. Tonight, for Willie, was something else again.

The last romantic note died away. Applause, led by the violinist in the band. At my elbow, a voice. "But there's something *odd* about her . . ." Lady Haddlewick. The soloist blew a kiss to her audience, and opened her mouth.

Then Willie, like a shot, stepped forward: loud and clear. "My dear, you've never played better" – handing the violin back to its owner – "I wanted it to be a little surprise for the King, you must be tired, a glass of wine with his Majesty?" And he held out his arm.

Belle took it, bowed loftily to the company, and they walked to the ante-room. The band played "God Save the King" – he needed saving – and I took leave of the last of my guests. The Ball was over.

But Cinderella – a new reading of the part – was still with us. I thanked the band, and was careful to look nonchalant as I strolled to the ante-room and banged the door behind me.

No need, the room was empty. And a back-door open. Trust Willie: on second thoughts, a chap who had once disposed of a Duke, nude and deceased, wouldn't have found it too difficult to spirit away a blotto female impersonator. As I walked out again, past the little lurking army of housemaids and cleaners waiting till the coast was clear for mopping and sweeping, I took comfort from the fact that nobody had heard Belle utter one word. I collapsed into bed.

But not to sleep.

Kathy and Bruce. Practical Jokers Inc . . . If you want to take an estranged friend for a ride, this prank was what the doctor ordered. Even better than ruining a costly stage tableau with a big yawn. Damn and blast her . . .

Then, before my closed eyes, there formed the picture of Mr and Mrs Baldwin, standing there placidly watching Belle's act, and I started to laugh. You had to see the funny side, *had to* . . .

Then I stopped laughing, because I was missing her. I dived into an exhausted dreamless sleep. How could any dream compete with Belle at the Royal Ball?

Next morning, I slept late, as arranged, and at noon Willie came in with the Red Boxes and List of Appointments.

The rest of his night, he filled in for me. After he had helped our music-maker to the promised glass of champagne, they had quickly left by the back-door, then down a back stairway. The descent had been a bit of a stagger, but nobody about; just as well, because one of the staggers had been more of a lurch, pitching the tight-curled wig to the bottom step and revealing the scant locks I knew well.

Out by a second back-door, to Willie's car parked in Stable Yard. He had then driven the lolling lady to her Chelsea flat. (Luckily Belle had had the foresight to transfer keys to the Baroness Lydyeff's property hand-bag.)

As soon as Willie had stopped the car outside, he had given his passenger a smart shake, which produced a mild attack of hysteria. Poor Belle must have been a sorry sight, make-up blotched with tears, wig on the blink: the stately Cinderella transformed into Widow Twankey.

Having told me all this, Willie opened a small case he had brought in: a dictaphone which (I was impressed to hear) often travelled with him, "you never know".

He then played me the record of Belle's replies to his questions; before me, I have the typed transcript which he later made for me.

His first demand, of course, concerned Kathy and Bruce, and the answer was emphatic: the escapade had had absolutely nothing to do with them. "Cross me 'eart, dear . . ." I filled up with relief; I had done them an injustice.

"Well, dear, it started – let me see – ooh I feel terrible, you're not goin' to arrest me are you, it would kill my poor old mother, she's eighty y'see . . . Oh thank Gawd . . . Yes dear I'll pull meself together, but don't call me Mr Dell, it puts me off, call me Belle . . . Well, it was like this, on the Monday it was, three nights ago, well I got to the Lane for the perf, mindin' me own business, an' there it was, a note for me – 'ere it is, in me bag, can you see by the street-lamp, oh these stays are killin' me . . .

"An' *anonymous*! IF YOU MEET GENTLEMAN IN CORNER CAFE AFTER SHOW, YOU WILL HEAR SOMETHING TO YOUR ADVANTAGE, KEEP THIS NOTE QUIET – see? Gave me quite a turn, but curiosity got the better of the cat an' there I am at 11.15, in me old mac but feelin' like Marlene in *Morocco*, waitin' for Gary Cooper.

"Well, in walks Gary's seedy old uncle, in the same mac as me, but over a black striped suit, an' talkin' ever so well-off. I sized 'im up as one o' them Whitehall queens – pardon me – who spend all day postin' off nasty forms to annoy tax-payers, an' spend all night chattin' in queer pubs an' takin' till closin' time to get to the point.

"Oh but wi' me 'e gets straight to the crunch, quite rude. 'Belle,' 'e says, wasn't that *forward* – 'Belle, d'you want to earn this?' An' before you could say Jack Hulbert 'e spreads ten fivers on the table as if they was a feather fan. I felt ever so insulted but at the same time (if you know what I mean, dear) high-priced . . .

" 'What for, pray?' I says. An' 'e says, 'For a 'armless practical joke which a certain 'Igh Personage graciously wishes to play. 'Is Majesty the K. It is 'is wish for you to get into the female attire with which you are not unfamiliar' – oh 'e *was* posh – 'and then it is 'is wish that you should bring this invitation with your name on it – Countess Something – proceed to the Palace and mingle with the guests, to whom the King will have explained the joke, you might even acquire a small decoration out of it!' Oh I *was* shocked, I did think Jack would 'ave more loyalty to 'is Crown than that, then the shock wore off and I got intrigued, it was like bein' caught up in *The Prisoner of Zenda* up to date.

"So off I go to the A.S.M. – the one that replaced Jack when Jack transferred to the Palace – an' tell 'im I've been asked to a private drag party in Mayfair, then I persuade 'im to slip me the key to a certain dressin'-room where would be 'angin' up a certain costume ('e knew I'd take good care, looks good on me doesn't it?). Well, the show over an' everybody gone, I 'ad a couple o' nips, Dutch courage, then up to the stage-door rolls the car, I creep past the fireman – in the Land o' Nod as per usual – an' I'm off.

"With the booze I got that excited, an' when the car drove right in the Palace gates, I could 'a died. But once I got up there into the middle of everythin', an' caught a glimpse of Jack, I thought, that's not Jack it's the King . . . An' I got stage-fright an' jus' walked away to the champagne, oh what a beautiful show, dear, the décor an' the *costumes*, oh I *couldn't* ha' mingled! An' the idea o' *campin'* . . . The ballroom scene in *Glamorous N.* will *never* look the same to me after this . . .

"I can only 'ope Jack got a laugh out of it, oh it *was* naughty, I'm *disappointed* in 'im, 'ow can 'e be a good King, as 'e promised on the wireless, when 'e's up to this sort o' joke?

"Apart from all that, dear, 'ow did you enjoy my performance? . . . Yes, when I didn't go in for the violin professionally it broke me mother's 'eart . . . Oh no, dear, not a word, believe me now I'm soberin' up I do realize the trouble I could get into, not a word to a *soul*, you've been so kind an' understandin', where's me other shoe – I'm ever so glad you enjoyed 'In a Monastery Garden', goodnight, dear!"

It was the truth, every word; in Belle, there was a lot of silly day-dreaming, but no trickery. I said, "I think Mr Dell'll be too frightened to talk, don't you?"

"Oh, absolutely." It was once more a comfort to know that Kathy and Bruce were out of it. But I felt vaguely alarmed, and I could tell Willie did too. A smooth posh man in striped trousers under a dirty raincoat . . . It had to be a mean little try-on, to make a fool of me.

In other words – more alarm-sounding – a plot to discredit the King of England.

CHAPTER SIXTEEN

The Pen Pal

Two days later, *Sat. 31st August 1935, 81st Day of Reign.* Waking up, I had a premonition. And grabbed the newspapers.

I was right. Had somebody blabbed?

Daily Express, William Hickey. CLEAN-UP. "*At long-awaited 1st ball of new reign, wonder which young beauty spilt face-powder on exquisite upper lip, and who was gallant gent who removed same with crested hanky?*"

But wait for the *Mail* . . . WAS IT A STRAD? "*For those who stayed to the bitter end, the highlight was a performance, on the violin, by a titled lady who bore quite a resemblance to Lady Oxford (Margot to her friends, and foes). But Lady O. is reputed not to have a tune in her head (A tongue? That's different.) Could it have been foreign royalty travelling incognito? A visiting Queen?*"

And next day, Sunday, *The People.* "*It is rumoured that the titled fiddler-ess has apartments (Grace and Favour) in the region of Chelsea. The Countess of King's Road? And who else should that Road belong to?*"

I shut my eyes. Somebody *had* blabbed. From now on, in Drury Lane and throughout the London musical theatre, Bill Dell would answer to the name of Belle, Countess of King's Road.

Keep cool Jacko, keep cool. The Palace never answers back.

But somebody's against me. Who?

". . . And our Jack, dont you take to heart the ole rubbish in the cheep papers. At that big Social you had in your Palace, well, if there *was* High Jinks – well, *why not?* I have my Faith, but I am the 1st to admit that a boy as igh-spirited as you, cannot spend his whole time bent in prayer.

"You was always playin tricks that had the cats laughin, so what if there was such jokes at your Social, such as takin away a chair just as some person is goin to set down? I used to scold you, but no real harm."

I stopped reading, for the pleasure of pulling an imaginary chair from under my Prime Minister.

"One paper (& on a Sunday too) was pokin fun on account of you allowin a Lady in with a white moustache. But how can the poor thing help herself? Many a Lady has that burden wi gettin on in life, look at our organist Mrs Pennell, a nice face but bristly. Impudence, I remain Your Lovin Mother & Subject . . ."

A loyal subject, at that. To the last ditch.

Next morning, Sunday, in the *Observer*, a short leader. But not sweet. IS CHARM ENOUGH? "*Youth is allowed its fling nowadays, but in certain cases, surely, caution should be the watchword. Our King had a sacred duty which – so far – he seems to have performed admirably (that first-rate broadcast speech!). So we can only deplore rumours which one hopes will be scotched, of dubious goings on in high places.*"

Nothing definite; just a mysterious hint, which was worse. I thought of the letters which must be piling up, signed or otherwise, and which Willie was shielding me fom.

Next morning, just as my waking thoughts started to creep towards the worry, they were pulled – hard – a different way. On a coded envelope, unfamiliar writing. Precise, careful.

And yet familiar. I'd known it as a scrawl. Kathy. I nearly knocked my teapot over. (She was always self-conscious about her handwriting, claiming that "it goes back to the Orphanage . . ." I remembered it on scraps of paper. *Milk on window-sill . . . Gone to have hair done.*)

The first paragraph displayed the same dignified hand, and she had embarked on it without addressing me, as if writing an article. And the text was as dignified as the writing; she was remembering my dictionary, and falling back on hers. The Battle of the Books, Cassell's *v.* Oxford.

"I am cognizant of the fact that I shall ultimately have to in-scribe on my envelope the words 'His Majesty the King', but I choose to temporize on that score. It frightens me."

Then the tone turned more human, and with it the calligraphy. (Good word, on the show-off side, but it's catching.)

"The reason I'm writing is that Bruce has persuaded me to, we're both worried about you. Very worried. You see, Belle came straight to us – oh she's talked to *nobody* else, but (as she explained) the fact she couldn't was driving her mad, so she had to come to the only two she could trust *not* to talk, or she would burst.

"Oh, she *is* upset, and so contrite, once she knew she'd been tricked into it. She says she would willingly give the £50 back, but of course that dreadful man will never bother her again. And she's spent it anyway. But she said for me to apologize for it all, and to say that you looked 'lovely at the Ball'.

"You are doing a wonderful job. How dare the cheap Press snipe at you, when they're aware that three months ago you were working a four-hour day (eight on the two matinee days) pulling switches and doing a couple of dances and such – and how your working day starts at seven a.m. (Bruce and I know it all) and ends at eleven p.m., sixteen hours – how *dare* the skunks try to bitch you, makes my blood boil!" [That's more like our Kathy.]

"We are both confident that you will ignore this set-back and wish you the good fortune you deserve."

Which sounded like my mother finishing a letter. Except that there was no signature, and no word of affection.

But anything was better than the nothing which had been there before. I went straight to my desk, to uncrested notepaper.

"My darling Kathy, Tell Bruce to persuade you to write again. And again. And I'll write back. And we'll forget those Diction-aries. Any minute when I'm not working, I miss you both. Your loving Jack."

Fri. Sept. 6th 1935, 87th Day of Reign. 8.30 a.m., H.M. will drive to Lancaster to inaugurate the new Langthwaite Reservoir. 1 p.m., Lord Mayor's Luncheon, then return to London by 7. 9 p.m., Great

Western Railway Centenary Dinner, H.M. will propose toast of the G.W.R.

This last turned out to be a particularly wearing marathon followed by five speeches, not including mine, each taking an average of twenty monotonous minutes relieved only by a couple of laboured quips. My effort turned out the shortest, eight minutes, but it sounded as monotonous as any.

As the evening crawled on, I could see glasses being filled and refilled, and the faces of male guests reddening and serenely decomposing under the blessed influence. For me, toying throughout with a glass of sherry, then one of white wine, then one of red, there no such short cut to dreamland; I *had* to look interested – not only was there never a moment when fewer than twenty pairs of eyes were fixed on me, any second there might come the click of a camera. I did notice, during my speech, several nodding heads. *People were getting used to me.*

An evening of interminable hell, only lightened by one exchange with the Lady on my Right, the one detail I remember. She informed me that her husband had not had a cold for ten years, his secret being the sucking of three lemons a day. I congratulated him, in his absence, and suggested he should make public an important discovery. "Oh," she said, "he couldn't do that, he passed away six years ago, pneumonia, isn't it ironic?" I agreed.

Back in my bedroom, Footman Wilkins explained that the Valet on duty was in bed with a cold and that he and Fielding were deputizing. He got me into my slippers and quilted dressing-gown as if helping a child, then noiselessly poured me a whisky and water, next to a plate of biscuits, while Footman Fielding noiselessly laid down my evening correspondence, and with it the list of tomorrow's engagements.

As they moved, I took a fleet look at one face, then at the other; indistinguishable they were too, as usual, being both blank. But for the fact that these two faces were young, they were the same as the ones which had stared at me, mildly inquisitive, all the evening. The looks I was stuck with for the rest of my life.

The two bowed and left. Noiselessly. I slumped back and drank my whisky. As I shut my eyes, I thought, this isn't natural, I'm overtired . . . Because a feeling was creeping over me, which seemed to be recurring, and it bothered me. A sensation of drifting, of . . . the present being unreal. This time it was more definite.

But my first day here, I had had an equal feeling of unreality, with regard to my previous life. Was I to end up in a vacuum?

I felt disembodied. Neither fish nor fowl, neither for land nor for sea. I started on land, I said to myself, I spent twenty-four years on land, the sea was another world . . . and here I am, swimming!

And every stroke, slow but sure, is taking me further and further away from the solid earth where I belong. The day I started off, I could see the land, crystal-clear by daylight, enough for me to wave back to the friends on the shore, loved ones I was never to see again.

Since that day – twelve-odd weeks ago – the land has been receding, just a bit, every time I look. And any minute now, it'll be just a thin line on the horizon. Then . . . nothing at all. No communication, not even a message in a bottle to catch a current.

And in front of me, nothing either. No hope of a port, no chance of loving hands held out to help me ashore, to a pub, to a stage-door, to a fireside. Oh for a slap on the back, a kiss, an anonymous kiss, anything . . .

I pulled myself together. Then for no reason, I imagined, on my bedside table, a glass of milk. The bedtime drink my mother used to coddle me with, on the Farm. It was a craving, I *must* have that glass of milk . . .

I got up, padded out into the corridor and along to a small recessed pantry, where I picked up a bottle of milk and a tumbler. I was just turning to go back, when I heard a burst of laughter. Peering through a glass partition next to me, I saw two boys in shirt-sleeves, wrestling and yapping like a pair of Cockney puppies. "Oh Jimmy give over, you twat, you'll 'ave me bleedin' arm orf!" . . . "You wait till I grab you by the balls, chum, I'll give yer what's what!"

I watched the two flushed faces, lit up and alive with laughing. They could have been in a school playground, letting off steam. Footman Wilkins and Footman Fielding.

As I moved to go, they both saw me. And they both snapped upright, in unison, and stared, panting. I watched the life drain from their faces, leaving the sweat of painful embarrassment.

As I said, "I felt like a glass of milk – please don't bother, goodnight . . ." I tried to sound friendly, but my voice sounded cold, distant.

"Goodnight, your Majesty." And I knew I was never again to catch a glimpse of those two boys.

In bed, I didn't drink the milk. It would have made me sick. Home-sick. Lying staring up at that damned coffin-lid over my head.

I thought . . . How can it end, except in death? Can't there be a twist, like in films and musical plays? Suppose a Document turns up, proving – up to the hilt – that the day my Quaker grandmother gave birth to the Duke of Clarence's son, the child turned out to be an idiot and had to be put away, and a new-born substitute was smuggled out of the Foundling Hospital round the corner – i.e. my real father, a changeling . . .

Fat chance.

Next morning, the milk looked curdled.

But next to the milk, the scrawl. Trying not to be one.

"Dear Jack." That's a bit better.

> "It was more of a pleasure than I can say, to get your letter. So Bruce has twisted my arm again, he's even suggested that if you send a second letter I must write back and so on, once a week, since it is a Royal Command.
>
> "And it's a good idea, isn't it, to make a plan like that? And it won't be like those eighteenth-century novels with two people writing reams to each other every evening in spite of the fact they were in each other's company every other day – no, this is different because, since you and I can never meet again (cue for song, but darling Jack it is true, and you knew it was true when we left you at the Palace that day, I know you did) I can put on paper what I feel, which I couldn't then. I'll also put in bits of gossip and nonsense, I know you miss all that.
>
> "And anything you write, I'll put straight under lock and key, most important.
>
> " 'Once a week?' I can hear you say, 'She'll never keep that up!' I know I won't, knowing me – all I know is, I'll try. That sentence has got too many 'knows' and I'm supposed to be a budding writer, but writing to you is different, I'll just ramble along the paper and keep the Literary Discipline (and the Dictionary, except when essential) for my daily life.
>
> "Oh that first morning, when Bruce and I read the papers and realized it *was* true, that you'd been taken from us . . . Because, my darling, that's what it was. As if you had . . . no, I won't say it. And I mustn't get sentimental or Bruce will upbraid me for it (sorry, I mean scold, Mr Cassell the lexicographer will rear his head occasionally).
>
> "But it's no good pretending, you have been taken from us.

And we miss you more than anybody would think possible. Is it, I wonder, that we value you more now because of what you've become? Which would mean that we're not quite the non-snobs we think we are . . .

"The second day, what do you think I did? I emptied that big bottom drawer – you won't remember it – and I tidied all your clothes away into it, shoes, hair-brush, the lot, down to your tooth-brush, then said *Fool* as I put it away. I'd washed some socks and shirts and ironed them (not the socks) and I put them with the rest, they're all still in there. I couldn't help myself.

"Yesterday, in Brompton Road, Bruce ran into Sally, our wardrobe mistress in *Sleeping Beauty*, she's now with *Revudeville* at the Windmill – funny you never worked there, considering your old hobby – well, she told us about a madcap female in it called Bibi La Marr, contortionist and Speciality Act, in which she's in a crinoline and whirls round by her teeth, sounds special all right, let's hope her teeth are more real than her name.

"She also does the Dance of the Seven Veils. Or *did*, she gave in her notice saying she'd seen the light and was going to turn into a Nun. ('Ah,' Bruce said, 'comin' up for the Eighth Veil!').

"Well, apparently Bibi did leave, but it wasn't religion, it was appendicitis. Except that Sally has an idea it wasn't that either, because Bibi had talked to one of the girls and you don't try to get rid of an appendix by sitting on the tops of buses jumping up and down. Sally even mentioned the word 'abortionist', very modern for her.

"But surely the one lady who could shut the door to an abortionist, is a contortionist? Bibi's back in the show, and studying to be a Buddhist.

"This morning, a photo of you bowing to the Archb. of York, and smiling as if he'd just said something funny (is that probable?). We've made a habit of cutting them out and pushing them into your drawer, there are so many we'll have to stop. Yesterday Bruce came home from the fishmonger's and I didn't know whether to laugh or cry – the man had wrapped the kippers in the *Daily Express*, and there you were, waving to us and swimming in oil. Bruce didn't like dropping you into the dustbin, but there it was.

"My darling, I did enjoy our way of life, of course I did, but

I was assuming that – like so many experiences with our kind of people – it would taper off in time, and leave a happy memory. But when I pushed that drawer shut, I knew once again that I love you, for good.

"Writing that down is already a help, thank God – I can feel the relief creeping from the paper into my pen and into my arm. Oh my darling . . . Won't be intense next time, Your Kathy."

Then Bruce. Careful, orderly.

"My dear Friend Jack, I am no letter-writer and honestly don't know what to put. Our Kathy will have told you how we miss you, but there is nothing to be done about that. Just to say that with her being up in the air one minute and down in the dumps the next – not too much of a problem – she's like the girl in *Oh Kay*, needs Someone to Watch over Her, so that someone is Yours truly. From now on she will write for the two of us, but rest assured of my thoughts. I must close now, knowing that your time is occupied. Cheerio and all the best, Your Faithful Friend Bruce."

I did my best day's work since my Accession.

Except at the Privy Council, 11 a.m. Because there, I had no work to do. Oh, those Privy Councils! It was at them that I felt the un-reality most. I would make the occasional comment or suggestion, unambitious, sensible, just to prove that my head was not empty. But I never lost my original impression of being the one schoolboy at a posse of schoolmasters. A humoured child.

Sitting in bed that night, exhausted, I opened the *Evening News*.

A blurred photo of me that morning, taken through the Daimler window at a traffic light, with in the foreground the miniature Royal Standard on the car bonnet, and the silhouette of the detective next to the chauffeur; we were in the first stage of my journey to Portsmouth, where *H.M. will inspect 2nd Battalion of the Middlesex Regiment at Victoria Barracks, Staff Luncheon afterwards.* I was looking down at my (inevitable) typed speech and memorizing it, and since it didn't include anything to amuse me, I had quite a serious look on my face. I may also have been embarrassed by having just noticed, next to the car, a red Royal Mail van, with *J ii R* on it under a big crown.

WHERE'S THAT SMILE? "*Something seems to be on the King's mind.* What *is the document? A State Paper? A worried letter from the Prime Minister?? After all, one can't be reading fan mail all the time!*"

In a rage, I tore it up, clenched my fists and leafed through another evening paper, the really gossipy one. "*If the Duke and Duchess are* not *divorcing, why the smoke if there's no fire? . . . Item – does a good dancer make a good life-partner and parent? The question is prompted by a remarkable demonstration of the art at a recent august function. Dancers . . . Jack Buchanan, Pavlova, Fred Astaire, Ginger Rogers, Massine – one somehow does not associate such worthies with the domestic virtues . . . Rumours of a rift between a certain shipping magnate . . .*"

I lay awake. *Something was going on.* Eyes shut, I kept seeing the mysterious man in the café, hunched opposite poor gullible Belle, with between them the five-pound notes "spread like a fan". And an invitation-card. Who was he? And who was the enemy employing him?

Sir God? It was true he disliked me, with enthusiasm: but he was also painfully righteous. No.

A Communist? I remembered the *Daily Worker*, on my Accession: my only bad notice. Was the man in the raincoat in the pay of the paper, bent on overthrowing the Monarchy?

Or employed by some man with a grudge against someone I've been close to?

The Beast? I opened my eyes, and in the dark I saw his face on that unforgettable First Night, staring at Kathy, the Snoring Beauty, with a look of pure hate – and who could blame him? He must well know, from the papers, that I had shared a flat with her . . . But surely a plot against the King would be a fairly roundabout way of revenging oneself on a chorus-girl? It didn't make sense.

Plot against the King . . . Revenge . . . It was out of a novel by Baroness Orczy.

Well, when you're important these things can happen. A year ago, if a madman had shot at me in the street, fatally, it would have been called murder. Now it would be Assassination.

On which thought – and it was, somehow, comforting – I switched on the light and wrote to Kathy – "As well as missing you, and Bruce, I love you" – and so we fell into the routine of a (roughly) weekly letter. I made no mention of the new worry, it would have alarmed them; instead, I told them about the White Moustache and the dictaphone record of Belle's confession to Willie, "Apart from all that, dear, 'ow did you enjoy my performance?"

Then –

> "I'm writing this at midnight, in the bed *you* would be sharing with me if the world was a different place. But I do see now what I refused to see when you both came here and said good-bye. Things can't be different and that's that, let's say no more about it, it only makes me sad.
>
> "I note that you write that I won't remember the big bottom-drawer, well in case it interests you, I do. A pile of folded-up brown paper and string, which you always put by for a rainy day; a scrap-book you'd started when first on the stage and got sick of; Bruce's School Certificate, framed, the glass cracked; a few tools, screw-driver, etc.
>
> "Does Bruce still sit in the high armchair that shows the stuffing underneath? And you in your sofa corner, with the blue cushion you made, with the bobbles? Kindly notify of any changes . . ."

It did me good to write, and I was to look forward intensely to that little weekly vigil when I would feel the tiredness seep away as I scribbled.

Thurs. Sept. 19th 1935, 100th Day of Reign. 9.30 a.m., H.M. will sit to Mr Gerald Kelly, R.A. (for hour, portrait, 4th sitting). 10.45 a.m. H.M. will receive the French Ambassador (M. Charles Corbin) and Members of War-Graves Commission. 12 noon. The Earl of Shaftesbury will have an Audience of the King and will present addresses from the House of Lords, to which His Majesty will be graciously pleased to reply. Colonel Sir Lambert Ward will present addresses from the House of Commons. Etc., Etc. . . .

And never – at all that, or at the Luncheons and Dinners – during mile after mile of talk, never one mention of the Ball.

Willie was his tactful self. "These things, Sir, come in psycho-logical waves – if you like, I'll look up some of the things they said about your great-great-grandmother and John Brown, there were even caricatures which would cheer you up considerably." But I knew that he too needed cheering up.

> "My darling Jack, You write that you love me. Well, it's reci-procated.

"I did relish your ordeal with Cocaine Connie (and we both appreciate your trusting us so implicitly that you just know it won't go any further). Since Belle can't talk about that night to a soul *but* us, she's always popping over. She swears that in the middle of 'In a Monastery Garden' Mr Baldwin winked at her, is that possible!!

"What is more believable (only just!) is that while she was standing about drinking bubbly before her act, she overheard one old boy smothered in medals say to another, 'His grandfather Clarence was homo y'know, painted water-colours!' 'What?' the other said, '*Water-colours?* He should ha' been shot!'

"Bruce has an understudy rehearsal, I'll get him to put a P.S. next time. In case you're curious, he and I are just as much brother and sister as we've been since we moved into 82a, only more so. And it seems so right somehow, don't ask me why. He's like a big handsome dependable dog without a bark, we love him don't we, only it's different. What helps it to feel right is that I've never had a brother nor him a sister, and now we have! That's not grammar but I'll leave it.

"The flat? It looks exactly the same, my darling, and Bruce and I sit just as you describe, which makes it that bit harder *not* to miss you in your low armchair with the leather thing over one arm with the brass ashtray. The only difference is over the mantelpiece – instead of that Sickert copy you never liked, a Medici print (Canaletto) of Venice, which you would love. Do you remember how we decided that Venice is what Heaven must be like, and the three of us day-dreamed that once we'd all been in a year's run, we would go? . . ."

It hadn't been a day-dream: a firm plan. Venice . . .

The Doge's Palace, a State Banquet given for me by the British Ambassador, and my Spanish no good to me. "No, Marchesa, my first visit, so restful without the cars . . ." I shivered.

Tues. Oct. 8th 1935, 119th Day of Reign. 9.30 a.m., H.M. will sit to Mr R. G. Eves, R.A. (for an hour, for portrait, 1st sitting, 4 more to follow.) 11 a.m., the Duke of Buccleuch and Queensberry will have the honour of being received, and will deliver up the Insignia of the Order of the Thistle worn by His Majesty's great-grandfather King Edward VII. 1 p.m., Luncheon Party for His Excellency the Spanish Ambassador,

the Siamese Minister and the Mexican Minister. 3 p.m., Coinage Com-
mittee Meeting, to discuss profile of His Majesty with the Mint, to be
minted on coins early 1936, Mr W. R. Dick (Sculptor) having been
suggested. (I remember there was quite a discussion as to *which* profile, there being a tradition that with each Monarch the profile should
be the opposite to the last.) *5 p.m., H.M. will preside at Council Meet-*
ing of Institute of Medical Psychology. Etc., etc.

> "Alhambra Theatre, 9.30 p.m. . . . I've got ten minutes, have
> just done my change from schoolgirl in clogs and flaxen plaits
> (this bore of a show is set in Holland, so you can imagine the
> rehearsal jokes about Dutch caps, thank God that's died down)
> and I'm dressed for the ballet after the Interval, as a Tulip (!)
> A good thing that it isn't one of your Ceremonial Musts to have
> to sit in a box at *Tulip T*.
>
> "This morning I did ballet practice here, then this afternoon
> – perfect St Martin's Summer weather – for the first time since
> you left, I went for our old Walk in the Park. Not a cloud, I
> thought of you cooped up having coffee with His Majesty's
> Ambassador Extraordinary and Plenipotentiary to Chile. (Court
> Circular.) But to me you weren't sitting there nodding and try-
> ing to remember what you'd looked up about S. America – you
> weren't there at all, you were by my side on our walk. You even,
> once or twice, pulled my arm inside yours, as you used to do.
>
> "Rotten Row, then across the Serpentine and up to the foun-
> tains, then round past Peter Pan and up to the Round Pond,
> then the Flower Walk and out by the Albert Memorial – re-
> member all the old people playing bowls, and you wondering if
> we'd ever get so old we'd be playing bowls too?
>
> "At first the walk wasn't easy, but I perked up. I can hear the
> other girls clattering up the stairs for the Interval so won't get
> any peace, love love love, and 4th love from Bruce, Kathy."

When I read that about the Park, I felt once more that dizzy feeling. Of unreality. Combined with a nameless hunger. It must be
what prisoners go through after months in solitary. It was then it
crossed my mind that while this correspondence was creating, for
me, a vital escape-hatch, it was also stirring a frustration which was
becoming unbearable. I shot out of bed, pulled on a dressing-gown,
and walked smartly out to a corridor-window overlooking the
Garden. My Garden.
As on most days, it was sunlit and at its best. Not a breath of wind,

no leaf stirring. A landscape without figures. And as I looked, I blinked. Because it wasn't a living view. It was the painting of a view. Perfectly painted at that, like those Pre-Raphaelite ones at school, Art Class: every twig, every petal standing out, just like real life only brighter. But not real life. If a human being had appeared in the distance and walked along a path, I would have been startled.

I shut my eyes. And with all my heart, and all my body, I wanted, at this minute and under this same sun, to be doing that walk in the Park. Past the trippers lying in the deck-chairs dozing over the racing and the football: past the half-naked sun-bathing bodies drugged by the heat, past the sleeping tramps and the entwined couples clamped together, without shame, by love: past the dogs frisking into the forbidden water after sticks and ploughing back to splash everybody, past kids carrying toy boats and kites to the Round Pond – people people *people*, each relaxing from a private intense life.

And as I walk, none of them turn a head. All sublimely indifferent, to unknown Jack Green . . . All? Maybe, once in a hundred yards, a girl might glance my way, or a man, thinking – where's he from, what does he do . . . To unknown Jack Green, it's a compliment.

I sent a letter by messenger.

"My darling Kathy, I sound a bit mad, but will you do something for me? The next fine afternoon, will you go again for our old Park Walk?

"Do you remember, when we used to go, how you used to tease me about not knowing a rose from a rhubarb? Well, I want you to look at those flower-beds along that Walk – whatever it's called, by the Albert Memorial. And the people you pass, as if you were describing it in a novel, good practice for your writing. It's as if I'm being starved, don't take any notice, it's not serious. The Albert Memorial, God he's my great-great-grandfather, it's too bloody much, don't forget . . ."

Th. Oct 10th 1935, 121st Day of Reign. 10 a.m., H.M. will receive the Earl of Radnor, Lord Warden of the Stannaries. 11 a.m., H.M. will hear details of Memorial Service for the Lord Cornwallis. 1 p.m. Luncheon for Canadian Pilgrims and Wives, 50 Guests. 3 p.m., Presentation, in Hyde Park, of New Colours to Battalion of Foot Guards. Final March Past of the Palace Guards. H.M. will ride back to Buckingham Palace at head of Troops.

This last, of course, was pure irony. There I was, in my Park. On a perfect afternoon, St Martin's Summer; on horseback, and on show. Travelling slowly about, inside a mobile glass bell – imagined – and spouting through a megaphone, real. "You Soldiers of the Empire will discover, in these days of peace, the same chance to distinguish yourselves as you did on the battlefield." (But, thank God, with more of a chance of getting home all in one piece.) Twice, after sudden bursts of cheering, my horse nearly bolted, but I managed. It was a relief to guess that Kathy wasn't anywhere about.

But next day, she did go round the Park.

". . . Oh Jack, the Flower Walk is gorgeous now (I started our walk that end, in reverse like we did sometimes) all sorts of autumn flowers – the names wouldn't mean much to you, but the colours! – and even a special kind of rose, so delicate you wouldn't think they'd be on the scene, so late.

"And the squirrels were scampering about, being fed by the same old girl we saw sitting there last year, 'Come along Kiddywinks, eat your din-din!' Her grey hair looked as if it hadn't been combed since you saw her last, talk about a nest! A sparrow perched on her shoulder, and seemed about to hop right in.

"This time I heard her speak, and very much the lady. Slumped next to her was an old tramp sipping something out of a bottle (not milk) and when those greedy pigeons started strutting up and she threw stuff to them, he said, 'Madam, you know they're vermin, don't you?'

" 'Vermin yourself,' she said politely, 'come along my dears, din-din!'

"You see life in the Park.

"The Round Pond, quite a breeze – oh I nearly forgot – then she said to the squirrels, 'Vermin indeed, I'm going to treat you like *Royalty*!' There now . . .

"The Round Pond. A breeze, and if you looked up, there were the children's kites biting the wind and swooping; a fleet of toy boats. Then I sat on our old bench facing the Energy Statue, next to two women with shopping-bags, one telling about her husband. 'Oh, 'e's been quite poorly, on account of the doctor findin' this vagina in 'is chest . . .' When I told Bruce this he said, very straight-faced, you know how he can surprise one sometimes – 'D'ye reckon he said, "Doctor, all those years I've wondered what it was".'

"The Statue looked glorious in the sun, the horse seemed to be vibrating, waiting to hear the starting gun. Walking along the Serpentine, north side, I could see that chariot statue at Hyde Park Corner, the winged lady (Peace?) standing on it, and I re-membered that from your side you can see it too, from your Garden. It looked miles away, which made you further still of course! Then, crossing the grass, I passed only a few yards from a boy and girl lying under a tree, she with her eyes closed and he smoothing her breasts as if they were alone on a desert island. The fountains were playing . . ."

I found it hard to read further, and laid the letter aside to finish later. Then I would put it away in the drawer with the others. They would start mounting up. And up.

For years.

CHAPTER SEVENTEEN

Uneasy Lies the Head

Fri. Oct. 11th 1935, 122nd Day of Reign. 9.30 a.m., Portrait Sitting to Mr Eves. 11.30 a.m., H.M. will inspect 1st Battalion of the King's Own Cornish Guards, at the Tower of London. Walking down the long lines of identical busbied ramrods, I wondered if my old chum Harry Kellow could be somewhere among this lot. If I had spotted him, I would not have been able to resist winking.

Back in my study for Gram and Voc, I was asked by Willie if we could make a break at five, his Aunt Rose was coming to tea.

"But Willie, I thought you found her a crashing bore?"

"Oh she is! But she wants my advice about something, and sounded fussed. One hopes that Dreardy hasn't – in an absent-minded moment – got into the family way."

He left me at five, and I was glad of the hour; I conned my speech for a particularly heavy banquet at the Egyptian Embassy, the Ambassador having expressed "a deeply cherished dream that the King will one day augustly deign to visit Cairo." At six Willie arrived back, looking distinctly worried. "Sir, may I bring in my Aunt?"

He was followed by Lady Haddlewick, dressed in . . . oh, a smart summer something – how can I remember, since every woman I met, young or older, was as smart as the last, and the next? It would have been refreshing to meet an Honourable Deb with fingers stained nicotine-yellow, or a Marchioness with a slip showing over laddered stockings. No, the nearest I'd got to a Lady who was . . . different, was Cocaine Connie.

But this time Aunt Rose was off the social gambit – positively subdued, even more worried than her nephew. I brought forward a chair, thinking how my life had enough complications, from one day to the next . . .

Willie went to the point. "I'm sorry, Sir, but my Aunt has received a disturbing letter."

Oh, God . . . I suppose because I'd thought of Harry Kellow that morning, my mind flew to him. Out of the question . . . "Yes, Lady Haddlewick?"

Without speaking, she opened her bag, took out a sheet of paper, looked at it with distaste and handed it to me. It was odd not to hear the typewriter voice, it gave dignity. And alarmed me.

Quite good writing.

> "To Lady Haddlewick. Your Ladyship, knowing that your nephew Mr W. F. Millingham is at present Private Sec. to H.M. the King, I beg leave (from me having worked for you 7 yrs ago in a domestic capacity) to approach you on a serious matter which is on my mind. (I am in financial straights owing to investments letting me down, but that is not the serious matter to which I refer.)
>
> "I will get to the point, which is that I am very anxious owing to being in possession of evidence which would be very embarasing to H.M. and dont know what to do about this. I have the idea that if the Police got to know that I am neglecting to give this evidence up to them, I am in danger of prosecution by the law. Would you kindly consult his Secretary? Perhaps he could write to me Box 526, Post Office, 11 High St, Ealing, London W5. Yours faithfully, R. S. Wardle."

I looked up at them. They waited. I had to say the word, and tried not to make it sound sensational. "Blackmail?"

Willie nodded slowly. His Aunt clasped her gloved hands, with a sharp intake of breath. I said, "Does it often come up?"

Willie thought. "Not lately – the last time, I believe, was about 1883, when your grandfather was kicking over the traces, the year before he married your grandmother."

"But I haven't been kicking over anything, I've behaved from the moment I was plonked where I am!"

"I am the first, Sir, to know that."

His Aunt spoke, for the first time. "I've never encountered such a thing before. It's frightening."

"I'm sorry," I said, "to be the cause of your being brought into it. Lady Haddlewick, do you remember this man?"

"Not at all, I'm afraid, so many changes of staff, over the years . . . Willie, what do we do?"

"It may be a try-on."

I said, "Or not." It was an unnecessary remark to make, in front of her. He thought so too: "I imagine a blackmailer makes it his business to put an ugly construction on the most innocent actions, and to call it 'evidence' until it's exposed as nonsense. It's unsettling, of course, but Aunt Rose, try not to worry, I'll look after it." She took her leave, he accompanied her out.

And it *was* unsettling. I had never been one to dwell on matters over and done with, but now I sat down to cast a steady look at what I was thinking of, by now, as "the old days". But there was so much that hadn't been important enough to stay in my mind, as an "incident".

Except one. The memory which had reared its head the evening I had thought the two Whitehall high-ups were the Police. I was again back to the party when – what was his name – Sir Simon Rawson had drugged my drink and I'd been photographed with two girls. Very dangerous.

When Willie came back, I told him. He listened with understanding, but also with the greatest concern. "I suggest a formal note from me to this box number suggesting a private meeting, and we'll wait and see."

He went, and one of the valets came in to lay out dress clothes for my stolid Middle-East evening; meanwhile, I studied a sketchy guide-book to Egypt. "It is a cherished dream of mine, Madame Fazullah, to have the Tutankhamen treasures lent to us for an Exhibition, I agree the Sphinx would be a trifle cumbersome, *vous restez longtemps en Angleterre . . .?*"

That night, for the first time since childhood, I had a nightmare. In it I stepped out on to the Palace Balcony to find an immense storm of thunder and lightning rocking the London sky. By its light, I looked down on the Mall. No carpet of human flowers, instead acre upon dark acre of gleaming twisting bodies. Snakes. Millions of eyes, glittering. Then a vile low steady noise, louder and louder. The snakes, hissing. I woke up in a sweat.

Keep busy. And thinking of Wednesday, May the 6th of next year, Westminster Abbey, I had no choice. I stayed awake.

By now Kathy and I had both waived our rule of writing once a week, we were corresponding irregularly and constantly.

". . . While I remember – tell Bruce there's a ceremony here, which makes me think of him for a quarter of an hour every morning – indeed I like to think it's in his honour, though it goes back to dear old John Brown – for that quarter of an hour, the pipe-major of the Sutherland and Argyll Highlanders plays the bagpipes outside my window! One gets used to everything.

"You mention having let your novel slide – you *must* persevere, in this last letter when you described the dresser telling you about her husband killed in the war, it came alive on the paper – you must stick to that foolscap and keep filling it up. Because, though female, you are a born writer. (That is a joke, to tease, in letters one has to be careful to make such things quite clear!)

"My darling, you are too easily discouraged, you must *not* be timid. That is, about yourself – God knows you're not, towards other people! Also I note that through writing to me in the dressing-room you were a minute late onstage for the Dutch-Clog Ensemble, and ticked off by the A.S.M. Quite right, *discipline must be maintained*. Or the show goes to pot. I'd have done the same . . ."

Wed. Oct. 16th 1935, 127th Day of Reign. Evening News: "The King today enjoyed a day of relaxation at Newmarket Races, watching the Cesarewitch". He didn't, and there was no relaxation. I hadn't warmed to the horses on the Farm, why should I start now?

Two days later, *Fri. Oct. 18th 1935, 129th Day of Reign*, and my twenty-fifth birthday. At twelve noon I stood at a window and listened to the Gun Salute from Hyde Park, and again at one p.m. to another from the Tower of London, roaring out each year of my life, through Farm and Theatre to Palace. *1.15, Birthday Luncheon Party, 50 guests, including most of Privy Council, Maharajah of Jammu and Kashmir, Duke of Braganza, etc. etc. 3 p.m. Visit to Sailor's Home, Dock St. E. 6 p.m. Audience to Mr Glyn Philpot R.A., to discuss future portrait. 8.30 p.m., Annual Dinner of Royal Marines Old Comrades Assoc.*

On my last birthday, my three presents had been a currant loaf from Mam and Dad, a sweater from Kathy and a bottle of gin from Bruce. Today, on my way to the Luncheon, I passed (no surprise to

me by now) a row of gifts which could have filled every window in
Harrods.

From my special four? Their presents, addressed to the code
number, had arrived with my breakfast. From the Farm, the currant
loaf, oven-fresh; from Yeoman's Row, two big beautiful expensive
books with paintings and photographs in colour: *Hyde Park and
Kensington Gardens, Flora and Fauna* and *Windmills of the World.*
Kathy's inscription: *In case William Hickey hears of this, these are
joint presents from Lily Langtry (London) and Mr John Brown
(Balmoral).*

I smiled but my eyes were prickly. Which was happening too
often.

Four days later, *Tues. Oct. 22nd 1935, 11 a.m. Funeral of the Duke
of Buccleuch and Queensberry. 3 p.m. Opening Ceremony of Royal Art
College, Bloomsbury Square.* Next morning, in the *Daily Express,*
under a photo of me and a simpering she-pupil of sixteen, COULD
THIS BE THE LADY HE'S LOOKING FOR? STAND BY,
1936!

On the steps of the Art College, I had been in the act of accepting,
from her, her own painting of the building, framed and hideous.
Biting into a piece of toast and studying my bemused look, I recalled that it had been caused – just as the photographer held up the
thing that flashes – by my hearing the girl behind her say, in a
strangled whisper, "Go on, kiss 'im, you *promised!*"

And in the second before the flash, I had thought, God, suppose
she does have a go, I can't score either way – if I let her kiss me I'm
letting the Cabinet down, if I don't they'll say I don't like girls. I'm
pleased to say she lost her nerve. And any minute now her painting,
together with quite a selection of my birthday presents, would be
finding its way upstairs to what Willie called the Junk Room.

I imagined it as the most enormous attic: enormous because, even
in my few months, it had been steadily fed with mementoes of my
forgotten speeches (to Distinguished Members, acknowledging Our
Great Honour and Our Great Pleasure and even Our Considerable
Emotion) and my thousands of gracious greetings and bowings.

Every single item was inscribed, for posterity. Regimental swords,
every conceivable make of gun; picnic-baskets, cuckoo-clocks,
shooting-sticks, cigarette-boxes that played – guess – "God Save
the King", cruet sets, copper kettles, meerschaum pipes; Union
Jack cushions, Red Indian head-dresses; sets of bezique, back-
gammon, dominoes, mah jong, draughts; pottery crowns, pottery

Cornish pasties – imagine that – cider mugs, paperweights, paper-knives, Toby jugs. Also, on top of the dozens and dozens of hideous framed photographs of official functions, a hundred amateur sketches of me, all with one thing in common. Unrecognizability.

There was even – a gesture from a monarch-minded toy factory – a giant doll with frilly underclothes who lay down, closed her eyes, and whispered, "Your Majesty". I had no wish to inspect the Junk Room.

Each of Kathy's letters caused a tug of longing, but they were a help.

". . . And on my way to the Alhambra this morning, I was afraid I'd be late for rehearsal (with George Gee's understudy in *Tulip Time*, G.G.'s down with 'flu) so I took a taxi. Driver said, 'This time o' day the quickest way is by Buckingham Palace and into the Mall.' 'Oh no,' I said, 'Knightsbridge and Piccadilly, *please!*'

"I was quite taken aback, I'd said it so quickly – you see, since that last day, I've not been near B.P. I want to feel I'm near you on paper, but not in actual fact. Can you understand that?

" 'Anyway,' the driver said, 'there'll be a crowd round the Palace front, isn't 'e openin' that new ward in St George's 'Ospital?' Strange, every time the King is mentioned (and he's still big news) I am somehow able to disconnect him from the 'you' I correspond with. And that's as it should be, isn't it?

"After your encouragement for my writing, what do you think? Yesterday morning, between washing up (9.30) and dusting (noon) I covered two pages of foolscap! I haven't said much about it, have I, but now that I've got to P. 33, I can, a bit. It's autobiographical, of course (what novel isn't!) but only up to a point. Neither you nor Bruce come into it, Heavens no. But I start the girl off in my Orphanage, Deptford rather than Stoke N., and I really think that marvellous Matron is beginning to come alive.

"Oh, after that I feel good! I'm going to do something I've not been up to before – that is, open that big drawer and hang everything up to air, your two suits etc. it'll look as if you're back home. Which I feel you are, when I write to you like this, but if you *were* back home I wouldn't have to write, would I? What nonsense, will finish this later.

"Later, midnight. Bruce just brought me a cup of cocoa, I'm writing this in bed. The bed you should be in, my darling, not *me* in the one *you're* in, if you follow me. I'm sipping luxuriously between sentences.

"And talking of this bed, who do you think is lying in it by my side at this minute, fast asleep? Bruce! It's like this – one night last week when I couldn't sleep he heard me crying – nothing serious – and came in and sat here till I went to sleep. And in the morning, when I apologized and explained that it was just that I hated waking up and finding myself alone in that big bed, he embarked on a serious talk with me. (What else would a talk with Bruce be, but serious?)

" 'Kathy', he said, solemn as an owl, 'I have a suggestion to make on the subject, a very *delicate* suggestion. Would it help – since we are now on a different footin' – would it help if I was to share the bed with you?'

" 'Oh Bruce!' I said – I was so touched and happy – 'of *course* it would!' (And it has helped.) 'The only thing is . . .' He looked hopelessly red and embarrassed. 'Yes, Bruce?' 'Well, you know I norrmally sleep in the nude – well, in case I might not find it easy to contrrol myself, I reckon it would be a gude idea to buy some pyjamas, don't you?' And here he is in his pyjamas, and so far they work like a charm.

"I said, 'Oh Bruce you're *beautiful*!' and he said, just as solemn, 'So I'm told, but gude looks don't last verra long' – can't you hear him? Then we discussed his future, he's typically sensible, he's getting like you were with your windmills, you remember how clever he was, tarting up the flat, well soon after you left he decorated one floor of a house for two friends, so marvellously that they urged him to take it up, and I've been prodding him as well – I just know he'll make a success of it.

"Well, next thing, the two friends put him on to a woman friend of theirs (rich, divorced) who wanted her flat done over, and she fell for him so heavily and permanently she proposed marriage. When he turned that down, she offered to keep him. You won't be surprised – knowing our Bruce – that he was mortally offended.

"But he's got fond of her 'noo she's stopped offerin' me pr-resents', and I have an idea that he'd quite like moving out, if it didn't mean leaving me on my own. But I've an idea, too, that it's still Kathy and Jack he loves best. And that any New Year, he'd still answer that his wish was that you and I would get *our* wish. I think the light being on is beginning to disturb him, so will finish in the morning.

"Morning. Oh my darling, the lady novelist has put away her ruled exercise-book and fountain pen, for the simple reason that I have in front of me, at this minute, a beautiful portable typewriter, delivered by Special Messenger from some mysterious Central Place. How did my benefactor guess that at the age of fifteen I took typing lessons, before I decided that my immediate future would be to do with feet and not with fingertips?

"Well, at the moment my life is to do with both, and you're so right to see alphabetical letters leap up in front of you and turn into printed words is magical for getting ideas in order.

"Am I the first budding writer to be getting words on paper BY ROYAL APPOINTMENT? (I won't type to you, of course, it wouldn't feel right) . . ."

Fri. Nov. 1st 1935, 142nd Day of Reign. 9.30 Final Sitting to Mr Eves. 11 a.m. His Majesty will give audience to the Prime Minister Mr Baldwin, to discuss New Year's Honours List. Etc., etc.

In between, one word rattled around in my head. Blackmail.

Next day, "Willie, when did you answer that letter, and suggest a meeting?"

"The same day we saw it."

"Eleven days ago. It's getting me down."

"Same here, Sir."

But, on the Monday, his face showed a sign of not-bad news. "Sir, I sent a man to check at the Ealing Post Office. There is no Box 526, and no F. Wardle under any other box number."

"A hoax?"

"Looks like it. A vindictive loony case. I must phone my Aunt, she'll be relieved."

I was more than relieved. Not that the threat had disappeared, it had merely moved slightly away: the negative of that photograph was *somewhere*. But I pushed that thought away. There was enough general pressure without that.

And not helped, that week, by a flare-up on the part of my Pen-

Pal. It had started from a letter of hers which struck an unexpectedly acid note.

"... *Tulip Time*'s a bore, and a boring company, and I've got a severe mental block over the novel, I stare at the page and tell myself I'm a stumbling illiterate amateur, the Orphanage refuses to come into focus.

"Also, I've just perused an idiotic article in some Woman's Page, discussing the answers to a competition on 'Who is the King's Ideal Mate?'. It starts: 'It is well-known that never a day passes without his Majesty eagerly scanning photographs and particulars of high-born young ladies who might qualify for a *Very Special Post*.'

"It goes on to say that your Ideal Mate will be flawlessly beautiful with slim *aristocratic* ankles. Now us common girls don't much care for that, because it's *just* possible to be a guttersnipe and still have slim ankles, here's one scribbling at this minute. Funny, nothing about the Sex Angle. Presumably because H.M. is indifferent to that department. But he can't be, not entirely, if there's to be an Heir to the Throne!

"Now I've got the blues again, because I realize that Bitchery will get me nowhere. Bruce keeps telling me I must try to like the idea of her, whoever she'll be. Robert Nesbitt asked me out to supper but I don't feel sociable and said no. Your loving Kathy."

I wrote back that night.

"... You should have gone to supper with Bob Nesbitt, he's not only an important young producer, he's a very nice fellow.

"I'm worried about you, my darling. Your future. Knowing the uncertainties of the profession – how lucky *I* was, to work as often as I did – well, I worry.

"I'm on delicate ground, but once again my mind goes back to last New Year's Eve, to our discussion about what we hoped for in life – and when you implied that you'd only be happy if you had security, and you used the word 'kept' – well, I'd like to think of you as *married*. Not necessarily in love with your husband, but contented. Secure.

"We've seen it happen, do you remember Betty Maloney in *The Sleeping Beauty*, who was having a fling with that stock-broker she called Monkey-face, and at the end of the run married him, and we heard she was very happy in a big house in Sunningdale and expecting a baby?

"I do think you should have a look round. Oh, I know you have your writing, and how I've bullied you about going on with it – but surely unless you're immensely well-known in another field – like Tallulah writing a novel, or Queen Marie of Rumania – it's slow work financially? *Not* security.

"My darling you're so attractive (so long as you don't speak your mind *too* often) that it'll be as easy as falling off a log.

"There, got that off my chest. Back to the grindstone. I'm in Rep, a different part every day, *and* every night . . ."

As I licked the envelope, I had an uneasy feeling that it was not the most tactful gesture I had ever made . . . Well – I thought – try and write a sensible letter any *more* tactfully! I had done my best.

Mon. Nov. 11th 1935, 152nd Day of Reign, Armistice Day. 9.30 a.m. H.M. will sit for Portrait Bust by Mr. W. R. Dick, R.A. 11 a.m., Ceremony at Cenotaph, Laying of Wreath by H.M. Etc., etc.

I soon learnt that my best, in the way of friendly advice, was not up to standard. Two days later, on my breakfast-table, a surprise. An envelope in Bruce's meticulous hand.

"My dear Friend, I hope you don't mind, but K. showed me your letter. I told her it is a *good letter*, from a busy man, but she does not agree. At the moment of writing she is curled up in her reglar corner of the sofa, scratching at her letter to you, on that big Atlas. Smoking a cig (after giving it up two months ago) and handy next to her she's got the Cassell Dic. and (watch out) a gin and water, and we know (with her head) what that does to her, I'm glad I'm not on the receiving end of *this* one.

"She has made me have a gin as well, and you know what that does to me too. What it does at this minute, is to make me say (excuse me) that she's not the only one that loves you. Forget it. All the best, Bruce."

Scanning the theatre list in *The Times*, I read "GLAMOROUS NIGHT, last 3 wks." My final link gone. And Bruce would be out of work.

I was thankful, as a Busy Man, for the busy day before me. Waiting for me at six, the letter. Before tackling it, *I* had a gin. The envelope was more than usually scrawly; I slit it open as if to extract a bomb.

It *was* a bomb.

> "Your Majesty . . . Cognizant of your manifold responsibilities, I am speechless with admiration. *How* can a youth just turned twenty-five run (at one and the same time) an Empire and a marriage bureau?
>
> "What would your Majesty suggest as my first step? An S.O.S. in the Agony Column? Or a dignified ad in *The Stage*? 'Young performer dreading her thirtieth birthday and having turned down an offer of Royal patronage, seeks the shelter of . . .'?
>
> "I was immensely cheered by your information that Betty Maloney is happily married and living in Sunningdale. (What it must be to have so many vital facts on the tip of one's tongue! Could your Majesty have spotted this one in a gossip column while scanning the paper for news of your good self?)
>
> "And how good to hear that Betty is happy in a *big house*! So perhaps the reason I'm not always on top of the world, is that the flat is so *small*. Oh, Sunningdale sounds *scrumptious*, so near Ascot, which means (natch) the Royal Enclosure. So felicitous, for by next June she'll be able to make it, having got the bun well out of the oven.
>
> "I am also fascinated by the information that I can become a best-seller by the simple process of turning into Miss Bankhead or the Queen of Rumania. But what confounds me here, is that the Queen takes second place! To an *actress*? And the Queen of R. a distant relation, surely? Oh Sir . . .!
>
> "May it please your Majesty, don't worry about me. I can always eschew both histrionics and literature, by starting a brothel in Cleveland Street and you could pop in for a chat, there might even be an old girl about who remembers your Grandad.
>
> "You're right, in that letter you were on delicate ground. And (to quote the Honourable Cocaine Connie) the fucking ice has cracked.
>
> "This correspondence must now cease, Your livid Subject."

I laid the pages down, expecting wisps of smoke to rise from them.

And Mr Cassell had done her proud. Felicitous, histrionics, eschew . . .

Eschew, wow! I must look that one up.

All of which, of course, lowered my morale even further. So much so that I made up my mind to raise it, at least a peg or two, at the Privy Council next morning. Fed up with nodding my head and making the odd remark, I decided to make a gesture. Nothing sensational, just an act of commonsense, and one which Kathy would definitely have approved of.

"My Lords and Gentlemen, I have a suggestion to make. It seems to me a shame that except for the privileged few, the nation is allowed no glimpse of the unique treasures here in the Palace. I propose that on (say) one day a week the Picture Gallery should be thrown open to the public, and that if a charge is made the proceeds should go to a charity."

You'd have thought, from their faces, that I'd suggested converting the Private Chapel into a Palais de Danse.

Sir God spoke first, of course. "An interesting idea, your Majesty, which nevertheless presents complications . . . And such a gesture, however well-meant, might in the long run involve the Administration in a problem of the invasion of Royal privacy which must be safeguarded . . ." And he waffled on to something else.

It was the politest of snubs, and made me angry. Suppose I said, "That's my wish, and will you see it's carried out?"

Looking back, I should have seen the red light.

But I didn't. So I was expected to spend the rest of my life "doing a good job", and what did that consist of? Smiling, bowing, chatting, examining machinery with unseeing eyes, planting trees, wishing speedy good health to ailing subjects, breaking champagne against ships, laying the foundation stones of nameless buildings – and next year? I tormented myself by glancing at a book on Edward Prince of Wales. "In 1925 he visited 45 countries and travelled 150,000 miles . . ." Oh, no . . . He had chafed at it all, but hadn't openly rebelled.

But then again, he had been only a Prince . . .

And didn't the official announcement always run, *His Majesty will hold a Privy Council*? But His Majesty did no such thing. He just sat there, useless.

Willie was watching me get more and more desperate, I could tell. Once he asked me if I felt I was being overworked, and I was very definite that, overworked or not, I must keep occupied. "Otherwise I'll go mad." I was using the shop-worn exaggeration, but there were moments when it didn't seem as exaggerated as all that. And unless I was to be thrown a life-line from somewhere, I was heading for a crack-up.

The life-line came. From – of all places – the Farm.

CHAPTER EIGHTEEN

Idée Fixe

Fri. Nov. 22nd 1935, 163rd Day of Reign.

"Enclosed photo in Western Morning News of you on my knee aged 2, next to phot of Queen Mary with the Prince of Wales on her knee aged 2 & underneath WHAT A LIKENESS. I do not see it, since all babies look the same.

"Your Father & Self are upset about something.

"My sister your Auntie Harriet that you staed with in Jarrow when you wus fourteen, well I inclose her leter recieved this mornin."

Auntie Harriet.

"My dear Sister and Bro, I am writing for Fergus and me, he is depressed which is most unusual, the same with me. We are all right in ourselves, it is like this.

"We have not gone harping in letters to you about the Unemployment here, the Shipyards etc, it would make such poor reading but with every year, as everybody knew it would, it has got worse, Men who fought in the Great War are dyin of starvation and – just as bad – dyin of nothing to do. They say London remembered them in 1914 when they were needed, but London has clean forgot them by now.

"It's a poor thing to say, but over the years Fergus and me have got used to it, like you get used to everything, and it takes a shock for you to see the thing as the terrible thing it is.

"Well, the shock is that last week our old friend Walter Riverthorpe, quite a scholar also choirmaster, aged only 49 and with wife and 3 children, climbed over a wall in the ship-yard area that has not been operating all these years and found a cross-beam and hanged himself. Oh the pity of it.

"Well, you know how to Fergus, being an Undertaker is just a job, well he couldnt face this and went to bed for 2 days, can you imagine that? They had to go elsewhere.

"Oh it has hit us hard. They are talking of organizing a March from Jarrow to London of the Unemployed, to prove to Parliament how bad it is, but others feel it will do no good, Fergus says people will only stand and stare and do nothing. Then he said – and he was crying, I never saw him cry before, that we should get on to our Jack will do something.

"When you think of all those pages of fuss about him in the London papers and hardly a mention of the trouble up here, it isn't right. Excuse the sorrow, Your Affec. Sister Harriet and Bro. Fergus."

I didn't eat my breakfast, I couldn't touch it. I just stared at the careful writing. And at the sober words, which understated the tragedy more effectively than a raised voice would have done: *the trouble up here, it isn't right, excuse the sorrow* . . . I looked round the room, as familiar to me by now as the farm kitchen had once been. And the same thing happened as had happened, in this very place, in the company of my parents: I saw the walls melt away and found myself somewhere else, like a dissolve in a film.

I was walking along that endless Jarrow road, past rows of faces staring at me. No uniforms, no medals, no coronets, no ermine. Cloth caps and shawls, shoes with holes. Starved shame, starved pride.

I had half an hour, and went walking in the Garden. Slowly.

No, not in the day-dream, everything had swum into sharp focus. And though my feet moved slowly, my thoughts did not. Swift, steady.

My situation during this time – such as, at this moment, finding myself strolling alone in the Garden of Buckingham Palace – of course it was fantastic enough to seem – over and over again – unreal . . . But *it was real*. I stopped and turned round. I could just see the flag Kathy had written about. The Royal Standard, floating high over the Palace, to tell London the master was at home. My flag, my Palace.

"I am the King."

I had said the words aloud, and felt growingly excited by an impulse, right inside me, which was crying for release: the only way I had ever been similarly excited, was by sex. This was new; I was aware of a part of me which had always been asleep, which I'd never attempted to shake into life. The urge to do something. *One thing.* I had never – ever – created, inside myself and on my own initiative, a determination to attain a specified goal. From the Farm I had drifted into school and then into the theatre, jobs I'd not had to fight for, they just came. Hadn't Kathy once said that since I was born under Libra, I was lazy until forced to take up the cudgels, when the whole picture might change?

It had changed. I had a fight on my hands.

Mon. Nov. 25th 1935, 167th Day of Reign. Funeral of the Admiral of the Fleet Lord Jellicoe, St Paul's Cathedral. Etc., etc.

Next morning, the scrawl. I dreaded opening the envelope.

"My darling Jack, After thirteen days of unremitting Scottish bullying, I hereby cave in. I haven't smoked since the one I was chewing when I wrote you-know-what, nor have I toyed with a gin. No question, love, of my apologizing for what I wrote, because I haven't the faintest recollection of *what* I wrote, so that takes care of that.

"My giving in to the bullying, started on Sunday, a wireless debate on 'Is the Youth of the Thirties Irresponsible?' An Oxford Don, a Judge and a doctor and a woman barrister, all pretty sharp and scathing . . ."

I thought, *scathing*. What about the letter she couldn't remember one word of?

"I was just going to switch off when I heard the words 'Our present King' and I listened. Oh, they were marvellous about you, all of them, 'integrity, humanity, modesty, dignity, patience . . .' I had a lump in my throat and I turned to Bruce, 'I *must* write and tell him!'

"And when he said, 'I was underr the imprression that the corrrespondence had ceased,' I nearly threw a book at him. (No, not the Dictionary.)

"Of course you're right, I must *not* reject the idea of a prospective husband. If it happens, I can afford to give time to my writing, which you have encouraged me about, without worrying about earning my living.

"On Wednesday mornings (matinee day) I've taken to catching the 11 bus – to Trafalgar Square – half an hour before I need. (a) so I can have twenty minutes in the National Gall. (b) so I can stand – for a minute – under Admiralty Arch, from where I can see – miles away at the other end of the Mall – B.P. with the Royal Standard flying at the top.

"The last time I did this, I found two nice American matrons doing the same thing. One said, 'That flag is to show *he's* in there! My, he's pretty . . .' Then she turned to me, 'Wouldn't you just *love* to see him in the flesh?'

"I must have gone a bit red. I muttered something like 'Oh I don't know' and went my way, matinee of *Tulip Time*. They must have thought, that's one Britisher who doesn't sound too patriotic . . . Love love love from your marriageable Kathy.

"P.S. As I started this letter in my sofa corner, I called out to B., 'If you hear a funny choking noise, it'll be me swallowing my pride'."

That cheered me immensely, and I was doubly glad to note that my pleasure was unmixed with the usual sense of frustration: which was because of the new force fermenting at the back of my mind. I longed for the off-duty chat with Willie.

He noticed something at once. "Sir, you look remarkably untired."

"I feel it. I have a plan."

I described my Tyneside visit, then read out my Aunt Harriet's letter. As I finished, I tried to steady the tremble in my voice, but did not succeed. He had listened with care. I waited. He looked thoughtful.

I said, "Well?"

"It's certainly a very disturbing situation."

"More than disturbing, surely. Shocking. And has been for years."

"I know. People are very much concerned."

For the first time, Willie irritated me. He had said it with conviction, but . . . was it my intensity which made his reaction seem a bit . . . cold-blooded?

As usual he read my eyes. "Please believe me, I am touched by your distress. It does you the greatest credit."

"Do you think others would agree with you?"

"Others?"

"The Powers-That-Be. Sir God, with behind him Baldwin, MacDonald, Neville Chamberlain, Hoare and the rest."

"They could not fail to appreciate your anxiety."

"Good. Because I intend to tackle them on the subject."

Again he did not speak at once. Then, carefully – "What procedure, Sir, had you in mind?"

"Don't be alarmed, Willie, nothing drastic. A sort of special smaller Privy Council, round a table?"

And so it was to be, a couple of days later. Seeing that I had got away with composing a speech to be read out to millions, I now wrote one to be read out to the chosen few – and a speech free of their usual rigmarole. I sat up most of that night preparing it, and the next evening corrected it and made a clean copy, like a proper writer.

"My darling Kathy, Oh I *was* glad to get your letter, I hope you didn't find your Pride too indigestible. I'm sure it wasn't that easy to chew, but I've an idea it isn't as tough as it pretends to be. And of course there could be no question of your apologizing for the previous letter, because not only have you no recollection of its contents – neither have I. It does simplify life, doesn't it?

"I certainly won't bring the subject up again, I'll just content myself wishing you everything you wish for yourself.

"Just off to shake hands with two hundred Girl Guides, care to take over? But your account of the wireless debate has done me a power of good. Kathy, I HAVE A PLAN. Will tell you more later.

"Here's to the girl with the head that spits fire, and the heart of gold. Your loving Jack. Always."

The "Council" I called was confined to Baldwin, MacDonald, and the Minister of Labour (Mr Oliver Stanley): joined by the inevitable Sir God. I sat at the head of the table, in the usual striped trousers, black coat and hard collar, like the others; Willie just behind me. He had purposely given them no idea of my intentions; I wondered if their guess might be that I had in mind an even bigger

Royal Ball, where I could show off my dancing with even more panache.

The first ten minutes were spent in sober leisurely discussion of a proposed statue and its problems, how and when the appeal for funds would be launched, and so on; during it, I noted that Mr Baldwin had a bad head-cold. The discussion over, as he blew his nose, blinked and wrote a couple of stolid words, I thought of Belle at the Ball, of the wink Kathy had written about. That imagination was even more vivid than one had thought.

I saw my chance and rose to my feet. As I did so, I glanced at Sir God; his face wore the same look of respectful wariness as on that first morning of shock. But I had changed. I was now a King. I wondered if that crossed his mind too.

"Gentlemen, with due deference to seniority, may I read you my views on something?"

One by one the heads came up; behind the gleam of spectacles, eyes blank with polite inquiry. I was once more reminded how much younger I was. They looked like a covey of sharp old birds. Then the quick exchange of looks: views, he has views?

Sir God was, as always, correct. "Your Majesty?"

"I would like to talk to you, for exactly five minutes, about the tragedy of Tyneside." In the silence, I took out my two type-written sheets; starting to read from them, I was careful to try and speak as simply as I had on the wireless. "Several years ago – and things have got infinitely worse since then – I walked along a road –"

A loud sneeze, echoing round the cathedral of a room. They were all too polite to turn a hair, except the Prime Minister himself, red and apologetic. "I'm so very sorry . . ."

". . . Next to shipyards which had been idle for many months –"

Another sneeze, louder. The culprit stuffed his handkerchief into his mouth, which meant that the next attack turned into a bellow. "I do apologize . . ." These things happen in theatre auditoriums, but there the offender can sneak abjectly out and indulge himself. Not here. "I'm so very sorry . . ."

Not a good start.

I persevered, describing that morning walk down the long straight road; reading from the two sheets of paper which later would be filed and used to give the account of it earlier in this book. Then – "If you, gentlemen, had witnessed all that, I am certain you would need no persuading from me that the situation constitutes a national disgrace."

I was not certain at all: apart from the certainty that half their attention – including Mr Baldwin's – was fixed on whether he was going to sneeze or not. I had the wrong audience; I had just seen the Labour Minister's pencil doodling on his pad. I might as well have been Shakespeare reading *Romeo and Juliet* to a round table of clergymen.

"A situation, moreover, which is the direct and appalling result of Government neglect. Money must be spent, a very great deal of money. We must act, and act immediately."

As my voice died away, I felt I had read well: firmly, but with no undue emotional emphasis. I looked round, and saw that the faces showed nothing. Dead silence. Then Mr Baldwin gave an outsize sneeze; the poor fellow must have been suffering, trying to keep it under.

A couple of embarrassed coughs, then Sir God cleared his throat. Here we go. "I venture to think that I speak for the entire Privy Council, for those present today and for those *in absentia*, when I express the sentiment that we . . ." Waffle waffle. "That we deeply appreciate the motive behind your Majesty's spontaneous expression of a natural solicitude for the underdog . . ." Get to the snub, old boy.

It came. "The ramifications of Government in relation to reforms in the immensely complex legal system of this country, are understandably not to be grasped by an outsider –"

"But we are not an outsider." In the circumstances, I felt that the "we" was called for.

A flurry from Chamberlain. "Of course not! More – if I may say so – an *in*sider!"

That sounded like prison, but I didn't say so. What I did say was, "However complex the legal system, is it not manifestly in my power, as King, to call for immediate emergency measures? I propose a meeting, later today, between myself and the Chancellor of the Exchequer."

The faces froze. No sneeze, not even a clearing of throats. I was doing something which had not happened during my speech: I was holding their attention.

Sir God spoke for them all. "Your Majesty, with all due respect, I would venture to point out that this most difficult problem can hardly vanish into thin air by means of a chat with the Chancellor." The alliteration of "chat" and "Chancellor" was lightly flicked with irony, just this side of insolence. In court, he must have made a deadly lawyer. "You see, Sir, a state of emergency is not easy to define –"

I heard my voice get louder, and didn't like that. "Would you not describe a state of starvation as a state of emergency?"

"In law, not quite yet –"

"How many people have to die before an emergency is recognized as one? Are not these shipworkers and their families more important than the exact spot in Parliament Square where a statue of Mr Asquith should stand, and where the money's coming from for it?" I was losing my temper and the Cornish accent was uppermost; Miss Fogerty would not have been pleased. My anger was turning me into a spoilt child bent on getting his way, and them into a bunch of nervous Nannies.

"Sir . . ." Chamberlain this time. "Nobody could applaud your sentiments more heartily than this assembly . . ." From the assembly, a quarter-hearted croak of "Hear hear!"

Sir God took over again. "Sentiments so well-meant as to do credit to a young man not yet versed in the labyrinth of constitutional procedure . . . In the meantime, your Majesty and gentlemen, shall we move for a moment to the question of the House of Lords Refurbishing Bill?"

And they did move on, to the urgent consideration of what kind of new cushions to be placed in rows to await the titled bottoms which might occasionally repose on them.

End of session. I got up, they got up, I bowed, they bowed, I left.

I had jumped the gun. And was I mad.

The fight was on.

Chapter Nineteen

Idée More Fixe

". . . With regard to your kind sugestion for your Father &
Self, since you are feelin so keen on buyin a house for us, then it
do seem right for us to give in, with your Father 6o next yr – so
long as there will be a nice garden for his hobby & I have my
eyesite for my Needlework & it is near St Austell since we belong here. Thank you very much. Yesterday a nice photo, you
bendin down to shake hands with a little girl . . ."

I waited for Willie to mention my late confrontation with the
Powers-That-Be, but knew he wouldn't. He was maintaining the
same inscrutably tactful stance he had kept up before I made that
wireless speech: more so.

I had ten minutes between chores, and sat and thought . . . What I
need is a guiding hand. An *old* hand, who knows enough to tell me
how to cut through the ropes and get things done. A man who
doesn't mind being called unpredictable, a hot-head . . .

And instantly I knew who he was – and who more emotionally in
sympathy with the project, than a Welshman? Lloyd George. I
looked up his letter to me all those weeks ago. *If you ever feel the need
of my advice, please send for me.*

I wrote him a note, conscious that it was a fateful gesture. "Uncle
David, the new boy appeals to the Master. Help. John R.I."

I showed it to Willie. The expected reaction: the thoughtful pause.
"You don't mind, Sir, if I say one thing?"

"Say it."

"The old boy can be very . . . persuasive. I'll make the arrangements."

". . . I was calling for Bruce last Sat. after the last night of *Glamorous N.* and ran into Ivor and he's writing a new musical play for himself and Dorothy Dickson, *Careless Rapture*, and he's going to try and work me and Bruce into it, isn't that good?

"And before then, Bruce goes straight into the Drury Lane Panto with Binnie Hale, and what do you think it's called? *Jack and the Beanstalk!*"

Mon. Dec. 2nd 1935, 173rd Day of Reign. At six in the evening he strode into my study, the Welshman of legend: the white mane flowing, the body square and peasant-strong, the seventy-two-year-old eyes gleaming with a mischievous vitality which was almost sexual. "Your Majesty, my boy!" And he shook my hand, vigorously. It was obvious to me, and touching, that he was delighted I had made my gesture. The footman served us with whisky and water, and went.

He asked after my parents, and talked of my childhood in Cornwall and his own in North Wales. "May I congratulate you, Sir, most warmly, on your wireless speech? You wish to ask for a little help?" Here was the man who had been the World Statesman who, in the eyes of the majority of the British people, had won the Great War.

I told him the whole thing: Jarrow, the street of forgotten men. The vivid old face listened and nodded, nodded and listened. I read him my Privy Council speech, and the effect was as different as fire from water. When I finished, the bright eyes had misted over. "In 1918, end of the War, I publicly said something which, for seventeen years, has echoed in my mind. I said, 'We must make this a fit country for heroes to live in.' It's true I wasn't Prime Minister for long after that, but the thought still haunts me that I could have done more. This has brought it all back to me."

I described my session with Sir God and Co., and his restless vitality came to the boil. As he paced up and down, the room became too small for him; the vitality was so strong that you felt if you touched his sleeve, you'd experience an electric shock.

"Ah, poor old Baldwin! He should have settled, years ago, for slippers in front of the fire, a soothing puff at that pipe, and a drowsy evening with any novel by Mary Webb. The trouble with them all is, they let life catch up with them and pass them by, without it ever occurring to them that it's up to them to try and catch up with life! They have the coward's fear of cutting the corners, of slashing the red tape. It was the same in the War – with the guns on the Western Front pounding so damned hard you could hear them from Kent, I'd get something like 'We feel we should adjourn while the Hon. Member makes further inquiries into the feasibility of his rather impulsive suggestion' – in the name of Almighty God! Oh my boy, you've no idea what I went through . . ."

This was all the best stuff. "Another thing," he went on, "there's every chance of a General Election next year" – and explained to my naïve mind the psychology of that, with a grin. "It means that each Party makes very careful plans!" I said, "The one thing I need to be sure of – is there enough money to cope with this crisis on the right massive scale?"

He snorted. "Of course there is, and nobody, Sir, knows that better than yourself, from those endless Red Boxes! You must have cast an occasional look at the staggering sums mentioned almost casually in document after document, and if you knew the way they can be squandered . . .

"Before the War, when I was Chancellor of the Exchequer and introduced what I called – ironically enough – the War-against-Poverty Budget, the opposition was something you wouldn't believe, the nation couldn't possibly afford this or that, it would spell ruin! Then – only a few years later – I'm Prime Minister, the real War is on: and to pay for it, untold millions gush mysteriously out, one after the other – of *course* the money's there, we're still an incredibly rich country, you've just damned well got to get *at it*! I tell you what . . ."

I had not even finished my weak whisky-and-water, but I was as elated as if I had drunk half a bottle. I understood perfectly why he had been dubbed "the Welsh Wizard"; I was hearing phrases emotional and yet practical, grappling with a fearful problem, of this minute.

He stopped pacing. "I have an idea!" And he beat a fist into the other palm, it sounded like a pistol-shot. "The man for you, my boy, is Maynard Keynes of King's College Cambridge, the most brilliant economist of the age, was at the Treasury during the War and invaluable to me, you send for him, today! Good luck!"

After he left, I sat back exhausted, and not – as so often – through boredom. Through excitement. I sent for Maynard Keynes.

Next day, *Tues. Dec. 3rd 1935, 174th Day of Reign. At 12 noon, H.M. will give audience to Sir John Reith.* I looked across at Willie. "Reith?"

"Director-General of the British Broadcasting Corporation."

"You make it sound severely official."

"He *is* severely official."

"Oh Gawd . . . What's he after being official about?"

"You will remember, Sir, that King George broadcast three Christmas Messages, with enormous effect. The Powers-That-Be felt – and I must say I agree – that your Majesty should follow suit."

"Agreed, as usual."

"It's a routine procedure. When Reith brought the suggested speech to King George, the interview lasted less than ten minutes."

The Director of the B.B.C. turned out to be official all right: a tall pillar of grey Caledonian granite. It was a surprise that he could fold up enough to sit down. "Your Majesty, I had a most satisfactory interview with Sir Godwin and the P.M." But of course. "We decided that the themes your Majesty might touch on, lightly, would be the tragedy of Abyssinia . . ." How the hell does one touch on a tragedy lightly?

"Then the eternal problem of the Irish, then a delicate indirect reference to Russia, closing with family life at this festive season." Not with my family life, I had none.

As he took typewritten sheets from his briefcase, a knock. "Sir Godwin Rodd."

My surprise must have shown. Sir God: "I telephoned your Secretary and he intimated that you would have no objection to my presence this morning." What else could Willie have intimated? "Please sit down." What else could *I* have said? I was not pleased. I went on, "Sir John was about to acquaint me with my Christmas Message by reading it out."

No reaction, except "Capital!" Sir John cleared his throat.

"I address you on this auspicious and traditional day, when our families are gathered together to exchange memories of Christmasses gone by, and to dream of Yuletides to come." The granite voice rasped on. "Let me first speak of the momentous issues which we, as a nation, face and will continue to face.

"The Abyssinian crisis, of course has loomed larger and larger, and we and our Ministers have kept well abreast of the situation and in constant collaboration with the League of Nations. The economic outlook, in spite of regrettable set-backs . . ." *Regrettable set-backs*!

It was then that I stopped trying to listen, for I had felt a click in my head. I had *heard* it, almost. I was going to do what I had done before: write my own speech. And I knew, too, what it was going to be about.

On and on, to the non-bitter end. ". . . Solidarity and freedom from panic must be the watchwords. On which optimistic note, we wish you all a happy Christmas, and for our beloved country and Empire a prosperous New Year."

I waited for him to speak first, which he did in a comparatively human voice. "May I ask if that meets with your Majesty's approval?"

I could feel Sir God's eyes fixed on me. I spoke carefully, as if he were not there, which I knew would anger him. "Sir John . . ."

Reith met me halfway, which was quick. "We are, of course, more than willing to examine any minor criticism you might think to make –"

"Sir John, it's not easy." He looked quite surprised. "Your Majesty, there is nothing, I hope, which you find too controversial?"

Too *controversial*? "No, no," I said, "now if the speech were to touch on the subject of a probable General Election next year, then that *would* be controversial."

A pause. Then Sir God's voice, with a cutting edge to it. "I understand, Sir, that you had a meeting with Mr Lloyd George?"

For the first time since his arrival, I took a square look at him. "A private meeting. Evidently not as private as I thought."

"Mr Lloyd George is a great talker."

"He is indeed, Sir Godwin, an orator."

"And a dangerous man." Reith's head was turning rhythmically from me to him and back as if watching tennis.

I said, "So I understand. *The Welsh Wizard has a morally disintegrating effect on all whom he has to deal with.*"

He stared at me. "Who said that?"

"You did."

"Sir . . . May I ask who told you?"

"Mr Lloyd George."

I was winning, a love game. He came to the point. "May I ask, Sir, if you broached the subject of unemployment in the North of England?"

"Naturally."

"Your Majesty will recall that we recently met your laudable concern for the underdog with a most sympathetic response."

I had expected that. "So sympathetic that you told me to mind my own business."

"I don't, Sir, recall any use of that expression."

"It was not used, that would have been much too direct. It was wrapped up in circumlocutions." Not a bad shot, considering. I pressed my advantage. "I took in Mr Lloyd George's point about next year's Election. Your party, the Conservatives, would prefer to wait till the eve of such an event, before promising any new move against Unemployment."

Sir God began to steam, with political indignation. "Lloyd George, as the head of a rival party, and a still-ambitious Liberal at that, may have convinced himself that this issue is a party one, but it is untrue. Lloyd George is a devious man."

"A great man."

"The two, Sir, have been known to go together." Point. "In the meantime" – and his voice was even sharper – "may we take it that what Sir John here is offering us, will be the text of your Majesty's Christmas Message?"

The direct question. I answered it carefully. "As I'm sure you are aware, Sir Godwin, quick decisions can be rash ones. I have not yet examined the text in detail."

Which was true; on the other hand, I was making no promise to do so, and then report. Double talk. Well, I had learnt from masters. And got up. "I mustn't make you late for your next appointments, is there anything else?"

They got up. They knew their power, but knew too that they couldn't say, straight out, "Listen chum, this is the speech, and either you read it out like a parrot, or it's the Tower of London." My lot, over the centuries, knew more about the Tower than they did.

Our parting was – predictably – polite. They might suspect, but couldn't be certain. The certainty being that my mind was made up. I felt sure, and secure.

Then, a cloud no bigger than a man's hand. So small that I didn't yet notice it.

". . . Bruce says this will make you smile.

"As you know, I've had a *couple* of propositions over the years, do you remember the stockbroker who wrote to me when I was in *Streamline* asking for one of my pairs of black silk shorts in the Apache dance, so he could have them made into gloves for himself?

"Well, last Friday when I got to the stage-door, an enormous bouquet of red tulips (*Tulip Time*, get it?), Constance Spry, must have cost half my week's salary, 'Thank you for the pleasure your performance has given me during 7 performances, Peter Fothergill.' I thought it was a joke for a minute, but there were the flowers, I left half in the dressing-room for the girls to enjoy and took the rest home for me and Bruce.

"Then Babs Hennery (a bit of a snob, her nose never out of the Tatler) says, 'You know dear who he is, or rather *going* to be, any minute since his Daddy is getting on for 80? The Duke of Lynchester!' I turned the card over and sure enough there was the address, Lynchester Castle, Lynchester, Suffolk.

"Well, I thought that sort of thing stopped with the Gaiety Girls and (pardon me) your great-grandfather! I must look my beau up in the Chelsea Library next time we pop in to have a look at the latest on you, also must find out how to address him and then write a thank-you note before the tulips die and I forget.

"Two of the girls have your picture over their mirror, in among Cagney and Gable and Chevalier. One asked me why *I* haven't got you over my mirror, I said I didn't know" . . .

Fri. Dec. 6th 1935, 177th Day of Reign. 9.30 a.m., H.M. will sit for Portrait (3rd Sitting out of 4) to Mr Oswald Birley, R.A., 11 a.m. H.M. will give audience to Mr Keynes. Things were moving swiftly.

And a gratifying audience it was: a quiet unassuming man in his early fifties, but looking younger. You just knew there was nothing he didn't know about finance, but he never for a moment set out to impress me, just explained things I asked about in a way I could grasp, simply, clearly.

Without mentioning my (imminent) Christmas Message, I explained that I intended, immediately after that day, to recall the same special Privy Council and face them with a concrete plan. Keynes and I then spent two hours incorporating his suggestions into a speech which I would make at that Council. Here is the relevant part of that speech.

"I have plans. *Two* plans, on a scale big enough for me to have sought expert advice. The first is Top Priority in the face of emergency: since the current Unemployment Allowances – the Dole –

are disgracefully inadequate in the face of acute hardship, these allowances must be increased, massively, overnight.

"That will serve, of course, as a powerful remedy, but a temporary one. My second plan is to look further, much further, to the one thing that must be created – the only answer. Work.

"Over this plan, which I am the first to admit is ambitious and complex, I have consulted one of our great economists, Maynard Keynes, and he has put forward many suggestions which should be immediately examined by a panel of specialists – suggestions too detailed to go into here. In these pages he has set out – one by one, simply and clearly – the salient necessities for each project. It is enough here to indicate that they cover not only plans to reopen mines and shipyards and to restore ships standing unfinished, but also the practical possibilities of supplying, for the unemployed shipworker, docker and miner, a job different from his former one *but* one using his qualifications, by building new training schools or converting derelict buildings into such schools, for the continued and valuable use of those qualifications.

"Since these include manual skills, toughness, adaptability, endurance, the workers could be siphoned into such occupations as the building trade, underground repairs and extensions, also roadworks, which would be the most suitable, involving – as it does – mountain rock-breaking and blasting. And many other businesses I can't know about. Those are my plans."

It was an inspiring two hours.

Willie didn't mention that meeting, neither did I. Any more than we'd spoken of the one with Ll.G.

It was happening more and more. He was getting very quiet, and there were fewer and fewer of the sly jokes that had brightened up many a day; I was finding it impossible to guess what he was thinking. And whereas the impassive image had formerly amused and comforted me as the essence of tact, it was now a bother.

But who was I to feel like that, when I was consciously avoiding further discussion, with him, of what was uppermost in my mind? And why? Because I could not face discouragement, and indulged in half-confidences elsewhere, expressed in phrases that sometimes struck an attitude.

"My darling Kathy, I want you both to know that I haven't written this week not because I forgot, but because something very serious is on my mind and every day getting nearer, like a first night – oh not anything alarming – on the contrary, it's exciting!

"After being thwarted 'in my job' for six months, at last I see daylight. Because the time has come when this unique and daunting position I've found myself in, with all the sacrifices it calls for – and you know that, my darling, more than anybody – well, at last it is possible for me to reap the benefits of that position, by *doing something*.

"Not for myself – hence the excitement – but for other people, a lot of them, and I love them. I won't say any more, for now. Happy Christmas, in twenty days' time! Is your wireless in trim?"

Reading that now, in the glare of hindsight, I can see that I was in a state of . . . what's the word that's always cropping up . . . Euphoria.

False well-being. A state of mind not quite normal, desperately anxious to find an outlet for stresses created by overwork and – yes – sexual frustration.

I was living on hope. And hope can get out of hand.

I now switched to a topic I still thought of as small talk, little knowing that later it was to loom larger.

"Darling, we must congratulate (no, felicitate, better) our Favourite Subject on being bunched back-stage. We have made inquiries of our Private Sec. and he assures us that the stage-door Johnnie in question is indeed no slouch, and heir to a goodly slice of Suffolk. (That, of course, don't mean a sausage where I live.)

"Don't forget to write and thank the gent, before you throw his tulips out. Because if this goes through, it'll be the biggest thing since Rosie Boote sang *Rhoda Had A Pagoda* and turned into the Marchioness of Headfort!

"If he asks you to a meal you *must* go, if only to satisfy the others in the dressing-room. I hate to sound discouraging, but if his Dad is rising 80, he'll be 50 if he's a day, tall and skinny, Guards moustache, old Etonian tie, squeaky drawl, doncher-know, how you stage people remember your lines every night beats me my deah . . .

"I meet them in dozens every day. I can't wait to hear . . ."

Next morning, *The Times*. "*We warmly welcome the official announcement that in seventeen days' time, on Christmas afternoon at 3 p.m., HIS MAJESTY will follow the precedent created by KING GEORGE V, and broadcast a Christmas message to the nation. The unforgettably vivid impact of his Accession Speech in June is still with us: an address which proved to the world that this was the voice of a young but responsible Monarch who is also of the People.*

"*The country looks eagerly forward to this unique Christmas present. Long live KING JOHN THE SECOND!*"

". . . Your Father & Self thank you very much for Xmas invitation but our idea is that we are best here where we can set by the fire & listen to you on the Wireless. Keep up your strength & Heart . . ."

With regard to the Powers-That-Be, my relationship with Maynard Keynes – I said to my pleased self – had made me even more secure.

But you never know the minute. From the other quarter, without warning, there loomed a cause for concern. Unreasonable concern too, on my part.

". . . Bruce and I are thrilled that you have a *Plan*, and are once more pleased that you trust us to keep it to ourselves. It makes all your drudgery worth while, to be able to use your position to *do* something beyond the scope of any of us. Marvellous.

"To change the subject – I've met my Stage-door Johnnie I wrote you about!

"I sent him a note – as you suggested – thanking him for the tulips, cordial but non-committal, he wrote by return asking me to lunch at the *Ivy*! My first visit to the Ivy, ever . . .

"Well I got into my best, the same I wore the last time you saw me, with the halo hat, and there was Ivor sitting facing the door, with Isabel Jeans on one side and Dorothy Dickson on the other, and as I passed he whispered, 'Our love to you-know-who!' It was a joke of course, because nobody knows you and I write to each other, except Bruce and he would never tell.

"Well, I pass Marie Tempest's table, then a table with a very handsome young star, he was looking at the menu but I couldn't place him, dark hair, bronzed, twenty-eight about, small clipped moustache, sort of between Ronald Colman and L. Olivier, I thought I wonder if he's in a show, then I went on and looked round for my aged admirer when – you've guessed it – I hear a voice, 'Miss Tripp? Good morning!' I turned round, he'd got up. Six-foot two!

"Very nice smile, lovely teeth, firm masculine lips and nice voice too, not a bit lah-dee-dah, more like a Shakespearean actor taking it quietly, if you know what I mean, really charming."

For the first time ever, she sounded . . . vapid. A vapid fan. Six-foot two, fancy. If I'm Jack, he's the Beanstalk. I had a shot at saying, "Miss Tripp, good morning!" in the manner of a titled Hamlet "taking it quietly', but couldn't make much of it. He must have what they call a velvet voice. I turned the page, with a flick.

"My first visit to the Ivy, and the surprise of his being so different meant I just couldn't concentrate on the marvellous menu!"

What was this, a gossip column in *Woman's World*? Why hadn't I, instead of being in this ridiculous man-trap – why hadn't I been discovered as a dancing star the way Jack Buchanan had been, so *I* could have taken her to the Ivy – oh no, Sandring waits till he steps on a Royal firecracker, namely the news that he has a certain Grandfather, so step this way lad – and Jack wakes up.

Too late. Somebody's got to the Ivy before me. Via inherited wealth. Oozing it. But hark at me, 180,000 acres in England alone . . . Back to *Woman's World*.

"He wasn't a bit the type you imagined, you *have* been unlucky with your aristocracy! How right you were to advise me to look around – he was so *easy*, attentive without being a fusspot – 'would you care for a dry white wine, if you would I'll get Mario to scratch up the very special one . . .' The food of course was out of this world but I hardly noticed, he was such a good talker! His father's title goes back to 1600 and something . . ."

A talker, through lovely teeth and firm masculine lips.

"Not a bit stuffy politically either, quite a Liberal, thinks it's an awfully interesting idea to have somebody like you on the throne, says it's new blood . . ."

I looked him up in Debrett's. My new blood was roughly six hundred years older than his. And boiling.

Tues. Dec. 10th 1935, 181st Day of Reign. 9.30 a.m., H.M. will journey by car to Liverpool for visit in connection with National Association of Boys' Clubs. Luncheon with Lord Mayor. Will occupy whole day. Etc., etc.

During this time, two bulky letters with outside "From J. M. Keynes, King's College, Cambridge." Though they were obviously as official as all the correspondence Willie dealt with for me before weeding it out, he left them on my desk unopened. Next to the letters, Reith's version of my Christmas Day speech; I confess it was there in the hope of reassuring Willie.

So I had extra homework: secret late-night work. Cutting, re-shaping, cutting. Rehearsing. Words, words, words . . . But as my mind raced day by day, there was the second horse between the shafts, demanding attention. Neck and neck.

I had never experienced jealousy, and had sometimes asked what it felt like. Each time, the answer had been "Painful".

Now I knew. And "painful" is the word.

"Our dear Bruce, For obvious reasons I'm addressing this to Drury Lane Th., where you must be rehearsing the Panto.

"I need your help. This titled character – is there any way you can be introduced to him, and then post me a memo? Have a shot.

"Bruce love, I *am* grateful to you for looking after her as you are doing, a big weight off my mind. Oh I know the three of us would do the same each for the other two, but I do appreciate it.

"Brucie, I ain't happy. Too long to go into, but I have a feeling you understand. Your loving Jack.

"P.S. Excuse me – is that pyjama-cord double-knotted? Please check."

I settled down to the trickier letter. I ended up rather pleased with it, but scanning it now, I don't think I hid my feelings as well as I thought.

". . . What splendid news! Well-born, cultured, tall, hand-some . . . And (I imagine) sexy . . . ? Sounds almost – it may be just me, the cautious side I get from my mother – too good to be true. Could the gent be – over the ladies – not unlike a certain gent even higher up in the social scale, my Grandad Clarence, blowing hot and then cold? Careful now.

"But look on the bright side. And since you've never been

any more of a connoisseur than I have, it's good that he's an authority on wines.

"It says in *Who's Who* that one of his hobbies is Croquet. (I didn't know it was a man's game??) Watch out my girl, I once read that once Croquet gets a hold on players it brings out the worst in them, makes them throw the mallet at their opponents. We can't have the Duchess of Lynchester presiding at a banquet with a black eye. Frankly, to me you don't suggest Croquet. Not the type.

"Talking of type, will you keep your typewriter? In the library perhaps, overlooking the Park? (It's got two Gazebos, it's in a Book of Famous Gardens lying about here somewhere.) You *must* go on with your writing, though it won't be easy with a Castle to run.

"It does sound good my darling but don't rush, you know what a creature of emotion you are. I do want you to be happy, and so does Bruce. Good luck and love, Jack."

Yes, quite a bit spilling out, from between those lines. Which I so little realized, that I was hurt by the tone of her next letter. It wasn't as bad as the blasting one, but hardly toast-warm.

". . . I'm so glad you approve of my Stage-door Johnnie, but you're jumping to conclusions darling – just because he turned out not to be a bore but an *attractive companion*, doesn't mean I plan to dive headlong into the marriage bed. I first set eyes on him exactly a week ago!

"But it's gratifying to be one of a pair openly admired – at the Ivy several heads turned to look at us and Martita Hunt stopped on her way out (he and I had sat on for ages chatting, coffee, etc.) and she said 'Bumpy darling!' and he introduced me and she said, 'It's so good to see young people at the Ivy, you make *un couple ravissant*!' (He was nicknamed 'Bumpy' as a child because he had bumps on his forehead which he grew out of.)

"Last night I took your letters out of the locked drawer and re-read the one where you so rightly advised me to 'shop around', and I must admit that this first thing that's been slapped down on the counter is not to be sneezed at. (A realistic approach of which you'll approve.)"

But, I thought, does it have to be expressed so vulgarly?

"Bumpy came to the show both Tuesday and Thursday nights, the first time with his younger brother, the second with his mother, and tomorrow night he's taking me to supper at the Embassy Club."

Then "Love, love Kathy", so scrawled as to be illegible. Absent-minded, like a signature in an autograph-book.

Nice that the bumps had cleared up . . . The Embassy Club, *well*! During the last few years Royalty had often patronized it, supping and dancing the night away, and I had once been tempted to make up a party there: it was apparently a good spot for *me* to go shopping around in, for *my* future mate. Then Willie and I had decided that it might be labelled (by public and press) a frivolous gesture; not worth it.

I wondered what Bumpy's dancing was like. And hoped it lived up to his nickname.

Mon. Dec. 16th 1935, 187th Day of Reign. Nine days to Christmas. And it wasn't shopping days I was counting. Waiting ones.

I could think of nothing else but the afternoon of December 25th. Except, of course Kathy's future, and I was thankful that the one could take my mind off the other. Every night, sitting up in bed, I worked on my couple of handwritten sheets, cutting, rephrasing, polishing by simplifications; I would then lock them up in the drawer set aside for Kathy's letters.

A third problem – minor, but obsessive – was Christmas Presents. Willie was easy, we made a pact not to exchange any, and he of course took care of the official cards I would seem to have thought of sending out – hundreds of them, I spent two hours signing, each an etching of the Palace, safe safe safe – and I imagined there were obligatory presents with a printed card – but what was I to give (a) my parents (b) Kathy and Bruce?

After a sleepless night working that one out – for my mother, a diamond ring? for Da, the contents of a hot-house in Kew Gardens? for Kathy, a life-ticket to Chanel? for Bruce, twelve cases of whisky which he would take fifty years to drink – I wrote to them all explaining that I wasn't sending anything. Yet another indication that I was getting a bit neurotic.

Back to Kathy. News from Bruce, and not reassuring.

"My dear Friend Jack, Well I have met him, came to tea after playing polo at Roehampton."

Of course . . .

"I'd brought some cakes in and China tea in case he fancied it."

Forget the props, Brucie, get *on* with it . . .

"Well, we'd had a thorough spring-clean of the sitting-room and bathroom, but left the bedroom as it did not seem necessary."

I should think so, straight from a spot of Polo and a trifle pooped, what?

"Kathy was right about him having no side, he was v. natural with me. About his looks and personality – hard to say really, me being no writer. I would say he's not quite what she had described, i.e. the Answer to a Maiden's Prayer – just a pleasant-looking chap, the public-school type but not offensive with it. Good physique, a bit heavy.

"He was something in the City but with his father being delicate he has for 2 years been running the estate, which is a full-time job. Good teeth, dark hair going a bit thin at the front. They got to chatting about books, and Kathy got what you used to call 'one of her Dictionary attacks', that's when I went into the kitchen to boil some fresh water, and when I came back he was remarking that he likes Hugh Walpole (Rogue Herries etc) because W. spins a good yarn.

"Then other authors came up, you remember those heavy books of hers, and she says, 'But nothing can compare with Proost's evocation of the past' (I think those were the words). On that he says, 'Sorry, who's Proost?' and she looks a bit disappointed. Anyway, who *is* Proost when he's at home? (I did not say that out loud.) I hardly said anything, of course, except 'Another cake?' and such. He can hardly have known I was there, and that suited me.

"Then they talk a bit about politics, Anthony Eden, Lady Astor, etc, then back to other authors, then they seemed to get into a bit of a muddle. (I don't know if this will interest you.)"

Oh it will Brucie, it will, go on . . .

"Well, Kathy mentions that hot-stuff one called 'Ulysses' and says, 'I don't agree with people who label Joyce as indecent, do you?'

"Well, Bumpy looks a bit lost and says, 'Joyce Grenfell *indecent* ?' Then he explains she's a girl our age whom he knows quite well, in journalism and does impersonations and some relation to Lady Astor, hence the confusion.

"Then Kathy says, 'No, James Joyce.' Then Conrad came up and I thought he was going to say, 'Conrad who, Veidt ?' but he didn't. Then she says, 'I do find a lot of James fairly essiteric.' (Is that right ?)

" 'Oh,' he says, quite surprised, 'you know him well enough to call him by his first name ?' Then *she* looks puzzled, 'Who ?' And he says, 'James Joyce.' 'No,' she says, 'I was referring to *Henry* James.' Too tricky for me.

"One thing for sure, he's dead keen, never took his eyes off her. Hard to tell what she feels, she's certainly not nervous with him, quite lofty really (hence the Dictionary trend) – she certainly isn't making any effort to gush over him, which could be the right technique. You could easily imagine she was the Lady of the Manor, and him one of the tenants being favoured with a cup of tea.

"He liked the China and ate four of the cakes.

"Sorry I can't give you more of a picture, this is not a good letter, though by far the longest I have ever written, Your Faithful Friend Bruce."

No, Bruce, it *is* a good letter.

I tried to feel sorry that the future Duke of Lynchester was getting a bit thin on top. I didn't succeed.

And if he's already a bit heavy, he'd better watch those cakes.

Thurs. Dec. 19th 1935, 190th Day of Reign. 10 a.m., H.M. will inspect Royal Air Force Establishments (also aircraft and crews) at Northolt and Hendon. The day ending with 8 p.m., Centenary Dinner of the Association of Municipal Corporations, Presentation and Mingling with Guests. That night, in bed, I made the final clean copy of my sheets of paper, in a round hand, almost copperplate.

Next morning, the scrawl. A second version of the tea-party. Hostess's-Eye-View.

"Well, for the first time, Bumpy came to the flat, he was so easy and knowledgeable, quite a reader, we talked about Proust, Joyce, James etc. . . . The only slight embarrassment was to do with our Bruce – oh he was a duck, shopping beforehand and running the little event as smoothly as one of your Equerries would have done.

"I hadn't noticed anything odd, but when I saw Bumpy down to his car (a sensational Rolls, plus chauffeur, quite a little crowd) he said, about Bruce – 'Nice fellow, but he kept staring at me and looking me up and down as if looking for copy for an article or something, is he all right?'

"I said that of course he was – oh I hope Bruce didn't give the impression of being smitten with him, that's not our Bruce at *all*! He's asked me to the Castle for Christmas Day, to meet his parents – but I've ducked it, it's too early, I'd be so shy with them all – and anyway I couldn't listen to your broadcast with a roomful of people I'd only just met . . ."

She had been invited to a family party. This was serious.
But get Christmas Day over first.

Chapter Twenty

Into Action and Under Fire

Wed. Dec. 25th 1935, 196th Day of Reign.

From the moment of waking, it was a unique Christmas. To begin with, since it was traditionally the one day of the year which the Monarch was free to enjoy in the bosom of his family, and since I had no family, and Willie was in the bosom of *his* family . . . once my breakfast had been brought in by Fielding – his home was up in Scotland – I spent the morning alone.

With my breakfast, the two presents I had hoped for. From my parents, a box of my mother's mince-pies; from Yeoman's Row, a fine framed photograph (taken by a professional friend of Bruce's) of the sitting-room. This caused a pang which would have distressed them. Today I must forget all that, must must.

I walked down into the brumous Garden, but it was such a . . . (Sorry, I'll cross out the "brumous", it's just that I came across it in my Oxford Dic. yesterday and rather fancied it. And "fancy" is the word for it, it means "foggy".)

Anyway, the Garden was such a bleak winter desert that soon I turned and wandered back, and down the draughty corridors to my fire. Sitting in front of it listening to the inevitable carols on the wireless, I was once more reminded of those mornings creeping slowly, minute by minute, towards a First Night: the heartbeat, the tightening, the crackle in the air.

Seizing the valid excuse that Sir God, Sir John Reith and Co must be allowed to have their midday Yuletide family dinner, at the season of the Good Cheer which they could hardly be said to exude, I was able to have my meal on my own: a sliver of turkey and a couple of my Ma's mince-pies. What a time Kathy could have had in Bumpy's castle, watching him lash into the Christmas pudding . . .

At a quarter past two I changed into a formal black suit (for the wireless) then sat waiting. The B.B.C. technicians arrived, and watching them organize their set-up, I found myself, blankly and literally, twiddling my thumbs. I welcomed the arrival of an official photographer, and posed for him sitting at the microphone.

At twenty to three, Fielding came for me; I slipped my sheets of paper into a pocket and followed him out, past a table piled with letters and greetings telegrams. We then skirted an immense glittering tinselled Everest of presents from people I did not know. Banks of flowers. The hospitals, as well as the Junk Room, were in for a bumper New Year.

In the Music Room, my handful of guests stood waiting for me. Including, of course, Sir God and Sir John Reith. All in morning dress, they were a delegation of distinguished undertakers. My Uncle Fred, the genuine article, would have looked – next to them – like Santa Claus.

A polite criss-cross of bows and handshakes, then a partaking of cut-glass thimbles of brandy, ah well since it *is* the Festive Season, here's to a post-prandial libation, what? Cheers . . . I was taking no chances, and ostentatiously asked for an orange-juice. My visitors sipped their holiday tipple as if it were Communion wine.

The conversation was even more non-existent than usual. I'm sure, Sir, you'll agree that it's strange how the old carols bring a lump to the throat, sad that such a very special birth should become every year more and more commercialized. When Fielding came up to me, I almost waited for him to say "Overture and beginners, please!" I bowed to them all, and left. And I *was* a beginner, still. After one hundred and ninety-six interminable days.

Back into the study, where the curtains were closed against the cold grey city. From my pocket I took my sheets of paper and spread them in front of me. At last, no need to hide them. This was it.

Except for Willie's absence, the same scene and procedure as for my first broadcast. The table-lamp the only light, behind me the noiseless shadowy technicians. Somebody switched on the portable wireless: a burst of audience laughter, then another joke from Arthur Askey, "which reminds me, playmates . . ."

I thought, marvellous for him to have the millions catch the end of his programme – that time I was Sandy with *Dandy and Sandy*, when we had a talking routine as well as the tap-dancing, what luck it would have been for us, to be broadcasting at this moment! . . . And then I saw, in the shadows behind their shadows, a desolate riverside with, against the empty sky, rows of rotting masts and ropes. Hanging in the middle of all that – and I was not being fanciful, it had happened – the dead body of a broken man. *I am doing the right thing.*

Big Ben died away; a blare of trumpets, the wireless clicked off, the green bulb flashed on, then off. As it did, I knew I had stopped being nervous, this was beyond nerves.

I had phrased the first paragraph formally, to be spoken formally. And in my routine reference to the religious side of the holiday, I had tried to be respectful without committing myself insincerely. From then on, I had kept the speech as simple as I possibly could.

A voice. "From Buckingham Palace. His Majesty the King."

I spoke.

"On my first Christmas as King, I am happy to join my people as you celebrate a very special birth. A birth which – as every true Christian believes – was God's gift, to the world, of a son who would inspire mankind to make that world . . . better.

"And with that in mind, as the appointed head of our Empire, I feel compelled to grasp the opportunity given me by this unique medium, to remind you of a tragedy in our midst. A tragedy which has never been adequately faced. I emphasize that there has been no guilty party; statesmen, departments, committees – all have done their best." I was bending backwards to be generous, there had been some disgraceful cases of passing the buck but no harm in being tactful. "I refer to the running sore of Unemployment."

Then, no longer formal, sitting alone with each of the listening millions, I told the story. "Once, when I was fourteen, I went to stay with my mother's sister on Tyneside . . ." It didn't take long.

"Things were bad then, but by now – the end of 1935 – they are . . . worse. We have, on our hands, a patient who is wasting away. That patient is an entire community, many of them men of forty who fought in the Great War and have since been stripped of their self-respect and cannot understand why. Unless first-aid is available *immediately*, the patient will – hopelessly, bitterly – the patient will die. The case is Emergency Number One.

"You may well be thinking, what a depressing Christmas message – it isn't! Because I am here to tell you that I, who have been called upon to be your King, am going to use my power to do something about it. Which means – and this is where I can strike a note of definite optimism – which means that you, through me, will be doing something about it too. Millions of pounds are essential – I don't have to tell you that – and the millions are there. I give you my word, *as* your King, that they are available, *now*. So I hope that every true Christian will feel – in the name of the Christ who said 'Blessed are the poor' – that the anniversary of his birth is a good time to remind ourselves that the time has come to grapple with a vital emergency. 1936 will be a good year. I promise you. My best wishes to you all."

Then the silence: the deep silence which – so it seemed, for that moment – was spread over the whole world. Then music; when I got up and turned, I remembered that after that first time, although the head man of the B.B.C. crew had been too busy to listen properly, he had given me an appreciative smile. This time, he was looking thoughtfully at the carpet.

Making my way to the Music Room, I braced myself to face the group waiting for me.

They weren't. The enormous perfect room was empty. The Monarch's guests had walked out on him.

On my way back, the mammoth pile of presents looked bigger than ever. The fag-end of the festive day, I again spent on my own. I read a bit, listened to a concert (on the wireless!), doodled an idea for wheels for a windmill, pottered. Drank, was brought something on a tray, ate mechanically and drank again.

Got quite drunk. Turned the wireless on again, heard a couple of bars of *Silent Night* and switched off. Another drink. The telephone had not rung once, it was Silent Night all right. I could have been one of those film stars so adored that nobody dares ask them out, so they spend Christmas – incredibly – alone. Or, conversely, I was an old-age pensioner in a combined room.

I had a large nightcap and went to bed. The drink induced sleep.

Next day, *Thurs. Dec. 26th 1935, 197th Day of Reign.*

Though I had slept, at seven in the morning I lurched awake, with – of course – a slight hangover. And lay inert, my mind as drained of thought as I could make it, till eight o'clock chimed and Fielding brought my breakfast.

But, since it was Boxing Day, no newspapers. No phone calls either, everybody's waiting for tomorrow's Press. I waited too, interminably.

Fri. Dec. 27th 1935, 198th Day of Reign. With breakfast, the newspapers.

Knowing that once I looked at them I would neither drink tea nor eat, I forced myself to do both, for five long minutes. I picked up the top paper.

The first thing I saw was the photo of me, very big, at the microphone, in profile, good picture, serious without being dreary; it would be in all the papers and couldn't do any harm. I looked across at the printed matter.

Often in the theatre – once more the parallel is inevitable – after a disastrous opening performance the first review you pick up with trembling fingers is, for no reason, a rave notice. WONDERFUL XMAS MESSAGE, BEST EVER!! I couldn't believe my eyes, and looked at the top of the page. The *Daily Worker*.

"*The day before yesterday, history was made. A nation hitherto blind to unpalatable facts (especially at Christmas) listened to a young man who, though holding an outdated post, has remembered that half of his heritage stems from the working classes. We salute his guts. Will his speech produce the sweeping reforms he promises us? We'll see. In the meantime, three cheers for Jack Green!*"

Well, I thought, thanks for a compliment which will get me absolutely nowhere. The *Telegraph*: ROYAL MESSAGE A DISCONCERTING SURPRISE. "*After the fatherly and comforting tones of the late King George's Christmas Message, it was a radical change to hear a young man's voice, just as measured but hardly as comforting, telling us what is wrong with our country.*"

Like a crazed flagellant baring his back for more, I offered myself to the next lash. And each stroke drew a little more blood than the last.

Mail, KING JACKANAPES! "*Reminded by the King's Accession Broadcast that he is acquainted with the French language, one hesitates to touch on the phrase 'Lèse Majesté!' Which we are about to (almost) commit by suggesting that the King* can *do wrong – he can indeed! One thinks sadly of his first wireless speech on his Accession, displaying as it did such admirable humility, and now this – a display of . . . what?*"

Of leadership! My hands were shaking. Was I being reminded that the key to Royal popularity is – humility?

Express, JACK THE BRICK-LAYER! "*We have to ask ourselves whether (however worthy the motive) Christmas afternoon is the right time to talk to millions about hardship and starvation at a moment when most of them have just enjoyed a particularly delicious Yuletide dinner?"*

Fair enough: I had been so anxious to justify my gesture in the eyes of the Christ whose Christmas it was, that I'd forgotten about Christmas Pudding.

Star, A BLIGHTED CHRISTMAS, MILLIONS OF RAISED EYEBROWS, CORNISH TERRIER BARKS UP WRONG XMAS TREE . . . *"While he spoke with restraint, His Majesty is a born actor".*

Really? Throughout those tours as Buttons, Sandy etc., my hoarded reviews had praised my dancing and my "winning personality", but not once had I been described as a born actor. *"Has the Boy King bitten off more than he can chew?"*

Morning Post. KING PUTS MINISTERS IN DOCK. THE PROMISED LAND OVERNIGHT? *"Between the quiet phrases, one sensed an antagonism towards the edifice of Democracy which, at the season of goodwill, hardly augurs well for the future. Yesterday, a well-meaning young man seems to have overreached himself and (as it were) fallen over the footlights into the orchestra pit"* . . .

As often happens, the most damning judgement was the one which seemed to be trying to be fair: the first leader in *The Times*. As I turned to it, my eye caught an obituary; the Princess ("Victoria Matilda of Meiningen-Anmisch") had died in her sleep on the eve of her 89th birthday. This hardly cheered me up, but I could at least be glad she was not reading the papers this morning.

A MAJOR BLUNDER. *"It is with real regret that we (and surely millions of his subjects) suggest that HIS MAJESTY'S 'Christmas Message' was a grave mistake.*

"Compared with other administrations, the government of this country – to any unprejudiced mind – has never turned a blind eye to the problems, social and industrial, which face any post-war nation: those problems are a constant and deeply felt responsibility –"

I stopped reading, I couldn't take any more. As I put the paper down, I knew that with the approach of 1936, life was going to quicken its pace.

In the same way that the victim of a car smash will scramble up and walk for minutes before the shock hits him, I got out of bed and went methodically through the mechanics of shaving, bathing and having my clothes handed me by Fielding. After being overworked for weeks, how was I to get through this second holiday day?

At all costs, no brooding; wait and see. This afternoon, I would do Languages, then a walk in the Garden, then a letter to Kathy. This morning? I sat down and forced myself to read: Trollope, Kathy had recommended *Barchester Towers*. It was hard work at first, but by noon I was actually enjoying the sly humour. Not one telephone call, then who should arrive but Willie.

I was startled first by his being there at all, then by his appearance: he looked haggard, as if he had not slept. I said, "But it's only the day after Boxing Day, you've got till the day after tomorrow . . ."

"I felt I must come up, in case I'm needed."

"Thank you Willie, you are needed." I plunged straight in. "You guessed I was going to cheat?"

He was just as direct. "I had a good idea. So did the others."

"Why didn't you give me your advice?"

"Because I was not asked for it. I'm here to oil the wheels, not to put a spoke in them. You followed your conscience, Sir, and that has to be to your credit."

"When I followed my conscience, was it going the wrong way?"

He was about to say "Yes", then softened the blow. "It's happened before, through history."

"Such as?"

"Christ followed his conscience, when he chased the money-changers out of the Temple."

"But Willie, wasn't that right?"

"It may have been right, but it was rude. And they didn't like it. Considerably later, an ancestor of yours followed his conscience when he attempted to seize the Tower of London by force. Charles the First."

I tried to laugh. "You mean I'm on my way to . . . Nice Christmas present!"

He seemed to set his teeth, as if he couldn't, at this moment, bear any facetiousness. I plunged again, "Willie, what do I do now?"

"The Powers-That-Be rang me up yesterday evening. The situation, Sir, is critical."

That shook me. "Critical?"

"I've just had another talk with the P.M. He would be very much obliged if this afternoon you would grant an audience to Sir Godwin and Sir John Reith."

"And himself?"

"His apologies, but he has a top priority meeting in Glasgow, with the Scottish Coal Board –"

"The Coal Board? Was this arranged last evening?"

"Sorry Sir, I'm not in a position to know."

"You bet it was, and a clever move too. There'll be a lot of pub-licity. And no harm done to the Scottish miners."

"But a little more harm done to you." He looked pale and con-cerned.

"The harm to me, Willie, is already done. Self-inflicted . . . About this afternoon – what time does the Star Chamber trial start?"

"Would three-thirty suit you, Sir?"

"It had better. I'd planned a half-hour with my Spanish records, but that can wait. Unless I'm due to be deported at once to Mexico. Shall I wear a bullet-proof vest?"

He didn't move a muscle, I couldn't blame him. After he crossed to his office, "to catch up", I went to my desk and worked on the speech I would be making at the Meeting.

After an hour Fielding brought in a letter. I told him to keep the evening papers from me. No stamp on the envelope, just the code-number, and *By Hand.*

"My particularly darling Jack, No good pretending they're not *terrible notices* because they just are, and there can't be the usual alibis – we can't blame them on the fact the Critics were drunk or came in late or left early so didn't get the plot right, or that they got into cahoots during the interval or that the show is Years before its Time – they're just *terrible notices.*

"But . . . if it's any comfort, my darling, though I was nervous when you started (and upset, of course, to hear your voice) after the very first sentence I sat riveted, I forgot it was you, and it was so obvious that you meant every word – and that's why people are mad at you. You announced what has to be done and that *you are going to do it.* At the end I was too moved to cry, or even to speak. Then Bruce said 'That was verra fine.' And coming from him . . .!

"He's going to drop this round at your place. On the chance of somebody being in. So proud of you, my darling, and Bruce says to Keep Smiling, love love love, Your Kathy."

That helped, considerably. And – not a bad sign – no mention of Bumpy. I rang for Fielding and asked him to telephone a telegram to her, *Lovely letter stop morale is high.* No signature. With the letter in my pocket, I went for my brisk two-mile walk, under grey skies, on and on past flowerless soggy brown beds, under bare skeleton branches. Even Royal gardeners can't forbid green leaves to turn yellow and abandon their posts. I hoped I wouldn't come face to face with Methuselah, this time he might not turn tail and run. Would he taunt me with a leer? Or a graveyard sigh? "Blimey you *'ave* blotted yer copy-book, 'aven't yer?" No sign of a soul.

Except for the far rumble of cars behind the high spiked wall, I might have been alone in the centre of a desert. But the walk helped; if you're a prisoner, take the exercise. Kathy was right: I had been clubbed, but the performance must continue.

3.30 p.m., Music Room. Confrontation. Rex *versus* Rodd and Reith.

The ceremonial bows were the stiffest yet. I sat, they sat, and as they produced papers I was disconcerted to see that both men looked as strung-up and exhausted as Willie did, sitting at my elbow with his note-pad. Sir God's eyes were slightly blood-shot.

A knock. The Right Hon. Viscount Sankey, the Right Hon. Neville Chamberlain. Who were, respectively, Lord High Chancellor and the Chancellor of the Exchequer. A high-powered little get-together. Sir God said, "We felt, your Majesty, that these two eminent gentlemen – to whom our thanks – should be with us today, not to participate, but to observe." To watch the fight.

Not a newspaper in sight.

I had decided to make the first move, and a crisp one. I was about to say, "My Lords and Gentlemen, shall we get down to brass tacks?" then decided it would be *too* crisp. "I suggest I aim straight away at the heart of the matter." They looked relieved. "By all means, your Majesty."

I got up and opened my folder; I had papers too. "My complete preoccupation, at this moment, is the problem of Unemployment."

Sir B.B.C. was the one to deal with that. "So one gathered, Christmas afternoon." It was just this side of insolence. If they were waiting for me to climb down, they were in for something.

"My Lords and Gentlemen, what I said, then, is too fresh in your minds for me to have to repeat my speech to you now. All I will say is, that I stand by it, every word."

It was like flinging down one of those gauntlets, and I meant it that way. They sat like statues. "I will only remind you of one sentence. 'We have on our hands a patient who is wasting away, and unless first-aid is available immediately, the patient will die.'"

That had to have some effect, enough to push me forward. "I have plans. Two plans . . ."

And I read those plans out, the ones I copied for you – increase of allowances, restarting mines, miners switched to building, road-works, etc., etc. As I read, Keynes' brilliant practical vision gave my voice the confidence it needed. "Those are my plans."

And I sat again. The ball was in their court.

Silence. A silence so cold that it could have been waiting for the drip-drip from stalactites. I was determined not to speak before one of them did, and glanced from one to another, as impersonally as I could. They evidently did not need to exchange looks.

Sir Godwin Rodd spoke. "Your Majesty." Correct, as usual; but there was the shade of an intonation which said just that, "I'm being correct, as usual" . . . "Your Majesty, let me say, before we proceed, how impressed we all are" – the sugar before the pill – "by the thoroughness of your suggested plunge into the troubled waters of economic and social reform. But I have regrettably to break it to you . . ." The pill, smoothly held out between fastidious fingers. . . . "To break to you that the Prime Minister wishes me to express his grave concern and displeasure –"

That hit me. "If he . . ." Keep the voice down . . . "If he feels like that, why isn't he here, instead of up North furthering the interests of a political party?" And that hit *them*.

I pursued my advantage. "Which causes us to express *our* displeasure. And whose displeasure comes first? I would remind the Prime Minister, and you, his colleagues, that while the King rules this country, as his family before him – the oldest Royal House in Europe for over nine hundred years, and when I said that over the wireless after my Accession, nobody contradicted me – I would remind the Prime Minister that *his* title is non-existent, the law of this country is unacquainted with it. The phrase 'Prime Minister' was first coined by Disraeli when he signed the Treaty of Berlin fifty-seven years ago. And Disraeli was an upstart. Mr Baldwin is merely my Senior Minister."

They did look a bit taken aback, at such proof that the schoolboy had been burning midnight oil. But their recovery was a swift one, and Sir God was as bland as a blancmange. (As a child, how I hated them!)

"Forgive me Sir, for suggesting that (a) that was an amusing quibble which might have done credit, in the House of Commons, to a back-bencher, (b) your historical research might have been better directed – before your Majesty embarked on the most rash speech in living memory – to the standard works which the Cabinet so strongly recommended to your Majesty."

He paused in order to produce, from his brief-case, two books. My two heavy friends, Bagehot and Kerr-Mallinson, on the Constitution. "I remember," I said, "I read them soon after my Accession –"

"If I may say so, *not carefully enough*." That was rapped out. "We'll come to that in a moment. Let me first – if I may, Sir – impress upon you that we feel – and we have the whole of the Cabinet behind us – that we feel, emphatically, that your Majesty is living in an unreal world."

Still wearing the gloves, but a jab straight from the polite shoulder. I thought of the times when I *had* felt unreal . . .

"Are you saying, Sir Godwin, that to face squarely the necessity to deal overnight with a national disaster, is to live in an unreal world?"

"We are all, here, familiar with – and deeply concerned about – the situation in question, but . . ." He turned to Reith. "Sir John." They were as thick as thieves.

Sir John took his cue. "To help your Majesty to understand that the view Sir Godwin has just expressed – of your own mistaken attitude – is not exaggerated, I draw your attention to a disagreeable fact. Throughout your Christmas Message, I had – sitting next to me with the requisite machinery – my head engineer; he was there in case of emergency. Two emergencies approached, and each time I held my hand. Had that hand fallen, your speech would have been – all over the world – faded out. Obliterated."

I tried to ease the strain out of my voice. "May I ask if I uttered a word never before heard over the wireless – a word unfamiliar to any respectable listener? Please make yourself clearer."

"With pleasure." He consulted a paper. "The first occasion was when you declared to the world that . . . 'Millions of pounds are essential . . . and the millions are there. I give you my word, as King, that they are available, now.' "

I said, "But that is a statement of fact –"

Sir God looked at me over his pince-nez. "It is not, *it is not*." It was the Civil Service speaking: accusing, withering.

I was bewildered. "Are you implying that this country cannot *afford* to salvage a disaster on British soil? Are you under the impression that all these weeks, I haven't taken in the contents of those endless Red Boxes? Documents where the millions are shovelled out as if they were shillings and pence? Millions for Army, Navy, Air Force, Government Buildings, Purchase of Treasures, Restoration of Ecclesiastic Property, money poured into every kind of ostentatious display, from the Coronation down –"

"Your Majesty!" They were all shocked, I suppose quite rightly: I was on the edge of something I had hoped to avoid. I was about to lose my temper.

Sir God's face had gone a dull purple. "We can only be thankful that this meeting is *in camera* . . . Sir, it would take me wearisome hours to explain, to a novice, the intricate ramifications of the English legal structure: ramifications with which I have had to make myself familiar years before your Majesty was born: the thousand careful sub-clauses – and sub-*sub*-clauses which exist in order to forestall abuses – oh, endless, has it not crossed your mind how long it takes for the simplest reform to be voted through the two Houses? You must surely have observed the frequency of the expressions, *Second* Reading of Bill, *Committee* Stage of Bill – all representing a veritable log-jam of legislation!"

I *must* fight back. "Will you answer one question – suppose that telephone rang now, this minute, to inform me, and you, that a foreign power has just declared war on Britain, and that we must declare war back . . . would the millions not be automatically available? And would not the essential Acts of Parliament be rushed through at express speed?"

"Certainly." They all looked at me as if I had asked why Newton's apple fell to the ground. "War is war, and produces emergency laws, automatically."

"And peace is peace? When my starving subjects can wait?"

A shrug. "I'm afraid so, short of martial law. And anarchy."

I tried another tack. "Lloyd George got things done!"

"He did indeed, and I have no doubt that he reminded your Majesty of the fact. I've no doubt, either, that he failed to remind you that the reason he *could* get things done was – precisely – that there was a war on. A war in which he was allowed to play the part of Dictator. After 1918, he found his position very different, which is why he is now . . . out."

I was losing. He went on, without mercy. "No, your Majesty is an idealist, and it is impossible to argue with naïveté. Which brings us to the second public statement in the course of the broadcast, which so alarmed Sir John here: when you spoke the words, 'I, who have been called upon to be your King, am going to use my power'."

I was again bewildered. "Are you trying to tell me that I am not the King? That there is no such thing as the Royal Prerogative?"

Another pause, while he drew *The Times* from his briefcase, open at the leader page. He read out, from the part I had not reached in the morning, when I had put the paper aside. "*Yesterday's Royal speech, from a source which (from time immemorial) has been rightly regarded as above politics, can only be viewed as a public attack.*

"*We move on to an even more serious aspect of the case. It must be obvious to anyone with knowledge of the way our country is run, that this unfortunate gesture was made – in medias res – without any consultation with, or advice from, the institutions which are there for that very purpose. The incident must be viewed with the gravest concern.*' "

Not for nothing had *The Times* been nicknamed "The Thunderer". Another pause, while he opened Kerr-Mallinson at a bookmark. " 'The British Constitution, representing a democracy headed by Royalty, is a unique phenomenon, admired and envied by the rest of the world, by reason of the completely special relationship between King and State, a relationship befitting a Constitutional Monarchy.

" 'The People speak, through the Prime Minister' – on whose office, Sir" – he looked at me sternly, over his pince-nez – "we were pained, just now, to hear you pour some scorn – 'through the Prime Minister, the Cabinet and the two Houses of Parliament. The King is loved by his people, personifying as he does the perfect father and embodying the middle-class ideals of domestic virtue, good works and discipline.' "

I felt impelled to speak. And said the wrong thing. "I feel a bit young for a Father Figure!"

The Judge pounced. "May I suggest, your Majesty, that that could be the trouble?"

Having scored, he went on. "Oddly enough, your Majesty will find, under a glass case in the Blue Room, a Cabinet Paper in which King George recommended to the Cabinet that work should be created for the unemployed. *Recommended*, mark you, *not* commanded – ah here we are . . ." He read again, this time from Bagehot. "It is the Sovereign's duty to advise his Prime Minister and his Cabinet: to advise, encourage and warn . . ." Then he looked up and his voice rang out like brass. "But . . . *not to dictate. The King has no power. He reigns, but he does not rule.* So can you wonder, Sir, that on Christmas

Day Sir John Reith was appalled when you used the words 'I, who have been called upon to rule, am going to use my power' et cetera?"

He closed the book. "King George knew his Bagehot from cover to cover, it was his Bible. And as for the Royal Prerogative to which your Majesty referred, King George (by reason of the early enlightenment of which you, Sir, were so sadly deprived) understood it perfectly. He understood that though, *in theory, the King can act as he feels (without the permission of Parliament) either by Order in Council, Proclamation or Sign Manual* – in reality, and we have in the end, to get back to reality, the Royal Prerogative is . . . obsolete.

"In conclusion, your Majesty . . . The young are understandably inclined to regard any man over fifty – particularly if he is a statesman – as an old fogey." Twitching smiles, all round. "It is a little ironic, seeing that the Divine Right of Kings is as dead as the dodo, that your Majesty should yesterday have made a speech three hundred years behind the times.

"The King-Emperor is a beloved Symbol, and no more. And I can assure your Majesty that if your predecessor on the Throne had heard your Christmas Message – had listened to you make impossible promises (over the air, to the world, without having consulted one single Minister) he would have been inexpressibly shocked and distressed. Having heard your defence of that speech, Sir, I can only respectfully repeat that a King of England who has convinced himself that he can reform his country, single-handed and overnight, is living in an unreal world. I don't think we need usurp any more of your Majesty's valuable time."

One after the other, he took up his two Bibles and banged each one shut. The schoolboy took the hint and dismissed himself, his knuckles smarting from the invisible rulers with which his masters had steadily rapped them. Rulers for the Ruler who does not Rule.

Willie stayed behind with them. Returning to my study, trudging along my endless corridors (of No Power), I looked into one of the gigantic mirrors, framed in gold and ormolu, and was surprised to see myself. The glass should have been empty.

I walked on, to my Red Boxes. A Symbol. And (I felt, at this moment in history) not much beloved.

CHAPTER TWENTY-ONE

Waiting for the Verdict

I sank heavily into an armchair, as I had done so often after a big day. But this time it was more than tiredness. I was battered. Punch drunk.

So might as well get properly drunk. It was only four o'clock, but I drank a large whisky which had no effect at all. Willie arrived, paler and more drawn than before.

I raised my glass to him. "I'm trying to get plastered."

"I can't blame you, Sir. Godwin Rodd is a cruel man."

"Willie, this is awful for you. I'm sorry."

"I blame myself for not having put you firmly in the picture about the Constitution and all that. When I gave you the Bagehot and the Kerr-Mallinson, I thought that would do it."

"Well, it didn't, I skipped. No, I'm the one to blame – over that broadcast, I had no business to keep you in the dark . . . When you described it all as a machine, how right you were. I'm caught in it good and proper, aren't I? I mean 'good and proper *am I not*' . . . Will you go back to your family for the rest of the day?"

"No, Sir, the P.M. wants me to stick around."

Which sounded serious, but it did mean that Willie would be within reach through the yawning week-end I had on my hands. A note from Lloyd George.

> "Your Majesty, I'm sorry you have been misunderstood. I hadn't thought you would go as far as you did; if I had seen the speech beforehand I could have helped you to put the points

more diplomatically. We politicians have to be experts at that! Be tough, my boy, pick up the pieces and get on with it. Your Uncle David."

I showed it to Willie before he left. "You once warned me against flattery, was he flattering me? If he was, I certainly fell for it."

"Let's say that he meant well." . . . Alone, before pouring a second drink, I wrote to Kathy.

". . . You've always said the trouble with me is that I'm a sunny-headed optimist – well, at this minute you'd find no trouble with me at *all*. Through ignorance and wishful thinking, or (depends how you look at it) through colossal conceit, I have made a fool of myself on a scale (thanks to a little contraption called the Wireless) unknown in the previous history of the world.

"On consideration, I've done it through conceit. My crown has gone to my head.

"If you beat your skull against a wall, all that happens is, you're a hospital case; the wall stays as it was and always will be, it's called Tradition. They're a smug lot, Sir God and Sir B.B.C. and most of the others, but they know the ropes and they call the tune. I was living in Cloud-Cuckoo-Land. To hell with Christmas, and ban all radio-sets everywhere!

"What did I think I was doing, when I'm nothing more than a smashed electric bulb, for the simple reason that I have *No Power*? There's a Junk Room here, for useless old presents – well, I feel I'm one more present to Buckingham Palace that's heading that way. I'm as low as I can go. I'll write when (and if) I pick myself up . . ."

I was wrong, I was to go lower. I gave up attempting to get drunk enough to forget my problems, and tried Trollope again. It began to get dark. I could hear the rain outside, but I hadn't the heart to turn lights on. A knock, it was Footman Fielding, looking worried and uncertain. "I beg your pardon, your Majesty, there's a crowd at the Gates."

I felt my hands clench. I was in no mood to be booed. "Have you any idea who they are?"

"I took the liberty, Sir, of slipping on a raincoat an' goin' out and minglin' for a bit. A couple told me they're Tyneside people living in London and wi' relatives up there, an' that they're hopin' you'll come out on the Balcony for a minute."

I followed him out and along the empty echoing corridors, dimly lit over the holiday and draughtier than ever. He unlocked the windows and I stepped out.

By the light of the Gate lamps, I could distinguish a huddle of heads. There were probably a hundred of them, but from this height they looked a mere handful. I remembered that other time, in July. As far as the eye could reach.

They looked up, saw me, and cheered. Lustily, so that a meagre gathering seemed to swell into a multitude. I waved to them. And they sang. In harmony, *God Save the King*. The many times I had heard it since my Accession, I had of course been excited; but as these voices wafted up through the bleak London evening, I felt the tears come into my eyes. I was moved, deeply and not for myself. Moved out of pity, out of grief.

As the last note died beautifully away, I blessed the architect who had designed the enormous Forecourt between the Balcony and the Gates, so that a speech from me would be out of the question. I waved again, for almost a minute, and when I stumbled backwards into the room, they were still cheering. I followed tradition (yes, Tradition!) by waiting a little as the cheering continued, and then taking an extra call. I waved again, then again retreated; crossing to a corridor, I felt I was walking back to the star dressing-room. If only . . . if only I were . . .

But there was none of the exhilaration which players can delight in after a reception as loving as that. As I passed a couple of Staff, I found it hard to control the gulping sob which kept pushing up into my throat, like hiccups. I hurried into my bedroom and threw myself on the bed.

I thought of Christmas Day: of what I had said, to Tyneside. "1936 will be a good year. I promise you."

I let the sobs do their damnedest.

Sitting with Willie, I wondered if he had heard the cheering from his office, but did not mention it. I said, "I've nothing till Monday, have I? The National Monuments Luncheon at Londonderry House?"

He hesitated. And these days, damn it, he was always hesitating. "I'm afraid, Sir, it's off."

"Off? Thank God – is Londonderry ill?"

"No, Sir." More hesitation. "You are."

"Me?"

"It seemed prudent to issue a bulletin that the Royal Physician Lord Dawson of Penn has advised a week's rest. Overwork."

"Suits me . . . No, it doesn't, of course it doesn't . . ."

"It appears that feelings are running so high that the Powers-That-Be feel it would be unwise for your Majesty to venture out in public before the New Year."

"What do you mean, feelings are running high?"

"There is a very sharp difference of opinion. The younger generation and the working classes are for you, while the older lot, the Traditionalists . . ."

"Are behind Sir Godwin Rodd?"

"I'm afraid so. There's already been a clash in a big crowd outside the House of Commons – nothing serious, but . . . ominous."

"Willie, this is terrible."

"I know."

He had dinner with me, but it was not a good idea. We were bad for each other.

And when I finally got to sleep I had a nightmare, about those snakes, then woke up with a piercing sense of foreboding. Remembering vaguely a certain sword I'd read about somewhere, I got out of bed and looked it up. "*The Sword of Damocles* hung above the hapless courtier by a single hair; at any moment the hair would snap and he could be decapitated."

I wished I hadn't bothered. Goodnight, my great-great-ever-so-great Grandad. Charles the First.

My Black Christmas was over. But the interminable abysmal week-end which followed was as bad; I was not to see Willie again, it rained every day and all day, and – since I had requested "*No newspapers*", and found no difficulty in keeping away from the wireless, it meant living in a self-imposed void. In the circumstances, I welcomed it. I recall only two things.

Sat. Dec. 28th 1935, 199th Day of Reign. From the Farm, the expected reaction.

"It was not quite what your Father & Self was expectin, nor anybody else, I reckon. I could only think of your Auntie Harriet ect in Jarrow & sayin, God bless the King.

"Your Fathers idea is that you acted rite tho it brought a sad note to the happiest day of the year esp. for the children what with carrols & presents & mince pies. Well I make a good Mince Pie as you well know but the Lord understands, so never mind the Mince Pies, think of the Loaves & Fishes, Your Lovin Mother & Subject . . ."

The second thing I remember was just silly – and yet it was to turn out to have its own importance. The continuous rain meant that I could not even indulge in the penance of striding round and round the desolate dripping garden, which would at least have done my body some good; so by Sunday afternoon my feet were itching for any kind of violent exercise – anything to drive the thoughts out of my ailing mind. As I sat inert in an armchair, they started to tap.

On an impulse, I leapt up and crossed to a cupboard which I knew contained a stack of old jazz records; Willie had told me that the Prince of Wales used to put them on as an accompaniment to his ukulele. I fished out "Mountain Greenery", from *The Girl Friend*, wound up the portable gramophone which I had never played, and the tinny music filled the room.

I rolled back the rugs, placed myself in front of the long mirror, as I had done years ago to rehearse with Eric Dandy for *Dandy and Sandy* – whatever happened to Dandy? – and started to dance. It was misery, I was falling over myself like the rankest amateur – such misery that I set my teeth, started the music again and went on and on; until, suddenly, something clicked, feet and brain flashed recognition at each other . . . and I danced. I was hoofing it with Dandy, on the stage of the Chelsea Palace.

One by one the swift routines came back – *watch that shuffle-hop . . . when you do Trenches don't get the left hand working with the right foot, get the right hand working with the right foot* – even the little impudent extra twirls which had always drawn a burst of applause. I went on and on as if possessed, stopping only to run to the machine and wind it up again – on and on until I fell exhausted and panting into a chair.

I felt better, tried again to get drunk, and again failed.

Mon. Dec. 30th 1935, 201st Day of Reign.

The rain had stopped, there was even a glimmer of sun. But stagnation still hung in the air. Even if it was to lead nowhere, I must see Willie. At eleven in the morning I crossed to his office.

He was out; there was only Sec-Sec in his corner, typing busily.

He got up and gave a sharp click of the heels, I asked him not to let me interrupt, he smiled, bowed and went back to his work. Smooth. I wondered what he thought of it all. Neither pro nor con, was my guess. Just wanted to keep his job and go on from there. A sturdy climber, up the steep slopes of Mount Civil Service. I asked where Mr Millingham was.

"I'm not sure, your Majesty."

"Where's his next appointment?"

"He didn't tell me, Sir."

As I turned to go, I saw Willie's diary open on his desk. What caught my eye, interested me. The door opened and there he was. With that dreaded closed look.

"Good morning, Willie." I walked back to my study, he followed me. And I sensed how Sec-Sec was longing to be in on whatever would be said.

"Willie, I happened to see your diary."

"Yes, Sir?"

"I'm sorry if I did the wrong thing I'd have thought your list of official engagements would be . . . well an open book. I see you've been twice on Saturday and again at midnight last night to a certain address."

"Yes, Sir."

"Ten Downing Street. How was the Prime Minister?"

He did not answer. Evasive. No doubt about it.

I couldn't stand it any longer. "Willie . . . If you don't come clean with me, I'm bloody well going off my rocker, they won't have seen anything like it in this joint since George the Third. You'll have me foaming at the mouth in a strait-jacket and fighting my way into Broadcasting House to tell the world, over the wireless, that it's all the fault of my Private Secretary."

But he looked so tired that I again felt sorry for him. "I'm afraid, Sir, it's a crisis. The biggest since 1926, the General Strike. Or even since 1914, the outbreak of war."

I wondered if I was as pale as he was. "Have the newspapers got worse?"

"Yes. Saturday's *Times* was headed AN IRRESPONSIBLE DESPOT. Not even a question-mark. The official attitude has stiffened considerably, and last night's emergency meeting was joined by J. H. Thomas."

"Representing the Labour Party?"

"They wanted to get the Party's point of view."

"Which is?"

"The Labour people naturally see it differently. While they acknowledge the rashness of the speech, they have to salute its motive: to strike a blow for the workers. For the Monarch to have come out with an uncompromising – if unprecedented – statement of his personal opinion is – for Labour – a tremendous fillip."

"And for the Conservative Party?"

"A tremendous smack in the face."

"And then?"

"They suggest leaving you undisturbed till New Year's Day, to think things out. Then, that afternoon, a meeting to discuss what they feel might be the next step."

"Yes?"

"A *possible* next step. Even J.H. finally agreed."

"Willie, let's have it!"

"Your Majesty, it is my duty as your Private Secretary to inform you that . . ." He blurted it out. "They feel you should abdicate."

CHAPTER TWENTY-TWO

Acceleration towards the New Year

No wonder he had shirked it.

The word, echoing down the years from my shadowy history lessons, was fraught with disaster. And shame. What had those Kings done, we wondered in class, to make them *abdicate*?

I sat down, to sort things out. Which I failed to do: this was a development too immediate and drastic for a cool appraisal of something which could never be as simple as it might look. Emotion got the upper hand.

And I leaned back, as if into a warm bath, and dwelt only on the sudden, unbelievable possibility of . . . escape. "Willie, if I did this – what would be my next move?"

His reaction was so ready, so practically thought-out, that the prospect became steadily more credible. "If your Majesty *did* accept the idea, the suggestion is that you would leave tonight –"

"Tonight?"

"And then the plan would be that, first thing tomorrow morning, suitcases would be packed with belongings befitting a reasonably prosperous commoner and delivered to Yeoman's Row. A temporary secretary would work there for a few days, dealing with the mail which would be bound to flood in. The telephone would hardly be a problem, as the number would have been changed and made ex-directory."

"But after all this, how could I possibly arrive at leading a normal life?"

"It'd be a problem, but two factors would help. First, careful im-

mediate planning. An extraordinary situation calls for extraordinary
measures. It sounds melodramatic, but what I would suggest would
be a scheme involving a complete disappearance."

I was getting caught up. "A complete disappearance . . . For how
long?"

"A couple of years. Your old names would of course have become
out of the question – not only John Sandring, but also John Green.
Would you visualize, Sir, being shocked at the idea of assuming –
with the help of a passport – a new identity?"

"Hardly more of a shock than when I was yanked in here on June
the 12th . . . I know – I could turn into the reincarnation of Victoria's invisible son of the soil – from John Green to John Brown!"

"Excellent! Mr Brown would – under top secrecy provided by the
Powers-That-Be – find himself spirited out of the country, pre-
ferably moustached or even bearded, and of course innocent of the
King's Curl –"

"Of course – and Mr Brown's destination?"

"The other day, Sir, you joked about being deported to Mexico.
Would a couple of years there, of your own accord, appeal to you?"

"The nearest I've ever got to going abroad was once on tour
playing Dover, when I swam out to sea, a good quarter of a mile –
yes it *would* appeal to me! And when Kathy was on tour was the only
time she's ever been out of London even, it would appeal to her too,
I know it . . . But at the end of the two years, when Mr Brown
would be spirited back to London with his wife – wouldn't the
difficulties start?"

Willie smiled. "An Abdication, of course, would have to figure
permanently in future history books – but during the rest of your
own lifetime . . . if it did happen, I have an idea you'd be agreeably
surprised. Just now I mentioned two things which would help, the
first being careful planning. Well, the second is simple – just time.
Two years is quite a gap. At the moment you naturally picture the
danger of being suddenly spotted in public and mobbed like a film
star, theatre foyers besieged by autograph hunters and so on – but I
have experience, from my travels, of how fickle the public memory
can be.

"Oh I do agree, Sir, that during those first days in Yeoman's Row
there would be sackloads of telegrams and cables, hysterically high
sums being waved at you for a Frank Account of Life at the Palace –
can't you picture it? But after that, something tells me that with
every edition and news bulletin, less and less attention would be paid,

so making your disappearance to Mexico that much more practical."

Mexico . . . Would John Brown sit back there in the tropical sun, a semi-blueblooded layabout?

No. "Making windmills" sounds like a children's game. It isn't. And since I was more and more convinced that that was something only I could do – that it could be my vocation – it would be my chance to make up for lost time. It's amazing the amount to be learnt about windmills, and the lovely outlandishness of the terms – even at that moment I could remember bressummer, neck-box, pintle, grapnel, centrifugal governors, luffing gear . . .

I would relearn it all, and go on from there. My books and tools would be waiting in Yeoman's Row, and before Mexico my temporary secretary would shop for whatever else I needed. And in Mexico City, there must be at least one store specializing in requirements as I went along. Then again, since my initial publicity had somehow missed out on my "hobby", Mr John Brown could plan ahead with a hope of success without complications. I would work towards an Exhibition, if necessary stipulating that it would be publicized "solely as the output of the said John Brown, with no exploitations of his personal life".

My mind was on the move. Upward, towards fulfilment. Towards happiness. "And Willie, after the two years?"

"Oh, there'd be the odd moment when somebody might say, 'See that young chap walking into the Tube station – looks to me a bit like the last King, remember the silly fuss about a Christmas message? But sooner than you think, you'd be able to circulate in and out of your flat without embarrassment."

The walk round the Park . . . By now this hypothetical future of mine – I was powerless to resist it – was becoming a fact. Travelling on top of the 16 bus down Grosvenor Place for a glimpse, over the spiked wall, of the Palace Garden. And a flat . . . Must be grander than Yeoman's Row, but not grand. An extra room for Kathy to work in, a novel about Mexico maybe . . . Then I had a fanciful idea.

"Willie, about where we would live – guess the part of town we'd go in for straight away, we'd just have to!"

"Which?"

"Buckingham Palace Road."

"Of course!"

"The Ebury Bridge end, I wouldn't want to be too near. The King is dead and living in Buckingham Palace Road!"

Then – as had to happen, sooner or later – my mother's legacy of down-to-earthness took over, and I . . . came down to earth. "If I did abd . . . If I did what they want me to do, what are they planning, for the country?"

"That had to come up, of course. At half-past one in the morning, not a good time. The P.M. faced it very candidly."

"Faced what?"

"The possibility, in the unprecedented circumstances, of what happened to France."

I was slow. "How do you mean?"

"A Republic." He waited for me to take it in. "It was first brought up by J. H. Thomas, who intimated that Labour might declare itself in favour of Abdication, *if* the idea of a Republic were to be seriously considered. That is the position."

"I see." I felt a need to think, a need so strong that I had to be in the open air, and alone. I got up. "I'm going for a walk."

"When you want me, Sir, I'll be in my office." At the door, a routine question occurred to me. "If I am officially requested to go, can I refuse?"

"Certainly. There is no power, short of anarchy, that can depose the British Sovereign."

I went on looking at him, but he turned away and looked out of the window. Once again, it was impossible to read his thoughts.

Out in the Garden, I looked up at the scowling winter sky, was glad of it, and paced slowly, deliberately, in rhythm with the slow deliberation of my thoughts. I looked down at the water-fowl; even they seemed to be waiting for a decision. (Were they called that? I ought to know, considering they were mine.)

Mine, for how long?

I sat down and stared across at the stern face of the Palace. I knew that to step outside oneself and take a good look at oneself, is as impossible mentally as it is physically – but I wanted to have a try.

I recalled my recurring interior litany of the past months, "I'd give anything to get out, *anything* . . ." Although I had dutifully pushed it into the back of my mind, it had been so persistent that I never knew when it might crop up – not only when I lay awake, but in the middle of an official speech, or of pretending to listen to the Luncheon Lady on my Right. And yet now, at this moment of reckoning, I knew – for certain – that over those same months since I had stepped into this place, I had – gradually, without realizing it – I had changed.

Shutting my eyes with the effort of reconstruction, I forced my-self back, in time, to the evening before that had happened. An evening when the country was – after thirty-two days – still waiting and wondering. Drury Lane Theatre, the top chorus-room. And nobody in the room waiting much, or wondering – "superficial" was the word for us. I could smell the fresh sweat and the scent of make-up, I could hear the chat. Guess what I heard Miss Ellis say to Ivor, Jill auditioned but lost the part because she looked too like Frances Day isn't it the limit, did you know Max Factor have in-vented a new powder that won't rub off . . .

Suppose Belle bursts in, always the first with the news. "What d'you think – we're going to be a Republic, isn't it camp?"

"You don't say, well what's wrong with the people running the people, time marches on . . ." Anybody in that room could have said that. Including me.

But I had changed. Those months here had gradually injected into my system, slow but sure, an influence which was now taking me over. I was viewing the present crisis through the eyes of people standing in line up to the horizon, and all looking at me. Ancestors. Only once, when the upstart Oliver Cromwell reared his head – only that one time had the line been broken.

I concentrated on the gravel at my feet. Suppose – I said to my-self – suppose that tomorrow is your sixtieth birthday, you've been on the throne for thirty-six years, a King who married at twenty-seven and a couple of years later fathered a son, the popular Heir-Apparent now aged – say – thirty. The Cabinet has just suggested, tactfully, that it would be a fine gesture, on your part, to give way to new blood. To abdicate.

No shadow of a doubt, I would leap at it. So what is holding me back now?

Answer – the idea of there being nobody to take over. The idea of a Republic.

Then, there came back to me a phrase Willie had used earlier. "An Abdication, of course, would have to figure permanently in future history books." Still staring at the ground, I again travelled to my class-room in St Austell County School. But this time, not back-ward. Forward. A hundred years forward.

"We now reach a fatal New Year, please copy down the date, 1935 to 1936. This marked the melancholy end of Europe's longest dyn-asty, and the removal of the Crown to the British Museum. This tragic collapse was caused by the sad inability of the last King of

England, John the Second, to face up to his responsibilities. A true grandson of the feckless Duke of Clarence.

"Having started off with reasonable promise, he made the mistake of exceeding his powers with an unconstitutional speech – but then made a far graver mistake. He abdicated. In doing so, he caused irreparable damage to the British image, worst of all in America but indeed all over the world: an image which has still not recovered its former glory, and (some say) never will.

"It seems clear now, a century later, that if only John the Second had had the courage to stand up to his Ministers and claim that he had learnt from his one mistake and was determined to fight to the bitter end, for himself and his forebears, he would have won through and today Britain would be very different. As it is, he has come down to history as King John the Faint-hearted. Write thirty lines on 'The Monarch Who Gave Up' . . . "

I was not like my grandfather. I was not feckless. There can't be a republic. Hello 1936, Windsor, Sandringham, Balmoral, Canada, India, Australia . . . I'll cope. No. We shall cope.

I got up and walked back. At a different pace. Brisker. With purpose.

Ten minutes later.

"Kathy, Please tear that last miserable letter into tiny pieces. Because I *have* picked myself up. You wrote you were proud of me, you'll be proud again. Bruce sent a message to keep smiling, and I will. I come from a long tough line, and I'll survive. (Come to think of it, my mother's tough, too, in her view of Duty.)

"So we'll give the Coronation Coach a dab of gold paint, send the old Abbey red carpet to the cleaners, and get the trumpeters into their livery, to tell the world that the rumour that this family is putting its notice up on the board is unfounded, because the show is extending its run, indefinitely. I wish it didn't have to be me – God how I wish it didn't – but there it is.

"Sorry your audition for *Follow the Sun* didn't work (Cochran, isn't it, for the Adelphi?). I think, my darling, you made a mistake, at the audition, singing 'Too Many Rings Around Rosie', too coy for you, your forte is dead-pan comedy, letting the jokes speak for themselves – next time do try something like

Gertie Lawrence's 'Experiment', from *Nymph Errant*. Not a Command, just a suggestion!

"Think of me, as I think of you, and Bruce . . ."

Ten minutes later than that, my first hurdle: tricky meeting with Willie. I prepared myself for the non-committal look, which would mask his disapproval. Of my obstinacy.

"May I say, Sir, how glad I am to see you looking more cheerful?"

"I'm *feeling* more cheerful. Willie, brace yourself for a shock."

He did. "Sir?"

"John the Second will not abdicate. We repeat. *Will* . . . *not* . . . *abdicate*. If by a miracle the right man for the job turned up, and there would be no question of a Republic, of course I'd go. As it is, no Abdication."

I waited for the expected reaction . . . And was I taken unawares! His face opened like a flower.

I would not have believed it possible, "Congratulations, Sir!" Then came the first spontaneous thing I'd ever seen him do. He took my hand and gripped it.

"But Willie – earlier this morning I'd have sworn you wanted me to give in –"

"I was anxious to sound impartial, so as not to influence you one way or the other. I'm delighted."

What a relief. Then, by the second post, Kathy; I realized she had not yet received my depressed letter.

". . . Oh I was happy to get your telegram saying your morale is high – of *course* you must resist the fuddy-duddies and show the stuff you're made of . . ."

It could have been the answer to the letter I had just written to her; so far so good.

Then, at a moment when my head was still hot from my decision not to walk out of my job, the timing of the next paragraph was cruel. My premonition had been right, things were accelerating towards the New Year.

"And my darling, I have good news for you. Bumpy and I were getting into more and more of a state of indecision as to our future (after knowing each other for a fortnight, barely, can you beat it!!) He had kissed me a couple of times, while dancing, etc., but nothing more. Well, this afternoon, walking in the Park, he told me, quite calmly, that days ago he had talked to the

Tulip Time management and they're releasing me from the show as from tonight (Sat.) – I have to admire his nerve – and on Thurs. next (Jan 2nd) he's taking me for Two Guilty Weeks ... where do you think? Venice! I had told him I'd always longed to go, and he says it's magical in the winter, not a tourist in sight (except us!). We'll be at the Danieli, terribly grand, Signore and Signora Nobody, all that rubbish.

"It's to see if we're all right together, he says he *knows* it's all right but I think it's only sensible, don't you? And if it *is* all right ... He's very sweet and thoughtful, isn't it exciting?

"Tomorrow (Sun.) he's taking me to stay with old friends in the country, then we'll be back Tues. (Dec. 31st, my birthday!) for the Chelsea Arts Ball, Albert Hall! Remember the fun the three of us had there last year? I hope it doesn't get *too* wild in the small hours – not that Bumpy's stuffy, not a bit!

"I'll write again (of course) before he and I leave Thurs. for Venice. Exciting about you too darling ..."

There's nothing like reading about a pair of lovers planning their future, it warms the cockles of your heart. I felt, more acutely than ever before, the familiar symptom, across my chest. What I minded most – even more, somehow, than the idea of Venice, which had once been a plan – was the walk in the Park.

It mustn't happen. It can't. Because she belongs to me.

But she doesn't. And who was the one who loftily advised her to plan for a secure future? And the future is certainly that – a year ago she would never have walked out of a show in the middle of the run.

But it mustn't happen.

I looked at the letter again. The Chelsea Arts Ball ... Yes, we had fun last year, the three of us, Columbine and the Two Pierrots; we had held hands for "Auld Lang Syne", then danced and drank wine till 6 a.m. and then weaved home. *Should Old Acquaintance Be Forgot* ...

It mustn't be forgot. Oh my love, it mustn't be ...

Then I recalled phrases in her letters. *You and I can never meet again ... You've been taken away from us.* It's true, now more than ever. *But this must not happen* ...

And something started to drive me, which I had no way of resisting. No way in the world. A madness.

I've got to see her, got to stop her. But I've no idea where she is, or where she'll be, until ...

The Chelsea Arts Ball, New Year's Eve. Tomorrow night. *I've got to see her*, if it's the last thing I do in 1935. Or the first in 1936.

A clock was striking noon. I sat at my desk, took out a sheet of paper, and for half-an-hour I thought hard, made a note, thought again, made another note. I was hatching a plan. No, a Plot. And once it had acquired a shape, like any Secret Agent I memorized my notes and put them in the fire.

I sent for a Special Messenger, sat down and dashed off a letter. It was so frantic that, as I copy it out now, I'm going to find it only just legible.

"Our dear dear Bruce – do something for me. First thing tomorrow morning – New Yr's Eve – an errand. Bit of a shopping list . . ."

And I ticked off the finicky details.

"And then will you deliver same here by noon, in cardboard box? To stop the staff here suspecting it might have a bomb in it. I've left special messages at Gates and at Privy Purse Door that I'm expecting a suit from Hawes and Curtis, so will you mark box clearly FROM HAWES & CURTIS TAILORS. Don't hire, buy, I enclose £20. Your Friend always, for Auld Lang Syne, Jack."

Idiotically, the snag (*Royalty does not handle money*) was now to get hold of the £20 in cash. I crossed to Willie's office, knowing the coast was clear, he was at a business meeting with the Keeper of the Privy Purse. Just Sec-Sec in his corner, looking rather bored till he saw who it was and sprang to his feet. I explained that I needed the money for a delayed Christmas present to Staff, and would he get it from the Comptroller's Office, at once.

He did, the messenger arrived, I addressed the envelope; I wanted it to be waiting when Bruce would report for the evening show.

I enjoyed addressing it, too. "To Bruce Renfrew Esq. c/o JACK AND THE BEANSTALK Theatre Royal Drury Lane."

I crossed again to Willie's office where Sec-Sec again sprang to attention.

I had never looked at him properly before: an eager face, boyishly diffident. I wished I'd been in more official contact with him, it would have made my present task that much easier. Go carefully.

But what was Sec-Sec's first name? I had to look it up. Lionel, Captain Lionel Sellison.

"Lionel, would you help me out? I need to dictate an urgent memo."

He flushed with pleasure at my calling him Lionel, took up his writing-pad, bowed and followed me into my study. From my desk I took the draft of a speech Willie had worked on with me two weeks ago, to be made next year at Oxford when I would receive an Honorary Degree; since there was no immediate hurry, we had shelved the preparation for more pressing business.

I dictated carefully, and tritely. "The signal academic honour which you are bestowing on me today . . ." It did not take long and Lionel got up to go. "A glass of sherry, before lunch?"

Again his face lit up. "Thank you, Sir."

I offered him a cigarette. "Cheers," and we sipped. "Ah" I said "nice to relax, it's been the hell of a week."

"I know. Your Majesty, dare I take this opportunity to express my deep sympathy and concern?" Smooth. I saw that the diffidence had gone, he was quietly at his ease. Never mind, I needed all the concern he could give me. "After being cooped up in here for seven months," I said, "there are moments when the desire to escape, if only for a few hours, is unbearable."

"I do understand Sir, is there any way I can help? Could I take you for a drive? I have my car by the Stables, it's only a little Austin Seven, nobody'd notice it. What about a run down to the Hotel de Paris at Bray?"

This was helping me along no end. "I have a better idea. It's a crazy one, but I feel like doing something crazy."

"Sir?"

"Lionel, I am about to ask you a great favour." The use of his name worked again. "Certainly Sir . . ."

"But if you say no, I shall completely understand. First, you've obviously got tomorrow night planned, a New Year's Eve party?"

"*Rather*! Down in Berkshire, my Aunt Rose is giving a big family do."

"Oh? You have an Aunt Rose? Did you know Willie has one too?"

He smiled and looked a bit embarrassed. "Yes Sir, it's the same Aunt Rose. My father married one of her sisters, and Willie's father the other."

"Really? Willie never told me!"

He looked more embarrassed. "I can understand that, Sir. You see, he was rather peeved because he felt that Aunt Rose had gone a bit behind his back to the P.M. to get me this job. He said it smelt of nepotism."

"I suppose he'd got something there." It occurred to me that Lionel might have inherited his ambitious streak from Auntie. "Lionel . . . if you were unable to turn up tomorrow night for Aunt Rose's party, owing to a sudden pile of clerical work at Buck House . . . would she be very much put out?"

He answered without hesitation. "Not that much, Sir, no, it'll be a pretty big show. And she knows that if you need me, that comes first."

Good. Very good. But my tricky patch was to come; I felt that in fairness to him I must give a warning. "I should first make it clear that if anything went wrong and I . . . I got into trouble, it would be next to impossible for *you* not to get into trouble as well."

"Oh." He looked suspicious. Cautious. Since his career came first . . . I sensed failure. But I was determined not to mince matters. "You'll soon see the danger involved, when I explain to you that I want to – it's childish, I know – I want to see the New Year in at the Chelsea Arts Ball."

He sat speechless. Yes, it sounded ridiculous. Then he found words. "But – excuse me, Sir – you *can't* – you'd be mobbed – I don't mean the crowd would be against you, the kind of people there might be mostly in favour of your Christmas Day Speech – but you'd be crushed to death, it would be appalling . . ."

"I've gone into that, Lionel, of course – don't forget it's a Fancy Dress affair . . . *If* you consented to take the risk you'd have to trust me, on all the details. All I'd ask you to do beforehand, would be (a) to let Security, sentries and so forth know that you'll be driving out in your car, at about 11.15, to a New Year's Party – why not tell the truth, that it's the Chelsea Arts Ball? – (b) to find out, discreetly, what the situation would be tomorrow night, between eleven and midnight, round about the Stables where your Austin Seven would be parked – I mean, would there be policemen hanging about, *et cetera*. The rest you'd leave to me. What d'you say?"

He drank his sherry, slowly. His mind was ticking. I said, "Well?"

"I'll risk it." I had expected "Sorry, Sir, I have my future to consider." I had misjudged him, he was a sport. We shook hands – conspirators – and clinked glasses. I said, "Will you see that everybody's told that tomorrow night I'll be seeing in the New Year spending an early night in bed, as I have a heavy January the First? And will you see that the footmen are told they're free from eight on, for the Staff Party – and will you be here, in dinner-jacket, by ten?"

We got up. He said, "I'll telephone Aunt Rose straight away and put her off because I'll be working with you, Sir, but Willie will know I'm not, so I'll tell him I made it an excuse to get out of her party and join a girl friend." And he went. Not missing a trick. Eager to please, glossy.

Why couldn't I take to him? No point in going into that, he was essential to me.

In the afternoon, I walked round and round the Garden, absent-minded, then at six met Willie. Now that he knew I was not going to give in to the Powers-That-Be, and was himself free of them until the momentous meeting on New Year's afternoon, he was his old serene self.

Over our comfortable drinks, we worked on the announcement I was to make at the meeting. The first sentence would be impressively formal. "We, John the Second, King of England and the Dominions beyond the Seas and Emperor of India, hereby declare our firm and solemn decision not to abdicate."

The rest of the statement would strike quite the other way: chastened without grovelling.

"I would like to apologize for my mistaken Christmas Message, and hope that you will put that mistake down to inexperience and the enthusiasm of youth. I am now more aware of the delicacy of the Monarch's position, and pledge myself to respect it."

Willie suggested a postscript. "John Two thanks his elders for the caning and – cross his heart – will do better next term." We decided against it. I unlocked my private drawer and laid the document carefully on top of the stack of letters from Yeoman's Row.

Then he explained that he was going home, and tomorrow would proceed from there with wife and son to see the New Year in at Aunt Rose's party in Old Grange House – "Would have been difficult to get out of" – they would spend the night, and he would return in the morning for the meeting. We wished each other a happy New Year. He left.

I locked the secret drawer, and sat looking at it. Why was one side of my mind engaged on the most solemn commitment a man could make, while the other was equally engrossed in concocting as daring and wilful an escapade as anything in the *Boy's Own Paper*?

Don't ask me.

CHAPTER TWENTY-THREE

The Vagabond King

Tues. Dec. 31st 1935, 202nd Day of Reign.

I was awake with the dawn. New Year's Eve, and all day I would be ticking off the hours as they crept towards the witching one. Midnight.

As I lay back in the warm morning bed, the idle moment could – formerly – have been one of those when the brain is turned the other way and the healthy body, craving release, takes over. No chance: for me, love had shifted from the once familiar area of physical pleasure, out to a place far more mysterious. All I knew was that it meant pain.

I got up quickly and walked, in the wilderness of Garden. And walked. Once again my fingers yearned to be busy over balsa-wood and emery boards and shavings and tiny wheels and chains; making a windmill would have speeded up this particular day no end.

At twenty to one, a large cardboard box, FROM HAWES AND CURTIS, TAILORS. Good old Bruce . . . I opened it, checked the contents, shut it again and pushed it under the bed.

The rest of the day passed somehow, I can't remember; I would have liked to switch the wireless on, music would have helped, but I dreaded hearing something about myself. At half-past seven Wilkins brought my dinner and went off to change for the Staff Party. The evening was mine. And Sec-Sec's.

After my meal I had a whisky (only one, must have my wits about me) and felt it rise to my head like a purring cat. I was having an idea of what a cold-blooded murderer must feel beforehand: no pang of conscience, just the excitement of wrong-doing, spiced with secrecy, and danger. I had an hour, and made it my pre-First-Night rest: eyes closed, arms and legs limp. Heart missing an occasional beat, but quickly making up for it.

At five minutes to ten I went into the bedroom, closed the door and dressed for the Ball. I was almost ready when I heard a brisk knock at the other door; I went through finishing touches, then opened my door, softly, an inch.

Sec-Sec was standing next to my desk, perfectly groomed in dinner-jacket and black tie, a red rose in his button-hole. He was looking down at my papers. Then he moved them around, and examined a couple.

That took me aback. Perhaps he's doing his job, making sure that he hadn't forgotten something . . . but how he is to know there's not something private in there? I was glad of the locked drawer . . . Then I brushed all that aside, for the simple reason that I was standing in the wings, exhilarated, about to make my entrance.

I knocked loudly on my door, called out "Ta-RAH!", flung it open, waddled into the study and struck a pose.

I could feel Sec-Sec standing there, galvanized. I was galvanized too, for in my pose I was staring into the big mirror next to him. Staring at Charlie Chaplin.

At Clarkson's – the "Theatrical Costumier's" – Bruce had carried out my instructions to the comma. The battered bowler, frizzy black wig, black tooth-brush moustache, baggy trousers, ancient pathetic too-big boots – there stood the Little Tramp. (I was a shade too tall, but no matter.)

With Sec-Sec's eyes glued on me, I did a quick strut on to parquet (I had previously rolled back the rugs) and danced to "Mountain Greenery" as I sang it, very high, in a sort of clown's voice. After my exhausting "exercise" on Sunday, I was step-perfect and the boots felt good, they were so heavy they gave resounding smacks, almost as if fitted with taps. I finished with a flourish, my eyes fixed – in a wide music-hall grin – on my audience of one.

Sec-Sec's eyes were fixed too, in astonishment. I took off bowler, wig and moustache and turned to him as if nothing had happened. "Lionel, a drink?" As I poured for both of us, "How long before you cottoned on?"

"Quite a few seconds, Sir, it was uncanny. If I hadn't known you were planning a disguise, I wouldn't have guessed for a minute!"

"Good, now the plan." He leant forward to listen, keen as

mustard, and when I had finished, made a couple of suggestions, excellent ones. When we had gone through the thing again, to double-check, Sec-Sec rubbed his hands – "Capital!"

We had a second drink, and made it last till it was time to move. I filled a small silver flask with whisky, dropped it into one of the loose pockets of my baggy trousers, then realized that the one thing I had forgotten to put on Bruce's list was important. The Tramp's cane.

I was in luck – there it was! I lifted it out. It looked pretty shabby by now, except for the small silver band round the handle. I studied the tiny inscription, *To Prince A.V. on 21st B'thday 1885, fr. Sandringham Tenants.*

But how to travel it? My fellow-felon helped me on with my (own) overcoat, hooked the cane into the sleeve inside the coat, and buttoned the coat. It worked a treat. He then carefully took up my bowler, squeezed my boots inside it, as well as a tiny box containing wig, moustache and small bottle of spirit-gum: then draped his overcoat over his arm to hide what he was holding. I picked up a writing-pad and pencil and placed them in his hand. We left.

For the following account of an extraordinary night, I am able to draw on my detailed notes later.

Nobody about. As we passed a door leading down to the Staff Quarters, there were faint subterranean party noises; a gramophone was playing "Lullaby of Broadway". On a night like this, along those corridors it was darkish, so when two maids came along, they failed to spot my boots and baggy trousers; but what they did notice, was that I was dictating a memorandum to my Second Secretary, his writing-pad at the ready. I broke off to wish them a happy New Year. Tonight the corridors were particularly chilly, which made it plausible that I was walking around in an overcoat without necessarily planning to leave the premises.

As Sec-Sec opened the door to Stable Yard, I hung back in the shadows like the Scarlet Pimpernel. He walked out into the dead quiet, then his footsteps stopped. I peered out. Two policemen. I drew back.

Sec-Sec: "Sorry, gentlemen, but we just had a phone call from Gerald Road Police Station, they'd been rung up with a report that two suspicious characters had been spotted out there in Lower Grosvenor Place, carrying a ladder. In view of the scare last year, if you remember, the drunk trying to climb the wall, you never know . . ."

"Of course, sir." The echo of all their footsteps dying away, the rattle of keys, the clang of gates being opened. Silence.

I crossed quickly to Sec-Sec's little Austin Seven – the only car there – climbed into the back, pulled the door quietly shut, crouched on the floor and made myself as comfortable as was feasible.

A tight fit. During the minute's wait, I wondered who had been the last King of England to travel on the floor, in disguise, and decided it was Charles the Second before his accession, in danger of his life. Then I remembered the Palace boot-boy who had drunk boot-polish and tonic, and been rushed to St. George's Hospital on the floor of a Daimler. This wasn't a Daimler.

The footsteps. Sec-Sec: "They must have got the wind up and moved on, sorry, gentlemen!"

"You did right, sir, you never know!"

Sec-Sec's footsteps, approaching. A front door opened and I felt his overcoat being delicately lowered over me, and with it what had been hidden underneath. He settled at the wheel, then whispered. "All right Sir?"

"Snug as a bug." I felt us move, slowly, cautiously, then stop.

The noise of the gates being reopened, then murmurs of "Happy New Year" from the two policemen as Captain Sellison drove out into Lower Grosvenor Place. Alone. On his way to see 1936 in with a couple of pals. We were off.

I felt us turn left, left again and up Constitution Hill to Hyde Park Corner, where the traffic sounded brisker: there were snatches of revelry by night, Happy New Year Happy New Year ... Then along Knightsbridge, a slow turn to the left, stop. "O.K. Sir?"

A bit cramped, I levered myself up on to the seat; we were parked in a small deserted side-street. I pulled my stuff from under Sec-Sec's overcoat and swiftly organized myself: got out of my overcoat, smeared my upper lip with the spirit-gum and firmly fixed the little moustache, then the wig – as I did so, I almost peered into an imaginary dressing-room mirror – then the boots, the bowler and the cane.

I said "Right..." and sat back. The car turned round into Kensington Road and went sailing west.

Adventure-bound: on a journey which had nothing to do with the staid and stately expeditions of the last months. I was an excited child playing truant, I might never before have been out after nightfall: the street-lamps and the car-lights dazzled and bewitched me, every pedestrian seemed to be hurrying to meet 1936 head on. We stopped for a moment at a traffic light, and two people in the next car, in paper hats, pointed at me, laughed and waved, "Happy New Year, Charlie!" I was anonymous at last, at last . . .

At the portico of the Albert Hall (named after my . . . forget it) we drew up behind several others. I said, "See you exactly here, two a.m.? Enjoy yourself!" (He too would attend the ball, the cost of his ticket to be recovered from the Comptroller, as Incidental Expenses.)

"Two a.m. Good luck, Sir."

I had opened the car-door and was just climbing out when he called, sharply. "Just a minute, Sir!" I sat quickly back, he must have spotted somebody tricky . . . But no, I must have confidence, in this get-up *nobody* would recognize me . . . I said, "Yes, what is it?"

His hand dived into a breast-pocket. "Your cash, Sir, for entrance ticket and sundries."

The child's pocket-money. "Good for you, Lionel, thank you." I did feel a fool. I'd have felt a bigger one if he'd driven off to park and left me penniless. Admirably efficient, was Sec-Sec. He drove round a corner, and I followed people into the foyer, or whatever they call it.

And was deafened. By the din of a crowd chattering and laughing; it gave me a dizzy feeling, almost of panic, and I could not understand why. Then of course did: for seven months, apart from the cheering of crowds, I had heard *no noise*: at my entrance into any room anywhere, voices had become automatically hushed, and stayed hushed. This was life as lived by ordinary people, and it had knocked me sideways.

I pulled myself together; threading my way to the box-office, I was pushed three times. As I approached it, for the benefit of the girl selling tickets I gave a twirl to my cane and the familiar Charlie sniff, sending the little moustache to one side. I knew I was good.

I waited for her to stare and then giggle appreciatively. She did neither, looked straight through me. "Just yourself, dear?"

I paid my three guineas and moved on, somewhat dashed. I wanted to be anonymous, indeed I did – but hardly (as an actor) ignored.

Then I began to understand why I had gone unnoticed. In front of me, a ticket had been bought by a St Bernard dog with a barrel labelled "BRANDY XXX" slung under hairy jaws carefully decked with painted dribble. In order to buy its way in, the animal must have had to hoist itself up on its hind legs, with the entrance money clenched between its cardboard teeth.

The poor creature staggered forward, looking fairly worn out before the event, which it must have hoped would include winning the First Prize for the Most Original Costume. Then, under a poster belatedly announcing XMAS EVE ST DAMIEN'S CHURCH CHOIR AND DAGENHAM GIRL PIPERS IN A FEAST OF HYMNS OF PRAISE! the St Bernard was knocked flying by a pair of nymphs, near-naked and each waving a bottle of wine. XMAS EVE seemed a long time ago.

I understood the box-office girl's indifference to me even better when I turned and thought I was looking at myself in a mirror. Charlie Chaplin, complete with bowler, boots, moustache and cane. I watched him amble jauntily round a corner, in search of a happy New Year.

I thought, I'm better than he is, even though he *is* two inches shorter and therefore the right height. Feeling almost huffed, I walked on with no attempt at the Chaplin waddle: tonight, it would be a waste of stage talent. But I was at least safe.

As I climbed up some stairs, it struck me – for the first time – that I had no idea of Kathy's costume, or of that of her . . . What should one call him? Were they officially engaged, or would that have to wait till after Venice? The thought of that didn't help me up the stairs, and my boots were so awkward that I tripped, twice. A girl running down sang out, merrily, "Charlie's blotto, Charlie's blotto!"

I got to the big arched passage, like a street, circling round most of the vast building, and the first thing to hit me was the thunderous music from below, one big rhythmic throb: Harry Roy and his Band, live, playing "Tiger Rag".

I was hovering on the edge of an immense globe of blinding light, and of noise a hundred times worse than that in the foyer: a globe in which seethed and bubbled a swaying mass of colour – a thousand dancing couples, while above them shimmered rows of boxes one on top of the other, each a jewel-case overflowing with still more colour. From all that, I turned to the passage on each side of me, filled with shadowy figures scurrying and whooping and shrieking as if there was a fire.

There I stood – a dazed convict-monk on a couple of hours' leave from his cell, and ridiculously disguised – adrift in a Never-Never Land of Cleopatras, Regency Rakes, Red-Riding-Hoods, Cave-

Men, Salvation-Army Lasses, Rasputins, Shirley Temples, Fauns in search of an *Après-Minuit*: an enormous sexual jumble-sale with an inexhaustible procession of bargains.

Two impersonations were to stick in my memory. First, an overweight mermaid, wearing a long flaxen wig and a tail with each glittering scale in place, who had solved the problem of getting about, even if it meant acute discomfort. While one foot seemed to be twisted upwards into some part of the lady's fishy stomach, the other was masked by the tail-end and so, in a high-heeled shoe, was able to propel the owner forward with the aid of a pair of crutches presumably found washed up on the beach. She must have had to give up any hope of shining on the dance floor.

I came upon the second costume through remembering my flask of whisky, extracting it and taking a swig. I spluttered and choked – oh but it did taste good! I looked again around me, and what had seemed nightmarishly real, gradually melted into a rosy dream, unreal but cosy. Rosy and cosy. His Majesty was mixing with his subjects! God if they only knew . . . The band was playing "You and the Night and the Music", and I moved my shoulders as I remembered dancing to it with Cocaine Connie . . .

A tap on my shoulder, and I froze. A warder from Buckingham Jail . . . I turned, to find a flushed face, swaying a foot away. "Charlie ducks, adored ya in *City Lights*, could ya spare a wee drop for a dry ole Gladdie?"

I said, "Sure, baby!" took a second swig myself and handed him the flask, "Help yourself, happy New Year, Gladdie!" As he gurgled away, I vaguely wondered why he called himself Gladdie; looking down, I saw that he was dressed, carelessly and unsuitably, as a Roman gladiator. He handed me back the flask with a sweeping Restoration bow. "Charlie ducks, we who are about to die, salute ya!"

As he staggered on, he almost collided with the second Charlie, who came hopping and skipping – in character – twirling his cane: saw me, stopped in his tracks, stared, sniffed and hurried on. But he was wearing brown boots instead of black. It wasn't the same Charlie. A third.

Could there be enough of us to start a Fan Club?

The effect of the whisky soon wearing off, the whole phantasmagoria came at me again and I wandered on, more dazed than before. And not helped by running into a pretty girl in a Swan-Lake ballet-skirt, enough like Kathy to make my heart jump. She gave me a look and brushed past, and that riled me; I wasn't used to people giving me a look and brushing past.

Where was she? They wouldn't be in a box, the boxes were all for more than two occupants; but I recalled that presentable guests were often invited into any of the big ones forming the immense horse-shoe round the dance-floor, for a drink and a close view of the passing show. I made my way carefully downstairs, feeling clumsy and stupid in my get-up; I should have come in dinner-jacket and a mask. I looked in a mirror and hated myself; I was just turning away when a buxom Britannia called out, "You're right dear, no luck tonight!" and walked on. I felt very depressed.

I was swept down by the crowd, to the dance-floor. Glancing at the jostle of the tango-ing couples – a lot of close work and lingering kisses – I caught a glimpse of Sec-Sec, dancing gracefully with a self-possessed young lady in full evening fig, no fancy dress for her. Ten to one, she was an ex-Deb late of *Country Life*. Then I lost him again.

I skirted the crowd and joined the slow queue of unabashed oglers moving past the fabulously expensive boxes, at a distance of six feet, as if examining Harrods' windows.

And what was on view caught the eye more than any shop display. Each framed picture was as crammed as any cornucopia: with fashion-plate Restoration beauties and gallants – powder and patches, snuff-boxes, fans: Sylphides, Elizabethan pages; flashes of jewellery, the real thing; whiffs of perfume, sparkling glasses of the best champagne, poured out by flunkeys, themselves also the real thing, accompanying their employers for a serving night-out.

I recognized "stars of stage, screen and society": Evelyn Laye signing an autograph-book, Oliver Messel as Beau Brummel, Madeleine Carroll, Massine, Tilly Losch. Getting to Ivor's box I quickened my step, though there was no possibility of my being looked at by any of his entourage. I also spotted several young nota-bilities who had come to *my* Ball, or who had been presented to me at any of a hundred functions: Margaret Whigham, Bob Boothby, the Earl and Countess of Rosse, Randolph Churchill. And I noted, sadly, that it wasn't that easy to recognize them, because this time they were enjoying themselves.

Why couldn't Willie have taken a box for *me*? The Shrine of Shrines, the *Royal* Box? He could have filled it with the choicest human flowers a King should have the Divine Right to pick . . . I slunk on, invisible, the Chaplin waif off to wander alone into the sunset. At least twice I plodded round on the sight-seeing treadmill, looking hopelessly about for the sought-for face.

Until the moment when even I could feel a tension in the air, as it mounted gradually to crackling point. I looked up at the giant clock.

One minute to midnight.

Harry Roy signalled to the band to fade gently down, and as they did so, a shrill concert took over: the noise of a thousand chattering voices. As the lights dimmed, so the voices dimmed too. Then the ritual of the balloons.

They had hung, unnoticed, in an enormous cloud, from the dark ceiling high out of sight. Caught by the sudden spotlights, they seemed – by magic – to stir and wake up; watched by the murmuring sea of faces, the multi-coloured cloud floated down and disintegrated into hundreds of single drifters. As they reached the faces, there came the steady gun-fire of a thousand shrieking destructive children bursting the balloons one by one.

From a monster wireless loud-speaker, Big Ben striking the quarters; as the midnight strokes started to boom, a general crossing of arms and the ragged half-facetious chant of *Should Old Acquaintance* . . . I thought of last year, wanted to be crossing arms with Kathy and Bruce, and felt the welling of maudlin tears.

A hand on my shoulder. By a miracle, Bruce. In dinner-jacket, and so excited to see me he could hardly speak. "It *is* you? I've already tried two Chaplins!" He was glowing with pleasure, as I was.

Against the singing, I had to shout. "What did she come as? Are they in a box?"

He shouted back. "No, they changed their minds and went to the Savoy Grill, they're not here!"

And the last stroke died away. The raucous singing stopped as well, because the crowd was waiting for the traditional ceremony introducing the New Year. I again thought of last time, the rubber model of the Sky Whale, with 1935 across it.

Through a megaphone, the blare of a stern announcement. "Ladies and Gentlemen, Attention please for news of the most sensational presentation of a New Year ever offered at the Chelsea Arts Ball. It is our unique honour, ladies and gentlemen, to pay homage – as he steps forward to welcome the year 1936 – to pay homage to . . . His Majesty King John the Second!"

Bruce and I were so hemmed in that his arm was pressed against mine; I felt it give a convulsive jerk. We looked at each other, then straight ahead at the raised centre platform, quite near to us. The band had crowded outwards to the edges of this platform, leaving the middle part clear, while Harry Roy himself stood at a corner, as if waiting to conduct.

The announcement had sounded so solemnly genuine that there was a thousandfold intake of breath so sharp as to be almost audible. The crowd seemed to recognize a bad joke, and started to laugh and mutter. There was even a scatter of ironic applause. Next, Roy signalled to the band and they played, slowly, impressively, a familiar opening phrase. *God Save The King.*

It even offended the ribald element, there were shouts of "Bad taste!" "Stop it!". Then dead silence; a single spotlight was fixed on curtains at the back of the platform. The curtains parted, and a figure walked forward, in dinner jacket and black trousers, and stood still. The jacket was open, displaying a white polo sweater emblazoned with the numbers 1,9,3,6. This time, the general gasp was violent enough to sound like a cry from an audience of astounded children.

It was me.

Or rather it wasn't. It was Eric Dandy Esquire, Dandy of *Dandy and Sandy.* The wig was new, and exactly my present haircut, down to the famous King's Curl.

He bowed and smiled: evidently enough like the real thing to cause a second gasp. Then he looked at Roy, who signalled to his pianist, who went straight into "I Want To Be Happy". Dandy – masquerading as Sandy – started to tap (he had his tap-shoes on, of course), and it dawned on his audience that this was a brilliant stunt. The applause was terrific, and they settled down to enjoyment.

What makes a human being, at certain shock moments, able to perform a series of actions as if manipulated, with a swiftness so sure that the whole thing could look rehearsed in every detail? I moved.

Too fast even for Bruce to grab my arm. In front of me, I spotted steps up to the platform, enough to the side for the crowd not to notice me dart up them and stand hidden next to the band. Dart, in those boots? Well, I did . . .

Until I Make You Happy Too-oo . . . I slid out from among the band, flung away my cane, held out my arms in joyous control, took up the dance-step as if I had given two performances that day at the Palladium, and tapped my way to my partner. Excellent floor for tap, my steps were like pistol-shots.

God, please let Dandy be pro enough to cope with the shock . . . He swivelled his head, saw me there, had a second of dismay, then another of recognizing in the clownish intruder a performer in his own class, who was unaccountably familiar with his routine. To reassure our audience, he faked exaggerated surprise at being joined by a beloved comedian and held out his arms. It was admirable.

I arrived at his side, faced front, laid my hand on his shoulder, and we were off. *Don't bounce, this is Tap – press, into the ground!* For me, the troubles of the last month dissolved miraculously into thin air, blown away by music.

As we worked up to the finale, faster and faster, my mind spurted ahead. First thought: on the last flourish, at the moment of freezing into the routine tableau, I would yank off his wig and point to the wealth of red hair I remembered well. Second thought: they would yell for an encore, but I knew better. If ever a performer needed a swift exit without a hitch, it was me.

We finished perfectly – marvellous pianist – and we froze. To the wildest applause, I bowed stiffly to my partner, lifted my hand to his shoulder and then to behind his neck, and tugged at his wig. Hard.

It wasn't a wig. His hair had been expertly dyed to my colour, then expertly cut, to my cut.

Dandy didn't even look surprised (by now he was beyond it) and our audience must have taken my gesture as one of affection. And to a roar of cheering, I was through the back curtains like an arrow, tore into a passage, and off. A fugitive, hell-bent on the run.

It had got about like wild-fire that there was a Show you had to Catch, and the whole of the front was deserted, except for faithful Sec-Sec holding the door open of his Austin Seven, its engine running, "I guessed Sir you'd want to get straight out . . ." I dived in, he got to the wheel, the car lunged forward. We were off.

At the corner, to make sure we were not being followed, I turned my head: just in time to see, through the rear window, a figure dash out and climb into another car which overtook us and tore ahead.

It was Dandy. King Dandy. I sank down, beyond any more surprises, and settled on to the floor.

The Show was over. And I wasn't even out of breath.

CHAPTER TWENTY-FOUR

Acceleration from the New Year

On the floor, I had plenty of time – and needed it – to put away wig and moustache, wriggle into my overcoat and organize myself generally. Then, lying there, I thought . . . did I really see Bruce, for that second?

B.P. The gates closed behind us, the car circled and came to a halt, Sec-Sec whispered, "Coast clear, Sir" – we had not said one word on the journey – and I climbed stiffly out. Not a soul, the police officers, thank God, must be patrolling.

Walking to my quarters, we only spoke once. I said, "What the *hell* was all that about?" And Sec-Sec said, "Just what I was thinking, Sir – search me!" What did Harry Roy and the Ball organizers have against me, thinking up such a stunt?

As we reached my door, I felt a powerful heave of tiredness. I was just able to say, "Thank you for everything, I ought to ask you in for a drink, but . . ." If he hadn't caught me I would have fallen, but I insisted I'd be all right.

As I closed my door the telephone rang. It could only be Willie. "It's you, Sir? Oh . . ." It sounded like a sigh of relief. "I hope I didn't wake you?"

"No no, I'm in bed reading, just about to turn out my light. Anything happened?"

"No, Sir, just to wish you a happy New Year, good night, Sir . . ." He sounded in a bit of a hurry.

I even managed to push all the Chaplin stuff under the bed before I collapsed into blessed sleep. I only woke once, to find myself

moaning, "Don't go . . . Venice . . . don't go . . . Venice . . ." then
sank back into nothingness.

Wed. Jan. 1st 1936, 203rd Day of Reign.
Fog, which had even seeped into my bedroom. But the newspaper
headlines leapt out clear enough. Was I never to escape them? (The
reporters must have dashed to telephones the second after *I* had
dashed.)
AMAZING SCENES! . . . *WAS* IT THE KING? . . .
KING JACK ON TAP! . . . The first breathless piece which I
skimmed through, typified them all. "*Today a few thousand people
saw the New Year in at the Albert Hall, will be talking of nothing else,
and – by now – so will the whole of London. The King of England
walked on to a stage, where he was joined – from the audience – by a
stooge got up as Charlie Chaplin; the pair then performed a brilliant
tap-dance which – since it was 12.3 a.m., approx., on January 1st –
could be described as the Turn of the Year.*" (Not a bad quip, considering the pressure of the deadline.)
"*At the end, to ear-splitting applause, the King vanished, from the
stage and from the building, into the night, while, remarkably quickly,
the Chaplin impersonator was spotted in the crowd.*"
Not as remarkable as all that, considering there were at least two
of him around.
"*He was immediately interrogated by security police and – incredibly
– flatly denied the evidence. In any case, there was no concrete offence
with which he could be charged.*" I wondered which unlucky Charlie
they had picked on.
"*While the die-hard minority refuse to believe that the other performer was the King, the majority are convinced (unbelievable though it
may seem) that he was. More details in our later edition. (Which, we
warn our readers, will be immediately sold out!)*"
STOP PRESS. "*A cane, a present inscribed to the King's grandfather the Duke of Clarence, has been retrieved from stage at Albert Hall,
which seems positive proof that it* was *the King.*"
I pictured two certain gents reading all that and thinking, Is 1936
to be *all* like this? Sir Godwin Rodd and Sir John Reith.
The thought of the latter put me in mind of the 9 a.m. news, and I
switched on the wireless. Sir John had artfully seen to it that the
bomb-shell took third place, being preceded by a dull bit about the
crowds in Trafalgar Square and a drunk who had climbed one of the
lions. And when it did come, it wasn't a bomb-shell at all. From the

bloodless reading voice, you'd have thought that Royalty went tap-dancing in public at least once a week. The incident was described as "presumably meant to amuse, but in extremely bad taste. A per-former presented an impersonation of His Majesty the King and then left. A malicious rumour, claiming that he *was* the King, has been scotched by the fact that immediately following, His Majesty's Pri-vate Secretary telephoned the Palace and spoke to the King, who had retired some time before." No wonder that Willie, on the phone, had sounded relieved.

"It is not yet decided whether a complaint must be lodged with the Lord Chamberlain, or even the Police, on the grounds that a law has been broken: the law declaring that neither the Deity nor Roy-alty may be depicted on the stage. The weather. An anti-cyclone . . ."

It was gratifying to hear myself teamed with God. *Deity and Royalty*, it made us sound like a couple of stand-up comics. On a par with *Dandy and Sandy*.

I returned to my newspapers, and in no way did the *Daily Express* tally with the B.B.C. It delivered the bomb-shell.

IT *WAS* HIM!!! *"From our immediate inquiries around 12.15 a.m., via a phone call by our enterprising man-on-the-spot, to a theatrical chum who has a library of bound copies of the* Stage, *one significant fact has emerged. One of His Majesty's early activities, while still a private person, was a music-hall double act. The* Stage, *November 1930 :*

> 'Dandy and Sandy are a nifty duo. The presentation is extra-ordinary, leaving the audience buzzing with 'Are they real twins?' The secret is that while Sandy (Jack Sandring) is him-self, red-haired Dandy is sporting a wig modelled on Sandy's hair, and the rest to match. A miracle!'

"So spake the *Stage.*

"From which we deduce the unassailable facts. The King (alias Sandy, begging his Majesty's pardon, short for Sandring, short for Sandringham, the imagination boggles) – the King got into touch – for reasons best known to himself – with his former professional partner, the very same Mr Dandy, and persuaded Mr Dandy to disguise himself as Charlie Chaplin for the Chelsea Arts Ball and join him on the stage for their act.

"Another conclusive detail. Since dawn, this newspaper has been telephoned by no less than five taxi-drivers reporting that round about 12.30 last night (or New Year's morning, rather) as they were travel-ling in the neighbourhood of Hyde Park Corner, they had to wait at

various traffic-lights and so were able to take in, at leisure, a car travelling east (i.e. from the direction of the Albert Hall).

"Each driver has separately informed us that he was tremendously impressed to observe that the sole passenger was the King. The car turned into Constitution Hill, the direct route (of course) to the Palace. The British people hardly need Sherlock Holmes to help them draw their own conclusions."

To this (proven) evidence, the *Star* added a verdict of "Guilty" and pulled no punches. *"We, his people, are grieved and reluctant to face the ugly truth."* But they, his people, faced the ugly truth just the same. *"Which seems to be that we have been subjected to the most disgraceful piece of Imperial exhibitionism since Caligula made his horse a Senator."*

A knock at the door. Willie. The same pale, sleepless face. I gave him the story. He sat.

"Willie, now I've told you everything – what happens?"

"Your Majesty, it's my turn to tell *you* everything."

Your Majesty . . . It was the first time, since the day we met, that he had called me that. Something was coming. "Sir, would you mind if I ask Lady Haddlewick to join us?"

His Aunt Rose? I instantly thought of the last time he had brought her in. "Willie . . . has she had another blackmail letter?"

"No, no – anyway I wrote to Sir Simon Rawson about that party of his which you were at, and finally heard from him last week, from abroad, I should have told you – he had thought better of it and had destroyed the negatives the day after it happened." Well, that was one ray of light.

He went to fetch Aunt Rose. What was this about?

As he returned with her, I remembered how concerned she had been, over the blackmail threat – frightened, almost. Today no trace of that, nor of the social prattler I had first met: she was herself at last, poised and in command. She nearly forgot to curtsey. I motioned her to a chair, sat again myself and turned to Willie. He opened his brief-case and took out papers.

"You will remember, Sir, an incident some time ago: a letter from a blackmailer, to my Aunt here, which she brought to the attention of us both."

"Yes?"

"You will recall, too, that nothing more was heard from that quarter. For the simple reason that there was no blackmailer."

"But – I saw the letter – the three of us did!" Kathy would have said it sounded like a play: not *Bulldog Drummond*, more like a high drama I'd been with once, in rep. Oscar Wilde, *A Woman of No Importance*.

Willie took up a sheet of paper, and I recognized the neat loathsome writing. Clipped to it, another sheet, blank except for some squiggles.

"Early this morning, at 12.45 a.m., the Press rang up my home from the Albert Hall, then tracked me down at my Aunt's house. My wife and I were just going to bed. It was then, Sir, that I telephoned you. That reassured me, but I was still extremely disturbed by what the Press had reported, dressed again and walked about the grounds, trying to sort things out. At 7 a.m. – nobody up yet – I went to the library, sat at a desk to make notes, pulled out this blank piece of paper, and took up a pen lying in a tray in front of me. I noticed something.

"I happened to have this" – holding up the blackmail letter – "in my brief-case, as usual. I took it out, and held both sheets up to the light. The same water-mark, and I know enough about water-marks to spot an unusual one. I then tried the pen out on the blank sheet – you see? The pen was the one used to write the letter."

He looked at his Aunt Rose, and waited.

Her voice was crisp, like frost. "Yes, I wrote it." I turned back to Willie.

"As you can imagine, Sir, my talk with Lady Haddlewick, over breakfast, was a thorough one." He hesitated, then decided to say what he had to say. "Aunt, I don't think it's exactly news that I've never been . . . very close to you. But we've kept up appearances. Today that's not possible. I have to speak frankly, and so has the King."

I turned to Aunt Rose. "Lady Haddlewick, you wrote this letter to yourself. Why?"

She was crisper than before. "You're looking at me as if it's something I should be ashamed of. I have *nothing* to be ashamed of. It was a perfectly legitimate device, to put people off the scent who might have the impertinence to pry into my private business. Anyway, as you implied when you were shown the letter, your conscience was clear, so it cannot have worried you unduly."

That was clever of her. She was as composed as if she were sitting at a matinee with a tea-tray on her knee, watching Marie Tempest in an interesting society comedy. "I have *nothing* to be ashamed of, quite the contrary. I may sound pompously stuffy, Sir, to one brought up in a theatrical milieu, when I say that everything I have done was for my country." She sounded like Nurse Cavell facing the Prussian firing-squad. Except that all that this heroine had to cope with was . . . my solitary self. I was the one with my back to the wall.

And Willie wasn't going to let her get away with it. "So concerned was my Aunt for the welfare of her country, that from the moment she realized that her daughter was never to become Queen-Consort, by a coincidence she began to realize, more and more, your Majesty's unsuitability for the position which you occupy. Not to mince matters, she was determined to undermine you, and has been ever since.

"Her first move in what she, just now, called her 'private business', was to engage a private detective to bribe a friend of yours at Drury Lane Theatre to gate-crash a Royal ball; at the same ball she deliberately manoeuvred that your first dance should be with a girl whom she knew to be completely unreliable, and later paid the same man to plant hints in the Press discrediting yourself."

He consulted his notes. "I don't know if you are aware, Sir, that your Second Secretary is – like myself – a nephew of Lady Haddlewick?" I nodded. "She worked at getting him the job with the idea that he might come in useful. And last night he did."

"Last night?"

"You, Sir, thought he was doing you a service. He was not, you were playing into his hands. As soon as you confided in him your plan to get to the Albert Hall, he telephoned Lady Haddlewick, she telephoned the same private detective. That gentleman, from the beginning, had been intrigued by the saga of *Dandy and Sandy* – of your partner's successful stunt as your twin – and had made it his business to strike up an acquaintance with Mr Dandy.

"Two days ago, as soon as he heard about your plan for the Albert Hall, he telephoned Dandy and asked him if – for two hundred pounds – he would participate in a harmless and amusing New Year hoax which might considerably advance his career. They had twenty-four hours to work it out – hair dyed and cut, mustn't speak, just come on for the solo dance: Harry Roy to be alerted, a car waiting which – your twin, Sir, wasn't aware of this – which had instructions to drive towards Buckingham Palace, so that he could be recognized as yourself. So much for last night."

"And," I added for him, "so much for the harm it has done." I thought of my Christmas Message. "Lady Haddlewick, you must have been gratified by my talk on the wireless."

Her voice cut in, swish. "It did indeed make me happy, since it confirmed my conviction that you were unfitted to be the head of this particular State."

No holds barred. I said, "Willie must have mentioned the danger of your country being turned into a Republic. You must surely be distressed by the possibility of *that*?"

She said nothing. He said nothing.

She looked more sure of herself than anybody I'd ever seen: as sure as any saint bullied by any Inquisition. The same fixed half-smile you couldn't get past. The scorn of the fanatic.

Their silence mystified me. "Lady Haddlewick . . . I am baffled by something. I can understand your feeling – and, for that matter, many other people's feeling – that I am not right for my job. But the lengths to which you have gone to try and get me out! They go so far beyond patriotism that you sound – I'm sorry – a bit mad."

"I'm not, you know." Then a chuckle. Dry, good-humoured.

I tried again. "But however firm your convictions – to have been faced, at this moment, and by your own nephew, ought to have shaken you considerably. It hasn't. Why?"

As she gave her answer, her expression stayed exactly the same. "Because, your Majesty, I have a card up my sleeve." The "your Majesty" had sarcasm in it. She turned to Willie. "What's this about the danger of a Republic?"

It was an order to him to take charge again. And very ill at ease he looked as he did so: it was the way his Aunt should be looking, and wasn't. "Sir, you will remember that after the meetings at Ten Downing Street over the week-end, I reported the conversations to you. I am ashamed to confess – but I must – that I did not report quite accurately. I distorted. And suppressed . . . The question of a Republic was indeed brought up, but not for long; to you I ex-aggerated the danger, because I wanted you to get the idea that you must fight it. To your eternal credit, you *did* decide that it was your duty to stay."

"Thank you."

From Auntie, another little laugh. "Don't be too grateful, Willie wasn't thinking so much of *you*! Not *that* unselfish . . . Willie, spill the beans!"

He got up, formally, as if we were in court. Whatever this was, it was plainly very serious. I felt a surge of fright, then controlled it.

"Your Majesty . . . Those meetings this week-end in Downing Street, were not the first I had attended there. On June the 12th last, the night preceding . . . your Accession, I was at the same address till two in the morning – Baldwin was already Prime Minister of course – and at the end of the session they asked if I would accept the post of Private Secretary, and I did."

"But Willie . . . what happened *before* the end of it?"

"A long and complex discussion. The problem was so extraordinary that it could be nothing else."

This was getting more and more strange. I persevered. "But the documents Sir Godwin showed me next morning were surely plain-sailing, since they included my grandfather's marriage certificate, my father's birth certificate, *and* mine . . .? What –"

"Besides Sir Godwin, present at the meeting were the Lord Chancellor and the Master of the Rolls."

"A Summit affair!"

"It had to be, and top secret. But now it's got to come out. You see, Sir, there was another candidate."

I sat up. "What? But I was direct in line –"

"I know, but it didn't have to be as clear-cut as that. You see, if a course of action is considered by the Government to be 'for the weal public' as they used to phrase it – pro bono publico – there are legitimate ways of slightly . . . adjusting the law to fit a particular case. The second candidate was not in as immediate a line as yourself, but . . ."

Lady Haddlewick put it for him. "Not as immediate, but just as direct. And with – of course – considerably purer blood on the distaff side."

I ignored that slap at my mother, I was too puzzled by the whole thing. "Willie, was the second candidate present at that meeting?"

Again Aunt Rose. "He was."

A horrible thought hit me. "He's not . . . Sir Godwin?"

She smiled. "Heavens no. Sir Godwin's grandfather was born, and worked, in Sheffield. Sharpening cutlery." The scorn in her voice was rather splendid.

"What was the feeling, at the meeting, about this second candidate?"

Again Lady Haddlewick. "A highly favourable one." She took her hand-bag and took out a piece of paper. Well, more than that – an important-looking document. "This is the text of part of the speech made at that same meeting by the Prime Minister." She read out.

"On August 3rd 1800, Queen Charlotte of Wurttemberg, formerly Charlotte Augusta Princess Royal of Great Britain and Ireland, and daughter of King George the Third, gave birth to a son. The boy – an only child – became the first Marquess of Traybrooke; his son, born on February 8th 1827, became in turn the second Marquess. The grandson of that second Marquess, gentlemen, is alive and – at this moment – sitting with us in this room, as the second candidate for the throne. And, you must agree, a strong one. The grandson of the great-grandson of King George the Third."

I was as puzzled as ever. "Then why wasn't he chosen?"

"He stood down."

I stared. "Stood down?"

Willie explained. "Well, let us say that he begged to be let off. He insisted that he was by nature a private person, unsuited to the position in question, with all its frightening responsibilities – I don't, Sir, have to go into that with *you*. People might call it cowardly . . ."

He looked at me. He was breathing in jerks, and clasping his knuckles round the arms of his chair.

Then he said four words. "I couldn't face it."

CHAPTER TWENTY-FIVE

The Outcome

They waited for me to take it in. I wasn't able to. I just stammered, in a lame way – "But Willie, you're *Mister* Millingham. How can a Mister . . ."

"Very simple. The fact is that I too have an ancestor who changed his name by deed poll, but for a completely different reason." He was about to continue, then looked at Lady Haddlewick. She referred to the document and read out again, clear and cutting.

" 'The second Marquess of Traybrooke – the said great-grandson of King George the Third, born on February 8th 1827 – was, to put it mildly, an eccentric. While still at Oxford, he became a rabid Radical – nowadays he might be dubbed a Communist – and changed his name, by deed poll, to Francis Parkes Millingham: an amalgam of the names of the three leading Radicals of that time – Francis Place, Joseph Parkes and Robert Millingham. The Marquess was clearly as ashamed of his antecedents as the most snobbish of low-born parvenus would be of his.

" 'Anybody who chanced to sound him out, concerning a rumour of his real family history, would be fobbed off with a scoffing denial, often accompanied by a hint at illegitimacy. His obsession was so strong that he swore his wife to secrecy, and his son Robert Jordan Millingham (born on April 9th 1871) grew up, and died, with no idea that the rumour he might occasionally have heard, could be the truth; while to *his* only son – Mr Millingham here – the rumour would have seemed more far-fetched still.

" 'So completely had the first Millingham managed to obscure his

279

family history, that not only would nobody have considered inviting his grandson to attend the send-off of the fatal Sky-Whale – not once, during the subsequent endless Press speculations as to the future of the Monarchy – not once has his name come up. It was only four days ago, through the diligence of the same officials who had tracked down the other candidate, that the all-important fact was brought to our notice. The fact that Mr Millingham here is the grandson of the great-grandson of King George the Third'."

She had not been able to resist ending that with a note of rising triumph. "Last paragraph. 'In view of the fact that compared with him, the other candidate is an unknown quantity, I would strongly advise that we invite our guest here tonight to accept his responsibilities as our future Monarch.'"

She folded the document carefully and replaced it in her bag. "And Willie," I said, "you begged to be let off?"

"Yes. Then they pressed me to stay on as your Private Secretary."

"So that you'd get to know the ropes, just in case . . .?"

"Yes. But the reason I consented was the opposite one. I was determined to help you do the job so well that the other contingency would never arise." Till this moment, I had never seen him vehement, he was white to the lips. "My only thought was to protect my wife and son from it. She's had no idea, I kept it from her –"

His aunt raised her hand. "She knows now. I made Willie tell her first thing this morning."

I looked at her as coldly as I could, then back at Willie. "And when did Lady Haddlewick get on to all this?"

"At about the time when she was hoping you'd be interested in her daughter, and went to Sir Godwin for help. He was mischievous enough to let her have that copy of a vitally private document, revealing to her that what she had dismissed years ago as an old wives' tale – namely my descent from George the Third – was the truth. So from the moment when it was clear you had no interest in her daughter, she's given me no peace. That paper she's holding is the Gospel according to St. Rose."

Said Lady Haddlewick, unruffled, "It also happens to be, at this moment, the Gospel according to the Cabinet."

I turned again to her. Even at this crucial moment in my life, I had to look at her from a new and curious angle – to reflect to what lengths ambition can drive a human being. The self-righteous single-mindedness behind those sharp eyes was terrifying. Her nephew had once described her as innocuous; I thought, she's about as innocuous as prussic acid.

She saw, like us, that it was now to be between me and Willie, and got up. "Willie, I'll be in your office."

As I opened the door for her, in Willie's office across the way I saw a woman getting up from a chair, I stepped forward, she advanced: Willie's wife Anne. As she curtseyed, her face was pale from shock and unhappiness. I tried to say something, could think of nothing, pressed her hand, turned, walked past Aunt Rose, returned to the study, closed the door, and sat opposite the direct descendant of King George the Third.

We looked at each other, knowing that this was the most important moment in both our lives.

I spoke first. "What are you imagining I've decided to do?"

He smiled, sadly. "I can make a guess. You'll do what the Cabinet hope you'll do."

"Step down?"

"Step down."

"Well, you've guessed wrong. I stay on."

"What?"

"They want me to go, but they can't force me."

"But you want to go yourself, I know you do –"

"That's as it may be, Willie, but out there just now, I caught a glimpse of a face. Your wife's."

"Yes?"

"She looked so sad I can't forget it. I can't let you and your family in for this."

The reference to Anne's distress had hit him, but he pressed on. "Sir, only a day or two ago you told me that if by a miracle the right man materialized, so making a Republic out of the question – you would go."

"I remember."

"Well, hasn't the miracle happened?" Then a twinkle. "Or don't you think the right man *has* materialized?"

"I can't quarrel with that."

"And, Sir . . . since you spoke of my Anne's feelings – may I tell you there's another face *I* can't get out of my mind?"

"Oh?"

"Your Kathy. Those two meetings I had with them, when she talked of you. Above all, that day I brought them to visit you in this room, the way she looked at you when she walked in. She deserves consideration, for the simple reason that she loves you very dearly. And Anne will get used to it all, as I will. I beg your Majesty to reconsider your decision."

He held out his hand, I took it. We were both too moved to look at each other, and as he turned his face away from me, I looked at the splendid head, then at the sculpted aquiline profile, and my heart filled with happiness. For I could see that profile proudly outlined, when the time would come, on a coin of the realm.

His realm. For a vivid second, I looked into the future: Wednesday May the 6th. The Coronation: the crowds in the Mall cheering and waving to the Palace Balcony. To King William. And to Queen Anne – a Cavendish, a cousin of the Duke of Devonshire and therefore acceptable even to Sir Godwin Rodd. With them, a son and heir aged ten. John, the future Prince of Wales. And the future King. John the Third. Strange.

I said, "Willie, I'm sorry to have done this to you, but . . ." I searched for the right words, and from me they were inevitable. "You'll be perfect in the part."

"Thank you, Sir."

"You ought to be, you've been rehearsing for close on thirty weeks . . . During which time you gave me a friendship I couldn't have done without."

A knock at the door, Aunt Rose. "Do come in," I said, "it's all settled." I felt elated enough to be able to tease her. "Lady Haddlewick, has it occurred to you that once I'm out of here, I am in a position to do you a lot of harm?"

She looked at me, from a height. "What do you mean?"

"What is to stop me from telephoning Fleet Street, and offering the Story of the Century to the *News of the World*, for untold riches? The tale of the Adventuress who Stopped at Nothing – not at forgery, not at bribery and corruption, not at malicious misrepresentation? Suppose, Lady Haddlewick, that my story resulted in a knock at your door? From the law? Suppose I said I'd do just that . . . what would you do?"

She looked at me, from the same height, and smiled. "I would merely remind you that the sister of the King's mother . . . will be *above* the law."

And she went.

You have to take your hat off.

It was still only half past nine in the morning. My first thought . . .
"My parents?"

"Croydon Aerodrome is waiting for a phone call from me, there's a plane standing by to fly to a private strip between Plymouth and St Austell. I'm sending a dependable man – *not* Sec-Sec – who'll put them wise, gently, before the news breaks."

"Once more our thanks, Private Secretary." Then my second thought. "Willie, would you – this minute – try and get Kathy before she might leave for Venice? It's early, there's a chance –"

"What shall I say?"

"Just . . . two words. *Don't go*. Tell her that within an hour she'll have a letter."

He left, I unlocked my secret drawer and took out the top paper. *We, John the Second . . . hereby declare . . . our decision not to abdicate.* I crumpled it up and put it in the fire. Willie was soon back. "They were due to leave at noon. She was bewildered, needless to say, quite upset, but finally agreed to postpone till tomorrow."

Then a brisk business talk, and Willie telephoned Sir Godwin Rodd, of the Sheffield Cutlery. The Powers-That-Be can take their time (how well I knew) but the present situation must have seemed, to them, as urgent as a Declaration of War; the wheels of the Number Ten Network fairly whizzed round, one telephone call after another to the Dominions in order to ensure their consent, and then Sir John Reith would be contacted *at once*. Willie rang for a Special Messenger, while I settled at my desk.

"My darling Kathy, In haste, though this is a vital letter. Bruce will have told you the details of my Star Guest Appearance at the Albert Hall. Here are two Royal Commands. (1) This eve., 9 p.m., tune in to B.B.C, then *don't go out*. (2) Phone Bruce Drury Lane stage door, care of Jack and his Beanstalk, and ask him if he'd mind spending the night with his chums whose flat he decorated, I know our Bruce will understand. Jack."

Another business talk with Willie, beginning with his quoting from the Civil List Act, *which provides for the honour and dignity of the Royal Family.* "Sir, the Chancellor of the Exchequer suggests, for your approval, a Life Pension of fifty thousand pounds a year, free of income tax."

That meant nothing to me, and I asked how much a week it was. "A thousand." I couldn't believe it, strongly disagreed, and finally beat myself down to a hundred a week: in those days a fortune. He then brought up the question of my parents, and I insisted that I would look after them, out of my Pension. I could tell he approved.

I then had a good thought – I asked him to promise that every year the difference between my agreed pension and the much larger sum which "they" had suggested, should be paid into a Relief Fund for the Tyneside Unemployed, my name not to be mentioned. Again I must emphasize that I can't look upon that as a magnificent gesture. What *could* have been magnificent, would have been if I had pledged to devote the rest of my life to the cause. Well, I didn't. Nobody's perfect, and I'm not anywhere near the top of the list.

We then went even more closely into the details of my future which we had touched upon the day before yesterday – but whereas at that moment that future had in no way been confirmed – moustached John Brown in Mexico – it was now a solid fact.

All this brought us to past midday, when Willie took his leave: a hundred things to see to. After an absent-minded picking at a tray of food, my disturbed night caught up with me and I slept solidly for over four hours. Waking up refreshed, I saw that an evening paper had been slid under my door. Across the front page, THE KING WILL SPEAK TONIGHT, WHAT IS HAPPENING?

It was beginning to get dark; the 204th – and last – day of the reign of King John the Second was drawing quietly to its close. The Two Hundred Days, give or take. Twice as many, I thought, as Napoleon's after Elba – and so far, I hadn't been handed a one-way ticket to St Helena.

8.15 p.m. A letter, delivered by hand, written – hard to believe – this morning and brought by the plane on its return journey from Cornwall.

"Our dear Son Jack, Your Da & me think that you are rite to do what you feel to be rite. I cryed a bit. All them months – tho I never wanted ee to know – I got the feelin that you was under a terrible big strain. And you made a brave job of it. And it is a good thing that from now on we will be blessed with little or no visiters, because Tregonissey Hill along up to the Farm will get steeper by the day.

"The Rev Blamey was in just now & offered to offer a prayer next Sabath Day, but I said no thank you, it would sound as if our Jack was on his last legs, which he is not.

"It was forward on his part, tho not so foward as that igorant Charlie Chaplin fellow that dared to jump on to the platform &

try to take the atention off you. I would like to be face to face
with im & give im a peice of my mind. I used to enjoy finishin
leters to ee wi the words YOUR LOVIN SUBJECT but I am
glad it will soon be over, Your Lovin Ma & Da, Bertram and
Alice Lavinia Green."

8.30 p.m. In my study, the same crew setting up the same microphone, with me conning my speech. A different one. And even
shorter.

I went into the bedroom to change into my dinner-jacket, before
I was to proceed to the Music Room for my five minutes with the
undertakers: the Powers-That-Were, who from tonight would
have no hold on me. I remembered the Chaplin stuff I had pushed
under the bed, and was tempted to dress up in it for the interview;
it would have given food for thought. I decided to put it all back in
the cardboard box and – later – take it with me. Let the Albert Hall
Mystery, like the Enigma of the *Marie Celeste*, remain a puzzle to the
world. Until the time would come.

In the Music Room, they were all standing formally round a table;
Willie was stationed in an unobtrusive corner, out of the light. On
the table, a large document, and a pen. I bowed and handed my
speech to Sir John Reith, who would hand it to Mr Baldwin, who
would hand it to Sir Godwin Rodd. While this was going on I sat at
the table and studied the document: INSTRUMENT OF AB-
DICATION. It sounded as if they were going to operate on me.

"I, John the Second, of Great Britain, Northern Ireland and the
British Dominions beyond the Seas, King, Emperor of India, Defender of the Faith, do hereby declare My irrevocable determination
to renounce the Throne for Myself and for My descendants, and
My desire that effect should be given to this Instrument of Abdication immediately.

"In token whereof I have hereunto set My hand this first day of
January, nineteen hundred and thirty six, in the presence of the
witnesses whose signatures are subscribed."

I signed it, eight times on eight copies ("John R.I."), got up, decided not to watch the witnesses signing, took my speech, bowed
and returned to my study.

8.59 p.m. So much was happening that I forgot to wonder if I was
nervous or not. A concert finished, Big Ben boomed and faded.
"From Buckingham Palace. His Majesty the King."

I spoke. "Tonight, I am grieved. And yet glad. Six months ago, I promised I would do my best. I have kept that promise. It turned out a not-good-enough best, and for that I am grieved. As you all know too well, on Christmas Day I made a mistake, but not – I ask you to believe – not out of mischief. And in spite of that mistake, I assure you that at this solemn moment I would be requesting a second chance – no, *insisting* on a second chance – if there were any risk of the Monarchy being replaced by . . . another form of Government. To a British Sovereign, the idea of a Republic is . . . un-- acceptable, just as – tonight – it is unacceptable to most of my people. But there is no danger of that, for a very simple reason.

"And for that reason, I am glad, and please be glad with me. I leave my place – the throne of nine hundred years – to a dear friend of mine who is ideally suited for his formidable task: so, to the great-great-great-grandson of King George the Third, I declare my allegiance. Long live William the Fifth, by the grace of God, King of the United Kingdom of Great Britain and Northern Ireland, Defender of the Faith, Emperor of India. God Save the King."

The National Anthem; I stood up for it, went into the bedroom and got out of my dinner suit. Hanging at the back of one of the wardrobes were the clothes I had been wearing the first day: sports jacket, wrinkled flannel trousers, brown shoes – even the bow tie was there. It seemed right that I should change back into it all. Without ringing for whichever valet was on duty, I did just that, then walked to the Music Room for the formal farewell. And it's no good pretending – the effect, on the undertakers, of my changed appearance gave me much enjoyment.

There was nothing to say – just the ritual of bowing and hand-shaking. Before Sir God could conform with that, I had to wait a couple of seconds while he finished feasting his eyes on what still lay on the table. My signature, on the Instrument.

The last in the queue (which was right) was King William the Fifth. His eyes were blurred with tears.

I knew I was never to meet him again. I also knew exactly what to do. I bent down, took his hand, kissed it, and went.

Following his plan, I crossed the Garden, under a full moon and carrying my cardboard box. No overcoat, but the January evening was unseasonably warmish. In the moonlight, everything looked as serene as I felt.

At the side gate, although the policeman on duty had been fore-warned, he looked at me in a bemused way and let me out without a word. He just didn't know what to say. As I walked on I imagined him telling his children, so that they could tell *their* children.

The gate clanged behind me. Goodbye Buckingham Jail, hello and goodbye Windsor, Sandringham and Balmoral. I thought of my mother's words in today's letter, you made a brave job of it. Well I'd like to think there was something in that.

At Hyde Park Corner, there stood a nearly empty 14 bus. It looked as if it had been standing there for seven months. Waiting for me. For 204 days.

In my trouser pocket I had enough change to pay the fare (an ex-king is allowed to carry seven-month-old money) and from the other pocket I drew out the keys to 82a. The conductor didn't look at me, I might have been anybody. I *was* anybody. A bell rang, and the bus moved. Homeward.

THE END